Miss Julia to the Rescue

Also by Ann B. Ross

Miss Julia to the Rescue

ANN B. ROSS

VIKING

VIKING
Published by the Penguin Group
Penguin Group (USA) Inc., 375 Hudson Street,
New York, New York 10014, U.S.A.
Penguin Group (Canada), 90 Eglinton Avenue East, Suite 700,
Toronto, Ontario, Canada M4P 2Y3
(a division of Pearson Penguin Canada Inc.)
Penguin Books Ltd, 80 Strand, London WC2R 0RL, England
Penguin Ireland, 25 St. Stephen's Green, Dublin 2, Ireland
(a division of Penguin Books Ltd)
Penguin Books Australia Ltd, 250 Camberwell Road, Camberwell,
Victoria 3124, Australia
(a division of Pearson Australia Group Pty Ltd)
Penguin Books India Pvt Ltd, 11 Community Centre, Panchsheel Park,
New Delhi – 110 017, India
Penguin Group (NZ), 67 Apollo Drive, Rosedale, Auckland 0632,
New Zealand (a division of Pearson New Zealand Ltd)
Penguin Books (South Africa) (Pty) Ltd, 24 Sturdee Avenue,
Rosebank, Johannesburg 2196, South Africa

Penguin Books Ltd, Registered Offices:
80 Strand, London WC2R 0RL, England

First published in 2012 by Viking Penguin,
a member of Penguin Group (USA) Inc.

Publisher's Note
This is a work of fiction. Names, characters, places, and incidents either are the product of the author's
imagination or are used fictitiously, and any resemblance to actual persons, living or dead, business estab-
lishments, events, or locales is entirely coincidental.

ISBN 978-0-670-02338-7

Printed in the United States of America
Set in Fairfield LH
Designed by Alissa Amell

This one is for The Book Club—the one in Mississippi that is so special to me, as well as for all the book clubs everywhere whose members buy, borrow, read, discuss, recommend and love books.

Miss Julia to the Rescue

Chapter 1

"Hazel Marie," I said as we sat at my kitchen table, "would you mind terribly if I redecorated your room?"

"Why, Miss Julia," she said, smiling at me, "it's your house. You can do whatever you want to it." Hazel Marie leaned over to replace a pacifier in one baby's mouth, then rocked the twin stroller back and forth with her foot.

She had strolled the babies over on this beautiful early June morning and now sat visiting with me. She was blooming—there was no other word for it. Second motherhood, late though it was, certainly agreed with her. Of course, a lot of it had to do with the fact that on this go-round she had a husband by her side. Well, not literally by her side today, for Mr. Pickens was off somewhere doing his private investigative work, while she reveled in her place as a well-situated matron, complete with spouse, three children, home and social standing.

It was all so different, you know, from her first foray into motherhood, when she had kept her head down, raising Lloyd essentially alone and avoiding notice as much as she could. That's what you do when you're a woman kept by a married man who wanted to keep his double life secret. Which he did until he keeled over one night in his new Buick Park Avenue and it all came out.

"What're you thinking of doing to it?" Hazel Marie asked, picturing, no doubt, the pink and gold room upstairs that she for the first time in her life had decorated exactly as she wished. She had chosen pink velvet armchairs—faintly French in style—pink taffeta bedskirt and quilted coverlet, pink striated wallpaper, pink lamps and pink carpet. Touches of gilt on picture and mirror frames and odds and ends throughout the room relieved the pink to some extent. It was a little much for my taste, but Sam and I had slept in it for months while she was on bed rest, relegated by her doctor to the large bedroom downstairs.

But now, she and Mr. Pickens, along with their baby girls, were ensconced in Sam's house, four blocks away, and Hazel Marie was loving every minute of it. That meant, however, that Sam no longer had a quiet and private place to work on the book that he'd been fiddling with for so long.

"Well, I'll tell you," I said, leaning my head against my hand, "the upstairs hall is stacked with boxes of Sam's papers and books—everything that was in his office at your house—so I have to make an office for him here. I've gone back and forth over this, and it comes down to either your room or the downstairs bedroom. Your room will be quieter for him and the downstairs room will be larger for the two of us, so that seems the best solution. The only thing, though, is the walk-in closet you put in upstairs. I hate to give that up."

"You wouldn't have to," she said. "You could use it for out-of-season clothes and for things you don't wear very often."

"Well, yes, I could." I sighed, trying to visualize Sam and me in each of the rooms. "I've even thought of turning the closet into Sam's office. Goodness knows it's big enough. What it comes down to, though, is that I hate to dismantle what you loved so much. It's like—I don't know—resigning myself to the fact that you are truly gone."

"Why, Miss Julia," she said, laying her hand on my arm. "That is so sweet. I thought you'd be glad to have me out of your hair and on my own. Well, on my own with J.D., I mean."

I knew what she was getting at—safely married with legitimate children. And I *was* glad, but I still missed her in spite of the rough start we'd had. The two of us had spent too many years together with me struggling to get over what she'd been to my now-deceased first husband—as hard as it still is to say, she had been his mistress and the proof of it, in the person of Lloyd, had the run of my house. And those same years had been spent with her trying to fit in with my respectable and unblemished way of living. We'd each done a good job of arriving at a meeting of minds and living in harmony, if I do say so myself. In fact, almost too good a job, because I was left with an empty space where she'd once been.

But I tend to look on the bright side of things, and the bright side of having her in Sam's house was not having little Julie and Lily Mae in mine. Oh, I was delighted with those twin babies, but I'd lived too many years in a quiet and well-organized home to adjust easily to the demands of growing children. Except for Lloyd, of course, whom I never minded having around, even though he was currently the reason for my unrelenting anxiety and feelings of dread.

Lillian pushed through the swinging door from the dining room and stopped. "I didn't know y'all was down here! Jus' look at them baby girls, they growin' like weeds." She leaned over the stroller and stroked the cheek of one of them—I never knew which was which. "Hey, little sweet girl, you come to see Lillian? I think you both need a sody cracker, don't you?"

The babies kicked and crowed and smiled at Lillian, reaching little hands for the saltines she offered. One immediately spat out the pacifier and crumbled the cracker against her mouth, while the other tried to get her cracker in without releasing the pacifier.

"How you doin', Miss Hazel Marie," Lillian asked, her eyes staying on the babies. "You gettin' much sleep?"

"They slept six hours straight last night. I couldn't believe it, but I'm getting them outside as much as I can. They sleep better if they have some exercise." Hazel Marie smiled ruefully. "Of course, pushing this stroller around means I'm the one getting the exercise. But I really need it." She looked down and patted her stomach under the loose top she was wearing. "I'm so stretched out of shape from carrying twins, it's unbelievable. I exercise like crazy, but I think the only hope is to have surgery to take up the slack."

"Oh, Hazel Marie, you're not thinking of going to South America, are you?"

She laughed. "No, my obstetrician said it can be done here, but to wait awhile before thinking about surgery. So I guess I'll just keep on exercising. Anyway," she went on, smiling down on her babies, "I have my hands full with these two little ones now. It takes all my energy to keep up with them."

By now—some five or so months after their birth—the babies were beginning to adjust their inner workings to fit in with the schedules of normal people, and I feared that Hazel Marie's days were getting easy enough for her to reconsider the arrangements we'd made, especially if she was thinking of having surgery. I would never bring up the subject, though. I just acted as if the way things were would be the way things stayed.

"I'm happy for you, Hazel Marie," I said, picking up where we'd left off, "but I do miss having you around."

"Shoo, I seem to be over here so much you hardly have time to miss me. But I know what you mean, because as happy as I am, I miss you, too."

We smiled at each other, then she said what I'd been dreading to hear. "But, Miss Julia," she said, her lovely face marred by a frown, "I miss Lloyd, too. I don't see how I can do without him much longer. I'd like us to think about when he can move in with us."

I knew it. I *knew* it would be coming sooner or later, and here it was.

Chapter 2

Every time Hazel Marie came to visit, which was two or three times a week, I would get that sinking feeling, sure that she'd come to tell me she wanted Lloyd living with the rest of the Pickens family. Up until this time, the boy had remained with Sam and me on the basis that he didn't need to be uprooted in the middle of a school year even though a move would not have meant a change of schools. The other, maybe more important, reason was that, try as they might, Lillian, Etta Mae Wiggins and Hazel Marie had been unable to get those two babies on any kind of reasonable schedule. One or the other of the twins, and often both at the same time, were awake and screaming half the night. Which meant that Hazel Marie had to sleep when they did—namely, half the day. And who wants a young boy wandering around a house alone while his mother is laid up in bed all afternoon?

And Lloyd himself had made the final decision, saying that he didn't have time to pack up and move all his stuff. That's what he called it, his *stuff*, which consisted of a computer, a printer, lengths of wires and cables, books, games and innumerable other electronic gadgets, to say nothing of tennis rackets, tennis shoes, books and collections of everything from rocks to compact disks. Frankly, though, I thought that he, too, preferred peace and quiet to the continuous turmoil that the babies created. But he occasionally spent a night or a weekend with his mother when Mr.

Pickens was out of town. Even though James lived in the apartment over the garage at Sam's house, Hazel Marie liked having someone in the house with her. So it wasn't as if the Pickenses had abandoned the boy, although Mr. Pickens worried about it at first.

"I don't want Lloyd thinking he's been replaced," Mr. Pickens had said to me. "He's a big part of our family and I want him with us."

Well, he was a big part of my family, too, and I wanted him with me. But I tried to stay out of it, simply suggesting that he stay at least until school was out, when he could unhook all his electronic appliances without needing them every day for homework.

So that's where we were, but school would be out for the summer before long and here Hazel Marie was, saying she wanted her boy back.

I thought about crying, which I was on the verge of anyway, but to use that as a method of getting my way was too low to consider for long. Hazel Marie loved that child, and regardless of how many other children she had, although I hoped the twins were the last, Lloyd was her firstborn and special to her.

I pulled myself together and said, "I understand, Hazel Marie, and I think he's planning on it as soon as school is out. Of course he's welcome here as long as he wants to stay."

I didn't mention that my heart would break if he left. One thing, however, was certain: I'd never dismantle and redecorate his room.

❦

"So," Sam said that evening while we sat in the living room after supper, "Lloyd will be leaving when school's out?" He folded the newspaper he'd been reading and watched as I separated yarn for the needlepoint piece I was working on.

"That's the way it looks." I cut a length of yarn and tried to thread the needle, then gave up in spite of the glasses I was wearing. "Oh, Sam, I don't think I can stand it. Just look at us, sitting here like two old people with nothing to do, and he's just away for a tennis match. We should've gone, too. I don't know why we didn't. The school they're playing is only two hours away. We could've gone."

"We go to the home matches," Sam reminded me. "He doesn't expect us to be at all of them."

"I know, I know." I sounded a little snippy because I was on edge. "But I'm thinking that this is the way it'll be all the time once he's gone. And that we ought to take advantage and be with him every minute of the time we have left."

"Julia, honey, it's not as if he's moving cross-country. He'll be in and out of here all the time. This is home for him."

"That'll change soon enough, as soon as he settles in over there. And I know I'm thinking only of myself, but I just don't know how I'll fill the days without him here."

"Well, I'll tell you one way. Go with me to the Holy Land."

I looked at him over my glasses. "Why're you bringing that up again?"

He shrugged. "I've wanted you to go all along, even before this came up. Traveling would take your mind off Lloyd during his first weeks away."

"No," I said, not having to even consider it. "I've not lost one thing in the Holy Land. Besides they're shooting at one another over there."

"It's safe enough," he said, somewhat complacently. "You'd enjoy the trip. I know I will."

"Yes, but you have wanderlust and I don't."

Sam grinned. "Restless foot syndrome."

"I believe it," I said, remembering the trip to Russia he'd taken awhile back. "I know you want to go and that's fine. Just count me out." I looked at the needlepoint piece, wondering if I'd ever finish it. "Besides, it's not as if you're going by yourself. You'll have plenty of company, won't you?"

"There're about nine or so who've signed up, but Ledbetter asked if I would talk you into going, or anybody else, for that matter. I think he'd hoped to have a bigger group so he'd get better tour rates."

"For goodness sake, Sam, why would anybody want a cut-rate tour? I still don't understand why you'd want to go with him in the first place." Pastor Ledbetter was not someone I'd choose to lead me around a strange land. He was hard enough to take on home ground.

"Oh, he'll do fine. This'll be his third trip, and I've heard good reports about the second one." Sam raised his eyebrows and gave me a wicked grin. "Not so good about the first one. Everybody got sick, including him."

"Preachers ought to stay where they belong," I pronounced. "I've never understood why they have to go running around all over the world. Next thing you know, he'll be wanting to go to Africa."

"Yeah, he's mentioned that. Wants to build a dam or a hospital or something one of these days."

"Well, count me out of that, too."

"Okay, but I'd like to count you in for the Israel trip. Give me one good reason why you don't want to go."

I looked at him. "I'll give you more than that. I have no desire to get in an airplane and let somebody else drive it. I don't like flying, and I wouldn't like traipsing all over the Holy Land with my knees aching and my feet hurting. And Pastor Ledbetter would drive me crazy, being with him every day, and I have to supervise a room remodel here. There's no way I'd turn a bunch of carpenters loose in this house with nobody watching them. And, finally, Hazel Marie might need me. She's still not in full control of those babies, and with Mr. Pickens gone so much she'll need help. And, well, I guess this is the final reason, but Lloyd might want to stay on awhile, so I need to be here in case he does." Then I said, "But I know how much you like to travel and see new places. Your plans are all made, bags ready to be packed and everything, so you go on and don't worry about me. Besides, I don't have a passport. That's really the final reason."

"I expect," Sam said mildly, "we could get you one, have the process expedited, so that's not a good reason."

"Well, I'll strike that one and let the others stand." I smiled at him, ready to let the conversation lapse.

"You don't mind my going?"

"Sam, I miss you every time you step out of this house, even to walk downtown. So, yes, I'll mind your being away for—what? Two weeks, isn't it?"

"Yeah, two and a couple of days for travel."

"I wouldn't keep you from doing something I know you'll enjoy. You just have a good time, and I'll try to have your office all set up and ready for you by the time you get back. Then we'll see if you can finish that book you've been working on for a hundred years."

"Setting me a challenge, huh?"

"That's right," I said, giving him a warm smile. "Actually, it would've been better if you'd had that book done by now. Then while everybody's reading it, you could be out of town."

Sam laughed. "I doubt everybody'll be reading it. There won't be many who'll be interested in the legal history of Abbot County. Although," he said, patting his fingers against his mouth, "it's not turning out to be quite as dry as I thought it would be. Might not be a bad idea to plan another trip when it does come out."

"Ooh," I said, teasing him. "You mean you've been writing a racy book all this time?"

"Well, you know what they say," he said, his eyes twinkling. "A writer should write what he knows."

I laughed, warmed by my husband's teasing. "You're too much, Sam." I held up the painted needlepoint canvas—Japanese or maybe Chinese chrysanthemums, only partially stitched. "Look at this thing. There's so much shading, I'll never figure out what color goes where."

"Pretty," he said and picked up the paper again.

I slipped the needle into the canvas and folded the piece, ready to leave it for the night. "Sam," I said, "I've just had a thought. Emma Sue's not going on the Holy Land tour, is she?"

"I don't think so. She planned to go on that first tour—the one that was a disaster—six or seven years ago, got a passport and was all ready. But at the last minute she backed out and ended up staying home, remember? And now I guess she's too busy with all her commitments." He turned a page of the newspaper, then looked at me. "Why?"

"Well, it seems to me that the pastor could make arrangements for his own wife to go at least once. And, yes, I know. She says she has too much to do to leave, but I'm wondering if the real reason has to do with thinking they can't afford it."

Sam lowered the paper. "That would be a big part of it, I expect."

"Then she can go in my place. I'll pay for it."

"You mean," Sam said, his eyebrows lifted high, "as *my* seatmate, roommate, whatever?"

"No," I said, laughing at the look on his face. "I want you to enjoy the trip."

"Well, seriously though, it would be a nice gesture on your part, Julia. I think Emma Sue uses her commitments as an excuse because it'd be too expensive for both of them to go."

"Yes, but you and I know what the pastor makes, and they could afford it if he'd just do it. Tell him tomorrow that *I* have too many commitments and that I want Emma Sue to go in my place."

"Okay, but what if the real reason is because he wants a break from her," Sam said, "or she wants one from him?"

"Too bad, because she's going." I laid aside the needlepoint and went over to his chair. "That's not the case with us, though, is it?" I sat on the arm of his chair and took his hand. "I expect you've noticed that we're all by ourselves. And, furthermore, it'll be a couple of hours before Lloyd gets home."

Chapter 3

With the question of my going to the Holy Land firmly settled—I was *not* going—I turned my mind the next morning to the other matter that needed settling. I was still going back and forth, trying to decide which room I wanted Sam to work in and which room I wanted him to sleep in. And the more I thought about it, the better I liked the idea of remodeling the downstairs bedroom into an office. Well, not an office, exactly, but more of a library with deep leather chairs and a sofa trimmed with brass nailheads, cherry or mahogany panels with bookshelves lining the walls, a few good oil paintings and, of course, a large mahogany desk for his work. And, I suddenly thought, a fireplace. Yes, we had to have a fireplace. I could already picture the room—a lush, quiet refuge for him during the day and for the two of us in the evenings.

To tell the truth, I was tired of the Victorian furnishings in our living room—tired especially of that stiff-backed, hard-stuffed neoclassical Duncan Phyfe sofa, which I'd never liked anyway. Even though I'd recovered every upholstered piece in the room in bright florals—as far from Victorian velvets and tapestries as I could get—as soon after Wesley Lloyd's demise as had seemed appropriate, the room was still a little too prim and stodgy for my taste.

So there was no way I'd carry the Victorian theme over into the rest of the house, now that I was in a redecorating state of mind. I'd just live with the living room the way it was, putting it on hold for the time being while I concentrated on Sam's new library. I wanted deep, soft leather—real leather, not Naugahyde, vinyl or plastic—and maybe carpet instead of an Oriental on the floor, and a colonial mantel with large brass candlesticks on each end or perhaps wall sconces on each side of an oil painting of a horse in the English countryside.

I would have a butler's tray with those brass hinges as a coffee table and lamps converted from porcelain vases, draperies with valances and fringed trim and a great leather executive's chair for Sam. It would be beautiful but, I realized with another one of my sinking feelings, not exactly suitable for a working office. The computer, a printer, cables and surge protectors strewn around would just ruin the decor.

Still, I wasn't ready to give up my vision because, to tell the truth, I'd just realized that the best place for Sam's office would be the sunroom upstairs at the back of the house. That was the room that then-Deputy Coleman Bates had rented soon after Wesley Lloyd passed and had more recently served as a guest room for Etta Mae Wiggins. It would be the quietest room in the house, and he could leave his books, notes and papers spread out all over the place without anyone seeing or disturbing them.

If I did that, I mused, it would mean that Sam and I would keep Hazel Marie's room as our bedroom, which in turn meant that it would need a complete overhaul, using a more suitable color scheme. Get rid of all that pink, first of all, because Sam kept telling me that pink wasn't his color. The room needed a color scheme that he would be comfortable with, something a little more masculine without ignoring the fact that a wife shared it as well.

It wouldn't take much, I thought as I tried to count the cost in my head, to remove wallpaper, then paint the room, replace the carpet and give Hazel Marie any pieces of furniture from the room that she wanted.

Wonder how pink would look on Mr. Pickens?

All of a sudden, I seemed to be planning some major remodeling, which would be a good thing, given my need to have something to occupy my mind. It would keep me busy throughout the summer and maybe ease some of the sadness of no longer having Lloyd around.

One other little niggling worry if I carried out these plans was how many more years Sam and I could manage to get up and down the stairs. I think that aging people, which we certainly were, should think ahead on such matters. Even now, I was sometimes so stiff I could hardly get out of bed in the mornings, and I didn't know how much longer I'd be able to trot up and down stairs a half dozen times a day.

Even so, I wasn't ready to give up my dream of an English library downstairs. If it got too difficult to climb the stairs, I'd put one of those little elevator chairs on the bannister. That would do the trick, although Sam and I would have to draw straws each night to see which one got the first ride up.

All of my dreaming and planning and musing came to a halt when the telephone rang halfway through the morning.

"Julia?" my neighbor Mildred Allen asked, although she knew my voice as well as I knew hers. "Did you hear that Emma Sue Ledbetter is going on that tour to Israel?"

"Why, yes, I did hear that, and I'm glad she's finally getting to go. In fact, it was becoming a scandal that the pastor kept leaving her at home, don't you think?"

"I certainly do. And I was thinking that I might slip her a few dollars to spend as she wants to."

"That'd be very thoughtful," I said, and restrained myself from mentioning the more-than-a-few dollars I'd slipped to enable Emma Sue to go. You lose the spiritual benefit of giving if you tell it, so I didn't.

"Anyway," Mildred went on, "I heard that Sam is going, and I wondered if you'd changed your mind."

"Not a chance, Mildred. I have no desire to go anywhere. I want to be here in case Hazel Marie needs me, and, of course, I still have Lloyd for a little while longer, and I'm planning to have some work done on the house."

"Oh, good. That means you'll have a big party when it's all done. I can't wait to hear what you're going to do. Why don't you bring your plans over and let me see them?"

"Shoo, Mildred, I'm just in the thinking stage. I don't have any plans yet, but now that you mention it, I probably should. Except the only real construction I'm thinking of is a fireplace. Oh, and bookshelves."

"You'd better have all that drawn out on a blueprint then. Believe me, I know what I'm talking about. You try to explain your ideas to even a master carpenter and if he doesn't have specific measurements and an exact picture of what you want, you won't get it. Take my advice, Julia, and use an architect. Tucker Caldwell is awfully good—he did my pool house, you know. You do have to be firm with him, though, and make sure his ideas don't take the place of yours. And when you're ready, I know a really good carpenter—Adam Waites. He is just excellent and easy to have around, except for one thing."

"Oh?"

"He's a Christian."

"Well," I laughed, "so are you and I. What's wrong with that?"

"He lets you know it all the time, that's what's wrong with it."

"You mean he's one of the witnessing kind?"

"Not exactly. Well, let me tell you what he did the first time I had him do some work in my kitchen. He drove up in his pickup, crawled out and turned his face up to the sky and started singing."

"Singing? Singing what?"

"Oh, I don't know. Some kind of hymn, like having joy down in his heart or something. Anyway, I was standing on the back porch waiting for him. Trying to be nice and friendly, I said, 'You sound mighty happy this morning.' You know, thinking that maybe his wife had just had a baby or something. And he said, 'I have Jesus in my heart and that makes me happy.' Well," Mildred said, taking a deep breath, "what can you say to that, 'I do, too'? Except I wasn't singing and didn't feel like singing, which would've made it sound as if Jesus had made him happy enough to sing but had left me out."

"So what did you say?"

"I said, 'Oh, well, good. You ready to work?' I mean, what else could I say? But he really is an excellent carpenter if you can overlook all that piety. But listen, Julia, that wasn't what I called about. Did you ever know the Whitmans?"

"Candy people?"

"No, banking."

"I guess not, then. Who are they?"

"They were a well-to-do, and I mean *very* well-to-do, family in Asheville, and they had one daughter late in life who was a trial to them the entire time they had left. I lost track of her after they passed. Well, I really never knew her—she's younger than we are by twenty or so years, I think. Maybe more. Actually, I knew the father more than I knew her because Daddy had done some business with him. Anyway, to get to the point of it all, that girl, woman, whatever she is, Agnes Whitman, traipsed all over creation from California to India, going from one crazy thing to another. You know, seeing gurus and wearing beads and caftans and things like that. And she was brought up in the *church*, Julia, can you believe that? Anyway, I've just heard that she's moved to Abbot County. She bought a good bit of acreage over in Fairfields and built what I heard is a mansion and is really making a showplace of it, with horses and everything."

"Well, she sounds interesting."

"Oh, you haven't heard anything yet. Actually, it's strange that you're looking for a carpenter because I heard that Adam Waites has done some work for her: built some stables, a pool house, and I don't know what all. What I'm getting around to telling you, even though it sounds like I've been rambling, is that it all ties together." Mildred stopped, and I realized it was time for me to say something.

"How?"

"Well, I'm not exactly sure. It's just that I've also heard that Agnes is mixed up with some sort of strange cult of some kind. Her parents would simply die if they knew, but they've passed on, so I guess it doesn't matter. And I was just wondering how she and Adam got along. You know, with one dabbling in weird Wiccan stuff and the other singing Gospel songs. I would think that'd make for a volatile situation."

"You mean she's a witch?"

"No, I don't think she dances around trees, although I wouldn't be surprised to learn she's tried it at one time or another. Now listen, don't think that Adam has been telling me all this. He's not a gossip, even though I admit I let him know I was interested when I learned he'd worked for her. No, I've heard from various people that she's involved in some kind of strange body-and-spirit religion, but nobody seems to know any details. I'm just surprised that she and Adam could work together."

I laughed. "Well, maybe one will convert the other. But seriously, Mildred, I doubt they'd have much to do with each other. I know I don't hang around any workmen I hire. I tell them what I want done and leave them to it. Anyway, if he's already done all that work for her, then he's through."

"No, that's what I'm trying to tell you. If you want him, you need to call him right away. She's redoing her entire landscape, and I mean to the extent of tearing down the pool house Adam has already built for her. He said she now wants a guesthouse that's either a miniature replica of the main house or a Palladian folly—you know, one of those eighteenth-century fun houses. She's just waiting for the blueprints to make up her mind, so you need to get him between jobs, which is to say, right away."

So Mildred gave me Adam Waites's business name, which was The Carpenter's Sons, and his phone number. With her assurance that he was the absolute best, I decided to take the plunge and secure Mr. Waites for my remodeling project. He could start removing pink wallpaper while I engaged an architect to draw the plan for the new library. No more dreaming and planning—I was now embarked on turning my house upside down.

Chapter 4

After discussing my plans with Sam and asking for his ideas on the remodeling project, I realized that I had a free hand to do whatever I wanted. He was so easy to please and easy to get along with that I congratulated myself again for having had the sense to marry him. Some men, you know, can't let anything happen without putting in their two cents, then they get mad if you don't agree with them. But Sam only wanted a place to work on his book, and as long as I arranged a room where he could spread out his notes and papers, he'd be happy. Actually, he was pleased that my summer would be full and busy, and he declared that the sunroom would be perfect for his office.

"It'll be out of the way," he said. "And it gets a lot of light with all the windows. I like the idea, and I'm glad you thought of it."

With that, I kept the appointment I'd immediately made with Mr. Tucker Caldwell, intending to set him to work transferring the visions in my head onto blueprint paper. Mr. Caldwell was a short, slender man who wore pleated slacks and a bow tie—most likely purchased in a boys' department. His straight brown hair flopped down over his brow, occasionally obscuring the black-framed glasses he wore. Something about him—maybe his precise, meticulous mannerisms or maybe his bow tie—reminded me of Wesley Lloyd Springer, my late, unlamented first husband, so I was momentarily put off when I first met him.

But he seemed to quickly grasp what I wanted for the new library. At Mildred's suggestion, I had brought a few books and some pages torn from magazines that illustrated the look I wanted to achieve.

"I'll need to come out and take some measurements," he said as he looked through the pages. "But I see what you want, and I like it." He glanced up from across his desk, giving me a quick smile, to see if his approval met with mine. "Now, how many windows are in the room?"

"Four," I said, then hesitantly passed another sheet of paper across the desk. "I've sketched out the room, but of course it's not to scale. I don't trust my measuring skills, but you can see there are two tall windows on the south side and two on the east. And on whichever wall you think best, I want a fireplace, and I want one of those big fat chimneys that you see in Williamsburg."

"No, you don't want that."

"I don't?"

"No," he said in a knowledgeable, almost a know-it-all, manner, "they're hugely expensive and nobody does them anymore. What we'll do is put in one of those ready-made fireplaces that comes in a kit, and all you'll need is a flue that runs up to the roof. It'll serve your purpose and save you a mint."

So this was what Mildred was talking about. "Stick to your guns," she'd told me, "or he'll talk you out of getting what you want."

"But it's what I want," I said.

"Believe me, you don't," Mr. Caldwell said with such firmness that I had to take myself in hand. "You won't be able to tell the difference from inside. We'll use a reeded surround and an Adam mantel on it, and you'll be pleased with all the money you save." He busied himself sketching an elevation of one wall with a fireplace to show what he was talking about, hardly bothering to look up to see how I was taking it.

"Mr. Caldwell," I said, and waited until he'd put down his pen and looked up. "Let's work it this way: you do what you do best, which is to design a plan of what I want, and I'll do what I do best, which is to pay for it. And what I want is a Williamsburg chimney because I care about the outside of my house as well as the inside. And because such a chimney would have a greater aesthetic impact than a metal pipe sticking up through the roof."

He tapped his pen on the desk, staring at me the whole time. I knew what he was thinking: *here's a live one.*

"And besides," I went on to stop that kind of thinking, "I've already investigated the cost of the workmanship required to build a huge chimney, so I'm quite prepared to have what I want at a price that I'm willing to pay."

"That being the case," he said, suddenly deciding that a Williamsburg chimney was a grand idea, "I'll have the preliminary plans in a couple of days. When would be convenient for me to do the measurements?"

We decided on a date and a time, and I stood to take my leave. "One more thing," I said, "because I've not worked with an architect before: I will pay you for today's consultation, but it's my understanding that you are not fully engaged until you produce a set of plans that meet my approval. Is that correct?"

He assured me that it was, and I left feeling that not only were we now reading from the same book, but we were also on the same page. I didn't want to have to fight him every step of the way, so it had been necessary and proper that he know with whom he was dealing.

❦

Adam Waites came rolling in the next morning, ladders tied to the roof of the camper shell on his pickup and the inside loaded with the tools of his trade. I watched from the kitchen window as he stepped out of his truck and fastened a work belt around his hips. He was a fine-looking young man, lean but muscular, with a shy reticence about him. He wore jeans that fit—no rear bagging, I was happy to see—and a gray T-shirt with a lion and a lamb printed on it, surrounded by the words RIDGETOP EVANGELICAL CAMPGROUND. As he walked to the back of the truck, I noted his heavy-duty high-top work boots, remarkable for the green patch on each tongue, which had the image of a yellow leaping deer. I recognized it as the logo of a plow and tractor maker. He looked capable and ready for work.

I counted myself fortunate for having reached him at just the right moment, when he was between jobs for that Whitman woman. My intention was to set him to work dismantling Hazel Marie's room, stripping the wallpaper and replacing it with a soothing, bedroomy paint color—just as soon as I could figure out what that was.

I waited for him at the back door, but Mr. Waites was not singing as he approached. He was humming. I didn't remark on it as Mildred had, but it was a tune I knew but couldn't at first dredge up the name of it. Don't you just hate that?

Finally, it came to me. I'd learned two dozen verses of "This Little Light of Mine" years before when I'd been talked into helping with Vacation Bible School, learning at the same time that I had not been given the gift of patience with thirty-some-odd boisterous five-year-olds. The only good thing that had come out of the experience was being able to say the following year, "Let somebody else have a turn. I've had mine."

Up close, Mr. Waites looked younger than I'd expected—late twenties, most likely—with a clean-shaven face and an open manner. He was pleasant enough, seemingly agreeable to all I pointed out that needed to be done both in Hazel Marie's room and in the sunroom.

"Let's build cabinets all across this wall under the windows," I said as we stood in the sunroom. I pointed to the hand-drawn plan that indicated the number, placement and color of the cabinets I wanted. "I want pullout shelves in some and file drawers in others. Then let's build bookcases on this other wall all the way to the ceiling. You'll want to match the crown molding and the baseboard. Will that be a problem?"

"No'm," he said softly.

I then directed him to the pink room, pointing out what I

wanted done. He nodded and went right to work moving Hazel Marie's furniture to the middle of the room and covering it with a heavy painter's cloth.

"Don't worry about the carpet," I told him. "That's coming up next. Of course, we'll have to do something with this furniture to get it out of the way."

Mr. Waites scratched his head. "I can bring some of my brothers and we'll move it if you have a place for it."

"Hm," I said, thinking. "Maybe we can put it in the sunroom temporarily, then shift it back when you finish in here—what's left of it anyway, because I'm giving some of it away. All that moving could be a big job. How many brothers do you have?"

"There's five of us, all sons of The Carpenter." He glanced sideways at me, perhaps to see if I got the allusion.

"Oh, so you learned your skills from your father?" I asked, deciding not to bite.

He smiled beatifically. "Yes, ma'am, we learned 'em from our earthly father and our heavenly father."

"Well, how nice." I knew, of course, that Joseph had been a carpenter and his young Son had worked alongside him. But if Mr. Waites wanted to play on words to test my scriptural knowledge, I would just let it go over my head. As long as he did good work, he could think what he wanted. I'd been around too many scripture-quoting contests to want to engage in one myself.

Chapter 5

It was still quite early the morning I returned home from taking Sam to the Asheville airport. I was feeling a little blue from watching his plane lift off, so I was comforted to find Lillian busy in the kitchen as the coffee made its last sighing perc.

"You get 'em off?" she asked.

"Finally," I said, pulling out a chair at the table. "I declare, it takes an act of Congress to get on an airplane these days. I'm just glad I didn't have to go through all that rigmarole. You wouldn't believe it, Lillian."

"What all they do?" She set a cup and saucer before me, pushed the cream forward and sat down with her own cup.

"Well, first off, we had to take Emma Sue with us, which put a crimp in our good-byes. Pastor Ledbetter had already arranged to go with the Dillards and they didn't have room for Emma Sue's luggage, so she ended up riding with us. And, Lillian, that woman talked the whole way to the airport, and a mile a minute, too. She was so excited she couldn't see straight, kept saying that she'd known the Lord would prepare a way for her if she'd just be patient. She went on and on about trusting the Lord's timing, going so far as to tell me that I should exercise more patience about Lloyd moving in with his mother. It was all I could do to hold my tongue." I took a sip of coffee and tried to exercise a little patience about Emma Sue. "Actually, though, I'm happy that she was excited about going and I hope she enjoys every minute. I just wish she'd given a little credit to those who made it possible by carrying out the Lord's will. I mean, he didn't, himself, leave a bag of money on her doorstep. It had to come *through* somebody."

"Yessum, an' I 'spect I know who that somebody was."

I smiled. "She thinks it was a group that contributed, which was the way I wanted it so she wouldn't feel obligated or embarrassed about it. But still, she could've expressed some gratitude to whoever was in the group. I've just never been comfortable with people who think there's a direct line between them and the Lord without any third-party help."

"Preachers is bad about that. Everybody dig down till it hurt to raise they salary, and they act like it found money come down from heaven 'specially for them."

"That's the truth," I agreed. "But, Lillian, that wasn't the end of it. They almost didn't let Emma Sue get on the plane. She'd packed some things she wasn't supposed to, so they unpacked everything right out there in front of everybody, and I mean everything. She was just mortified when they pulled out some feminine hygiene products that hadn't even been put in Ziploc bags. Which I wouldn't have known to do, either, but somebody should've told her how and what to pack. I can't imagine what'll happen when they change planes in New York and a full-body scan has to be done. But the worst of all was the pastor, who tried to defend her while halfway acting like she wasn't with his group. I really blame him for the whole embarrassing episode."

"Well," Lillian said, "I hope the pore little thing have a good time if she ever get there. And if she do get there, Mr. Sam'll look after her."

"I expect he'll have to." I sat back with a sigh at the thought of his being gone for a couple of weeks. "Why, good morning, Lloyd," I said, as the boy pushed through the swinging door from the dining room and Lillian got up to go to the stove. "Big day today, isn't it?"

He groaned. "Last day before exams is always a big day, but I could sure do without it. We'll be reviewing all day and studying all weekend—finals start on Monday. I wish it was this time next week."

"Scrambled or fried?" Lillian asked. "I already got some of them little link sausages you like. Miss Julia, which you want?"

Lloyd and I answered at the same time. "Scrambled."

"Mr. Sam get off okay?" Lloyd asked as he sat at the table to await breakfast. "Y'all sure did leave early."

"Yes, and we needed every minute of it, too," I said, able to laugh about it now as I told him about the search of Emma Sue's luggage, leaving out, of course, any mention of specifics. "I did feel sorry for her because it was such a public search, and of course she was weeping the whole way through it."

"I guess I would be, too," Lloyd said, "especially if they went through my underdrawers. Kinda embarrassing. Anyway, I think I'd like to go on one of those trips overseas one of these days."

"Why don't you plan to go to a college where they offer a junior year abroad? I might even come to visit if you were gone that long."

"Huh!" Lillian said, as she spooned scrambled eggs onto our plates. "I like to see you get on a airplane."

"You just might," I said, coming right back at her. "Because if I go, you're going, too."

"Wait a minute, wait a minute," Lloyd said before she could respond. "I'm not even in high school yet, so we have a long time to figure it out. Besides, I'm going to Chapel Hill if I can get in and I don't know if they have that junior year."

"Chapel Hill has anything you want, and you'll get in, don't worry about that. You just keep up your grades the way you've been doing, stay with your tennis and maybe some volunteer work and they'll take you. And, Lloyd," I went on, "let's put getting your Eagle Scout ranking at the top of the list. That'll look good on an application."

"Yessum, but I still have a few more badges to get before I can start my project. It might take another year or so."

"That's fine, just don't let it slide. Starting high school next year is just the time when a lot of boys give up Scouting. I know you're getting tired of it, but you're too close to let it lapse now."

"No'm, I won't." He took a last bite, wiped his mouth with his napkin and stood up. "Thanks, Lillian. I better get going or I'll be late. Miss Julia, we might get out early today, so I'll probably be home around two. I could start packing up some of my stuff this afternoon, 'less somebody wants to play tennis. I'll let you know."

After he banged out the back door, an almost empty backpack dangling from his shoulder, I sighed. "That's what I was afraid of. He's going to pack up and leave without a backward look."

"Don't be too sure about that," Lillian said as she cleared the table. "He's not gone yet, an' I 'spect you can come up with a few excuses for him to stay on. If you put yo' mind to it like you usually do."

"I guess I could," I said, agreeing because I'd already thought of a few. "But it wouldn't be right. Oh, Lillian, I'm just so torn up over this. He needs a mother and a father, and he has both just four blocks away, yet I hate to see him go."

"I know you do. But jus' think, a little while back you didn't have nobody. Now you got four chil'ren, if you count Latisha, who you might as well 'cause she think she b'long here, too. An' even better, you don't have 'em all underfoot all day long. I say, count yo' blessin's 'cause you got a lot of 'em."

So that's what I tried to do for the rest of the morning in between going in and out of Lloyd's room to look at all the stuff that would soon be gone and to enjoy the boy smell that permeated the room.

I thought of calling around to see if anybody wanted to go to lunch, but I didn't have the heart for it. I thought of working on that needlepoint canvas, but I couldn't sit still long enough.

The fact of the matter was that I dawdled all morning, becoming sadder and sadder at the realization that all my days from henceforth would be just like this one: empty of things to do and with nothing to look forward to at the end of each school day.

At just about the end of that particular school day, the telephone rang. Thinking it would be Lloyd calling to say that he'd be on the tennis court until suppertime, I answered it.

There was a lot of static on the line, and my first thought was that Sam was calling from miles above the ocean or, with a heart-stopping chill, that someone was calling about a disaster of some kind.

So it took me a second or two to concentrate on a vaguely familiar voice. "Miss Julia?"

"Yes?" I heard more voices in the background, low and constant, like a radio that needed to be turned down.

"Sam . . . ?" the voice said.

"I can't understand you. You sound like you're in a barrel. Who do you want to speak to?"

More static. ". . . need to speak to Sam."

"He's not here. He's on his way to the Holy Land. I can have him call you when he gets back, but it'll be awhile. Who is this, anyway?" I waited, listening to what sounded like rushing wind or maybe falling water. Then it hit me. "*Mr. Pickens?* Is that you? Are you all right? Where are you?"

I heard "Sam" again and maybe "Coleman," but I couldn't be sure, although I was holding the receiver so close that it was hurting my ear. Then, as clear as a bell, I heard another voice, heavier and harsher, say, "He can't talk no more." And the connection was broken.

"What in the world?" I said, then hung up the phone and stood there trying to make sense of the strange call.

Hearing Lloyd come into the kitchen, I wandered out to see him, still thinking over what more and more seemed to have been a call from Mr. Pickens wanting some kind of help from Sam. Which was strange to begin with, because Mr. Pickens knew Sam was off walking where Jesus walked, at least he should've known because that was all we'd talked about for weeks. And, yes, Mr. Pickens himself had left on a case—who knows whose footsteps *he* was walking in— a week or so before Sam flew off, so maybe he'd gotten the dates mixed up. But it was an unusual circumstance, to say the least, for him to need help from anybody at any time and the more worrisome because of it.

Chapter 6

"That was strange," I said as I pushed through the swinging door into the kitchen where Lloyd stood by the counter, eating a banana while watching Lillian smear peanut butter on graham crackers.

"What was?" Lloyd asked.

"That phone call I just got. I think it was Mr. Pickens, but the connection was so bad I could only pick up a few words. He was calling for Sam, I think."

"J.D. called?" Lloyd asked, the banana stopped halfway to his mouth. "Mama was expecting him home three days ago, but she's not heard from him. What did he want?"

"Well, that's the thing. I couldn't get much out of him. There was too much interference on the line. I heard him say 'Sam' and maybe 'Coleman,' but I'm not sure about that."

"Where he at?" Lillian asked.

"I don't know. He didn't say, and the odd thing about it was that somebody else—a different voice—broke in and said, "He can't talk no more," which was mighty poor grammar, and hung up. I feel as if I should be doing something, but I don't know what."

"Call him back," Lillian said.

"I can't. He didn't tell me where he was."

Lloyd's eyes had gotten bigger as we talked, then he seemed to shake himself and put his mind to work. "Anybody else call since he did?"

"No. I just hung up a minute ago."

"Then do the Return Call thing. You can make the last call reconnect. It might even clear the line."

"You do it, Lloyd. I might mess it up."

"Okay," he said, laying aside his half-eaten banana and going to the phone book under the kitchen phone. "I better look up the directions to be sure."

Then he turned back to me. "You reckon something's wrong? I know Mama's worried 'cause she hasn't heard from him."

"Let's not get ahead of ourselves," I said, although the more I thought of how weak and far away Mr. Pickens's voice had sounded, the more disturbed I became. If it even had been Mr. Pickens, though who else would've been calling for both Sam and Coleman? "Hurry and do that Return thing before somebody else calls."

He found the instructions in the phone book and carefully picked up the phone and punched in a few numbers. I leaned in close to try to hear who would answer.

Lloyd said, "It's ringing," then he jumped back and said, "Wup. Wrong number," and hung up.

"Who was it?" I asked. "Who answered? Lloyd, are you all right?" The child's face was as white as a sheet.

"They said . . . a man said—I think he said—'Deputy something or another,' of some kind of county sheriff's department. Then he said, 'Who's calling?' real sharp, like. It scared me, and now," Lloyd said, his face looking even more stricken, "I broke the connection and I don't know if we can get 'em back."

"Think real hard and see if you can remember what he said. Think which county he mentioned. What did it sound like?"

"Sounded like Carl or Carroll or something like that. I'm real sorry, Miss Julia. I don't know why I hung up so fast. It just surprised me so bad I didn't know what to do."

"It's all right," I said, patting his shoulder. "At least we now know that Mr. Pickens is in good hands. He'd have to be if he's with a sheriff's deputy."

"I don't know, Miss Julia," Lloyd said, a frown of worry on his forehead. "I don't like the sound of it. Not any of it. First off, why would J.D. be calling Mr. Sam? And why hasn't he called back if he needs help? And why would a deputy have his phone and be answering it?" Lloyd snapped his fingers. "And it *was* J.D.'s phone—his cell phone. Let's call it back. You do it this time, Miss Julia."

Lloyd took his own cell phone out of his backpack, accessed his list of numbers and pressed Send. "Here," he said, thrusting the phone at me, "it's ringing."

I held the phone and listened to the ringing, hoping to hear Mr. Pickens's voice. I heard a voice, all right, but it wasn't saying what I wanted to hear. "Voice mail," I whispered. Then, "Mr. Pickens? This is Julia Murdoch. We're worried about you. Please call me back as soon as you can."

Lillian, who'd been watching and listening to all this, said, "What we do now?"

"Let me think a minute," I said and proceeded to do so. "Lloyd, where was Mr. Pickens going when he left? And when did he leave exactly?"

"Around the first of last week, I think. Yes'm, that was it 'cause, remember? I spent every night this whole past weekend with Mama, and I'm pretty sure she said he'd be back Tuesday. And here it is Friday, and he hasn't called or anything to let her know when he'll be home. I think she was a little upset about it, said something about him having to remember he wasn't exactly free as a bird any longer."

"Well, I don't want to upset her any more than she already is. But we need to know where that phone call came from. You think your mother knows where he was going? Who he was working for or anything?"

Mr. Pickens could've been almost anywhere, well, anywhere in the country. I didn't think he was licensed as a private investigator in foreign lands, although who knew? For all I knew, his license could be limited to our own state and he'd strayed off the reservation. So to speak. Still, I couldn't believe that he would take off for parts unknown without letting his wife know. So, no, he was most likely somewhere in the southeast, most likely in the state, on some kind of case that he'd been hired to look into.

"I could ask her," Lloyd said. "He always tells her where he's going, but lots of times he ends up somewhere else. You know, he follows the case wherever it leads."

Lillian said, "I don't think y'all ought to worry that little woman 'fore you have to. He might already called her, too, lettin' her know where he at an' when he be home."

"That's true," I said, nodding my head, "and let's hope he has. Or," I went on, "he was trying to reach Sam because he didn't want to upset her. I mean if he's in trouble. And with a deputy answering his phone, I can't help but think something has happened. Maybe he's been hurt or injured or something."

"Well, what do we do? What can we do?" Lloyd was walking back and forth, wringing his hands.

"Two things," I said, trying to sound decisive and in control. "I think it's likely that he's somewhere in the state, so, Lloyd, you run up to your computer and see if you can find the names of all the North Carolina counties. Maybe you'll recognize the one you heard. And while you do that, I'll try to find Coleman and see if he's had a call. At least I think Mr. Pickens mentioned 'Coleman,' although he might have been saying the county he's in, because both start with a hard C."

"Don't stay on the telephone too long," Lillian said. "He might call back."

"Oh, my goodness, you're right. Lloyd, let me use your cell phone."

Lillian said, "He might call on that one, too."

Lloyd was on his way out of the room, but he turned back. "Use yours, Miss Julia."

"I can't. Which will teach me to keep the thing charged. Well, that's out, so I guess I'll have to take a chance and use this one. I won't stay on it long." Hoping that I wasn't giving Mr. Pickens a busy signal if he called back, I went to the kitchen phone and dialed the Sheriff's Department.

When the dispatcher answered, I said, "I need to speak to Sergeant Coleman Bates, please, on a matter of some urgency."

Somewhat surprised that I wasn't given a runaround, as they were prone to do on the nonemergency line, I waited only a few seconds until Coleman answered.

"Coleman, this is Julia Murdoch. Have you heard from Mr. Pickens?"

"What?" he said. "No. Should I have?"

"Well, we just hoped you had. See, Coleman, he called here, wanting to speak to Sam, but Sam's gone, as you well know, and won't be back for two weeks. Then Mr. Pickens mentioned you, or I think he did—the connection was so bad, I can't be sure—but anyway, he got cut off and when we did the Return thing, we got a sheriff's deputy but we don't know where he was, and when I called Mr. Pickens's cell phone, all I got was his voice mail. And now we don't know what to do."

"Sheriff's deputy, huh? You think he's in trouble?"

"That's all I can think, but we don't want to worry Hazel Marie with it until we know for sure, so I was hoping that he'd called you and you'd had a better connection. Lloyd's looking up North Carolina counties to see if he recognizes the county name, which he did hear but didn't quite catch."

"Uh, Miss Julia," Coleman said, "I'm not completely following you. Why don't I drop by on my way home. I'll be off duty in a few minutes."

"That's exactly what I wanted to hear, because I want to get off this line in case he tries to call back. You come right on, Coleman. We'll be waiting."

And I hung up fast. "There. The line's clear now. Maybe Mr. Pickens will call back."

"Let's hope," Lillian said.

Chapter 7

When Coleman came in, looking all official and professional and sharp as a tack in his dark blue uniform, with wide leather belt and straps creaking, along with clinking metallic sounds, I was relieved to turn everything over to him. Who better to track down an errant investigator? But as I thought about what Coleman was doing—immediately showing up, taking our concerns seriously and ignoring the slice of chocolate cake Lillian set before him—I was becoming more anxious. Frankly, I had assumed that Coleman would laugh it off and tell us that Mr. Pickens could handle any problem that came his way. Coleman wasn't doing that.

Lloyd told him that he'd found the names of seven or eight North Carolina counties starting with a hard C, but none of them rang a bell.

Coleman smiled and said, "We'd have a hard time tracking him down that way, so let's just ask your mother where he was going. That way we'll have a starting point."

"I don't know, Coleman," I said. "I wouldn't want to worry her. She has so much on her mind right now."

"Hmm," Coleman said, his handsome face serious and concerned. "You're right, I guess. No need to get her all worked up when it could be nothing. Tell you what. Why don't I ask her when he'll be home? I'll say that somebody wants him for a job, then ease around to asking where he is."

"That'd work," Lloyd said, nodding judiciously. "Better than us asking her anyway. She'd want to know why we wanted to know."

"Maybe so," Lillian said, "but y'all be careful and don't get her all scared and worried. She got them babies to look after."

"I'll be careful, Lillian," Coleman said. "In fact, I'll call her from here." He went to the phone as I marveled again at what a fine specimen of a man he was. He and Mr. Pickens were direct opposites in coloring—Mr. Pickens so dark and tannned looking while Coleman was blond and fair, yet both so fit and muscular. I would have a hard time judging between them if I was ever called upon to do so. If pushed, though, I'd probably come down on Coleman's side. The uniform, you know. But then, there was Mr. Pickens's mustache, so the matter would need more thought.

"I could go by and talk to her," Coleman was saying, as he picked up the phone. "But if she's already concerned, a deputy showing up at her door might really scare her."

"Might give her a heart attack," Lloyd said. "She's already thinking the worst 'cause he didn't come home when he was supposed to."

So we waited and watched as Coleman punched in Hazel Marie's number. And listened as he said, "Hazel Marie? Hi, this is Coleman. Yeah. . . . How you doin'? Oh, fine, fine. Listen, I just heard from somebody who's looking for a P.I. and was wondering if J.D. would be interested. . . . Uh-huh, yeah, well, when do you expect him? . . . And he was finishing up where? . . . Is that right? Well, you know how those hill people can be. We've got a few of 'em around here. . . . No, I wouldn't worry about him. He'll be dragging in before long. Just tell him I called, and you take care of yourself."

He hung up the phone, turned to us and said, "West Virginia."

"Law," Lillian said. "That's 'way off from here. What in the world he doin' up there?"

"She's not sure," Coleman said. "She thinks he was hired to look into some kind of missing person's case in Winston-Salem. But he called her last week and told her he had to check out some-

thing in West Virginia—he didn't say exactly where. Then he
called again last Friday and said he had to make one more stop
before coming on home."

"One more stop in West Virginia?" I asked.

Coleman nodded. "That's what she understood, and she's already worried. He's three days overdue getting home and she's not
heard from him since last Friday—a week ago."

"That don't sound good to me," Lillian said.

"Me, either," Lloyd said.

West Virginia, I thought, which might as well be a foreign
country, for all I knew about it. I knew a little about a few places
in Virginia, but I'd never been to the west of it, but the name
conjured up an image of mountains—it was located along the
same range as our own Blue Ridge Mountains on the Appalachian
range, or something like that. I wasn't too up on geography. Coal
country, I recalled from reading about mining disasters.

"What can we do, Coleman?" I asked. "Because the more I
think about that phone call, the more I feel that he needed help.
I mean, he didn't even sound like himself. It took me a minute to
recognize his voice, but it *was* him, I'm pretty sure, especially
because a deputy answered when we called back on his phone.
Wouldn't that mean Mr. Pickens wasn't able to use it himself?"

"Oh, me," Lloyd moaned, "maybe he's hurt, been in a car wreck
or in a fight or . . ."

"Hold on, Lloyd," Coleman said. "Let's not start thinking the
worst. I'll go back to the office and put in a call to the West Virginia State Police and to the sheriff in Charleston. They can check
hospitals, accident calls, and so forth, throughout the state. Might
take awhile, but it's worth doing."

Lillian had walked over to Lloyd and put her arm around his
shoulders. "He gonna be all right, Lloyd. Mr. Pickens never been
in bad trouble before, an' Coleman gonna find him, don't you
worry." Then she looked at Coleman. "I jus' don't know why you
callin' Charleston when it down in South Car'lina. How they
gonna know anything going on in West Virginia?"

"Two Charlestons," Coleman said with a brief grin. "Charleston, West Virginia, is the capital of that state, which makes it a good starting point for us."

"Oh," she said. "Wonder why they do that? Look like one of 'em would pick another name."

Nobody answered her because nobody knew. And it wasn't important anyway. We were all too focused on Mr. Pickens's personal state to worry about the names of cities.

Coleman was on his way out the door when I stopped him. "Should we tell Hazel Marie what's going on?"

He thought for a minute. "I hate to keep anything from her, but we really don't know anything. Let's wait until I talk to somebody up there and get a line on him. Time enough to tell her when we know something for sure."

I nodded, agreeing that we should wait. "Call or come by as soon as you hear anything. We'll be here waiting."

"I'll do it." And he was out the door and gone.

❦

"Well," I said, looking at the two worried faces staring after Coleman, "I don't care what we tell Hazel Marie or don't tell her. She's already fretting because Mr. Pickens hasn't come home, and she'll be doing even more if he doesn't soon call her. And if some deputy has his phone, he won't be calling her. Let's see if she'll come over for supper."

"Good idea," Lloyd said.

Lillian nodded and opened the silverware drawer. "'Least she won't be settin' home stewing all by herself. Onliest thing is, though, we ought not be talkin' 'bout Mr. Pickens when she get here."

"That's right. There're plenty of things we can talk about, and of course the babies will keep us all entertained, too. And Latisha will be here, so a lot will be going on, which is exactly what Hazel Marie needs to keep her mind occupied." I thought for a minute, then went on. "I wish I had something to occupy mine. All I'll be thinking about is what Coleman can find out."

Well, not exactly all I'd be thinking of. There was Sam still in an airplane miles above the earth with nothing but ocean under him—that was preying heavily on my mind. I declare, you let anybody you care about go traipsing off on their own and no telling what can happen. I liked my chickens all under my wing, and now I had two off and gone to fret over. To say nothing of the one who would soon be leaving, too.

"Lloyd, why don't you go ahead and check in with your mother? Tell her we're expecting her for dinner, but don't say anything about Mr. Pickens. Unless she's heard from him, of course. And in that case, let me know so we can tell Coleman to stop looking for him."

"Yes, ma'am, I will. And I think I won't call. I'll just go over there. That way I can help her with the babies and we'll all come back together." Lloyd started out the door, then turned back. "But if you hear anything from Coleman, call me and let me know. We can, maybe, speak in code or something so Mama won't know what's going on."

"You can speak in code if you want to since she'll be able to hear you. But I'll tell you straight out, probably no more than 'He's all right,' or 'You all better get over here,' or something like that."

He nodded agreement, a serious look on his face as our eyes met. We were of one mind as we usually were. My heart skipped a beat as I wondered how long that would last as he grew away from me.

Chapter 8

As soon as Lloyd left, I found myself staring at the telephone, willing it to ring. I wanted to hear from Mr. Pickens or from Coleman, or I'd even take that West Virginia deputy—anybody who could let us know what was happening. The phone just sat there like a stump.

"Lillian," I said, tapping my fingers on the table, "do you think Sam's cell phone would work in an airplane?"

"Law, Miss Julia, I don't know. Look like it be too long a reach. But you don't wanta be callin' him, 'cause what can he do, halfway 'round the world? No'm, I wouldn't do that. It jus' make him sick with worry not being able to stop that plane an' get off."

"Well, you're right. I ought to at least wait till he's on the ground, where he can get another plane to come home. If he needs to, that is."

"Now, you jus' quit 'spectin' the worst," Lillian said, walking over to the table and pulling out a chair. "That's what you always do— 'spect the worst an' sometimes you get it. Of all the folks we know, Mr. Pickens the best at lookin' after hisself, so you jus' think of something else 'stead of all them what-ifs goin' 'round in your head."

"That's good advice, Lillian," I said gratefully, "which is what you always give. So all right, here's something we can think about while we wait. Have you ever heard of Agnes Whitman? According to Mildred, she lives out in Fairfields on a big estate, so it sounds as if she's wealthy. I think she's fairly new in the area."

Lillian frowned at me and, for a minute, I thought she wasn't going to answer. "Widder lady?"

"I don't know. Either that or divorced, maybe. Mildred didn't mention a husband. Seems, though, that she's mixed up in some sort of strange religious goings-on. But," I said with a smile, "Mildred thinks anything that's not Presbyterian is strange."

"Well, you know I don't like to talk about folks you know, but. . ."

"Oh, I don't know her, so go right ahead."

Lillian nodded sagely. "An' maybe you better *not* get to know her, not from the talk I hear goin' 'round."

"So you have heard of her. Well, tell me. I need something else to think about."

Lillian squinched up her mouth as her eyes blinked several times. "Well, I don't know much, jus' some folks tellin' at the AME Zion Church that they's some kind of devilment goin' on out in the county. They say that lady part of it, an' the Rev'rend Abernathy, he say we better steer clear."

"Really? Well, I certainly respect the Reverend Abernathy's opinion." Then I leaned forward to hear more. "What kind of devilment?"

"They say it awful, but nobody know 'zactly what. Somethin' to do with earbobs an' tattoos is all I heard."

"My goodness, Lillian, half the young people in town have earrings and tattoos. And half the old men have tattoos if they've been in the navy—maybe the army, too—though they're less likely to have earrings. Don't tell me those people have drawn in impressionable young people—that would have a lot of parents up in arms. It's bad enough when a child comes home with one earring, much less with *Mom* written on his arm."

"No'm, I ain't heard nothin' like that. All I hear is they mostly like what used to be hippies till they went out of style. You know, people lookin' for somethin' new, then ending up with somethin' old as the hills they jus' think is new, but it jus' comin' back around."

"Oh, yes, like those groups of men who sit in a circle and beat drums until they get enlightened or something. Which just sounds like a bunch of red Indians getting themselves worked up to go on the warpath."

"Yessum, I guess," Lillian said. "I 'member, though, that that Whitman lady's name be part of it 'cause she a minister or something an' they meet at her big place. The reverend, though, he jus' zip his mouth up when folks start talkin' 'bout it. He say it bad doin's an' none of his flock better be messin' with it."

"That does sound strange," I said. Then, unable to sit still, I got up and paced the floor. "Well, things come and go, don't they? You never know what fad is going to be next. That's because people are always looking for answers when they don't even know the questions."

"You jus' said a mouthful," Lillian said.

The telephone rang then, and I nearly broke my neck getting to it. "Yes? I mean, hello."

"Miss Julia," Coleman said, "I just spoke with the Charleston Police Department, and they have no information on J.D. specifically, or on anything that's occurred in the vicinity that he might be involved in."

"Well, that's good, isn't it?"

"So far. It'll take awhile for the highway patrol to check all their areas, so we'll have to wait on that. It could be tomorrow before we hear from them."

"Oh, me, I don't know how I can wait that long. Coleman, is there nothing else we can do?"

"I can't think of anything. Just wait and hope J.D. calls in or the State Police get back to us."

"You don't suppose he's on the way home?"

Coleman didn't say anything for a moment. Then he said, "Not likely. He'd call if that was the case. He'd know Hazel Marie's waiting to hear from him."

"Yes, that's true," I agreed. "Well, she and the babies are coming over to eat with us, so if you hear anything, do let us know."

"I will. I've got everybody here on alert for a call, so I'll go on home. They'll let me know if any news comes in."

"Well, if it does, call me no matter what time of the day or night. I doubt I'll be doing much sleeping anyway, what with both Sam and Mr. Pickens gone."

"I'll let you know as soon as I know."

After thanking him, I hung up the phone and turned to Lillian. "He hasn't found out anything."

"Well, no news is good news, I guess," Lillian said.

"That's what they say, and I'd believe it if I hadn't gotten that strange call from Mr. Pickens. And if we'd been able to reach him again. As it is, I can't help but think that something is wrong."

"Jus' don't let Miss Hazel Marie know you thinkin' that. She get herself all wound up if she see you worried 'bout him."

"I know, and I'll keep it to myself."

❦

Lillian left to pick up Latisha from after-school care, so with an empty house I sat in the living room, trying to figure out a way to reach Mr. Pickens. I couldn't come up with anything that made any sense, but that didn't stop me from dreaming up all sorts of plots and plans.

It was with relief that I heard footsteps on the front porch and the ringing of the doorbell. Maybe somebody had heard something, I thought, then quickly discarded that on the basis that whoever it was would've called and not come by. Unless it was bad news.

In a way it was. LuAnne Conover breezed in as soon as I answered the door.

"Julia," she said, heading for my Duncan Phyfe sofa, "I haven't heard from you in I don't know how long, so since I had to be downtown anyway, I thought I'd stop by and see how you're doing."

"I've been busy, LuAnne, getting Sam ready to go on that tour and, well, you know, first one thing and another." There was no way in the world that I'd tell her our concerns about Mr. Pickens's welfare. With the best of intentions, she would feel she had to go comfort Hazel Marie, even though Hazel Marie wouldn't know what she was being comforted for. LuAnne was the worst when it came to keeping anything to herself.

"Well, you've got him off, so you ought to plan a few outings to keep yourself busy while he's gone. I know I would if Leonard ever decided to go on a tour. Not that he ever would, but I'd think of something."

After offering a glass of tea or lemonade and being turned down, I said, "I don't have any outings planned, but I'm about to tear this house up and do some remodeling. That'll keep me plenty busy."

"Really?" LuAnne said, leaning forward eagerly. "What're you going to do?"

"Well, you know, since Sam's lost his office at his house, I need to rearrange a few rooms and make a place here for him."

"Oh!" she nearly screeched. "You're going to make a man cave! He'll love it—I know Leonard would, but we don't have room in the condo."

"I don't know what a man cave is."

"Oh, Julia, it's a room for the man of the house where all his hobbies and interests can be located. Now, for Sam, you'd have his fishing poles and tackle stuff sort of placed decoratively around the room. And a television and a recliner, of course, and all of his trophies and plaques and things like that. And I guess a few books because Sam is such a big reader. You might want to put up a dartboard or some other game because it's sort of like a game room, where a man can entertain his man friends."

"LuAnne," I said, "if Sam wants to entertain his man friends, he can take them to the country club. I'm not having a man cave in my house, since I'm not married to a caveman. Sam is a civilized human being. The whole idea of a man cave is about the silliest thing I've ever heard of."

"Well, Julia," LuAnne said, getting a little snippy as she was wont to do whenever her enthusiasms weren't shared, "it's really the *in* thing to do these days."

"You know how much I care about that. Believe me, the last thing I want in my house is smelly old fishing tackle, and Sam would laugh his head off at the idea. But listen," I said, ready for a change of subject, "have you heard of a woman named Agnes Whitman?"

"No, should I have?"

"Well, let me tell you." And I went on to do so, repeating what I'd heard from Mildred and from Lillian, entrancing LuAnne and distracting her from any more talk of man caves.

"That's the strangest thing I've ever heard," she said, standing to leave. "We don't need such as that in this town. I'll look into it and let you know what I find out." And off she went.

Chapter 9

The phone rang at five-thirty the next morning, and even though it was a Saturday, when we were slow to rise, I popped up wide awake at the first ring.

Sure that it was Coleman with news or maybe Mr. Pickens with a better connection, I snatched it up.

"Miss Julia?" Coleman said. "He may be in a hospital."

"Oh, no! What's wrong with him?"

"Well, that's the thing. I didn't get much out of the state trooper who called. *He* didn't know much, but he'd had several feelers out to other troopers and just got the information that an unidentified male had been injured a few days ago in a little town back in the hills somewhere." Coleman gave a little laugh. "Looks like a lot of us are up early working on this thing. Anyway, whoever they're talking about was taken to a county hospital in Mill Run, West Virginia."

"Where's that?"

"About seventy miles or so southeast of Charleston—as the crow flies, that is. I just found it on a map."

"Well, is it him, Coleman? Could it be Mr. Pickens? And how could he be unidentified?" Coleman didn't answer right away, so I went on peppering him with questions, my voice trembling a little as I pictured massive injuries from a car wreck. "Should we get Hazel Marie there? How bad is he injured anyway?"

"The trooper didn't know. Said he's miles from there and

couldn't check on him himself. What information he had amounts to hearsay, more or less, just that the man might be a private cop and he'd been injured somewhere out back of nowhere."

"If the man's a private cop, then it has to be Mr. Pickens. How many of them can there be? But you'd think somebody would get in touch with us. Maybe we ought to go up there, Coleman, and find out what's going on."

"Yeah, I'm thinking that way, too. I'd go today if I could get away, but we're swamped. On the other hand, it'd be foolish to go flying off without knowing who we'd find. It could be a complete stranger."

"I guess," I said, fighting the urge to grab Hazel Marie and fly off to keep a vigil by a bedside. Well, not fly, exactly, but drive real fast.

"I'm still working on it, so let's wait till we know more. Oh, and I do have the hospital's number. You want to take it down?"

I certainly did, and did so. "Should I call or will you? Or should we go ahead and tell Hazel Marie and let her call?"

"Well, here's the thing, Miss Julia. I've already called, and even with telling them I'm a sheriff's deputy, they said they couldn't give out any information. It would have to come through their sheriff's office."

"Well, let's call that office."

"Yeah, well, I did, and got the runaround there, too. Told me that only the sheriff could discuss that, and the sheriff wasn't in. It's the damnedest thing I've ever run into. Oh, sorry 'bout that."

"Don't apologize. I feel the same way." I let a few moments elapse, wondering what to do next. Then I said, "I guess we better tell Hazel Marie, don't you?"

"Yeah, maybe so, now that it's probably him who's in trouble. Injured, and who knows what else." Coleman stopped, seemingly to adjust his thinking. "Except we're still not positive it's J.D. It could be some other private eye."

"What do you think, Coleman? You think it's him?"

"Yeah, I do. Too many things fit together. Anyway, the trooper will try to get over that way later today. Apparently, they're few and far between in that part of the state and he has a huge area to patrol. He has my cell number and he'll call if he learns any more."

"All right. I'll get dressed and go on over to Hazel Marie's, because I'm like you, Coleman, I think it's him, too. Let us know as soon as you hear anything."

❦

I stood staring at the long-distance number that I'd jotted down on a scrap of paper. Coleman had already called it and gotten nothing for his trouble. How was it that a hospital would refuse to give out information to a qualified, certified and official law officer? If a police officer or sheriff's deputy asked me a question, I'd answer it without another thought. But then, there were those new privacy laws, and maybe that was the reason the hospital had turned Coleman down. After all, anybody and his brother could say they were law officers over a telephone, and the hospital would have no way of checking the claim.

But maybe, maybe they'd tell me something.

I thought of getting dressed first—you know, to give myself a little confidence. It's hard to be firm and persistent when you're in a cotton batiste nightgown with your bare feet dangling off the side of a bed.

I couldn't wait. I dialed the number slowly and carefully, waited for an answer and heard a woman's twangy voice say, "Crayton County Hospital. How may I direct your call?"

"I'd like to speak to whoever is attending Mr. J. D. Pickens, please."

"Who?"

I repeated myself, then added, "He's a patient there, and I'll speak to anyone working on whatever floor he's on."

"Honey," the operator said, "there ain't but two floors, and everybody's busy."

"Well, could you just ring his room?"

"I could. If there was a phone in it. None of the rooms have 'em."

Getting a little exasperated, I said, "I just want a little information on his condition. How is he doing? And what's wrong with him anyway? We're all worried about him."

"I'm sorry, honey, but I got a note here saying no information to anybody about anybody. Hold on a minute. I got another call coming in."

She put me on hold while I wondered whether it was her way of getting rid of me. Still, she'd stayed on the line longer than the operator at our hospital would have. So I waited.

She came back on. "You still there?"

"Yes, I'm here. Will you just tell me one thing—is Mr. Pickens a patient there? His wife is most concerned because nobody will tell us anything. And they have little twin babies who're crying for their daddy and it's all so pitiful."

"Well," she said, "I guess it's all right to say that I got no Pickens on my list. But *somebody's* a patient here, but he's down as a John Doe. First time we ever had one of them, but whether he's who you're looking for or not, I don't know."

"John Doe?" I couldn't believe it. How could they not know who he was? Or was it him? I didn't know what to ask next. "Well, could you tell me how Mr. Doe is doing and what's wrong with him?"

"We can't give out that information to just anybody," the operator said, somewhat sorrowfully. I had begun to hear a little sympathy in her voice. "Would you happen to be a member of Mr. Doe's family?"

"Oh, yes," I said, chagrined that I hadn't made that clear in the first place. "I'm his . . . ah, mother?"

"Well, in that case, I guess I can tell you that he's doin' as well as can be expected with a gunshot wound."

"*What!* You mean he's been shot? Where? How bad is it?"

"That's all it says here and, uh-oh, I didn't see this. Says here anybody askin' is supposed to contact the sheriff. Honey, I wish I could help, but that's all I can tell you. And here comes another call, I gotta go."

I sagged against the head of the bed. Mr. Pickens shot? No wonder he didn't sound like himself when he called me. No wonder he'd wanted Sam or Coleman, or both. The man needed help.

Standing up, I dialed Coleman's cell phone and caught him as he was leaving home to go on duty. I told him what I'd learned and that I was going to Hazel Marie's right away.

"Can you meet us there, Coleman?" I asked. "I think your being there will give her some reassurance. We can decide on our next step."

"I've got to go to roll call, then I'll come over."

❦

Lord, I thought as I began dressing, Hazel Marie will climb the walls. She was already worried enough, a condition plain to see the night before. However much the babies and Latisha held our attention during and after supper, the unsaid concern had been present in her eyes.

Hearing Lillian come in downstairs, I quickly dressed, although my shaking hands fumbled with the buttons and I almost walked out in my bedroom slippers.

"What you doin' up so early?" Lillian asked before I could speak.

"Problems, Lillian." Then, seeing Latisha coloring in a *Princess Coloring Book* at the table, I said, "Good morning, Latisha. Would you like to go into the living room and do your coloring on the coffee table?"

"No, ma'am," she said, pressing down with an orange crayon. "I'm fine right here where Great-Granny can make me some breakfast."

"Oh, well, all right. Lillian, let me show you something in the dining room."

I walked out with Lillian behind me, then I turned and said, "Mr. Pickens is in a hospital somewhere in West Virginia, except they're calling him John Doe, so we don't know if it's him or not. But I think it is, because the highway patrolman told Coleman a private investigator was in that hospital. So how many of those could there be? Anyway, Lillian," I said, my voice catching in my throat as I clasped her arm, "anyway, I talked to the operator and she let it slip that Mr. Doe, who just *has* to be Mr. Pickens, is in the hospital with a gunshot wound."

"Oh, Law," Lillian said, her hand going to her throat. "What we gonna do?"

"First thing is to go over and tell Hazel Marie. I want you to go with me because we can't keep this from her any longer. Lloyd spent the night with her, so he'll be there. He and Latisha can entertain the babies while we talk it over and decide what to do."

"Yes, ma'am, let's us go now." She started back into the kitchen, then stopped. "What about everybody's breakfast?"

"We'll let James worry about that. I'll need your help with Hazel Marie."

We herded Latisha and all her crayons out to the car, while trying to answer her questions without really answering them. She was happy enough to go, settling down in the backseat, especially after we told her that we needed her to babysit for a little while.

"I can do that," she said in her sharp, piercing voice, completely confident in her ability. "I can take care of them babies jus' like they my very own."

Lillian rolled her eyes. "Don't be thinkin' nothin' like that. You got a long road ahead of you 'fore you havin' any babies."

Latisha's little legs stuck out over the seat as she rummaged through her pink backpack, making sure that all her necessities were in it. "That's why I'm doin' all my practicin' on Miss Hazel Marie's babies, so I be ready when the time come."

"Have mercy," Lillian mumbled.

I quickly drove the four blocks to Sam's old house, parked at the curb and climbed out. Latisha dashed up the sidewalk and onto the porch.

"You jus' wait a minute, young lady," Lillian called. "Don't go ringing that bell. Them babies might still be asleep."

"No'm, they wide awake. I hear 'em bawlin' in there."

And sure enough, so could we as Lillian and I approached the door.

"Oh, Lillian," I said, "I dread this."

"I do, too, but it got to be done." Lillian rang the doorbell and, thank goodness, Lloyd came to the door.

"Uh-oh," he said as soon as he saw us. "Bad news?"

"Not good," I said, "but maybe not terrible, either. At least as far as we know. Your mother busy?"

"Yes'm, she's feeding my sisters. Come on in, they're in the kitchen."

Chapter 10

Hazel Marie looked up with a surprised smile on her face as we trooped into the kitchen. She was still in her bathrobe, spooning baby cereal into two eager little mouths. The babies were each strapped into a carryall, and cereal was smeared in their hair and all over their faces.

"Why, Miss Julia," Hazel Marie said, a full spoon suspended on its way to an open mouth. "What are you doing out so early? And Lillian? My goodness. . ." Her face fell as she realized that our unusually timed visit did not bode well.

James turned from the stove, where he was frying bacon, a dripping fork held in his hand. A distressed look spread across his face. "Miss Lillian, what y'all doin' here? Something happen to Mr. Sam?"

"No, no," I said, "not that. Hazel Marie, we need to talk to you, honey. Are you about finished feeding the babies?"

"Oh," she moaned, her hand beginning to tremble as she realized that we had not come on a casual visit.

"Here," Lillian said, taking the spoon from her, "let me finish that. Miss Julia, you take her an' Lloyd on to the livin' room. I get these baby girls all done."

"I can help, Great-Granny," Latisha said, "soon as you clean that stuff off of 'em. They too messy now."

"Come on, Hazel Marie," I said, putting my arm around her shoulders and leading her to the sofa in the living room. "Lloyd, sit there by your mother."

"What is it?" Hazel Marie asked, her face becoming ashen as she realized that bad news was coming.

"Now listen, Hazel Marie," I said, as soothingly as I could. "We don't know a whole lot, but it seems that Mr. Pickens has been injured in some way—a small way, I'm sure—and it seems that he's in a hospital somewhere in West Virginia. Now before you think the worst, it's not confirmed that the injured man *is* Mr. Pickens. They're calling whoever it is John Doe, so it might not be him. Coleman is trying to learn more, as we speak. But we thought you needed to know that it might be."

Hazel Marie wrapped her arms around herself and swallowed hard. "How . . . how do you know all this?"

I told her of Mr. Pickens's phone call, looking for Sam or Coleman, and our further efforts to discover his location. "Those people, whoever they are, certainly play things close to their chests. We've not been able to speak to anyone with the authority to disclose any information. But, Hazel Marie, we are going to get to the bottom of this. We just didn't want to leave you in the dark while we do it."

To tell the truth, I had not known how Hazel Marie would take the news. I'd thought she might lose all self-control—cry, scream, throw herself around, go half crazy—who knew? But I saw none of that. Instead, she seemed to sink in on herself, growing smaller as her face became drawn and her eyes larger. It was as if she'd been struck a mortal blow.

"It'll be all right, Mama," Lloyd said, hugging her. "J.D. knows how to take care of himself. He's not going to let anything bad happen."

Hazel Marie's body began to tremble as she sat on the sofa. "I should've known," she mumbled, as she gazed down at her clasped hands. "It was all too good to last."

"Oh, honey, don't say that." I sat down beside her and held her hands. "Don't even think it. Look," I urged, "we don't know if it is him. And if it is, why, he was able to call for Sam, so he can't be too bad off. I think it's that sheriff up there who's holding things up, and as soon as Coleman reaches him, why, then, we'll know more of what's going on. So you just hold on and be strong."

Tears were flowing down her face by this time, but there was no sobbing or gasping. Tears simply ran down her face as if her eyes could no longer hold them.

The doorbell rang then, and I jumped up. "That's Coleman. Maybe he'll know something."

Lillian walked in as I went out into the hall. "The babies in they cribs," she said, and went to Hazel Marie. Gathering her up in her arms, she crooned, "Come here, little girl. It gonna be all right. See if it won't."

Hazel Marie clung to her as I ushered Coleman into the room.

"Here he is, Hazel Marie," I said, beginning to tremble a little myself. Anxiety is catching, you know.

Coleman pulled a chair up close to Hazel Marie as she released herself from Lillian and looked at him.

"Hazel Marie," he began, as he leaned forward, his elbows on his knees. "I talked to Sheriff Ardis McAfee in Crayton County, West Virginia, a few minutes ago, but I didn't get all the information I wanted. Apparently, a man they're calling John Doe was found out in the woods somewhere and he was brought to the hospital with a gunshot wound. The sheriff assured me that the wound is not life threatening, but by the time he was found, it had gotten infected. When they brought him in, he was running a fever and appeared confused and unable to give them any information. He had no identification of any kind on him, which is why they've labeled him a John Doe. So listen now," Coleman said, hunching forward and taking her hand, "it may not be J.D. The sheriff said they're getting the infection under control, and the man in question is telling them that he's a private investigator, but the sheriff said he didn't know what a private investigator would be doing in their neck of the woods, so he's not inclined to believe him."

"Why not?" Lloyd demanded. "If it is J.D., he'd tell 'em his name and everything, wouldn't he?"

"Well, I'll tell you," Coleman said, somewhat hesitantly, "what I just told you had to be pulled out of the sheriff—he was not the most cooperative person I've ever dealt with. I don't know what's going on up there, but the sheriff said that in the absence of proper identification, the man stays on the books as a John Doe."

"Maybe it's not him," Hazel Marie said. "J.D. didn't say anything about going out in the woods, so it could be somebody else. Couldn't it?"

"It could," Coleman said, nodding. "Because if it is J.D., I'd think he'd be calling you."

"No," I chimed in, "there're no telephones in the rooms in that hospital. That's what the telephone operator told me. So if he can't get out of bed, he can't call. And if they've taken his cell phone, he's up a creek." That didn't come out right, so I added, "As far as getting in touch with us, I mean."

That brought things to a standstill as we all wondered what kind of hospital it was. At that point, James reappeared to say that breakfast was just about cold and we'd better come on and eat. Lillian guided Hazel Marie to the dining room while she protested that she couldn't eat and Lillian telling her she had to. Lloyd, looking wan and worried, held his mother's hand and went with them.

I lingered behind with Coleman, wanting to hear what he really knew after having spoken with the Crayton County sheriff. "Did you tell her everything?" I asked.

He shook his head. "No, because there was no reason to worry her any more than she already is. But that sheriff has one thing on his mind, and he's not going to cooperate until he's convinced he's wrong. I'd sure like to get up there and shake some sense into him."

"Well, what in the world, Coleman?"

"Apparently, they're having a lot of trouble with marijuana growers and meth labs back in the hills around there, and he thinks this John Doe may be part of some of that. And," Coleman went on, looking down at me, "if it's not J.D., he may be right. Anyway, he's keeping this 'so-called private cop,' as he called him, under wraps until his identity is confirmed and the feds can get there."

"Oh, Coleman, this could be bad. You and I know that Mr. Pickens is not growing or making anything. Looks like that sheriff would realize that a private investigator would be working with him, not with a bunch of crooks."

"Sounds like the sheriff may have more than he can handle," Coleman said. "And he doesn't want one of 'em to slip away from him."

"Miss Julia?" Lillian stuck her head in the doorway. "Y'all come on an' eat something. Maybe Miss Hazel Marie will, too."

As we walked in, Hazel Marie was sitting at the table, staring at the food on her plate. "I don't know what to do," she said, her hands gripping the tabletop. Then she sprang up from her chair. "I do know, too. I'm going up there. It's him, I know it is, and he needs me. I've got to get there. Lloyd, will you call and see if I can get a plane? I've got to get ready. But no, maybe I better drive. I might need the car." She was beginning to flutter around, waving her hands, her eyes darting about the room, trying to plan a trip when nobody knew a destination.

"Wait, Hazel Marie," I said. "Honey, what're you going to do about the babies?"

"Oh," she said, stopping as if she'd suddenly remembered them. "Well, I'll just take them with me."

"You won't be any help to Mr. Pickens," Lillian said, "if you got them two babies with you. So I'll go an' help with 'em, but Latisha have to go, too."

"That won't work, Lillian," I said. "Maybe we can keep them."

"No," Hazel Marie said, sinking down on the chair again. "I can't leave them. I can't leave them and I can't take them, and I want to go but I need to stay here." And she covered her face and began crying again.

We all looked at one another, waiting for someone to come up with a suggestion. Then Hazel Marie gathered herself and asked, "Coleman, what do you think? You think it's J.D.?"

"I don't know, Hazel Marie," he said. "I wish I could go for you and make sure, but we've got deputies on vacation and I can't leave right now. But if you can hold on and we haven't learned anything more, I think I can get away about Wednesday. As for who the man is, the only other thing the sheriff said was that whoever it is can cuss a blue streak. Said as a church-going man, he'd never heard such language in his life. Does that sound like J.D. to you?"

"No," Hazel Marie said, looking up with hope in her eyes, "No, it doesn't. J.D. is the sweetest-talking man in the world. It can't be him, I'm sure of it." She wiped her face with the edge of her robe, then said, "At least I think I am."

I looked at Lillian, then glanced at Lloyd. None of us said a thing, but I thought to myself, *That settles it*. If the man in West Virginia known as John Doe was able to offend even a backwoods sheriff with his descriptive language, then he was indeed J. D. Pickens, P.I.

While everyone in the room reassured Hazel Marie, I slipped out into the hall and over to Sam's old office, which Hazel Marie was now using as a den. The telephone was on a side table, so I walked over to it, picked it up and, hoping my memory wouldn't let me down, dialed a number.

"Etta Mae?" I asked, as a sleep-filled voice answered. "How would you like to go to West Virginia today?"

Chapter 11

"What?"

"I'm driving to West Virginia today," I told her, "and I need you to go with me—not just for the company, but for your nursing ability. Can you be ready in about an hour?"

"What?" she asked again.

"Wake up, Etta Mae. This is a job offer because you'll be on duty. So call that woman you work for and tell her the same arrangement will apply now as the one we had when you took care of Hazel Marie. You can let her know that I expect to be back here on Monday, Tuesday at the latest, so you won't be gone long. Oh, Etta Mae, I do apologize," I belatedly said. "I've gotten ahead of myself because you don't know what's going on."

"No, ma'am, I don't. Did you say you're going to West Virginia?"

"Yes, I did. I'm going to see about Mr. Pickens." Then I went on to tell her the whole story, including Hazel Marie's anguish at not being able to leave the babies, Coleman's schedule that would keep him from going right away and Sam's being halfway around the world. "It's down to you and me, Etta Mae. I figure he's going to need some nursing care, which is where you come in. Between the two of us, we'll get him back here where he can be taken care of. That bunch up there, starting with the sheriff, does not inspire the least bit of confidence, especially with Mr. Pickens suffering a gunshot wound in a hospital room that doesn't even have a telephone."

"Gunshot wound! Good grief, is he hurt?"

"I expect he is, Etta Mae, as I would be if somebody had shot me. But apparently, it's not all that serious, although it's serious enough to keep him in the hospital. That's why it's vital that we get up there and see what's going on."

There was silence on the line for a few seconds, then Etta Mae said, "Ah, Miss Julia, I hate to tell you, but I've never nursed a gunshot wound. I might not be much use to you."

"Don't worry about that. You're more capable than any of us. Besides, you can bring your nursing book and read up on it as we go. Will you do it, Etta Mae? I really need you."

"Well, if you're sure, of course I'll go. This is the first weekend I've had off in a month, so it'll be fun to have something to do."

I wasn't too sure how much fun it would be, but I was grateful for her willingness to accompany me. She and I had been on a few other expeditions and she'd proved her worth many times over.

"I'll pick you up in about an hour," I said. "Oh, and, Etta Mae, you won't need to pack a lot, but be sure to bring your nurse's uniform. Mr. Pickens might require special nursing care. And also, his doctor might be more willing to discuss his condition with a fellow professional than with me."

There was another long pause as she considered the request. Then, in a halting way, she said, "Okay."

After hanging up and looking at the time—almost eight—I went back into the dining room. Hazel Marie was stirring scrambled eggs around on her plate, but not eating any, while Lillian urged her to keep up her strength. Lloyd sat next to his mother, but he'd hardly eaten anything, either. His face was almost as white and drawn as hers.

James stood in the door to the kitchen. "Miss Julia, you want some eggs? I can fix you some right now. Them on the table is already cold."

"No, thank you, James, I don't have time to eat. Now listen, everybody," I said as I stood by the table. "With Sam gone and Coleman held up here until later in the week, we have to make some plans on our own. So here's what we're going to do: I just spoke to Etta Mae Wiggins and she and I are leaving in about an hour to drive to West Virginia. We're going to bring Mr. Pickens home, come that sheriff or high water.

"Lillian, I want you and Latisha to stay here with Hazel Marie and help her, if you will. Lloyd, you'll finish the school year and help wherever you're needed, and, James, I'm leaving them all in your care. Now, I've got to get home and get ready to go."

Everybody sat still for a minute, staring at me, then they all began talking at once, telling me I shouldn't go and one of them should go with us and it was too long a trip for two women alone.

"I want to go, Miss Julia," Lloyd said. "I can help."

Lillian said, "You sure you know what you doin'?"

But James's face brightened after hearing the responsibility I'd given him. He drew himself up, straightened his shoulders, and went back into the kitchen. But Hazel Marie, who hadn't said a word, rose from the table and put her arms around me.

"Thank you," she whispered against my shoulder. "Thank you with all my heart."

"There, there," I murmured, slightly embarrassed by her display, but appreciative of it too. "Lloyd, if you've finished, I need you to come with me. While I pack, I want you to get on your computer and figure out how we should go, how long it will take and whatever else we'll need."

"I can do that," he said, getting to his feet. "Mama, I'll be back in a little while."

As he and I started out the door, James came running out with a sack. "Here, Miss Julia. Here's some bacon biscuits. You gonna be hungry 'fore long."

"Why, James, how thoughtful. Thank you so much. You watch over them now. I'm trusting you to do that."

He beamed, nodding his head. "They be safe with me, don't you worry. But y'all be careful goin' to whatever place you goin' to."

When Lloyd and I got in the car to return to our house, he said wistfully, "I sure wish I could go. I'm awful worried about J.D."

"I know you are, sugar. And I'd take you if you didn't have final exams and if we had room. But I'm planning to bring him home and he'll need the whole backseat, most likely. I hope you can see that Etta Mae is the best one to go because she has experience with sick people." I didn't mention that she'd had no experience with shot people. Even so, she was the pick of the litter under these circumstances and better qualified than any of the rest of us.

🐝

"Three-quarters of a tank," I said as I pulled into our driveway and glanced at the gas gauge. "That'll get us well on the way. Lloyd, you get on your computer and map out our route and I'll throw some things in a suitcase."

We hurried inside and Lloyd immediately went upstairs to his room to start the search. "Mill Run, West Virginia?" he called to me as I trudged more slowly up the stairs.

"That's what Coleman said. I hope you can find it."

"It'll be on MapQuest, and I'll print out the directions as well as a map. And with the GPS in the car, you won't get lost."

Going to my closet, I pulled out a medium-sized suitcase and began filling it with underclothes, gown, robe, slippers, comb, brush, toothbrush and toothpaste, and a jar of face cream. Then I stopped. I didn't know what else to take, so I stood there for a few minutes considering the matter. What kind of weather would they have? It was early June, so not too cold, but they were north of us, so the nights might be cool. I put in a heavy cardigan. What kind of people lived there? Some small towns could be quite dressy, so I put in a Sunday suit. Then again, people in a small town up in the mountains would most likely dress in a casual manner, so I put in an everyday dress, wishing again that I'd invested in a tailored pantsuit.

Then I pulled out a larger suitcase and repacked, knowing I was taking too much for a weekend trip, but wanting to be prepared for whatever we ran into.

Money. I would need some cash, and it was Saturday, when the banks were closed. Then I remembered my personal ATM cache and reached for a shoe box on the top shelf of the closet. *Speaking of being prepared,* I thought, smiling to myself as I drew out a wad of bills from the toe of a shoe I never wore, kept there just in case. In case of what, one might ask, and my answer would be: in case I need it, which I currently did.

"Miss Julia?" Lloyd said, as he came into the room with a handful of papers. "Here you go. And look, it's not such a long trip after all. MapQuest says it's about three hundred and sixty miles from Abbotsville to Mill Run. I figure it'll take you seven hours or so to get there. MapQuest says about six, but it doesn't count rest stops. I expect you'll be there before suppertime."

"That's wonderful, Lloyd. I was afraid it'd be much farther. With Etta Mae and me taking turns driving, we'll be in good shape. We could be back here tomorrow night. But," I quickly added, "don't worry if we aren't. I'm thinking Monday at the earliest."

"Just stay in touch," he said in his serious manner. "You have your cell phone?"

"Oh, my goodness, no. I forgot it."

"I'll get it. You ought to keep it in the car or in your pocketbook. And the charger. I'll put that in your suitcase, so don't forget to plug it in every night."

"Thank you, Lloyd. Is there anything else I'm forgetting?"

"No'm, I just wish I was going with you. If I could drive, I'd even go by myself. Then you wouldn't have to."

I drew him to me and held him close. It was not something I frequently did, both of us preferring to express our affection in other ways, but the boy needed reassurance. He loved Mr. Pickens dearly, and I knew he would fret until we rolled back in with the daddy he'd only recently gained with his mother's marriage.

"I better go, honey," I said as he straightened up. "Etta Mae will be waiting for me. You take care of everybody and try not to worry too much. I'll let you know what we find out and when we'll be home."

"Yes, ma'am, we'll be all right. And don't you worry, either, because I'm gonna be praying for y'all to have travel mercies the whole time you're gone."

I quickly turned and lifted the suitcase from the bed, not wanting him to see the tears that had sprung up in my eyes. From the way both of us were carrying on, you'd think I was flying off to the Holy Land instead of making a road trip to Mill Run, West Virginia.

Chapter 12

Etta Mae, grinning and waving, bounded out the door of her single-wide as soon as I pulled up beside the awning. She was dressed for travel or for anything else that came up. I could tell because she was wearing what she always wore when she wasn't working: tight jeans, plaid cotton shirt and pointy-toed cowboy boots, which she called her Dingos.

It wasn't until we'd loaded her suitcase in the trunk, buckled ourselves in, tapped in instructions on the GPS and pulled out of the Hillandale Trailer Park, where she lived, that it hit me. *What in the world were we doing?* Heading off north-northeast, according to Lloyd's map, into unknown country to meet with strangers, hoping to wrest Mr. Pickens from their clutches—it was enough to give a person pause.

But not me. I gritted my teeth and kept driving. We were packed and on the way, wholly committed to our rescue mission. But first I pulled into the drive-through at a McDonald's on the edge of Delmont so we could get coffee to go with James's bacon biscuits.

"Etta Mae," I said, as I merged onto Interstate 26 West, "when you finish eating, reach into that tote bag in the back and get the map and the directions Lloyd got for us. You'll have to help navigate because I'd feel better having a backup to this electronic voice. I'm not sure I trust some satellite roving around up there."

"Me, either," she said, leaning between the front seats to retrieve the papers. "We need some idea of where we're going. Even," she said with a giggle, as she brushed biscuit crumbs off her jeans, "some idea of where we are at any given time."

After several minutes of studying the map, Etta Mae folded it up, then read the printed directions with an intensity that meant she was memorizing them.

As we approached Asheville, barely thirty miles from Abbotsville, I took an off-ramp. "We better fill up," I said. "I get nervous when the tank's close to half empty."

Etta Mae proved her worth again, self-serving the gas as efficiently as she did everything else. I took advantage of the ladies' room, then she decided she should do the same.

Once we'd cleared Asheville and were on the beautiful stretch of interstate north of the city, Etta Mae said, "Now tell me again where we're going and what we'll do when we get there."

So I did, recounting to her each step that had brought us to the current point. "So you see," I summed up, "somebody has to do something, and we're the only ones who can. Mr. Pickens needs someone to speak up for him because it seems he's not able to speak for himself."

"Well, I don't understand why the sheriff is holding him incommunicado. Is he under arrest?"

I almost ran off the road. "I didn't think of that! But, no, he can't be. Surely the sheriff would've told Coleman if he was. At least you'd think he would. But that's a good question, Etta Mae, because it would explain why they're keeping Mr. Pickens from contacting anybody."

"Yes'm, but even a hardened criminal is allowed a phone call, and I know J.D. is not that."

"Of course he isn't," I said, although I wouldn't have been surprised if he'd come close a few times. "But it could be that that call he made, looking for Sam or Coleman, qualified as his one call, even if the connection was so bad I couldn't understand him."

We rode along in silence for a while as Etta Mae absorbed the information. Then she said, "Something else must be going on. A hospital doesn't withhold patient information from family members. Not that I've ever heard of anyway."

"Well, I didn't want to mention this because I didn't want to scare you. And I don't believe it anyway. But Coleman told me that the sheriff implied—take note of that, Etta Mae, he only implied—that Mr. Pickens is suspected of being mixed up in growing marijuana. Or making something in laboratories, which is ridiculous because Mr. Pickens is certainly no scientist."

Etta Mae's eyes nearly popped out of her head. "*Meth* labs? You're talking about meth labs? Listen, Miss Julia, the people who grow marijuana are bad enough, but we need to stay away from meth labs. Those people would as soon shoot you as look at you."

"Oh, Lord," I moaned, letting the car ease down below the speed limit. "That must be what happened to Mr. Pickens. He must've gotten too close. But, Etta Mae, if he did, it would be because he was trying to stop them, not because he was one of them."

"Then I guess we'll just have to convince the sheriff of that." Etta Mae thought about this for a while, then she said, "Wonder what kind of man he is. The sheriff, I mean."

By the time we'd gone through the easternmost tip of Tennessee and picked up Interstate 81 North into Virginia, I was feeling the effects of the coffee we'd had. I pulled off at the first rest area we came to and we both availed ourselves of the facilities.

When we were back on the road, Etta Mae adjusted her seat and dropped off to sleep. I kept myself alert by running over in my mind the various ploys we might use to get in to see Mr. Pickens. Should we go straight to the hospital? See the sheriff first? Try to find his doctor? Wander around like tourists until we knew more?

I drove on, watching the traffic, which was heavy with trucks, and fiddling with the radio. Stations came and went as we moved on through the rolling countryside of western Virgina, which was dotted with small towns off the interstate and farms along the side with cattle on seemingly a thousand hills. Giving up on finding a radio station with decent music, I listened for a while to a preacher who was exercised about the downward trend of our country while I became more and more exercised about finding another place to stop.

When Etta Mae stirred and sat up, I said, "There ought to be a rest area fairly near. Would you like to stop?"

"Would I ever!" she said, then yawned. "I'm getting hungry, too. Those biscuits you brought hit the spot, but it's getting close to lunchtime."

"I'd like to make just one stop, but I don't think I can wait to find a restaurant. See, there's a sign—rest area two miles. Let's make a quick stop there, then go on. There may be some restaurants around Wytheville, which is where we pick up 77 North."

"Suits me. I'm about to pop."

We came off the highway and nosed into a parking place as near the bathrooms as I could find. I locked the car, then hurried with Etta Mae to tend to what had become an urgent necessity. Remembering what Lloyd had said about praying for travel mercies, I gave thanks for the mercy of rest areas along the interstates.

"Want me to drive for a while?" Etta Mae asked when we returned to the car.

"Yes, if you'd like to. I want to study the map a little and see how far we have to go. But let's watch for a place to get off and eat. No telling what will be available in West Virginia."

It was a good thing that we found a fast-food place not far from our connection to the next interstate because the countryside became more sparsely settled along I-77. But the big trucks kept rolling along—behind, in front and alongside us.

Thankful that Etta Mae was driving, I clasped the armrest and closed my eyes when we went through a long, *long* tunnel. Then, almost before I could breathe easily again, we headed into another one.

Then we were on the West Virginia Turnpike, for which we had to pay to drive on. I'd thought that Virginia had rolling hills, but the ones now on each side of us were really rolling—knobby little hills, one after the other. Feeling comfortable with Etta

Mae's steady driving, I whiled away the afternoon by reading the signs along the way, astounded at the names of towns hidden away, off the beaten path—Kegler, Pipestem, Odd, Flat Top—and wondered at the stories behind them.

"You getting tired, Etta Mae?"

"Not too bad," she said. "We'll be in Beckley in about an hour, I think. We turn off there, don't we?"

I consulted the map again. "No, we turn off on 64 East before Beckley, but Beckley's not far from the turnoff. Let's stop there if we find a decent place and really look at this map. We'll start twisting and turning on back roads then, and I don't want to get lost."

So we made another stop off the interstate, had a soft drink and stretched our legs for a few minutes, then drove on into Beckley to a gas station to fill up again. While Etta Mae filled the tank, I glanced up at the sky, where clouds were rolling in from the west, covering the sun and threatening rain. That didn't bode well for traveling on unfamiliar roads, but I kept my disquiet to myself. Etta Mae was her usual perky little self, suggesting with a laugh that we ask for the key to the station's restroom because it might be our last chance.

She laughed again when we were back in the car, turning at the instructions of the robotic voice of the GPS onto a two-lane road that took us deeper and higher into dark wooded areas. "I hope we don't have to stop again. From the looks of this lonesome road, we'll have to find bushes to get behind."

One thing you could say for Etta Mae, she was the perfect travel companion as far as I was concerned because we were on the same wavelength. There's nothing worse than accompanying someone with a large capacity.

I smiled at the thought of tromping through the bushes, but I was uneasy at being where we were, with pine trees edging the ditches on both sides of the road, very little traffic and rain spattering on the windshield. The sky was overcast, at least what we could see of it through the trees and the mountain rearing straight up above the ledge we were riding on. And even though night was a few hours away by the clock, it seemed to be creeping nearer. To cap it off, wisps of fog slipped past us, an omen of more to come.

"Lord, Etta Mae, I'm feeling kind of lonely way up here. It's as if we're a million miles from home and we don't know a soul."

"Yeah, we do. We know J.D. Keep your mind on him and we'll make it."

That was comforting advice, which Etta Mae was good at giving, bolstering me enough to keep my mind on the prize. Excepting Sam, Coleman and Mr. Pickens himself, I couldn't think of another person I'd rather have with me than Etta Mae Wiggins.

Chapter 13

The rain continued to fall, never in heavy downpours, but steady enough to keep the windshield wipers going. With their monotonous flapping, I could've closed my eyes for a rest, but I didn't dare. The car continued to climb, and even though the two-lane road seemed to have been recently repaved, it was narrow; and the ditch, or rather the chasm, on one side—my side—was getting steeper.

A van passed us going the other way and after ten minutes or so, a pickup with the hood wired closed followed it. We were almost alone with roadside signs the only indication of human activity. To take my mind off the deep gorge on my side of the car, I read them—DEER CROSSING, DANGER: FALLING ROCK, SLIPPERY WHEN WET, S-CURVE AHEAD—they were enough to put a person on edge, which was exactly where I was.

As Etta Mae rounded a curve and topped a rise, the fog fell away and we both gasped at the sight. Far off, between clumps of trees, we could see the road dipping and rising, twisting and turning off in the distance. And not one thing between us and a horrendous drop-off but a measly little guardrail and a lot of air.

It wasn't often that I liked to relinquish control of anything, but I was glad Etta Mae was driving. She hunched over the wheel, holding it with both hands, and concentrated on the road as the car headed downhill and into a steep curve. Then we started climbing again.

"Oh, Lord," Etta Mae said as we crossed a bridge over a river far below, "look at that!"

A huge logging truck laden with logs was barreling down toward us. I rared back and clung to the armrest. The truck's passing swayed the car and threw up water from the road onto the windshield.

"Whew," Etta Mae said as the truck went by. "I would've pulled off if there'd been a place to pull off on." Then, as she maneuvered through another S-curve, she regained her confidence. "Something ought to be done about those loggers. They always speed and they're a menace on the road."

I couldn't reply. I was too busy trying to restart my heart.

Finally, as the rain began to slacken, I glanced at the GPS. "Just thirty-nine more miles, Etta Mae. But, I declare, I don't know what kind of town we'll find. Looks like nobody lives up here."

"I saw a house a little ways back. A cabin, maybe. It was way high up and I just got a glimpse of it. I don't know how in the world anybody'd get to it, though."

"Fog's getting thicker," I said, just to keep the conversation going. I was feeling more and more lonesome the farther we went. If Mr. Pickens hadn't been at the end of the road, I'd have told Etta Mae to turn around and go back—if there'd been a place to turn around in.

"It may be more cloud than fog," Etta Mae said. "We're pretty high up, and—look up there—you can't even see the tops of the mountains."

Not particularly wanting to look, I said, "You know, there hasn't been a crossroad, an intersection or anything the whole time we've been on this road."

"Well, look," Etta Mae said, raising one finger from the wheel to point ahead. "There's a filling station."

And sure enough, a two-pump gas station on a narrow gravel lot hunkered near the side of the road. It looked as lonesome as I felt.

"Closed, though," Etta Mae said. "I could use their restroom, if they had one and if it was open. But it's Saturday afternoon, so I guess they close for the weekend."

I wished she hadn't mentioned it, because I, too, would've welcomed a stop.

After a good while of steady driving, Etta Mae said, "I love this car, Miss Julia. It takes these climbs like they're nothing and it really hugs the curves." She laughed. "I feel like it could almost drive itself."

"Well, don't let it. Look, Etta Mae, there's a town limits sign." I sat up straight as we passed a sign reading MILL RUN, SPEED LIMIT 20. "I think we've made it."

Etta Mae eased our speed down, although we hadn't been going fast in the first place. Small houses began to appear on each side of the road, which had begun to level off to some extent. To our left, though, the terrain slanted upward, while trees covered the right side of the road. Gradually, with Etta Mae watching our speed, we drove into town. It looked as tired as we were. Hardly anyone was on the sidewalks and only a few cars and trucks on the streets.

"Goodness," Etta Mae said. "It's Saturday night and this place is dead." She stopped at a blinking traffic light—not enough traffic to warrant a stop light—at what seemed to be the main intersection. "Which way, Miss Julia? You want me to drive around, check the place out?"

"Yes, let's do that. Turn left here and let's see if we can find the sheriff's office. We have to find a place to stay, too."

"Oh." Etta Mae glanced at me. "We don't have reservations anywhere?"

"Well, no. Lloyd said he couldn't find any motels listed here, so we better look for rooms for rent. Or something." I belatedly realized that I'd been too anxious to get on the road and had failed to ensure that we had beds for the night. "I'm sorry, Etta Mae. We'll just have to make the best of it."

"I'm not worried. We can sleep in the car if we have to. Oh, look," she said, pointing to a building on the corner. "Is that the courthouse?" She pulled to the side of the street and stopped before a narrow two-story redbrick building that sat flush with the sidewalk. Double doors faced us, while above them the words CRAYTON COUNTY COURTHOUSE 1869 were carved in a stone pediment. "Not very big, is it? I'm gonna make a right turn here," and she went on and did so. "A lot of times the Sheriff's Department is close to the courthouse."

She was right. Attached to the back of the courthouse was a one-story cement-block addition with a sign out front that let us know we'd found the sheriff. Or at least his office, because from the looks of it neither he nor anybody else was there. A single light burned above the door, but none inside. A lone patrol car looked forgotten in the shadows of the parking lot.

"They must not have a very big force," Etta Mae said, leaning down to look through my window.

"Maybe they're all out on patrol. Let's go on, Etta Mae. I'd like to find the hospital before it gets too dark." A soft rain was still falling, the kind that seemed to have set in for the night. With the lowering clouds and high mountains around the town, the late afternoon was dark, lit only by a few streetlights and the few car headlights that passed by.

"I bet the hospital is on the outskirts. They usually are. Oh, look there," Etta Mae said. "It's a café. Why don't we stop and eat, and maybe ask around for the hospital and a place to stay."

"That's a good idea. I could use a stop, and I'm hungry, too."

She went around the block, then parked on the side near the restaurant behind four or five other cars. Reaching into the back floorboard, I drew out the umbrella I always kept there. "I only have one, Etta Mae, but we can both get under it."

"You use it," she said. "I don't need it." And she dashed from the car and waited under the awning that extended over the sidewalk. All the businesses that we passed on our way to the restaurant were closed, some apparently for the night, others forever. The restaurant seemed to be the busiest place in town, but it wasn't full. I hoped that Bud's Best Burgers, Etc. lived up to its name, while wondering what the Etc. entailed.

At least it was a family restaurant, for I saw a few children seated with their parents when we walked in. Maybe Saturday night was eat-out night and Bud's Best Burgers was a treat for the whole family. Everybody looked up at us as we stood by the cash register, not knowing whether to sit down or wait to be seated.

"Jus' grab any place you want," a waitress yelled from behind the counter. She wore a white uniform and had her blond hair tied up with a red ribbon.

We slid into a booth, one of five or so across from the counter. After studying the sticky laminated menus, we both decided on the special: meat loaf, mashed potatos, lima beans and sliced tomatoes. I guessed that was part of the Etc.

A young lank-haired girl, who kept looking up from her pad to glance at us from under her heavy eyebrows, took our order. "You want coffee?" she asked, a broad twang in her voice.

"Yes, thank you," I said. "Ah, miss, we're just passing through, but we need to stop for the night. Can you recommend a motel or inn where we can get a couple of rooms?"

She stared at me with her dark eyes, and I wondered for a minute how bright she was. "Ain't no motels, but they's cabins for rent all around. For the fishin', you know." She took our menus, leaned across the table and stuck them back behind the ketchup bottle, sugar, salt and pepper shakers. "I'll ask Bud. He might know who's got some empty 'uns."

Well, that brought out Bud himself, a short, overweight man with a toothpick in his mouth, his round body wrapped in a soiled apron. "Say you folks're lookin' for a place to stay? How long you here for?"

"Yes, we are," I said, although the man had addressed Etta Mae, as most men usually did. "And just overnight, I think."

"Well, Pearl Overstreet might have a cabin for you. I 'spect that's about the only place you'll find. She don't usually fill up till late in the season. Go back to the highway and turn left. Keep on a-goin' and you'll see her place about a mile out. You can't miss it. She's got a bait and tackle shop right in front. Turn in there and you'll see the cabins behind it. That'll be your best bet this late."

"Thank you so much. And," I said, as the young waitress slid our plates in front of us, "this looks delicious."

It wasn't bad, not exactly delicious, but welcome after a long day of travel and fast food. I dithered over the tip when we'd finished, not wanting to draw attention by being overly generous, but also wanting to leave good feelings behind us.

"Just do fifteen percent," Etta Mae whispered, understanding my dilemma. "That's probably more than she usually gets, but it's not too much."

Actually, it was the cheapest meal I'd had in a long time, so fifteen percent more hardly put a dent in my wallet. We waved and smiled at the waitress, who did not respond, and left the café with every eye in it following us.

"Let's go find Pearl's cabins, Etta Mae," I said. "We'll look for the hospital first thing tomorrow, but right now I am on my last legs."

Chapter 14

As we drove through town, following Bud's directions to Pearl's cabins, we passed a dark drugstore, a boarded-up movie house and a convenience store, which, besides Bud's, was the only downtown business open. On the edge of town, I saw a gas station selling a brand of gas I'd never heard of. Nonetheless, it was open, so I said, "We better stop and fill up, Etta Mae."

She glanced over and grinned. "Good idea. We're almost half empty."

"I like to be prepared," I said rather primly, then smiled at my own picky ways.

Before Etta Mae could get out to pump the gas, a young, coverall-clad man with a full head of red hair ran out from the station and leaned down to the window that Etta Mae lowered. "Fill 'er up?"

"Yes, please. Premium," she said, then turned to me. "I can't believe it. This must be the only full-service station in the country."

While the tank filled, the young man—Junior, from his sewn-on label—quickly cleaned the windshield, then he leaned in toward the window. "Pop 'er hood an' I'll check the oil."

When that was done and he'd slammed the hood closed, he ran around the car and disconnected the gas pump. Wiping his hands on an oily rag, he reappeared at the window.

"Mighty fine car you got there," he said, "but she sure takes the gas, don't she? That'll be twenty-eight, sixteen."

I handed two twenties to Etta Mae, who passed them to him. "Be right back with your change." And he dashed off, the oily rag flopping from his back pocket.

"Industrious young man, isn't he?" I said. When he returned with the change, I leaned over and asked, "Ah, Mr. Junior? Are we far from Pearl's cabins?"

Leaning over with his hands on his knees, he studied us for a few minutes. "No'm, not far. 'Bout a mile or so. Y'all not here for the fishin', are you?"

"Just passing through," Etta Mae said, picking up on what I had told Bud earlier, "but we need to stop for the night."

"Well," Junior said, "they mostly take them that wants to fish an' stuff like 'at. A few others slip in now an' then. But it'll do for the night, I reckon."

As Etta Mae thanked him and turned the ignition, he slapped the roof of the car and said, "Y'all be careful now."

Pulling out onto the road, Etta Mae said grimly, "He didn't quite give Pearl a glowing recommendation, did he?"

"Beggars can't be choosers, I guess," I said. Then sitting up, I pointed to a sign. "Look, Etta Mae, the hospital's up that street. Just think, Mr. Pickens is only a little way from us. We could go see him now."

Etta Mae took her lower lip in her teeth, then shook her head. "No, let's wait. I think we ought to check in at Pearl's first and be sure we have a place to sleep. Then if you're not too tired, we can come back. Visiting hours are usually till nine, so there's plenty of time."

"You're right," I agreed. "From the way everybody's talking, Pearl might be our only hope for a bed. Let's get that settled, then see how we feel." Actually, at the thought of Mr. Pickens being so near, I was feeling quite rejuvenated.

The feeling didn't last long as we passed small clapboard houses, looking dismal and rain sodden, interspersed with trailers, all with blue television lights emanating from their windows. Cars of all stripes and ages, a few up on blocks, filled the yards as well as the driveways. Large yellow plastic toys—tricycles and baby slides—had been abandoned in the yards.

After almost a mile of this unedifying stretch of road, Etta Mae turned in beside Pearl's Bait & Tackle and drew up in front of a small office with peeling paint and a listing porch. Several, but not many, other cabins were dotted around under the trees, and as we got out of the car, I could hear the rippling sound of a stream behind the cabins.

We walked into what seemed to be a one-room cabin and Etta Mae dinged the bell on the counter. A thin, morose-looking man, badly in need of a shave and dressed in overalls, came out of a bathroom. I knew because the sound of flushing followed him.

"Good evening," I said, as he approached the counter. "We'd like two cabins, please."

"Ain't got but one. Prob'ly the last empty 'un in the county. Number twelve, down by the creek."

"Oh, well. Well, we'll take it."

"Be fifty dollars," he said, "for one. Sixty-five for two. In advance."

Holding my pocketbook below the counter so he couldn't see what was in it, I handed him the exact amount. "We don't think it'll be necessary, but we might want to stay another night. Will that be all right?"

"Better decide early an' get it paid for," he said, turning a form around for me to sign. "These things go fast."

I can't imagine why, I thought but didn't say. The walls of the office were covered with signs and posters, fishing rods and mounted fish, and other piscatorial paraphernalia. I wondered if Sam, who loved to fish, would be impressed with the place. From what I'd seen so far, I wouldn't be recommending it.

Trying to be friendly as he passed a key attached to a wooden paddle across the counter, I asked, "Does Pearl come in tomorrow?"

He stared at me. "Naw, she's passed."

"Oh, I'm sorry. I didn't know."

"Been awhile, so it don't matter. And ma'am," he went on, as I realized he'd never given us a hint or even the pretense of a smile, "we don't allow no cookin' and no loud parties." His eyes slid over to Etta Mae, then he glared at me. "And no visitors in the cabins. Just the ones paid cash on the barrelhead right here in the office."

"Why, of course," I said, frowning at the unusual demand. "We're not expecting any visitors."

I had to hurry to catch up with Etta Mae, who'd slammed out of the office and plopped herself in the car.

"I'm sorry, Etta Mae," I said as I slid into my seat. "I wish we had better accommodations." When she didn't answer, I went on. "He wasn't very friendly, was he?"

"Friendly? He was downright rude and vulgar. The idea!" she fumed as she drove past the row of cabins, which I now saw were doubles. Each had a small porch with two doors that apparently opened into two rentable rooms.

"You know what he meant, don't you?" Etta Mae said, her temper obviously on the rise. "He thought we were here to entertain men."

"No! How could he think such a thing?"

"Probably because he's had the problem before."

"Oh, Etta Mae, maybe we ought to sleep in the car." As the full import of his implication sank in, I said, "I can see why he'd think you could do some entertaining, but *me*? Makes you wonder what kind of women have been here. Maybe I ought to be flattered, but I don't believe I could make a living at it."

She snorted, then began to laugh. I joined in because it was either that or cry.

Etta Mae parked in front of number twelve, then we got our bags from the trunk and walked up the one step onto the narrow porch. She unlocked the door and felt around on the wall for a light switch that turned on an overhead lightbulb. We would've been better off to have left the room dark. Unfinished paneling lined the walls, and one double bed took up most of the space. A small table held a one-cup coffeemaker and a few Styrofoam cups.

Two straight chairs were the only seating in the room. A lamp with a crooked shade stood on the only nightstand. The room was damp and chilly, and Etta Mae went immediately to the portable heater and turned it on.

She glanced into the bathroom and backed out with a grimace on her face. "Tee-ninesy," she said, "and rust everywhere." Then she turned around and took in all the amenities, or lack of same, in the room. "No television! And no telephone. Do these people live in the twenty-first century?"

My heart sank at the sight of the sad little room, especially at the one bed. I'd stayed in a similar place once before, but that had been in Florida and I'd slept in a chair by myself. Having become accustomed to sleeping alone after Wesley Lloyd Springer passed, it had taken months after Sam and I married for me to become used to sharing a bed again. Now I'd have to try to sleep with Etta Mae. Looking around at the crude accommodations, I wondered how I'd make it through the night. One thing was for sure: I was going to do all in my power to get Mr. Pickens out of that hospital tomorrow, thereby making this a one-night stand.

"Etta Mae," I said, "I'm not as tired as I thought. Let's go to the hospital and see what we can find out."

"Suits me. The only way we'll be able to sleep here is if we're too tired to care." She started toward the door, then turned around. "Let's put our bags back in the car. I don't much want to leave anything here."

"Good idea. But leave the heater and a light on so the manager won't think we've left for good. Though he probably wouldn't care now that he's been paid."

"Yeah," Etta Mae said as she held the door for me. "Except he might rent it to somebody else if he thinks we're gone." She giggled. "I'd hate to walk in and find a couple of strangers in our bed."

␝

Driving back toward town, I realized that the rain had stopped, although the street was still wet and the occasional passing truck splashed water up on the car. We both were silent while we looked for the small sign that had indicated the location of the hospital. It was full dark by this time, but I caught occasional glimpses of other signs, mostly for churches that were apparently set too far off the highway to be seen. SHILOH MISSIONARY BAPTIST was one, HOLY GHOST REVIVAL another and CHURCH OF GOD WITH. . . was one I didn't quite catch. We passed the gas station and saw Junior busily cleaning the windshield of a pickup.

"Turn around, Etta Mae," I said. "We saw that hospital sign when we were at the gas station, so we've passed it."

"Dang it," she said, "I thought I knew where it was. Okay, I'll turn around here." And she pulled into a lot that faced a string of open-sided sheds with a large sign above them reading LUTHER'S FLEA MARKET OPEN DAILY EXCEPT SUNDAY. She drove back the way we'd come, passed Junior's again, then turned left onto an even narrower blacktop street. We climbed steadily, went around two shallow curves and came out onto a flat area with a long white two-story building on our right.

"This is it," I said, "though it looks more like a nursing home than a hospital. Turn in here, Etta Mae."

"That's the emergency entrance," she said. "I see the visitors' lot farther down."

As we parked and got out, I looked around at the well-kept grounds, the lights glowing from the windows, many revealing patients propped up in bed. Groups of visitors were coming and going through the lobby doors. We got out of the car and followed one group, overhearing talk about Grandma and how much longer each of them reckoned she would last. One man said, "I'm gittin' tired of comin' up here ev'ry night that rolls around. An' I'll tell you this—I don't mean to miss *Dancin' with the Stars* another time."

The lobby was full—men, women, teenagers, children and babies—and I think every last one of them was wearing some kind of denim: flat front, pleated, hip-huggers, waist high, boot cut, straight leg, full legged, and bib. Etta Mae fit right in. I thought to myself that I would tell Binkie to put me in some denim stock when I got home. Binkie and Sam, both lawyers, managed my estate, but I occasionally offered some useful advice.

There was a shoulder-high counter at the back of the lobby, so we headed toward that. Able to see only the top of a beehive hairdo with a headset running across it, I stood on my tiptoes to get the attention of the operator.

"Good evening," I said. "We'd like to see Mr. J. D. Pickens. What room is he in, please?"

The woman looked up from her console, smiled in a friendly manner, and said, "I don't recognize the name, but let me check." Her lipstick was mostly eaten off, but otherwise she was an attractive middle-aged woman. I wondered if she'd been the one who'd tried to be helpful to me on the telephone.

She flipped through several pages, frowned, then said, "We don't have a patient by that name."

"Oh, well, I expect the word hasn't gotten to you. He may still be listed as Mr. John Doe."

Her eyes widened as she gave me—and would've given Etta Mae if Etta Mae had been tall enough for her to see—an inquiring look. "Well, we do have a John Doe, but, honey, he can't have visitors. Says so right here, by order of the sheriff."

"Oh, dear," I said, trying for pathetic, "we've come so far to see how he is. We've been driving all day. Can't we just peek in and let him know we're here?"

"I'm real sorry," she said, and truly looked as if she were, "but I can't let you do that. It'd mean my job and who knows what else. But tell you what. You go talk to the sheriff in the morning and see what he says. I bet he'll let you in, seein' as how you've come such a long way."

There was no use begging or flying off the handle, which I was tempted to do until Etta Mae tugged at my sleeve and pointed toward the door. So against my inclination, I thanked the operator and with Etta Mae in tow, left the lobby and walked out toward the parking lot.

"I didn't expect it to be easy," I said, fuming, "but I'm so frustrated and disappointed I don't know what to do."

"Tell you what," Etta Mae said, sounding exactly like the operator. "You go on to the car—here's the key—and wait for me. I'll be back in a minute."

"Where're you going?" I asked, thinking that if she was headed for a ladies' room, I'd go with her.

"To look around," she said, and before I could say a word she was up the steps, dodging departing visitors, and through the door into the lobby.

Chapter 15

"Well, for goodness sakes," I said, done in that she would just up and leave me stranded on the walk. I started to follow her, but fatique and my aching back stopped me, so I walked to the car. Sitting with the doors locked, wondering what Etta Mae was doing and feeling uneasy at being alone in the sparsely lit parking lot, I began to feel put upon. Etta Mae had gone off on a tangent, nobody in this town was helping us and we were going to have to sleep in a cabin by a creek. It'd been so long since Coleman had awakened me at five-thirty that morning and we were so far from home that I felt blue and depressed. Stiff, too, from sitting all day.

Etta Mae had parked under a rain-soaked tree that was dripping rainwater over the car, so it was difficult to see out as I waited. I could hear the crunching of feet on the gravel as the occasional visitor left the hospital and walked past the car. I was tempted each time to scoot down in the seat so they wouldn't wonder why I was just sitting there.

I was doing some wondering myself: Why was it taking Etta Mae so long? Where was she and what was she doing? Should I go look for her? But what if she came back and found me gone?

I didn't know what to do, but a sharp rap on the driver's side window nearly gave me a heart attack. "Hey, it's me," Etta Mae whispered. "Open up."

I did and she scooted in, raindrops glinting in her curly hair.

Her shirt was damp on the shoulders and back. "Whoo," she said, cranking the car, "let's get out of here. I'm about soaked."

"Where've you been, Etta Mae? What'd you do?"

She giggled, as she turned us onto the road that led to the highway. "I went back in and walked down the hall along with some visitors. When they stopped at a room, I kept on going just like I had good sense. There're only about a dozen or so rooms, and all the doors were open except the last two at the end of the hall. I'll bet you money that J.D.'s in one of 'em. In fact, he must be because the one on the right had a NO VISITORS sign." She giggled again and slowed the car on the wet road. "Anyway, I turned the knob to peek in to make sure and almost made it, but before I could push the door open a nurse came out of the room across the hall and asked what I was doing. Well, she *demanded* it, and wasn't too nice about it, either. Scared me so bad I said the first thing that popped into my head. I said, 'Looking for the ladies',' and she walked me all the way back to the restroom in the lobby, so I had to go in and go."

"Oh my, Etta Mae," I said as she turned onto the highway and headed back toward the cabin. "It sounds like they're treating him like a prisoner. I wish you could've at least looked in so we'd know for sure he's there."

"Well," she said, as she ran a hand through her hair, "I wasn't through. I left the ladies' and, figuring that nurse had her eye out for me—she was a witch—I decided there were two ways to skin a cat and came straight outside. I just slipped around the whole hospital—you know, between the wall and the bushes so nobody would see me. Well, I didn't bother with the emergency room, but I looked in the other windows to see if I could see him. Almost got caught by a security guy when I was around by the maternity wing in the back, but I knew J.D. wouldn't be there, so I left." She blew out her breath. "Whew, what a rush!"

"My goodness, that was a daring thing to do," I said, marveling at her courage. "Did you find him?"

"No, dang it. Well, I might have. Most of the rooms had blinds that were either open or cracked a little or pulled up a few inches, and the windows are low enough so I could see in okay. But those last two rooms at the end of the hall were closed up tight. I listened under both of them for a few minutes, but I couldn't hear a thing. The air-conditioning units were too loud.

"Anyway," she went on, "there's a fire door at the end of that hall between those two rooms. We can't get in that way, but we could sure get out. If we needed to, that is."

"You're not thinking we might have to *sneak* him out, are you?"

"Just being prepared," she said with a grin. Then she sobered up and said, "It just seems strange to me that they won't let anybody in. Or, I guess, let him out. And you know, if he's conscious at all, he'd tell them who he is, and he must be conscious because didn't the sheriff tell Coleman his wound wasn't all that serious? So I'm thinking he must be shot in the leg or foot, because if he could walk, he'd be up and out of there. Otherwise, I just don't understand it."

"Well, neither do I, and I'm worried sick about it. Of course, if they think he's some kind of chemist, I guess that would explain it."

"Who'd think that?"

"I told you, remember? Coleman mentioned something about laboratories."

"Oh, Miss Julia," she said, laughing. "It doesn't take a chemist to brew up a batch of meth. You can do it in a kitchen or anywhere. It's a drug, a homemade drug. They sell it on the street."

"My word," I murmured. Then, "Well, Mr. Pickens is not a cook, either." The more I thought about the whole situation, the more incensed I became, except I was so tired from the long day that I couldn't work up a full head of steam. "Let's get a good night's sleep, Etta Mae, then we'll track down that sheriff in the morning, get Mr. Pickens and take off for home."

"Suits me," she said, then yawned so wide her jaws creaked.

✤

After Etta Mae wondered aloud if Mill Run had cell phone reception, I was pleasantly surprised to get right through to Hazel Marie. Thank goodness, because I didn't have the energy to beg the use of a landline from Pearl's substitute in the office. I quickly gave Hazel Marie our nonreport, then had to spend an inordinate amount of long-distance time encouraging her. I spoke with Lillian and Lloyd for a few minutes, then I put the phone in the charger, which I usually forget to do, and crawled carefully into bed with Etta Mae. We were both on edge—literally—for we lay as far apart from each other as the double bed would allow.

Nonetheless, we slept until almost seven the next morning, but I don't know how—too tired to do anything else, I guess. The mattress was knobby, the linens damp and smelly, and I couldn't get comfortable with a strange body in bed with me. And on top of that, our next-door neighbors came in about midnight and the rumble of their talk seemed to go on for hours. At one point, Etta Mae flipped herself over and plopped a pillow over her head, mumbling something about thin walls and inconsiderate people.

"You want to go back to Bud's Best Burgers?" I asked as we dressed.

"I guess so, but I hope he's got more than that." Etta Mae wasn't much of a morning person. She dressed in silence and made no effort toward reaching her normal peak of perkiness, which I appreciated, not being a morning person myself.

I brewed two Styrofoam cups of coffee, handed her one, and tried to drink the other. The taste was more than enough incentive to keep moving so we could get the real thing.

❦

After a breakfast that was at least palatable, although neither of us ate very much, we drove to the sheriff's office, parking at the curb. There were three or four patrol cars—all with the usual PROTECT AND SERVE painted on the sides—in the lot next to the office, and even as we walked to the door, two of the cars pulled out, going in separate directions.

"I am determined to get some answers this morning, Etta

Mae," I said, pushing through the doors and into a small lobby with a counter across the back. "I'm tired of this runaround we've been getting. I say, no visitors, no information, no nothing."

I walked up to the deputy behind the counter and said, "I am Mrs. Julia Murdoch and this is Miss Etta Mae Wiggins. We're from North Carolina and we'd like to see the sheriff. Please tell him we're here."

He was a big man, tall and broad, reminiscent of Lieutenant Peavey, back home. He looked us over, then said, "Sheriff don't usually come in on a Sunday. You want to talk to somebody else or come back tomorrow?"

"Neither. My business is with your sheriff, and it can't wait till tomorrow. Please call him and tell him we have important information for him—information that he needs."

The deputy's eyebrows lifted as he gave us a skeptical look. To expedite matters, I said, "I wouldn't want to be the deputy who causes him to miss out on this."

"Have a seat," he said. "I'll see can I reach him."

Etta Mae and I sat down on the orange molded-plastic chairs that were bolted to the floor. They were supposed to be form fitting, but they didn't fit mine. We sat and squirmed for the longest time while I wondered if the deputy was just trying to outlast us. Maybe he hadn't even called the sheriff. Maybe he thought we'd eventually get tired and leave. He shuffled papers, walked around behind the counter and filled his coffee cup, all the while giving us sidelong glances now and then.

"Miss Julia?" Etta Mae whispered. "You reckon he's coming?"

"He better." I got up and walked to the counter, looked the deputy right in the eye and wished I were back in Abbotsville, where I knew enough influential people to have my demands met. "Sir," I said, "we've been sitting here for almost an entire hour, and you've not said one word to us. Did you call the sheriff? Is he coming in and, if so, when will he be here?"

"Sorry," he said, although he didn't sound it. "Most people don't wait. They just watch for his vehicle, then come on by."

"Well, I'm sorry, too. I thought I'd made it plain that we're not most people. When will he be here? You did call him, didn't you?"

"I did and he didn't like it, like I knew he wouldn't. But he said he'd come by on his way to church. If he wasn't runnin' late."

"Well, my word. When does his church start? How much longer do we have to wait?"

"Be 'bout ten-thirty, I 'spect."

"Well, thank you for letting us know." I was spitting mad by this time and had to rein myself in to keep my composure. "We'll go for coffee and be back in time to see him." I turned to leave, then went back to the counter. "And if he comes in early, you tell him he can just wait for us. Let's go, Etta Mae."

We left the office with me mumbling about the most poorly run sheriff's department I'd ever seen. " 'Protect and Serve,' " I said loudly enough for the deputy to hear as I went out the door. "Hah! I don't know about the protecting, but I haven't seen any serving to speak of."

Chapter 16

Etta Mae drove us around town, very carefully, I noted, possibly because she'd had enough run-ins with law enforcement personnel to know that you obey all traffic laws once you've made them mad, which I figured I had just done. She turned into a drive-through establishment and we got cold drinks, the day having heated up considerably.

"Let's go back now, Etta Mae," I said. "I think that sheriff might try to avoid us, and I don't want to give him an excuse to take off again."

Etta Mae laughed nervously. "I bet you he's just like that sheriff on *The Dukes of Hazzard*. Remember him? Sheriff Rosco P. Coltrane, and he was so goofy, those boys just ran rings around him. I bet that's what we'll have to deal with."

"I don't care what he's like," I said, although I was getting a little nervous myself about facing the man who held the keys to Mr. Pickens's room. "I just hope he'll listen to reason and do what I want him to do."

As we parked in front of the sheriff's office again, I counted the cars in the lot. There was a new one. Well, not so new, because it was a dark red, beat-up, mud-spattered sports utility vehicle that looked as if it had been worked half to death.

Marching right up to the deputy at the counter, I said, "We're back. Is he in?"

"Yes, ma'am. Just got here, an' he don't wanta miss church, so you better go on back." He hitched up his pants with his forearms, then unlatched a half door and led us through a hall to the last room on the left. Giving one rap on the door, he opened it and said, "They're here."

He stepped back and held the door for us. We walked into the small room, most of it taken up by a desk with two visitors' chairs in front of it. File cabinets lined the sides of the room, and a map of the county was pinned to the wall behind the desk. I took all that in at a glance because my attention was drawn to the lean, craggy-faced man who unfolded himself from the creaky chair behind the desk. He was as far from the picture Etta Mae had conjured up as I was from a Hollywood starlet.

Etta Mae took a deep breath beside me as I realized I wasn't quite immune to his presence, either. There was an air of competence and confidence about him that was both attractive and off-putting—off-putting because he could be a formidable opponent. His hair had started out brown but was mostly white, as was his bushy mustache. He had sharp, piercing blue eyes that looked us over, then tarried on Etta Mae. His craggy face was lined like old leather, but the closer I looked, the younger he seemed. He certainly wasn't too old to appreciate a young curly-headed woman, which he was obviously doing.

"Ladies," he said, holding out his hand, "Sheriff Ardis McAfee. How I can help you?"

I shook his hand and introduced ourselves, adding that we were from Abbotsville, North Carolina, so he'd know we hadn't just walked in off the street, then we took seats in front of his desk. I gave him the same kind of once-over he'd been giving Etta Mae. He was wearing jeans—denim again—and a white shirt. A black sport jacket hung on a coat tree behind him. His black string tie was, I guessed, his concession to church-going attire.

"Abbotsville, huh?" he said, his eyes lazing around as if he were sitting on a porch watching the world go by. "Near Asheville?"

"Fairly," I said with a terse nod.

"I got a niece livin' down that way if she's not moved again. You know a place called Fairfields?"

"Why, yes," I said, surprised at the connection. If we kept on, we might discover some kinship. "It's a wealthy enclave about ten miles outside of Abbotsville. What's your niece's name? I might know her."

"Cheyenne, last I heard." His mouth twitched. "Real name's Nellie McAfee, but who knows? She keeps changing it. One of them free spirits, I guess."

"My word," I murmured. Then, "There're a good many of those around these days, but I don't believe I've met her."

"You'd remember, if you had." His eyes swiveled to Etta Mae again. "What can I do for you ladies?"

"I understand," I said, getting down to business now that the niceties were out of the way, "that you have spoken with Sergeant Coleman Bates of the Abbot County Sheriff's Department, and from that conversation, he tells me that you may be holding a friend of ours, Mr. J. D. Pickens. We have come to take him home."

The sheriff let a few seconds pass, then he said, "Well, now, that may not be possible. For one thing, we're not holding anybody by that name."

"But you are. You just don't know it. You told Coleman that you have a John Doe, and we think that's Mr. Pickens. He called me, you see. Or rather he called my husband, who wasn't home because he's on a Holy Land tour, and the call got disconnected. Coleman had to track it down, and it led right here. So we'll identify him for you and take him off your hands."

"Well," the sheriff said again, leaning back in his creaky chair and drawing one leg over the other knee so that I saw he was partial to Dingo boots, too. "Fact is," he said in a lazy sort of way, "we got lots of problems here, which I won't go into. But because of 'em, I have my doubts that the man I have is the man you're looking for."

"But didn't he tell you who he is? We've heard he has a gunshot wound, but it's not in his throat, is it? He can talk, can't he?"

"Oh, he can talk," Sheriff McAfee said, rolling his eyes to the ceiling. "And he's said aplenty, all right. Lot of ugly talk, not much of which I can repeat, bein' a church-goin' man and a gentleman to boot. But I wouldn't be much of a sheriff to just take the word of a stranger, stripped of any and all identification and found in suspicious circumstances. There has to be an investigation, which is ongoing. We'll get to the bottom of it sooner or later."

"Sooner or later" didn't sit well with me, but I let it go for the time being and tried another tack. "Is the man of whom we're speaking under arrest?"

"No, ma'am, he's not. But he is injured and can't get around too good. So while we're pursuing the matter, the hospital's the best place for him."

"Etta Mae, here, is a nurse," I said, with a nod in her direction as I elevated her status just a tiny bit. "We can take care of him, don't worry about that."

"Look, Mrs. Murdoch," he said, sitting up straight while the chair complained loudly. "My deputies found this man shot and in shock way up in the hills. There wasn't a smidgen of ID on him, nothing to tell us who he is or what he was doing out there. When we brought him in, he was cold and wet and not making good sense. Now I've got feelers and queries out, and we ought to get confirmation of who he is in a few days. Then we can talk about what comes next. If, that is, you want to stick around that long." He cut his eyes toward Etta Mae. She ducked her head and blushed.

"But *I* can confirm who he is! I've known him for years."

He shook his head. "No'm, gotta be official. There's lots more going on than you know about, things he might be mixed up in. I can't just release a John Doe on your say-so."

"Well," I said, thinking furiously, trying to come up with something that would move this stubborn man. "Well, what if I told you that's his name."

"What?" he asked, a smile playing around his mouth. "John Doe?"

"Well, we call him J.D. for short."

Etta Mae's head snapped around and her mouth dropped open. Sheriff McAfee laughed. "Got me there," he said, "but it won't wash. Listen, ladies," he went on, his face hardening, "you just be patient, enjoy our little town, do a little fishin' maybe, and give us a few days. We'll get this straightened out one way or the other, then we can proceed."

"Proceed to what?" I asked.

"Well, I'll either arrest him because he's part of a crew we're roundin' up or I'll release him 'cause he ain't."

"And meanwhile," I said with some asperity, "you're just going to keep him closed up in that hospital, far from his family and friends, while you go about your business."

He nodded. "That's about the size of it."

"I think that's against the law, Sheriff."

He shook his head. "No, ma'am. He's injured. He needs medical care, and that's what we're giving him. Even if he turns out to be an innocent bystander, I'd be remiss if I didn't take care of a potential witness to a crime.

"Now then," he said, standing up and reaching for his jacket, "it's time for church, so I got to be going."

"One last question, if you don't mind. We'd like to see if your potential witness is who we think he is. Would you tell the hospital to allow us to visit?"

"Can't do that," he said, shrugging into his jacket. "The only way to keep him safe is to keep him isolated. Can't have any and everybody going in and out over there, and I don't have the manpower to stand guard."

That stopped me. "You mean he's in danger?"

"Could be. Depending on what he saw and what he knows, and if he's not part of some illegal goings-on, he could be. Let's just say he's in our own homegrown witness protection program for his own good."

None of it made sense to me, except one thing. "What it comes down to, then, is that you don't believe a word he's said. You don't believe he's J. D. Pickens or that he's a private investigator or that he's as law-abiding as, well, you are. If you are."

He gave me a frosty smile and opened the office door, indicating that the interview was over. "Just waitin' on confirmation. Now, if you ladies will excuse me, I have to get to church. I got the scripture readin' this morning."

Thinking to myself, *I hope it does you some good*, I stood, feeling completely stymied, and dejected because of it.

Etta Mae, who'd not said a word during the whole interview, sidled up beside the sheriff on our way out and asked, "You a Baptist, Sheriff?"

"Church of God," he said. "Be happy to have you go with me."

Etta Mae glanced down at her jeans-clad self, her pointy-toed Dingo boots peeking out at the bottom of her boot cuts, and said, "Well, I'm a Baptist myself, and I'm not exactly dressed for church. Thank you all the same."

"Looks fine to me," the sheriff said, ushering us out of his office.

"Maybe another time," Etta Mae murmured and followed me down the hall to the lobby.

❦

"Whoo," she said, fanning her face with her hand when we got into the car. "What a man!"

"What a stubborn mule, you mean," I said, slamming the door. "All that slow, down-home country talk he was doing didn't fool me. We didn't get to first base with him, so we're right back where we started. Which is nowhere."

Etta Mae cranked the car and, watching carefully, pulled out onto the street. She began to drive aimlessly around the town and, from the look on her frowning face, was giving something a lot of thought. I hoped it wasn't the sheriff she was mulling over.

"Miss Julia," she said at last, "what if it's not J.D.? What if we wait around and finally get in that room and it's somebody we don't even know? What if we've come all the way up here and we're in the wrong place?"

I was so sure of the rightness of what we were doing that I hadn't given that possibility much thought. But I did so then— gave it several thoughts, in fact. "No, Etta Mae," I said, finally and decisively, "we're in the right place and it is him. We know that because of the phone call he made to my house, which Coleman was able to trace. And that highway patrolman he talked to pretty much confirmed it. If we start second-guessing ourselves now, we're in bad trouble. We just have to keep after the sheriff until he lets us in to visit the man he's calling John Doe."

And with that and a few more minutes of thought, I had an inspired idea. "Tell you what, Etta Mae. Let's go to church."

Chapter 17

Etta Mae pinched up a plug of her stretch-denim boot cuts. "Like *this*?"

"Well, I wouldn't ordinarily approve, although you can see everything in church these days. But I'm not talking about actually going to church, I'm talking about going and waiting for church to be over. See, Etta Mae, we can catch the sheriff again when he comes out, and if he's ever in a compassionate and amiable mood, it ought to be right after he's heard a good sermon." I paused as Pastor Ledbetter passed briefly through my mind. "Let's hope his pastor has chosen an appropriate text, like visiting the prisoner."

"Yes, but what're you going to say that you haven't already said?"

"I'm going to give him another option. Instead of asking to let us visit Mr. Pickens or Mr. Doe, whichever it is, I'll suggest that the sheriff go with us and open the door—just crack it a tiny bit—just enough for us to peek in and see what the patient looks like. If it's Mr. Pickens, why, I'll tell the sheriff that we'll wait patiently for the official identification, and if it's not, why, then, we'll leave and not bother him anymore."

"That might work," Etta Mae murmured, turning down another side street. "Miss Julia, I've seen two Baptist churches and one Evangelical Mission Church, but I've not seen a Church of God anywhere."

"Oh, it's out on the highway, Etta Mae, on the way back to Pearl's. I'm sorry, I thought you'd seen the sign."

"Okay," she said, rounding the block to head in the right direction. "It's getting close to noon, so we should have time to find a shady parking place to wait, I hope. It's sure getting hot here in the middle of the day."

"The mountains are so close that the middle of the day is the only time it *can* get hot. I mean when the sun shines directly down.

"Go slow, Etta Mae," I went on, leaning forward to watch her side of the road. "It's a little way past the hospital turnoff. There it is! See the sign?"

Etta Mae turned off the highway onto a gravel road, then stopped to peer at the wooden sign with painted letters. "I've never heard of that kind before. Have you?"

CHURCH OF GOD WITH SIGNS FOLLOWING, I read. "Well, he said Church of God, so this must be it. Except I don't see a church."

"I'll go a little farther in," Etta Mae said, and eased the car onward. She went a little farther and a little farther, twisting and turning on the gravel road, until I didn't think we could go much farther without topping the mountain. The only sign of habitation was a cluster of cabins partially hidden by trees and bushes.

"Would you look at that!" Etta Mae said, slowing even more as she pointed at a handwritten sign nailed to a tree.

I gasped as I read:

WARNING!!

DRUNKS WITH GUNS LIVE HERE

YOU LOOT, WE SHOOT

"My word," I said, stiffening at the possibility of being mistaken for looters. "Move along, Etta Mae. If there's a church up here, let's get to it."

"I'm beginning to wonder if there is." She eased the car past the sign as gravel from the road tinked against the car.

"That must be it," I said, as the road ended in a wide level clearing bounded by trees and underbrush. A dozen or more vehicles, mostly pickups, some with camper shells, a few vans, and one dump truck, were haphazardly parked in the gravel lot. Looking for all the world like a neglected tenant house, a small wooden building, painted white, hunkered down on concrete blocks in the middle of the clearing.

"That's a *church*?" Etta Mae said, as she stopped the car and stared.

"It must be. See, it's got a big red cross on the door. No porch, though, or steeple. No stained glass windows, either. These are poor people, Etta Mae, and they're probably doing the best they can."

"I guess." She didn't sound convinced. "Uh-oh, somebody's coming."

A thin, almost gaunt, man, wearing dungarees and a long-sleeved shirt buttoned to the neck, walked between the cars and approached the driver's side.

"Don't tell him anything, Etta Mae," I whispered. "Just say we're visitors. He doesn't need to know our business. He might warn the sheriff."

"Okay," she said, lowering her window and plastering a smile on her face. "I hope we're not disturbing anyone," she said as the man leaned down to look at us. "We're visiting from out of town and had hoped to attend a service. I know we're late, though, so we'll just wait out here."

I quickly chimed in to clarify what we'd wait out here for. "Maybe we can speak to your pastor when the service is over."

"You ladies're just as welcome as you can be," the man said, holding the small of his back with one hand as he leaned in, smiling painfully. He rested one gnarled and atrophied hand on the windowsill. "My name's Chester Fields. I'm one of the deacons here. Most folks call me Chet, or just plain ole Deac—it don't matter. An' the afternoon service ain't even started yet. Y'all get on out an' eat with us. We're havin' dinner on the grounds over yonder behind the meetin' house."

"Why, that's very nice of you," I said as my stomach reminded me it was lunchtime. "But we wouldn't think of intruding. Besides, not knowing about dinner on the grounds, we didn't bring a covered dish."

"Lordamercy, ma'am," the deacon said, "don't let that stop you. We got enough to feed a army. Come on back with me. We'll just be tickled to have you."

I looked at Etta Mae and she looked at me. "Neither one of us ate much breakfast," she whispered. "And we might catch the sheriff before we have to attend anything."

With that prospect in mind, we got out of the car, thanking Deacon Chet profusely, and following him as he led us a zigzag path through the parked trucks. As we walked toward the back of the meeting house, I caught a glimpse of a vehicle with a dark red roof, convincing me that we were in the right place—unless there was more than one dark-red-roofed vehicle in town.

As we turned the corner, I saw a group of people gathered around two long tables, covered not only with what I later realized were white sheets but also with platters and Pyrex bowls and casseroles, bread baskets, and cake plates—all filled with food—and huge jugs of iced tea. The aroma of fried chicken made my knees weak.

And a good thing we were as hungry as we were, or out of courtesy, we might have begged off, thereby missing the best food I'd had since leaving Abbotsville. Deacon Chet picked up a rock and rapped the side of a metal bowl, getting the attention of the few who were not already staring at us.

"Brethren, the Lord has been good enough to put some strangers down in our midst. An' strangers is always welcome where the word of God is preached. Say amen!"

And they all did—loudly. Then we had to introduce ourselves and tell where we were from, and several of the ladies, all wearing cotton frocks down to their shins and hair down to their waists, came forward and urged us to fill our plates. "It's already been blessed," one of them said. "So dig right in."

So we did, edging along sideways around the tables, heaping our plates and marveling at the amount and variety of food fresh from the garden. There was even a huge bowl of green beans cooked the way Lillian did them—slow and with a chunk of fatback. I had to hold my paper plate under the bottom to keep it from folding up on me.

We were ushered to two kitchen chairs in the shade, while another lady brought over two jelly glasses full of sweetened tea. I ate like I hadn't had a decent meal since Friday night, which I hadn't. And Etta Mae groaned with each bite, it was all so good. When I didn't think I could hold another thing, we were offered our choices of pies and cakes.

"Etta Mae," I said softly, "this is a real dinner on the grounds. No wonder Sheriff McAfee was eager to get here. But I haven't seen him, have you?"

She shook her head, pointed at her full mouth, then swallowed and said, "No'm, I haven't. But all the men are sitting way over yonder, some of them in the sun, so I can't see them too good. He may be with them."

About that time, Deacon Chet banged the bowl with his rock again and announced that if everybody'd had their fill, it was time to start the service. The women had already begun to wrap tinfoil and Saran wrap around the dishes and stack them in baskets. Some of the men came over and took the baskets to the trucks while the women folded the tablecloths. In just a few minutes, remnants of the feast were all put away and people began to move toward the meetinghouse.

We had been so warmly welcomed and fed so generously that I could see no way to skip their services without being uncommonly rude. Thinking again of some of Pastor Ledbetter's monotonous sermons, I looked forward to a little catnap in the pew.

The interior of the meetinghouse pretty much matched the exterior, lacking the paint job. About six short rows of wooden pews were on each side of a center aisle that ended at a handmade lectern with a microphone on it. High on the wall behind the lectern hung a large wooden cross outlined with white blinking Christmas lights. It was my first clue that this would not be a Presbyterian service.

"Sit here, Etta Mae," I said, sliding onto the last pew in the back, leaving just enough room for her. It is so inconsiderate of people to do what I'd just done, that is, sit right on the aisle so everybody else has to crawl over them. I was feeling a little bit bad about it until four very large people—two men and two women—came in who had not had dinner with us. One of the heavyset women stood and stared at us until we had to slide on down. They kept coming, each one larger than the other, and we kept sliding until I ended up against the wall of the meetinghouse and could go no farther.

Etta Mae blew out her breath and whispered, "I don't guess we're gonna be slipping out early, are we?"

I didn't answer, for up at the front the most unnerving racket blared out, so startling that I couldn't answer. Four men had taken up instruments, one at the piano, another one strumming a guitar, one banging on a set of drums, and one beating a tambourine half to death. And they'd turned up the sound on the microphone. Everybody started singing, although there wasn't a hymnal in sight. The music was catchy, though, and when people began to rise, we did, too, and swayed with them. Etta Mae knew a few of the words, so she joined in—something about a beautiful, beautiful river, which had so many verses that by the time it was over I'd learned the chorus by heart.

After several more hymns, with first one person then another starting them off—not a choir director in sight—Deacon Chester went to the lectern. He'd seemed such a nice, gentle soul around the dinner table, but when he took the microphone in hand so he could wander around, something came over him. Now, I'm not one to sit in judgment on other people's manner of worship, but let me just say that that service was not even close to the manner to which I was accustomed.

The deacon became a changed man. He preached and

preached and preached, becoming more and more frenzied and rhythmic, almost hypnotic in his delivery. No chance for a nap in his service, for even though I couldn't understand a word he was saying, he'd bellow out loud every now and then, mop the sweat from his face and keep on going. People began to come out of the pews and walk around, encouraging him with "Amen!" and "Praise God!" and raised hands swaying overhead.

I grabbed Etta Mae's hand as she sat stiff as a board next to me. "I don't know about this, Etta Mae," I whispered. "I want to leave."

"Me, neither," she mumbled, and jumped when a woman shrieked. "I do, too."

But we were packed in the pew so tightly that I was crammed against the wall, with all those fat people between us and the aisle wedged in like Vienna sausages in a can.

A sudden commotion started up at the front of the church. People—men and women—gathered around the lectern, some moaning, some praying and some kneeling around a wooden box that a young man placed on the floor.

I didn't know the significance of the box and couldn't see what they were doing with it until Deacon Chester bent over it, darted his hand down and came up with a three-foot-long snake so angry that I could hear its rattles over the din.

Deacon Chester held that reptile up so that it was looking him right in the face. "If you got the faith, you can take up serpents," he shouted at it. "But if you ain't got it, you better stand clear. Don't tempt the Lord!"

Etta Mae's eyes popped wide and her mouth dropped open. The hand I held turned ice-cold, and sweat began to bead on her face. "I got to get outta here," she moaned.

Another shriek ripped through the air as a different man held up a coiling snake, its white mouth so wide it looked unhinged. The tail wrapped around his arm, and he reached down and picked up another one in his other hand. He held it aloft, its head darting toward him as he closed his eyes and hopped around on one foot.

But when he let the thing slither around his neck, Etta Mae screamed and jumped straight up. The fat lady next to her oozed into the space she'd vacated and yelled, "She's a-comin', Lord, she's a-comin'!"

Well, actually she was a-going, because—I don't know how she did it—crying and shivering, she scooted over all those mounded laps like a water bug skimming across a pond. She hit the aisle running. Out the door she went, with me bumbling along behind her. "Excuse me, excuse me," I kept mumbling, pushing hard past those larded knees, determined to get out of that place.

Finally, I got through, then had to dodge a woman whirling around in the aisle. Stumbling, I made it to the door, so anxious to get out that I almost forgot my manners. Recalling the excellent meal so generously shared with us, I pulled a fairly large bill out of my pocketbook, handed it to a man who looked only halfway entranced and said, "Put this in the collection plate, please. To cover our dinner."

I practically ran to the car, which Etta Mae already had cranked with the air-conditioning on high. She had to unlock the door to let me in.

"Let's go," I said, collapsing inside, wanting to pull my feet up on the seat.

Etta Mae, shivering and trembling, slammed the car in reverse, spun the wheel and threw up gravel as we headed away. "I have never, never, never in my life seen anything like that," she said between gulps of air. Big shudders ran through her body as she guided the car down the road and out onto the highway. "I won't sleep a wink tonight," she said. "I *hate* those things." Then she took a deep breath, trying to calm herself. "At least we'll have a tale to tell when we get home, if anybody will believe us. And if we ever get back."

"Lord, yes," I said, using a Kleenex to wipe perspiration from my face. A few shudders were running up and down my back. "But, Etta Mae, we have to do what Emma Sue Ledbetter always recommends and look on the bright side. Although I'm not sure it was worth what we've just been through, we did have a wonderful meal, much better than Bud's Best Burgers. I would never tell Lillian, but that fried chicken was almost better than hers."

My effort to bring about a little normalcy didn't seem to have much effect. Etta Mae kept driving toward Pearl's, an intent look on her face and her mind on the Sunday afternoon traffic. Four cars and a farm truck passed on their way to town.

Finally, she said, "They say rattlesnake tastes just like chicken."

I thought about that for a second or two, then my throat clutched up and I swallowed hard. My hand flew to my mouth. "Pull over, Etta Mae. Quick!"

Chapter 18

When we drove in at Pearl's, Etta Mae stopped by the office, saying she'd be back in a minute.

"Wait, Etta Mae," I said, opening my pocketbook. "Much as I hate to, we better pay for another night." I handed her the money, hoping our cabin had not been rented while we'd been witnessing what it meant to have "signs following" a church service.

"Okay, I'll be right back." And soon she was, bringing with her a broom that she put in the backseat.

I was feeling too weak to ask why she wanted to do some cleaning, but I soon found out. When we walked to the cabin door, she told me to wait there, and then, holding the broom, she took a flying leap and landed on the bed, Dingo boots and all. Then she commenced to swing that broom around, swishing it back and forth under the bed and across the tops of the windows and in the corners of the room. Then she jumped down and did the same thing in the closet and bathroom.

"Okay, Miss Julia," she said. "You can come on in now. No snakes, thank goodness."

Grateful for her thoughtfulness, I eased my way to the bed, took off my shoes and lay down. She brought in our bags again, locked the door, then stretched out beside me.

"I am wrung out," she said. "Remind me never to visit a strange church again. I'm sticking with the Baptists." She turned over, then said, "How are you feeling? Want me to try to find a drug-store and get something for your stomach?"

"Oh, no. It's much better. I'm just awfully tired. Let's try to get a little nap."

She mumbled agreement and we lay there, trying—or at least I did—to block out the image of writhing snakes going up and down arms and across shoulders.

After a while, I said, "Etta Mae?"

"Hm-m?"

"Sheriff McAfee wasn't there, was he?"

She turned back over. "No'm, I don't see how he could've been. As soon as we sat down, I looked at every man in the place. And he's tall. We would've seen him if he'd been there."

"I think so, too. Well, I guess we just went to the wrong place. Who would've thought there'd be more than one Church of God in such a small town. Now, if it had been the Baptists, I could understand it. Wherever there's one Baptist church, there's always another one. Or two. No offense, Etta Mae."

"Oh, you can't tell me anything about the Baptists I don't al-ready know. But, Miss Julia, I think we must've gone to the wrong place. I asked the man in the office if there was a plain ole Church of God without any signs following, but he didn't know. He said he liked the preaching on television because when they passed the plate, he didn't have to put anything in."

"I wish we'd asked somebody with some sense before we went," I said. Then after thinking about it for a few minutes, I went on. "There's one other possibility, Etta Mae. I hate to think the sheriff would do this, but he might've figured we'd follow him and told us the wrong church on purpose."

Etta Mae sprang straight up. "Would he *do* that?" she asked incredulously. Then she flopped back on the pillow. "Why, that sorry thing! And I thought he was so nice."

"Well, we don't know for sure. He could've been planning to be there, but got called away. I'll tell you one thing, though, you won't catch me going to a church with any kind of signs ever again. I don't care whether they're following or leading, I've had my fill of them."

"You and me," she said fervently.

❧

A roll of thunder wakened us sometime later. I looked out the window to see the trees being lashed by the wind as the day darkened. Rain came pouring down, and I wondered what we'd do with ourselves for the rest of the long night ahead. We'd missed our chance with the sheriff until morning at least. There was nothing in the room to help us pass the time—no television, no radio, and no books or magazines. Etta Mae was quite pleasant company, but as far as I was concerned, she didn't qualify as entertainment. Nor I for her.

She sat up in bed and yawned. "You hungry?"

"I guess I am," I said, checking inwardly on the state of my stomach. "I'm not sure I want to go out in this storm, though."

Etta Mae got up and looked out the window. "It'll stop in a few minutes—it's just a little mountain shower. They probably come every afternoon." She went into the bathroom, and when she came back, she said, "Why don't I go and see if I can find some sandwich makings? We can eat in here and you won't have to go out."

"Well, if you don't mind, that would suit me."

I handed her a few bills, then went on, "While you're out, go ahead and fill up with gas."

She grinned. "Okay, we've probably used almost a whole quarter of a tank."

"Well," I said, "I like—"

"To be prepared," she finished. "I know, and I will."

It was well over an hour later when she returned, bearing cold drinks and a sack filled with a loaf of bread, small jars of mayonnaise and mustard, a vacuum-packed package of ham and one of bologna, two small bags of potato chips, one plastic knife, and two bananas. We spread it all out on the tiny table and began to make sandwiches.

"Sure wish we had a tomato to go with this baloney," Etta Mae said, slapping on a slice of bread to top off her sandwich. "But," she went on, "I ought to be thankful for what we have. I drove all over town looking for a grocery store and the only thing open was a convenience store. These bananas were the only fresh things they had."

Limiting myself to the ham, because after my experience earlier in the day I didn't trust the ingredients in the other, I made a sandwich. "This is fine, Etta Mae, and I'm glad you didn't look any longer. I was beginning to get worried about you."

"Well, actually, I saw something that delayed me for a while." She put down her sandwich and propped her elbows on the table. "When I passed the sheriff's office, it looked like something big was going on: lots of cars and trucks in the lot with cops going and coming, a couple with dogs, even. And every one of them had these big, wicked-looking guns, and they were all bulked up with bulletproof vests. Well, I couldn't pass that by, so I went around the block and nosed out of a side street where I could see them, but they couldn't see me. I watched for a good while, trying to figure out what they were doing." She took a drink from her soda can. "And I'll tell you something else. Some of those cops were ATF guys. I saw it on their windbreakers."

"That's Alcohol and what?"

"Tobacco and Firearms. Miss Julia, I think they're going on a raid. And what I'm wondering is whether it has anything to do with J.D."

"Oh, my word, you reckon?"

"I don't know, but the sheriff sure implied that something was going on that J.D. might be a part of. Or rather, that he *suspected* J.D. was a part of."

"Yes, he did, but we know he's not." I put down my half-eaten sandwich and thought about this development. "Think about it, Etta Mae. The sheriff said that Mr. Pickens was found way back in the woods in suspicious circumstances. I don't know what he meant by suspicious circumstances, but when a person is found off in the woods, shot and stripped of identification, that'd be suspicious enough for anybody. So," I went on, trying to think it through, "maybe that's where they're going tonight—back into the woods where Mr. Pickens was found to search the surrounding circumstances." I pondered the matter a little longer, then went on some more. "But why have they waited until tonight to do it? They found Mr. Pickens days ago. Seems like they'd have jumped right on it at the time."

"Maybe they waited to see if J.D. could tell them anything. Or maybe the ATF was busy somewhere else, and they had to wait for them. But after what I saw tonight, they weren't just going to search somewhere. That was a bunch of guys getting ready to raid something. And it could be that meth lab Coleman heard about. Except," she paused, thinking, "it'd be the DEA if that was the case."

"I don't think it matters," I said, getting excited at finally being able to put a few things together. "But what I don't understand is why the sheriff thinks Mr. Pickens had anything to do with such a criminal enterprise."

"Why, that's easy. I'll bet you anything that J.D. was found close to where they think the lab is. And I bet you that's why he got shot. He got too close and saw too much."

"Well, it does stand to reason, doesn't it? And you know what else stands to reason? That if we could get Mr. Pickens out of that hospital, we could have him across the state line by the time Sheriff McAfee knows he's gone. I mean if they are raiding that laboratory, the sheriff is going to be pretty busy for the next few hours. We could be in and out and gone while he has his hands full."

Etta Mae's eyes got big and round. "You think we could? All three of us could end up in jail."

"I don't see why," I said, becoming more and more convinced that we needed to strike while the iron was hot, or while the sheriff was tromping through the woods. "Correct me if I'm wrong, but

I asked the sheriff directly if Mr. Pickens was under arrest, and he said no. He said he was either a criminal or a potential witness, and even if the sheriff doesn't know which one he is, *we* do."

Etta Mae sat still, her eyes roving about the room as she thought about it. "If we did," she said, "I mean, if we *could* do it, it'd make Sheriff McAfee really, really mad."

"At this point, I don't care. He either pulled a trick on us by sending us to that church this morning or he's a snake handler himself, so making him mad is the least of my worries.

"Listen, Etta Mae," I went on. "We can leave a note saying that Mr. Pickens will come back to testify if he's needed. That would be sufficient, don't you think?"

"Golly, I don't know." Etta Mae leaned back in her chair, sandwich and drink forgotten, as she considered what we'd have to do. "How would we get him out?"

"I've been giving that some thought, and here's what I've come up with. You brought your nurse's uniform, didn't you?"

She nodded. "Brought a scrub suit. But, Miss Julia, it won't do us any good. That ole biddy of a nurse would recognize me in a minute, I don't care what I had on."

"She wouldn't recognize me, though, would she?"

Chapter 19

So there I was, pulling on pants again, and because Etta Mae was a size small and not very tall, I filled them out almost too well. I knew Etta Mae had a collection of varicolored scrub suits—V-necked tops and drawstring pants, some blue and some green—but I was pleased that she'd brought a plain white set, because white looked more professional. I figured I'd need all the help I could get.

"Etta Mae," I said, looking down at my feet, which stuck out from those drawstring drawers that ended above my ankles, "I don't think these navy Ferragamo pumps go with the rest of my ensemble."

Etta Mae got tickled and started laughing. "They sure don't. Here, try these on." She handed me a pair of white running shoes that had soles thick enough to cushion a million steps. "They're what I wear."

"My word," I said, struggling to get them on, "I feel like an evil stepsister trying on a glass slipper. My toes are so cramped up, they'll never be the same." Have I mentioned that Etta Mae was a tiny girl and that her top was too tight on me and her pants too short and her shoes not even close to the size of my feet?

"Why don't you wear your own shoes till we get there? That way, you won't cripple yourself." She was still laughing, but I wasn't. "Okay," she said, trying to get with the program, "let's pin this on." She handed me a black plastic name tag reading E. M. WIGGINS, C.N.A., and showed me where to pin it.

"What does C.N.A. mean? In case somebody asks?"

"Certified Nursing Assistant," she said, then tapping a finger against her mouth, she studied the problem. "But if anybody questions you, tell them you're a certified nutrition aide. They'll think you're a kitchen worker and won't pay you any mind. The regular kitchen and the diet kitchen are sorta a no-man's-land to the nurses anyway."

"Well, but by the time we get there, it'll be way past suppertime. What would a kitchen worker be doing wandering the halls close to midnight?"

"Let me think a minute." She sat down while I waited. "I've got it. You can say that the head dietician left an order for you to do a random check with patients to see what they think of the food. You know, if they have any complaints about what they're served. And don't worry, we're going to get there way before midnight. In fact, we ought to be there just as visiting hours are ending, so it won't seem too odd for you to be in and out of patient rooms. They'll all still be awake."

"You mean I've got to really ask them what they think of the food? Oh, Etta Mae, I don't know if I can do that."

"Sure you can. I wish we had a clipboard for you, but here, here's a little pad and a pen. Just carry that around and jot down a few notes—room number, patient name, any complaints—like that. You'll look so official nobody'll say a thing. Now listen, Miss Julia," she went on, "the only people you have to worry about are the nurses—they think they're queen bees anyway, especially at night when the doctors aren't around. If anybody stops you, well, just remember to mention these words: *dietician* and *order*. And you can throw in *special diets* if you think of it. Other than that, you don't know anything. They don't expect you to know anything anyway. Kitchen help is just kitchen help, so being ignorant won't be suspicious. You're just doing what you've been told."

"Oh, Lord," I moaned, dreading what was to come. "Well, tell me this. How am I going to get into Mr. Pickens's room, if it is his room? From the way that nurse jumped on you, they're watching it all the time. I can't just waltz in there, can I?"

"No, don't do that. But here's the beauty of the plan: you can go in and out of the other rooms while there're nurses around to see you. But as soon as the coast is clear—you know, when they're working on charts or giving meds or whatever—you can scoot right into the last room on the right. And if he's not in there, scoot right back out and check the room across the hall. He's got to be in one of them, if he's there at all. And if he's not, then get out of there and we'll decide what to do next."

"Where will you be?"

"Waiting in the car, I guess. I don't want that old biddy to see me again. She might suspect something's going on." Etta Mae looked me over carefully. "But you'll be all right. Hospitals are full of all kinds of people—volunteers, Pink Ladies, orderlies, chaplains, visiting preachers, florists delivering flowers, doctors, X-ray techs, lab techs, OR techs, you name it, they're all running around the halls. You'll be just another one that the nurses pay no attention to."

"Well, my goodness," I said, "if I'd known I had all those types to choose from, I would've picked something other than kitchen help. I mean I could be doing a visitation from a church and handing out tracts. I think I'd be more suited to that."

"No, because some nurse would send you packing, especially after visiting hours. You need to be somebody who belongs at the hospital, and you're as close as we can get you just the way you are."

Etta Mae looked me up and down, checking to see if I passed muster. "Uh-oh," she said. "Let's swap watches. Yours is too fancy for a kitchen worker." She unbuckled her large round watch with a sweeping second hand and exchanged it for my small jeweled one. "I'll take good care of it. Okay, let's take our luggage with us—we don't want to have to come back here. Oh, one more thing. Keep your cell phone with you, and I'll have mine so you can call me if you need me."

I didn't like the sound of that. "You think I will?"

"No, I really don't. If you get caught, all they'll do is kick you out and that's no big deal. But wait, let me see your phone." She took it, punched a few buttons and handed it back. "I've fixed it so my number is the first one on your contact list. You won't have to scroll for it because I've spelled it *Aetta Mae*. Just hit Contacts, then OK, and it'll ring me."

"Oh, me," I moaned, "this is getting complicated."

"It's gonna work great. Just think, in less than an hour, we could be headed for home. Come on, let's get our bags in the car."

"Wait a minute, Etta Mae. What if I find Mr. Pickens, and he's too sick or too maimed or whatever to be moved?"

That stopped her, but only for a second. "Well, then, at least we'll know where he is. I mean for sure. And you can demand that he be moved to a city hospital where he'd get better care and we'd have easier access. You'd be well within your rights to do that, especially because Sheriff McAfee made such a big deal about taking care of his witness."

"You're worth your weight in gold, Etta Mae, and then some," I said, marveling at her perfect argument if I got called on the carpet by the sheriff. "All right," I said, putting my mind into acting mode, "let's go do this before I lose my nerve."

✲

"I'm still wondering about something," Etta Mae said as she drove along the highway toward town, our xenon headlights cutting a tunnel through the dark night. "Why would the ATF be raiding a meth lab? I still think the sheriff would call out the DEA for that."

"Etta Mae," I said, my mind on something other than alphabetized government agencies, "I don't know the difference between the DEA and the PTA."

She giggled. "Drug Enforcement Agency, which is not real close to the PTA. Anyway, what I'm thinking is that, with the ATF, it's more likely that they're after a liquor still, bootleg cigarettes or stolen guns and explosives. Any of those would make more sense than a meth lab, wouldn't it?"

"I declare, I don't know and don't much care. All I can think of is making this little charade work. I'm a nervous wreck just thinking about it."

She reached over and patted my arm. "Remember, I've seen you in action. Just act like you belong in there, and you'll do fine."

🐝

Etta Mae pulled into the visitors' lot at the hospital just as a few cars were leaving. She parked farther from the lights of the lobby than she had the night before, and we sat for a few minutes in the dark. I scanned the long facade of the hospital that extended on both sides of the central lobby. According to the signs we'd seen, the emergency room and X-ray department were to the right of the lobby, while our focus was on the left side, where there were two floors of patient rooms and wards. Most of the rooms were still lit with half of them open to public view through open blinds. I wondered if those patients knew that we could sit in the parking lot and watch as they lay in bed receiving visitors, taking medications, and watching television. A few, of course, just lay there, too sick, apparently, to care who was watching.

"Etta Mae," I said, "what if Mr. Pickens is on the second floor? Have you thought of that?"

"Yeah, I have. I just haven't mentioned it. But here's what you do: if you don't find him on the first floor and nobody's stopped you, go on up and try there. But I'm convinced he's in that last room on the right on the first floor because of the way that nurse was on me so quick and so hard. I mean if he's not there, I'd be really surprised." She craned her head, looking at the rows of lighted rooms. "I wish that room wasn't on the back side. We could at least see if a light's on." She turned to look at me. "Want me to make another run around the back and see?"

"I guess not." I shook my head. "Too dangerous with that security man wandering around."

Reaching for the door handle, I sighed and then said, "Well, this isn't getting it done."

"Wait, Miss Julia, there're people coming out. Let's wait till they're gone. Oh, you better leave your pocketbook here. Hanging it on your arm won't look too professional."

She was right, but I felt undressed without it. However, with what I was already wearing, why worry about accessories?

I waited until an old car with a broken muffler had left. Then without another word, I got out of the car, tightened the drawstring on the scrub suit pants and headed for the hospital to put on my act.

The lobby was almost empty, visiting hours being over, so I juggled my notepad and cell phone in one hand and held my pen at the ready with the other. Looking neither to the left nor the right and bending over a little so the operator behind the counter wouldn't see me, I scuttled across the lobby and went through the wide-open double doors that led to the hall. Patient rooms lined both sides, and nurses and other white-clad personnel went in and out of the rooms.

Deciding that the best method would be to avoid meeting the eye of anyone in authority, I put on a look of intense concentration, telling myself that I was there to carry out the head dietician's orders and nothing else.

The first room on the right had a nurse in it, so I quickly moved to the one across the hall. The patient was a husky man with a red face who had his bed cranked so high that he was practically sitting upright.

He glanced at me as I came in, then fastened his eyes on the television set high on the wall at the foot of his bed. "What now?" he demanded, and flapped the sheet indignantly. He was wearing only a little short hospital gown, so I almost got an eyeful.

Drawing on my long experience of pretending that a social blunder had not occurred, I acted as if I'd seen nothing. "Uh, I'm, ah, taking a survey for the kitchen. I mean for the dietician," I said, my pen poised over the pad. "How do you like the food here?"

"What kind of question is that? You know what they serve me? Jell-O, mashed potatoes and oatmeal. Supposed to help my ulcer, and I'm sick of it. I need real food, like a pizza or something."

"Yessir, I'll put that down." And I did, feeling very competent as I did so. It's quite rewarding to feel that you're of help to someone.

That wasn't so hard, I thought as I graded the man's response as an F. I headed for the next room, all the while watching for the nurses. They were swarming around the middle of the hall, where several were busy at the nurses' station. I ducked into a room where an elderly woman with white hair that had turned yellow lay huddled under a sheet.

"Ma'am?" I said, approaching the bed. "I hope I'm not disturbing you, but I'd like to ask you a few questions about the meals you're getting."

Her hand suddenly snaked out from the sheet and grasped my arm. "Will you take me?"

"What? Take you where?"

"To Walmart. I want to go to Walmart. Real bad."

"Well," I said, removing her hand and stepping away from the bed, "maybe tomorrow. How do you like the food here?"

"Okay," she said and closed her eyes.

Not knowing exactly what she was responding to, I gave her a C. Then, getting into the swing of it, I swished out into the hall, Etta Mae's thick-soled shoes squeaking on the waxed floor and my toes crimped up so bad that my swing had a list to it. And ran right into a nurse.

"Oops," she said, sidestepping away. "Sorry, didn't mean to run into you. You checking temps?"

Not sure how to answer, I ignored the question. "Dietician's orders. You know, special diets."

"Better you than me," she said breezily. She was a stout, dark-haired woman with a pleasant expression who seemed to accept my presence without a qualm. "The food is awful around here." Then she looked more closely at me. "You're new, aren't you?"

"No," I said, thinking quickly, "I'm usually in the kitchen." Then to distract her, I said, "That lady in there wants to go to Walmart."

She laughed. "Yeah, the sweet ole thing loves Walmart, but she's not too with it. Last week when I asked if she'd voided, she told me she hadn't voted in twenty years."

I smiled as the nurse went on about her business, leaving me to go on about mine with a little more confidence. I'd survived a close examination without arousing any questions as to my standing. To be on the safe side, though, I bypassed several rooms in case she decided to double back and check on me. Besides, I was anxious to find Mr. Pickens and get myself out of there.

As I neared the nurses' station, which I had to pass in order to get to the end of the hall and the last room on the right or on the left, whichever it turned out to be, I kept my eyes on the pad in my hand, lifting them only now and then to check room numbers— acting for all the world like I knew what I was doing and beginning to do it with a little more assurance.

Chapter 20

"What do you think you're doing?"

A hard-faced nurse who fit Etta Mae's description of an old biddy accosted me as I started into a room about midway down the hall.

She startled me so bad that I could only stand there and gape at her.

"Can't you read?" she demanded. "The sign says isolation. That means no one goes in without suiting up."

I started backing away. "Oh, sorry. I just . . ."

"If you have to go in, put on a gown and mask. Gloves, too."

"Yes, ma'am. I mean, no, ma'am, I don't have to go in. I'm just following orders. The dietician's, that is. Special orders. I mean, diets."

Her black eyes bored into me, her mouth a thin line, as I expected to be thrown out or arrested or otherwise publicly castigated. Instead, after giving me a swift up-and-down look, shaking her head with disdain, she said, "You can skip that one. She's on IVs, NPO."

"Right," I said, jotting a few scribbles on my pad, not knowing what NPO stood for and not daring to ask.

She turned away and went back to her station, leaving me trembling from the close call. I quickly tapped on the closed door of the next room, slipping in when I heard a response.

A fairly young woman, looking distressed and half angry, lay on the bed. "About time," she snapped. "I've had my light on for ten whole minutes and nobody's come."

"Well, I'm here for . . ."

"I don't care what you're here for. I need this bedpan emptied." She lifted her hips and slid a bedpan out from under the sheet. "Take it. You've left me on it for thirty minutes. I don't know what you people are doing, but this is no way to treat a patient on bed rest." She shoved it away. I had to catch it before it and its contents hit the floor.

I stood there holding the thing. "What do I do with it?"

"Empty it!" she said, ill-tempered as a hornet. "The bathroom's right in there. Don't they teach you anything around here?"

Finally finding my voice, I said, "I'm kitchen help. I don't think I'm supposed to be doing this, but," I went on as her angry eyes flashed, "I will."

And I did for the first and, believe me, last time in my life, then washed my hands until they were waterlogged. Going back into the room, I said, "How do you like the food here?"

"I don't. Now don't bother me anymore. I'm tired."

Giving her an F, I left the room, deciding that I'd only go into rooms that had open doors. No way would I risk another bathroom run behind a closed one—except for the two rooms at the end of the hall, which I was nearing with every step. But nurses were still going and coming across the hall and in and out of the rooms, preparing patients for the night, and at no time had I been out of sight of at least one of them.

With that in mind, I figured I'd better slow down my patient canvass or I'd run out of rooms before the nurses ran out of errands. If they didn't soon take a coffee break or something, I'd have to think up another question or two and start over from scratch. How long I could get away with doing that, I didn't know, because sooner or later someone would notice that I was going around and around the hall and in and out the same rooms over and over.

I didn't know what else to do. I hated to give up on finding Mr.

Pickens when he might be only a few steps away. Yet I was also getting concerned about Etta Mae. She wasn't the most patient soul in the world, and she might get tired of wondering what I was doing and come sailing in to look for me. That would really stir the pot, because once you'd seen Etta Mae in action, you wouldn't forget her, and I knew that sharp-eyed nurse would be onto both of us in a minute.

I thought of using my cell phone and telling her that everything was all right, that I was still making my rounds and that taking a random survey involved more than I'd thought—like emptying bedpans, for instance. But I didn't call for fear that any action out of the character I'd already established would draw attention I didn't want.

So I went on about my business, passed the nurses' station with averted eyes, and walked on into the back half of the hall. The farther I went, the dimmer and more shadowy the back hall became. Only a few recessed lights in the ceiling were on, and only a few room doors were open—most patients, I guessed, were already down for the night. Or maybe they were the sickest.

Across the hall from where I was standing while writing on my pad in an attempt to look busy, I saw a closed door with a light burning above it—a summons to the nurses, I assumed, and walked right on past it. I'd learned my lesson behind another closed door.

The room next to it was open, so I walked in to see a fairly young woman, all skin and bones, with big dark eyes sunk into her face. She didn't look healthy, and that was a fact, but she put a hand to her mouth and smiled behind it.

"Good evening," I said, holding up my pad in a professional manner. "I'm from the kitchen, and the dietician would like to know if you have any complaints about the food."

"Oh, no, ma'am. It's the best I ever eat. They's just not enough of it."

"Maybe we can fix that," I said, my heart going out to the lank-haired girl. Her color wasn't good, either. "Why don't I tell them that you'd like bigger servings?"

"Well, I wish that'd do it, but my stomach can't hold but a little at a time. That's why they feed me six times a day. See, my stomach's all shrunk up."

"My goodness, how did that happen?"

She shrugged her shoulders and looked away. "Jus' happened. Been coming on for years they said, and I got the low blood and not enough iron in it, either. Makes me real tired."

"Bless your heart, honey, I guess it does. Well, I'll tell you what. If I see any extra food around, I'll bring it to you."

"I wish you would," she said. "I've been thinking about getting up and seeing if any of the other patients left anything on their trays." To let me know she was kidding—I think—she smiled broadly before remembering to cover her mouth. And no wonder. She had the worst teeth I'd ever seen—they were decayed, broken and discolored. I didn't know how she could eat anything with them.

Just as I was moved to offer her the services of a dentist—my treat—we heard a commotion in the room next door that startled us both. Something metallic clanged to the floor and something heavy thumped along with it. Then a white-headed man in a short hospital gown ran past the door and down the hall toward freedom.

I hurried to look out and saw the nurses scrambling to stop him. Two of them, their arms spread wide, stood in the middle of the hall in an attempt to net him. He nimbly evaded them, his long thin legs high stepping toward the lobby. A clear tube bounced between his knobby knees, an unnamed yellow liquid spraying in his wake.

The nurses were in turmoil, all yelling at once. "Mr. Purvis! Stop, come back here! Head him off, Glenda. Grab him, somebody!" Charts clattered as they were thrown down, chairs pushed aside, and they were all in such a disordered flurry that a Pepsi bottle was knocked over and the brown liquid spread across the floor. One nurse shrieked when she slid in it, ending up entangling two others before all three fell together.

And through the chaotic scene on the floor by the nurses' station, I could see the old man elude arms reaching for him as he gained the lobby, yelling for a taxicab. I was mesmerized by the chase, fascinated especially by Mr. Purvis's flabby backside winkling in and out of the gap in his back-tied hospital gown.

Tearing my eyes away from that gruesome sight, I realized that for the first time the nurses were fully occupied and that this might be the last best chance I'd have.

Quickly excusing myself and telling the girl with the bad teeth that I'd try to see her later, I checked the hall again. Seeing a pile of nurses and maybe an orderly or a security man all wrestling with Mr. Purvis in the lobby, I scooted across the hall and slipped into the last room on the right, closing the door behind me.

I was in, at last.

Chapter 21

The room was as black as pitch. I stood against the door for a minute, my eyes squinched up, until forms gradually emerged and I began to get my bearings. I was able to make out a television set bolted high on one wall, the closed blinds with a little diffused light seeping through, and the bed with a long lump on it. But not the chair that I ran into as I crept toward the bed nor the night-stand that rattled as I bumped into it.

Fearing to turn on a light, I reached out to touch and arouse the unmoving lump on the bed. Then I hesitated. What if it wasn't Mr. Pickens? What would I say? How would I explain my creeping into a dark room and feeling up a strange patient?

So I stood there, trying to slow my rapid breathing and hoping for a clue as to the lump's identity before committing myself. I wondered how fast I could get out of the room if the patient screamed for help. I wondered how long I had before the nurses subdued Mr. Purvis and, concerned about their other patients, began to do bed checks.

Not long, I decided, and put my hand lightly on what I now could see was the patient's back—sleeping on his or her stomach, I concluded, pleased with my increasing ability to see in the dark.

Leaning over a mass of hair, I whispered, "Mr. Pickens? Is that you? It's me, Julia Murdoch."

He, she, it—I still didn't know what I was dealing with—

stirred, a dark head lifted from the pillow and turned toward me and mumbled, "What the hell. . . ?"

"Oh, Mr. Pickens, it *is* you! I can't believe it. I mean I can, because I thought all along it had to be you, but, well, I still wasn't sure."

"What? Who? Miss Julia? What's going on?" Mr. Pickens, still spraddled out on his stomach, had risen to his elbows to stare at me.

"Sh-h-h," I cautioned. "Not so loud. They'll throw me out if they find me here." Then hurriedly speaking to give him as much information as I could, I went on. "Now listen, we want to know what's wrong with you. Coleman heard you got shot, so are you all right? What can we do? I've got Etta Mae Wiggins with me—she's out in the car—and we'll do whatever we can to get you some help. That sheriff here is bound and determined to keep you isolated, but you're not under arrest, except you soon might be if he decides you have anything to do with whatever they're raiding. Which they're doing as we speak, so he's out of commission for the moment as far as you're concerned. So if you want out of here, now's the time."

"Huh? Hold on . . ." Mr. Pickens rested his face in his hands, like he needed a minute to think, which I completely understood because who would expect to be awakened by someone you thought was almost four hundred miles away?

He rubbed his face in his hands—I could see the movement, but little else except the uncombed mess his hair was in.

"Etta Mae's here?" he asked.

"She's waiting in the parking lot. But listen, Mr. Pickens, are you still wounded? Can you get up? We'll take you home if you want to go."

"Okay, let's go." His head dropped back down on the pillow. "Real sleepy," he mumbled. "Gimme a minute. Kinda messed up here."

"Oh, I understand. I've had dealings with Sheriff McAfee myself. But he's out of reach—Etta Mae saw them going on a raid, so they're all out in the hills somewhere. Now's your chance, if you want it."

"Oh, yeah. Jus' maybe. . . . Too tired."

"We'll help. Can you walk? Where were you shot? The sheriff said it wasn't life threatening and that you were getting better. We'll do whatever we can, but I don't want to cause any more damage. The first thing we have to decide is how to get you out of this room. Those nurses watch you like a hawk, but they have their hands full with Mr. Purvis. So if we hurry, we might be able to slip out the fire door, which is right next to yours. As quick as you are, Mr. Pickens, we could be outside in two seconds and nobody the wiser."

He gave a half laugh. "Not so quick. Can't get off the bed."

"How bad is it? Your wound, I mean. Is it in your leg? You can lean on me and hop. We don't have far to go. Or I can call Etta Mae and between us we'll get you out."

"Oh, Lord," he said in a despairing way as he rubbed his face again. "Head's buzzin'. Can't think. Had something for pain."

"Yes, I figured that," I said, getting a little exasperated with his slowness to be up and running. "We need to get a move on."

"Etta Mae's here? With a car?"

"Yes, and she's waiting for us. Now listen, it's good that you've had something for pain. Don't worry about thinking—just do what I tell you and jump out of this bed. We need to go."

"Miss Julia," he said, his words coming out muffled as if his tongue were thick. "I got shot in a place that connects to every muscle I have. Can't jump. Can't hop. Uh-uh, jus' can't."

"Well, my goodness, what place is that?"

He lifted his head and turned toward me. I could almost feel those black eyes boring into mine as his words came out clear as a bell. "My rear end—both sides, through and through."

"Oh," I said as an image of Mr. Purvis's shriveled backside flashed in my mind. A bullet fired at him would hit bone or nothing, but there was a good deal more to Mr. Pickens, which I'm ashamed to admit I had occasionally admired, and I assumed he had two entrance wounds and two exit wounds on a bullet's way in and out. "My goodness. That would be painful."

"Yeah," he said, dropping his forehead to the pillow, "I can't sit and can't turn over. Can't lie on my back and can't walk. Can't make it to the car."

"I've always said that where there's a will, there's a way. So you just put your mind to it, Mr. Pickens, and endure about five minutes of discomfort, which that pain pill should take care of, and we'll have you out of here. I'm calling Etta Mae."

So I did, whispering so that she could barely hear me. "He was shot in the rear, Etta Mae, and with all those big muscles running down his legs, he's not walking too well. He wouldn't be fast enough to get out of the fire door. So it's the window or nothing."

"Oh, wow," she said, "bottom shot, huh? Well, you're right, it'll have to be the window. I'll come around and meet you outside if you can get him to it. If you need help, open the window and I'll crawl in. Just watch for the security guy."

We clicked off, and I felt my way around the bed to the window to unlock it, hoping that it wasn't hermetically sealed. It wasn't, but it wouldn't slide up, either. I finally found a crank near the sill, turned it while fighting the blinds and was relieved to see that the entire lower pane opened out for about a foot or so. Enough, I hoped, to slip Mr. Pickens and then myself out onto the ground.

Leaving the window open and hoping the security man was still busy with Mr. Purvis, I went back to the bed.

"Okay, Mr. Pickens, we're going out the window. Come on now, we have to go."

He didn't move. I put my hand on his shoulder and shook him. "Are you *asleep*? Come on, Mr. Pickens, wake up."

"Okay," he mumbled. "I'm comin'."

But he wasn't. I threw the covers off him, grabbed his ankles and swiveled his body around until his legs hung off the bed. That woke him up.

"My pants!" he yelped. "Get my pants."

"Oh, good grief," I said, then realized that I was dealing with another short hospital gown that opened in the back, revealing a good bit of Mr. Pickens's posterior, although most of it was covered by a wide, thick bandage. "Well, just hang there while I look for your clothes."

Leaving him half on and half off the bed, I felt my way to what I thought was a closet, but found a bathroom instead. Finally I found the closet and pulled a shirt and a pair of jeans off a hanger. Snatching up his boots, I stumbled back to the bed.

"I've got them, Mr. Pickens, but if these jeans are the kind you usually wear, they won't go on over that bandage." He didn't respond. "Mr. Pickens? You hear me, Mr. Pickens? Wake up. I've got your clothes. See? I'm putting them out the window."

As I threw them out, Etta Mae stuck her head through the window, rattling the blinds. "Miss Julia? What you want me to do with this stuff?"

"I don't care. We'll take them if we can, but right now I can't get him to stay awake." I shook Mr. Pickens again. "Etta Mae's here. We're ready to get you out of here. Move, Mr. Pickens, move."

He lifted his head, mumbling, "Can't. Need to sleep."

"*Can't* never did anything. Now you just raise yourself up and get to that window."

I pulled and tugged at him, got his feet firmly on the floor and pushed myself under him enough to lift his top half off the bed. He moaned as I tried to stand him upright.

"Not so loud," I hissed in his ear as he leaned on me. My knees were about to give way, but I slid and twisted and turned and edged him toward the window. "On your knees, Mr. Pickens," I ordered. "Get down on your knees and stick your head out the window."

I don't know how I got him down because he didn't like any of it, but I got his head and shoulders over the sill, then poked first one arm, then the other through the window.

"Pull him, Etta Mae," I whispered. "Pull him on out."

I lifted his feet, straightening out his legs—another move he didn't like—while I pushed with all my might.

Unfortunately, the window pane wasn't high enough to slide him through without his backside rubbing against the metal frame. Mr. Pickens treated us to some of that ugly talk that had so offended Sheriff McAfee.

"Put a sock in his mouth, Etta Mae," I hissed, fearing that he would bring the entire roster of hospital personnel down on us. "He's as drunk as a lord."

Finally, as she pulled and I pushed, he went through the window, scraping knees and rump on his way, until he fell on Etta Mae and just ruined some foundation plantings.

Relieved, I hurriedly put a pillow under the covers, found a black sock I'd dropped and put it where a nurse might think it was his hair. Then I grabbed the blanket from the foot of the bed and threw it out the window. Then slipping under rattling blinds, I crawled through the window, a feat I will not recount, consisting as it did of some unladylike contortions and a little ugly talk of my own.

Chapter 22

Mr. Pickens lay sprawled out over a couple of bushes, which would never again be the same, groaning and carrying on, and making no effort to get up. That white bandage of his glowed in the dark, so I snatched the two sides of his gown and pulled them together.

"Need my pants," he mumbled.

"There's more to worry about than covering your privates," I snapped at him. "Nobody's looking anyway. Etta Mae, you all right?"

She was sitting on the ground with her knees drawn up and her head hanging down. "Yeah, yes'm. Just knocked the breath out of me for a minute. Boy, is he heavy!"

"Tell me about it," I said, still unrecovered from manhandling him through the window. "Let's get him up and out of here." Then, surveying our situation, I went on. "My word, with all those security lights, it's brighter out here than in his room. Come on, we've got to hurry."

Between the two of us, Etta Mae and I hoisted Mr. Pickens to his feet, Etta Mae under one arm and I under the other. He was such a dead weight, I felt like slapping some life into him.

"Wait, Etta Mae," I said, as Mr. Pickens swayed between us. "You got him? Don't let him get off center or he'll fall on you again."

I hurriedly grabbed the blanket I'd thrown out the window and wrapped it around Mr. Pickens's body, hoping that would allay his concern about being half naked. Although, believe me, neither Etta Mae nor I had any desire to see what he was so anxious to cover. That done, I snatched up his shirt, pants and boots, handing some to Etta Mae and keeping the rest.

Getting under Mr. Pickens's arm again, I said, "Walk, Mr. Pickens, walk. Put one foot in front of the other and move."

He groaned the whole way to the car, and don't ask me how we got him there. Every step was a trial, and how we were able to keep him from falling and dragging both of us down, I don't know. It's a flat wonder that we didn't draw the attention of every person in the place. *Thank you, Mr. Purvis.*

Etta Mae, puffing and blowing by this time, opened the back door of the car. "Crawl in, J.D. Crawl in and stretch out on the backseat."

Mr. Pickens just stood there. "Where are we now?" he mumbled.

"On the way home," I said. "To Hazel Marie and your baby girls, now get in the car."

We aimed him through the door, then pushed and shoved until he slid on his stomach across the backseat. Of course, it was too short for him even though I had the largest model, so he was half on the seat with his feet and most of his legs sticking out over the footwell.

Etta Mae opened the driver's door and slid behind the wheel. "Let's get out of here."

I hurried to my side, relieved not to be driving, and got my door closed just as she reversed out of the parking place and gunned it for the street.

"Careful, Etta Mae," I said, even though I was more than anxious to leave. "We don't want to attract attention now."

"Right," she said, her voice quavering. "Right. I'll slow down. I'll be careful."

Quickly and gratefully, I pulled Etta Mae's shoes off my cramped feet, wiggled my toes and hoped I hadn't maimed myself.

I can't tell you how good my Ferragamos felt—worth every penny they'd cost.

When we reached the highway, she turned right, away from Pearl's cabins—bait and tackle shop, too—and I hoped I'd seen the last of them all. Etta Mae drove carefully through town, although at one point she giggled nervously and said, "I don't guess you want to drive by the sheriff's office, see if they're back, do you?"

"Keep going," I replied, my hand clutching the armrest, fearing we'd be discovered at any moment. "The sooner this town's behind us, the better I'll like it."

And soon it was and we were on the treacherous curves of the long downhill drive to flat country. We seemed to be all alone on the dark two-lane road—no passing traffic, no lights behind or in front—just tree-covered mountains on one side and heart-stopping dropoffs on the other.

Etta Mae was a good driver, but even as we had climbed slowly upward on our way to Mill Run, so we were coasting steadily downward on our way out and occasionally the heavy car would take a mind of its own and almost get away from her. But she soon learned how to stay in control and I was able to turn loose the armrest.

Mr. Pickens had been quiet ever since we'd gotten him into the car, and I was thankful that he could now have the full benefit of his sleeping pill. Turning and glancing into the backseat, I was astounded at how he'd arranged himself.

"Look at him, Etta Mae! No, don't look. Keep driving, but he's on the seat with his knees drawn up under him and his back end sticking straight up. And he's sound asleep."

"Good grief," Etta Mae said, as she adjusted the rearview mirror to get a quick look. "He's in the knee-chest position. Just right," she giggled, "for a proctoscopic exam."

"From the looks of that bandage," I said wryly, "he's already had one."

Etta Mae started laughing. "We ought to put a sign on him: THIS END UP."

Then we both began laughing and couldn't stop—nervous relief, I guess—and kept on laughing until a deer bounded across the road in front of us and Etta Mae slammed on the brakes, throwing Mr. Pickens off the backseat onto the floor. He yelled out loud once, then set in with mumbling and groaning, until with a push from me, hanging between the front seats, he regained his upended position.

I kept looking over my shoulder, not only to check on Mr. Pickens, but also to see if there were any signs of pursuit. Each time I expected to see fast-gaining lights coming up behind us, but each time there was nothing to see. I sincerely hoped—in fact prayed a little—that the sheriff was fully occupied far from the reach of a nurse when a certain empty bed was discovered.

"Can you go a little faster, Etta Mae?"

"No'm, scared to on this road. Too many curves. I might lose it." She was intent on her driving, using the bright lights all the way because there were no other cars on the road. "We should hit a straightaway soon, then I'll speed up. Why don't you call Hazel Marie, let her know we have him."

"Oh, my, yes. I should've thought of that." I scrambled through my purse for the cell phone, hoping it was charged. It was, but it didn't work. "What's wrong with this thing? I'm not getting a dial tone."

"Oh, gosh, I bet you can't get reception with all these mountains. Well, we'll call her as soon as we get down."

About that time, Mr. Pickens started groaning and mumbling, and as I looked back, I saw him twisting and turning to find a comfortable position. He ended up on his side, facing the back, with his knees bent and his feet pushed against the back of my seat. Wedged in like that, he seemed to be in a less precarious position than the knee-chest one.

But he couldn't stay still. He kept trying to straighten out, kicking the back of my seat, then the door, all in an effort to relieve his discomfort.

"I wish we had some more of whatever they gave him," I said, feeling another kick in my back. "If he keeps on like this, he's going to be miserable by the time we get home."

"Look," Etta Mae said, "we've reached the main highway. Beckley's not far and it'll be easier driving from now on. Try Hazel Marie again, why don't you?"

So I did, and was pleased to hear the phone ring far away in Abbotsville. It was well after eleven o'clock, and I knew the sound of it would awaken and certainly frighten whoever heard it. Hazel Marie answered, but it took awhile because she dropped the phone in her haste.

"Hello? Hello? Who is it?"

"Hazel Marie? It's Julia, and we have him. Now, don't worry. He's all right. A little shot up, but not in any bad place. Well, it might be worrisome to him, but not to us. But I just wanted to relieve your mind. We're on the way home and should be there in five or six hours."

"You have him! Is he all right? Let me speak to him."

"Well, Hazel Marie, he's asleep, but he's all right. He had a sleeping pill before we left and he's out like a light. Hold on a minute." I got up on my knees and leaned over the seat, holding the phone next to Mr. Pickens's mouth so she could hear his steady soft snores. "Hear that?" I said, turning around.

"Oh, it *is* him!" Hazel Marie cried, literally, because I could hear the tears in her voice. "That's just the way he sleeps. Thank you, Miss Julia, thank you so much. And thank Etta Mae, too."

"All right. Now listen, Hazel Marie, we're going to need James's help getting him out of the car when we get there. You all need to get some sleep, but have James rest on the sofa in the living room. I'm going to be in no shape to climb those stairs to his apartment to wake him up."

"Are you going to drive all night? I hope you do. I can't wait to have my sweetheart home again."

"We're going to try to." I glanced at Etta Mae, wondering how tired she was. "It may be that we'll have to stop for the night, but I'll call and let you know if we do."

I was finally able to end the call, with Hazel Marie still thanking us and effusing over our having retrieved her husband.

By this time, we had entered the city limits of Beckley, and Etta Mae was easing the car along, carefully observing the speed limits. It felt to me as if we'd reentered civilization with the passing cars, the street lights, the well-marked lanes, and the neon-lit places of business.

"You want to stop anywhere?" Etta Mae asked.

"I'm going to have to before long, but let's see if we can get out of West Virginia first. We're near the state line, aren't we?"

"Another forty miles or so, I think. We can stop at the Virginia Welcome Center on the other side of the line. I'm like you—I want out of this state as soon as we can get out."

Chapter 23

That was the longest forty miles of my life. Not only did I fear that we'd be stopped before exiting the state, but Mr. Pickens was becoming more and more agitated. He couldn't get fixed, regardless of how often he turned and changed positions. He mumbled and moaned and groaned, talking out of his head and flopping around until I began to worry about his state of mind.

"He's getting worse," I said to Etta Mae. "You think we ought to do something?"

Etta Mae kept driving. "Sometimes those medications can have reverse reactions, but . . . whoops!" She slammed on the brakes at a red light on the outskirts of Beckley, and Mr. Pickens slammed to the floor again, yelling and cursing, as he scrambled back onto what he thought was the bed.

"What?" he mumbled. "What's happenin'? I'm hurtin', damn it." Then he yelled, "Nurse! Orderly! Somebody!" After crawling back onto the seat, he continued to moan and mumble.

"It's all right, Mr. Pickens," I said, trying to calm him. "We're getting you some help. Just stay real still so you won't hurt yourself."

He didn't hear me, but Etta Mae chimed in with something else to worry about. "I hope he hasn't opened up his wounds with all that falling around. We better check his bandage when we stop."

"Not *we*," I said. "I wouldn't know what to look for."

"Blood," she answered, as I shivered. "Hey, here's the interstate. We can make some time now."

And we did, heading for the state line as fast as the speed limit would allow. When we crossed into Virginia, Etta Mae and I glanced at each other and grinned. We both felt the anxiety of being chased and stopped by cars with blue lights flashing ease off. I knew we weren't entirely out of the danger zone—Sheriff McAfee had telephones, after all—but it felt better to be out of his immediate reach.

When Etta Mae put on the blinker and turned onto the ramp leading to the welcome center a few miles south of the line, I sat up to look around. The place was well lit with pole lights, and big trucks were already lined up with their night lights on. Etta Mae drove around to the parking area for cars, where she pulled in and stopped a good distance from the three cars there before us.

"If you have to use the ladies' room, you better run on," she said. "They probably close at midnight and it's almost that."

"What about you?" I asked, opening my door.

"I'll take my chances, but we can't leave J.D. by himself. I'm going to check his bandage, then I have an idea I want to look into."

Wondering about her idea, I didn't wait to hear about it, being in too much of a hurry to get to the restroom. As it was, I had to talk my way in, for a caretaker was headed for the doors with a key in his hand just as I pushed through.

When I got back to the car, I saw that it was the only one left in the parking area. And when I saw what Etta Mae's idea was, I was glad there was no one around to see us. She had the trunk open and was stacking our bags on top of each other in order to clear a space on one side.

"You're going to put him in there?" I couldn't believe he'd fit.

"No, not *in* here, but *through* here. If we can get him through." And she hopped up into the trunk and began fiddling with a latch. "I think, I *hope*, this will work. Miss Julia, go around and get him out of the car. I'm gonna push the back of the seat down and open this up. I can't do it if he's lying across the seat."

My goodness, I thought, *I didn't know my car would do that*. But I went around, opened the back door and began to coax Mr. Pickens out. It was a trial and a tribulation because he couldn't sit. The best he could do was to get down in the floorboard and crawl out, and it was a wonder he was willing to do that.

I found out why when he finally got out of the car and hung, bent almost double, onto the door. He told me in a graphic word what he needed to do.

"Just hold on to the door," I told him, propping him as well as I could. "And don't fall."

With that, I took myself back to the trunk to help Etta Mae, giving him some privacy in spite of the car's interior lights putting him on full display. That apparently didn't bother him because he went and went and *went* and went.

I knew that if I looked at Etta Mae, we'd both laugh our heads off—that nervous tension still with us—so we both pretended not to hear anything.

"Good thing we stopped," Etta Mae said dryly, and I almost lost it.

By the time silence reigned again, she and I hurried back and grabbed Mr. Pickens as he tried to walk away from the car. We held on to him and walked him to the trunk, where I told him to crawl into bed, hoping he wouldn't know the difference. He bent over and used his arms to pull himself part of the way in. With Etta Mae in the backseat guiding him through, I lifted his legs, bent and pushed them, one after the other, into the trunk. He was docile enough, probably much relieved and eager to lie down again.

Etta Mae guided his head, then his shoulders through the opening into the body of the car. His shoulders almost created a problem—they wouldn't squeeze through—so we had to angle him, then push and urge him on through so that he ended up on his stomach with his upper body from the waist up draped over the backseat and his lower parts stretched out into the trunk. It was unfortunate that the car seat wouldn't fold down flat, but the slight slant didn't seem to bother him. He sighed with relief at being able to stretch out, no longer scrunched up like a pretzel, and began snoring.

"Don't look, Miss Julia," Etta Mae said, as she came around and crawled into the trunk beside him, "unless you just want to, but I'm gonna check his bandage."

Not caring to witness a medical procedure, I went to get the blanket from the backseat, and in the doing, stepped in a soggy place on the ground. And in my good Ferragamos, too.

After covering Mr. Pickens's feet, legs and back end with the blanket, Etta Mae hopped out and we carefully closed the lid of the trunk.

"Looks like one side's bleeding a little," she said. "We could stop for the night and take care of it, but we don't have any bandages or medication, and no way to get any. So I think the best thing is just keep on going and get home as quick as we can.

"And speaking of going," she went on, "I really have to."

"The restrooms are all locked up now. Maybe we can stop a little farther down the road."

"No way," she said. "I'm finding a bush."

And that's what she did, with me standing as lookout, although I didn't know what I'd do if anybody came.

I blew out my breath as we at last left the welcome center, Etta Mae stepping on the gas as she merged onto the interstate. Mr. Pickens was sleeping peacefully, although at a slant, and I thought I might be able to nod off for a little while.

"Etta Mae?" I said. "Are you all right, driving? You want me to relieve you?"

"I don't think you can," she said with a laugh. "J.D.'s right up against my back, and I'm up closer to the wheel than you'd be. Besides, I'm okay, but let's stop at a McDonald's when we see one. I could use some coffee."

After a good while of steady driving, with me trying to stay awake out of courtesy to Etta Mae, who *had* to stay awake, she said, "I'm going back a different way from the way we came—too many big trucks on 81. We can stay on 77 and pick up I-40 at Statesville. That okay with you?"

"Whatever you think. I'm feeling bad for not relieving you. You've done nothing but drive almost the whole time we've been gone."

"I like to drive, so don't worry about that. We'll stop in Statesville and get some coffee, and I'll be good for the last two hours home."

And that's what we did, but to our dismay the McDonald's there was closed and we had to cross the street to a combination gas station and convenience store. Etta Mae filled the tank without my suggesting it, although I'd been fretting about getting low on gas. Then, one after the other in order for one of us to stay with Mr. Pickens, we went inside, used the facilities and looked around for something to eat besides corn chips and stale Little Debbie cakes.

It was my first experience of eating a hot dog off a rotating spit in a gas station, but it had been long hours since we'd made sandwiches in one of Pearl's cabins.

"Should we wake Mr. Pickens and see if he's hungry?" I asked when Etta Mae got back to the car, her hands filled with a coffee cup, two hot dogs, potato chips, a package of raisins and one of Twinkies. And napkins.

"I say let him sleep," she said, looking back at him. "He's easier to handle that way. Besides, we'd have to back him out of the trunk if we woke him up."

That was a job I could do without until we reached home, when we'd back him out for, I hoped, the only time. But with James's help. Then I had another thought.

"Etta Mae, should we take him home or to the hospital—in which case the orderlies can get him out?"

"I've been wondering about that, too," she said. "But I don't know. Once he's in a hospital, he's back in the system. We might have trouble keeping that sheriff away from him."

"Then let's take him home. We'll call Dr. Hargrove, who can just make a few house calls for a change. Mr. Pickens can get bed rest and sedation at home as well as anywhere else. That was all he was getting at the Mill Run hospital anyway."

"Well," Etta Mae said, stifling a yawn, "maybe some antibiotics, too. But whatever you say. I'm not too eager to hang around the emergency room a couple of hours while they decide what to do with him."

"Me, either. Let's go home."

☙

I declare, those last two hours on the road in the early morning hours were almost unendurable. I fought sleep, staying awake to talk with Etta Mae to keep her awake and listening in spite of myself to a preacher who was the only thing besides static on the radio. He was preaching about rich men who lived as if they could take it all with them. "I ain't never seen," he said, "a U-Haul trailer hitched to a hearse." And neither had I. Wesley Lloyd Springer, my grasping and long-gone first husband, learned that lesson the hard way—too late to mend his ways.

But it was all to the good when it came to Lloyd and me, because the two of us were Wesley Lloyd's beneficiaries, whether he liked it or not. I mean, once you're gone, you don't have any more say-so in what happens to what you left or who gets what.

I entertained myself with such thoughts as those, occasionally speaking to Etta Mae to be sure she was awake, and picturing Hazel Marie's joy when we got her sweetheart home. And also, occasionally, wondering what Sheriff McAfee would do when he discovered what we'd done. He claimed to be a church-going man who didn't like foul language, but I was willing to wager he'd have a few choice things to say when he found his prize witness had flown the coop. And if I found out that he'd deliberately sent us into a den of snakes, why, I just might have a few choice words of my own to say to him.

Chapter 24

As we came off the interstate onto the exit ramp, the lights of Abbotsville were a welcome sight even though I could barely keep my eyes open to see them. We drifted through the empty streets feeling as if we were the only two people in town awake. Half awake, I should say, because Etta Mae was looking awfully droopy and, of course, Mr. Pickens was still soundly, though noisily, sleeping.

When Etta Mae turned the car into the driveway at Sam's—now the Pickenses'—house, she sagged tiredly over the wheel. Her spirits, though, were still as perky as ever.

"Well, we made it," she said, grinning up at me. "First time I've ever run from the cops. Well, first time I'll admit to anyway."

The sconces on each side of the front door were on as well as the carriage light at the end of the walk. I could see several lights burning inside the house. I had little doubt that Hazel Marie hadn't had a wink of sleep since she'd learned we were on the way. As for Lillian, she'd be dozing in a chair somewhere, ready to be up and doing as soon as something needed to be done.

Just as I started to get out of the car, Hazel Marie came whizzing through the front door and raced down the steps. She flew to the car as Etta Mae opened her door.

"Where is he?" Hazel Marie cried. "Did you bring him? Where is he?"

Etta Mae pointed to the backseat. "There he is."

Hazel Marie bent over to look inside, pressing her face to the window. Then she jumped back and screamed. "They've cut him *off*! What happened to him? Oh, my Lord, they've cut him in two!"

Etta Mae grabbed her and held her tight—no small feat—for Hazel Marie was jittering all over the place. "No, no," Etta Mae said, "it's all right. His other half's in the trunk."

That didn't reassure Hazel Marie, for she threw her head back and screamed. "In the *trunk*! What've you *done* to him!"

Lloyd appeared by her side, his hair mussed up and his glasses askew. He cupped his hands on the window and peered in at Mr. Pickens, who was oblivious to the reaction he was causing.

"My word," Lloyd said, sounding like a little old man. And why shouldn't he? He was learning from a little old woman.

"It's okay, Mama," he went on, "he's still in one piece. You just can't see the other half. Hit the trunk release, Miss Julia, and let's get him out."

Getting Mr. Pickens out took the unified efforts of us all, for he didn't want to be moved and refused to help himself. For one thing, he was still under the influence, didn't know where he was and couldn't or wouldn't do what we told him to do.

James had come outside by then. He stood looking into the trunk, shaking his head and studying the problem before saying, "This gonna be a job." Which wasn't exactly news to those of us who'd gotten him in, in the first place.

Lloyd and I crawled into the backseat, trying to wake Mr. Pickens enough to understand what was required of him. "Scrooch on down, Mr. Pickens," I said, pushing on his shoulders. "Just scrunch back into the trunk."

He kept mumbling. "What? Who is it? What's goin' on?" None of which was any help.

Sticking my head close to where Mr. Pickens's posterior met the trunk, I called, "Etta Mae, maybe we ought to pull him out head first instead of pushing him back through the hole. What do you think?"

"I don't know, Miss Julia." She came around to the open door of the car and did a little studying herself. "Maybe we ought to do some measuring first—make sure his bandage won't scrape off if he comes out this way."

I cringed at the thought while Lloyd ran his hand past Mr. Pickens's waist to see how much room there was.

"Good grief," Lloyd said, wide-eyed at what he'd felt. "He was shot in the . . . *you-know*?"

I nodded. "Yes, but it's not life threatening."

"Well, if it was me," he said in that serious way of his, "I wouldn't take any chances of scraping anything. Let's push him out through the trunk."

We had a time of it, because what went through fairly easily on their way in—namely, his shoulders—had difficulty going the other way. As Lloyd and I pushed and guided from one end, and Etta Mae and James pulled on his legs, and Mr. Pickens struggled and complained the whole time, Hazel Marie stood by, wringing her hands and saying, "Don't hurt him. Don't hurt him." I was about ready to take a broomstick to such an uncooperative patient or just leave him stuck half in and half out. My patience had about run its course.

Mr. Pickens finally came awake enough to help get himself out, but only when Lillian crooned through the trunk, "Come on now, Mr. Pickens. I got a fine roast beef an' some gravy an' mashed potatoes, like you like, an' a great big choc'late cake jus' waitin' on you."

The poor man, unshaved, bent over and trying to pull down his hospital gown—which created a draft in the rear—was nearly driven to the ground when Hazel Marie flung herself on him. On top of that, he was confused as to where he was and how he'd gotten there, mumbling and half laughing in between whatever he was saying. Addled in his head, it seemed to me.

"Etta Mae," I said, sidling up to her, "I would've thought he'd be coming out of his daze by now. They must've given him a dose and a half."

She nodded, watching as James and Hazel Marie guided Mr.

Pickens up the steps onto the porch, with Lloyd right behind them. "Yeah, and I'm wondering if they've kept him sedated the whole time. I don't know, Miss Julia, but Dr. Hargrove ought to see him as soon as he can."

"That's going to be right away," I said, "and he better not tell us to take him to the hospital. Mr. Pickens needs to get in bed and stay there until his system is cleared out. He's had enough moving around for a while."

She agreed, then said she wanted to look at his bandage again.

On our way into the house, she was having second thoughts. "Maybe we should've taken him directly to the emergency room—let them look at it."

"If he needs to go, we'll call an ambulance. I don't want to get him in and out of that car another time." I looked at Etta Mae's watch, which I was still wearing, and saw that it was after three o'clock. "Take a look at him, Etta Mae, then let's get home and go to bed."

❧

That was quicker said than done, because by the time she'd checked the bandage and I'd taken her to her trailer in Delmont and gotten myself back home, there wasn't much time left for sleeping. But I went straight to the big downstairs bedroom and fell into bed after only a brief and hurried toilette. I'd left instructions with both Hazel Marie and Lillian to call Dr. Hargrove at six o'clock even if it woke him up.

Right before sleep overcame me, I started laughing as I recalled Mr. Pickens's reaction to having his bandage checked. Hazel Marie and James had led him to the bed, where he'd sprawled out on his stomach, heaving a mighty sigh of relief. At that point, Etta Mae had turned back the covers and lifted his bandage to check for bleeding. His head popped up off the pillow and his hand swatted at her. "Get away from there," he yelled. "That's private!" Which just goes to show how confused he was, because no telling how many people had had their hands on his privates since the day he'd been shot.

Then I had to laugh again, recalling Lillian's skeptical look at what I was wearing. "What you doin' in that getup?" she'd asked, looking up and down at Etta Mae's white scrub suit that had served me so well in the Mill Run hospital.

"Don't ask," I'd said, glancing down at my high waters, which revealed stockinged ankles between the end of the scrub pants and my stacked-heel Ferragamos.

Before long, though, I was sleeping like the dead, but was awakened too early by an awful racket banging somewhere in the house. Thinking the worst, I crawled out, put on a robe and stormed out to see what was happening.

"It's that carpenter," Lillian said as I got to the kitchen. "He start in hammerin' back in the sunroom, buildin' them cabinets and shelves you wanted. He worked all day Saturday, too, but not yesterday, it bein' Sunday. He got all that pink wallpaper off in the bedroom."

"Oh, my word, I'd forgotten about him." I dropped into a chair by the table, wondering if I should go back to bed or try to stay up. "Did you get any sleep, Lillian?"

"Yes'm, some. I jus' got here. I got the babies fed so Miss Hazel Marie could sleep in. She happy as a lark, now she got Mr. Pickens back."

"How was he when you left?"

"Still sleepin'. But Dr. Hargrove say he on his way, an' I 'spect he there by now."

"And Lloyd? And Latisha? They get off to school?"

"Yes'm. Here your coffee." She set a cup before me, and I decided I might as well stay up. "Now tell me what all you an' Miss Etta Mae get up to while you gone."

So I did, recounting everything that had happened, from attending a snake-handling service to becoming a kitchen aide worker, which accounted for the scrub suit I was still wearing when we arrived home. One might say that it had been a most unusual weekend for someone who was accustomed to slow and gentle days measured by respectable activities.

Lillian was wide-eyed at the telling, asking over and over about "them snake people," unable to understand how anybody could believe that fiddling with serpents was an act of faith.

"It's in the Bible," I told her, "somewhere, I'm not sure where, but the few verses may have been a later addition. At least, that's what I've heard."

"Who want to add something to the Holy Bible?" she demanded. "They's enough in there already to keep me busy all my life tryin' to live up to it. I don't hold no truck with anybody wantin' to put something else in. 'Specially something about snakes." She shuddered.

"Well, you and me," I agreed, getting to my feet. "I better get dressed, Lillian, and try to make it through the day. I declare, I feel as if I've been gone a week with all we've been through. And," I went on, "I've got to talk to Coleman because that West Virginia sheriff is sure to be looking for Mr. Pickens. And maybe Etta Mae and me, as well."

"Y'all in trouble with the law?"

"Well, yes, I guess we are. Which reminds me, I better talk to Dr. Hargrove, too. We'll make a case for Mr. Pickens getting poor treatment in the Mill Run hospital—being overly sedated or something—whatever we can think of that would require an immediate transfer to better facilities. No judge would hold us responsible under such dire circumstances."

"No judge 'round here anyway," Lillian said.

🐝

After dressing, I called Hazel Marie to get the latest word on Mr. Pickens's condition.

"Dr. Hargrove just left," she told me. "He was amazed at J.D.'s wounds. Said he'd never seen anything like it and J.D. was lucky it's not as bad as it could've been. I couldn't look, but I could picture it, bless his heart. Anyway, he started him on an antibiotic, but wouldn't give him anything for pain. He told me to give him nothing stronger than Tylenol if he really needs something."

"Is he awake?"

"Who? J.D.? About half awake, I'd say. I've told him twice how he got home, but he doesn't remember anything about last night."

"My goodness," I said, wondering how something so deeply etched on my memory could be blanked out of his. "What about his wounds? Etta Mae was afraid one of them had opened up. You know, when he fell off the seat."

"He fell off the *seat*!"

"Well, see, a deer crossed the road in front of us and Etta Mae had to slam on the brakes. Mr. Pickens tumbled off the backseat. He thought he'd fallen off the bed."

"Oh, my poor baby. Anyway, Dr. Hargrove cleaned it and put on a fresh bandage. He said he thought it'd be all right."

"That's good. Now listen, Hazel Marie, if a certain Sheriff McAfee from Mill Run, West Virginia, happens to call, just refer him to Coleman. Don't tell him anything else, not even that Mr. Pickens is there, or anything."

She didn't respond for a few seconds. Then she said, almost whispering, "You think he'll try to get J.D. back?"

"He might. But if he does, we'll put Mr. Pickens in *our* hospital under *our* sheriff's orders, and give Sheriff McAfee a taste of his own medicine." Try as I might, I couldn't see that lanky sheriff sneaking through our hospital as a kitchen aide worker.

Chapter 25

After tracking Coleman down to let him know we were back and had Mr. Pickens where he belonged, I had to go into detail about how we'd sprung him from Sheriff McAfee's clutches.

"You did *what*?" Coleman asked in some amazement.

So I told him again, then asked, "Now, Coleman, the big question is this: What's that sheriff going to do? Will he try to extradite him? Will he arrest me and Etta Mae? And by the way, Mr. Pickens was not under arrest. I specifically asked if he was, and was told by Sheriff McAfee that he was not, so we did not aid and abet an escape. It's important to remember that in whatever dealings you have with him."

"*Me*?"

"Yes, of course, you. I figure you'll be the one he'll contact—he knows where to reach you. I think the best recourse would be to firmly remind the sheriff that Mr. Pickens left of his own free will and will happily return to testify when and if he is needed. At least I assume he will—you can never tell what Mr. Pickens will do. You might also remind Sheriff McAfee that by that time Mr. Pickens should have all his marbles back in place and be able to testify because he'll no longer be so heavily medicated he doesn't know up from down."

"What?"

I was beginning to wonder about Coleman by this time. "Let me put it this way," I said, taking it slowly so he could follow my line of thought. "Etta Mae thinks they kept Mr. Pickens under heavy sedation. We know they kept him isolated, and we know they tried to keep us away from him. That to me smacks of unlawful imprisonment. Or something. So I think when that sheriff calls you, which he surely will, you ought to at least intimate that he is in big trouble, which I won't mind bringing down on his head."

"Ah, well, let me think about it, Miss Julia. First thing, though, I ought to talk to J.D. Get his take on what happened."

"Good idea. And lots of luck making sense of what he says. But go on and see for yourself what they did to him. Actually, that reminds me: I'm going to talk to Dr. Hargrove about defrocking whatever doctor took orders from a sheriff who's never been to medical school. I think steps should be taken against him. And I think I'd better get Binkie on board for me and Etta Mae. It never hurts to have a good lawyer on hand."

"Okay, you do whatever you want about that and I'll get my ducks in a row for when the sheriff calls."

🐝

After that satisfactory call, I went upstairs to see what Adam Waites, one of the carpenter's sons, was doing. The sunroom was in a mess, I can tell you that, with a table saw set up in the middle of the room, lumber stacked around, and sawdust everywhere.

"Mr. Waites," I said, as he removed his safety glasses, "tell me how you're progressing." From all the noise he'd been making, I'd thought he would've been further along than he was.

"Mornin', Mrs. Murdoch. It's a beautiful day that the Lord has made, isn't it?"

"Yes, yes, it is," I said, waving away the distraction. "Now, catch me up with what you're doing."

And what it amounted to was the building of the framework for the cabinets under the windows.

"Now, right here," he said, pointing to the middle window, "I thought I'd build a desk, then . . ."

"No, Mr. Waites, no built-in desk. Sam needs room to spread out, so I'm putting a table desk in here for him. Just build a straight wall of cabinets like the ones I drew out for you on the plan. Please don't add anything extra without checking with me first." Mildred hadn't warned me that Mr. Waites would have ideas of his own, but now that I knew, I'd have to watch him carefully. "And one other thing, we'll need to have a number of electrical outlets for the lower cabinets and around all the walls. You know, for his printer and copier and telephone and all the other gadgets he has."

"Have to get an electrician for that."

"Of course. I assumed you'd know who to get, so get him when you're ready."

Mr. Waites studied the wall for a minute. "Sure would be a good place for a desk. You want to go ahead and pick out the stain you want on the cabinets?"

"Mr. Waites, Adam," I said, trying for patience and about failing to get it. "No stain on the cabinets. See, right here on the plan, it says white. I want white cabinets. That means paint—good paint that won't chip. Enamel of some kind." Then, feeling quite efficient for my forethought, I went on. "In fact, the cabinets have been ordered and delivered. They're stacked up in boxes out in the garage, just waiting to be brought in and installed."

"Oh, yes, ma'am, I knew that. I'll bring my brother to help me get them in." He wiped his face with his sleeve, then looking at me with a sheepish expression, he said, "Just got my mind on too many other things, I guess."

"Well, let's get it on this job. Although," I said, not wanting to be too hard on him, "if you're having trouble at home or something, I'm sorry."

"No'm, I'm all right. The Lord will see me through."

Thinking to myself, *Let's hope He will*, I wondered if I'd been remiss by not employing Mr. Caldwell, the architect, to design and supervise the remodeling of the sunroom as well as the new library. But what was done was done, and I left feeling less than fully confident in Mr. Waites's ability to follow directions.

🐝

Then right after lunch, Mr. Tucker Caldwell himself showed up at my door right on time, although with all that had happened over the weekend, I'd forgotten he was coming. Which will teach me to check my calendar now and then.

"I've come to measure your room, Mrs. Murdoch," he said as I ushered him in.

This was the first time I'd seen him without his desk intervening and I was surprised at what a small man he was. Standing next to him, I saw he barely came to my shoulder, although in spite of his stature he gave off a sense of busy competence. He wore a brown suit with a red bow tie, which I could've told him did not add a whit to my confidence in him—reminding me, as it did, of another small man's affinity for bow ties.

I took him back to the large bedroom, pointing out the two possible sites for the fireplace with the Williamsburg chimney I wanted. He went right to work with a large metal tape measure, jotting down in his tiny handwriting the figures that he'd use in drawing a blueprint. I stood in the middle of the room next to the bed, watching as he worked with prissy efficiency. And gradually I began to realize that something was different from my first impression of him. I couldn't put my finger on what it was, for there was nothing unusual about his attire or his heavy glasses or the way his thick hair flopped over his forehead. But something *was* different. Perhaps, I mused, I just had not known him long enough.

"I think we'll need bookshelves, too," I reminded him. "Tall ones, all the way to the ceiling on the fireplace wall, with maybe cabinets underneath. Let's use mahogany or cherry or something along those lines. Remember, Mr. Caldwell, an English library is the look I want."

He nodded as he drew the room's outline on his pad. "I know what you want. I'll use a dark warm wood around the entire room with panels outlined by thin molding. Deep baseboards and crown moldings with dentils, too. I'll bring samples of the wood to show you and an elevation of each wall before we begin installation. And you might as well call me Tucker."

"Thank you," I said, but did not offer my first name to him. I believe in keeping a professional distance, at least until an employee has proved himself. It's awfully difficult to complain to or reprimand someone who views himself as your friend.

"You want to keep this Oriental rug?" he asked, as I stepped out into the hall to get out of his way.

"No, it has to go. It suffered a soaking not too long ago, and even though I've had it cleaned, I'd prefer carpet instead." As I considered the old, but not particularly valuable, rug, I couldn't help but recall Hazel Marie standing in the middle of a huge wet spot on the rug that frigid night her babies had been born.

Tucker Caldwell walked out into the hall, making me step back farther, and eyed the hardwood there. "Looks like the same. Sometimes in these old houses, the hardwood floors don't match from one room to the next."

"My house is not that old," I assured him, although because it wasn't a series of cantilevered modern boxes with solar panels on top he probably thought it was.

"Be a shame, though," he said, "to put carpet over this fine wood. I say we keep the wood and get a new rug."

"And I say that my feet get cold. Besides, the floor will still be there under the carpet. Now, Mr. Caldwell, I mean, Tucker, what do you think? Where would you put the fireplace?"

"I'm thinking the east wall," he said, walking back into the room. "It's a little hard to visualize with the bed in the way and that wall of closets. That'll have to go. But if we put the fireplace on this wall over here, it'll be the focal point and the first thing you see when you walk in."

"Perfect, and exactly what I was thinking," I said, pleased that he was seeing things my way and not going off on a tangent of his own.

He stood next to the bed, gazing around the room, looking up at the high ceiling and back around all the walls. "Take out those closets," he said as if he were thinking out loud, "and I'll have a symmetrical room with almost ideal proportions." Then, whirling around so quickly he almost startled me, he said, "Ordinarily, I don't like to copy what's already been done, but this room lends itself to replicating a typical Williamsburg library. Maybe you've seen them?"

"Yes, I showed you a picture. . ."

"Yes, indeedy," he said, rubbing his hands as if becoming more and more pleased with the idea. "Now, Mrs. Murdoch, you leave it all to me, because I can assure you that you will like how it turns out. And don't worry about its being too traditional or old-fashioned. The Williamsburg look never goes out of style."

I stared at him, hardly believing what I was hearing. "I know," I said. "I was the one who suggested. . ."

"So that's it. I have what I need, so I'll be going. Oh, by the way, do you have a preference for a builder?"

"Well, Adam Waites is doing some work for me upstairs, and I've mentioned the possibility of his doing this room, too."

"Good, good," he said, rubbing his hands together. "Adam is an excellent carpenter. I've worked with him before, so I'll get him lined up. But let me caution you, he tends to run ahead and add his own ideas."

"I've noticed," I said, somewhat dryly. "That's a fairly common tendency."

"He'll be working under my supervision, though," Tucker Caldwell said, as if he hadn't heard my comment, "so I'll have my eye on him. Thank you, Mrs. Murdoch, I'll call you as soon as I have the plan ready. Won't be long."

He'd already taken off down the hall, heading for the front door with me trailing along behind him. I was glad for the enthusiasm he was displaying, but would've liked to have had more of a conversation with him. It wasn't to be, however, for he was off like a shot, seemingly eager to get to his drafting table.

I stood by the door after closing it behind him as a wave of fatigue hit me—the consequence of our busy weekend. Then something else hit me—I suddenly realized what was different about Tucker Caldwell. *Earrings!* That fussy little man had a gold stud stuck in his left earlobe, which I *knew* had not been there when I'd met him in his office. It seemed as if Mr. Tucker Caldwell had had as interesting a weekend as Etta Mae and I, although I assure you we had not come home with any decorative souvenirs from our trip.

Chapter 26

For the rest of the day I had a sense of impending doom hanging over my head—all because there'd been no word from Sheriff McAfee. What was the man thinking? What would he do? Surely he'd do something. I didn't think he was the type to take an escape from isolation or protective custody or witness protection—whatever he called it—lying down.

But I decided not to dwell on it if I could manage to put it out of my mind. Sufficient unto the day is the evil thereof, I always say, although I couldn't always put it into practice. I understood the admonition against worrying about the future because there's always enough to keep us busy in the present, but what about the past? I couldn't get the previous day out of my head. Why, only twenty-four hours before, Etta Mae and I had been in one of Pearl's bleak cabins recovering from that church service and making plans to liberate Mr. Pickens. It all seemed so long ago, for here I was back at home going about my daily routine, broken only by the presence of a hymn-singing carpenter and a prissy, ear-studded architect.

All I'm saying is that it makes you think—how quickly circumstances can change and how disconnected it can make you feel. But a phone call late that afternoon began to put me back in focus.

"*Sam?* Is that you, Sam?" I wasn't sure at first who was calling, expecting a West Virginia twang, if anything. But the voice was

Sam's even though it wavered through the line, fluctuating over a roaring sound in the background. "How are you? Where are you? Are you having a good time?"

"We're all fine," he said, his voice suddenly loud and clear. Then as he began telling what they'd been doing, I could catch only a few words—Tel Aviv was one, the Wailing Wall another, then something about Emma Sue and the Dillards. "How're things there? Everybody okay?"

"Why, we're just fine," I said, images of Mr. Pickens's peppered posterior, a long night drive, an angry backwoods sheriff and snakes wrapped around an arm flitting through my mind. "Nothing unusual going on, just the same-old same-old. I can't wait for you to get back. Oh, Sam, I really miss you."

". . . miss you too," he said, then spoke a jumble of words, of which only a few came through clearly. But I heard enough to assure me that Sam's being half a world away had not dampened his ardor.

I hung up the phone, my heart lightened just from hearing his voice. I'd longed to tell him all that had happened, but it would've worried him and spoiled his trip, which I didn't want to do. There was nothing he could do from such a distance, and he'd be home soon enough. I'd wait and unload it all then. Besides, the connection hadn't been good.

Just as I turned away, the phone rang again. Still half expecting to hear Sheriff McAfee's voice, I gingerly answered it.

"Julia?" Mildred Allen said. "I've had a most interesting phone call and I want to know what you think."

"Who from?"

"Agnes Whitman. You know, the woman I told you about? She said that now that she's moved back to the area she wants to renew old acquaintances. Of course I hardly know her—just know *of* her and even at that, mostly about her escapades. She was just a child when daddy was doing business with her father. But they were all financial deals, so she was too young to be involved. I saw just enough of her to know she was spoiled rotten, but that's another story. Anyway, she tracked me down some way and invited me to a garden party she's giving."

"That sounds nice."

"I'm glad you think so because she wants me to give her a list of my friends so she can invite them, too."

"Well, how strange. Doesn't she have friends of her own?"

"She's been too busy to meet anybody," Mildred said. "At least that's what she told me. She said she's been heavily involved in getting her house built and the gardens designed and installed. Now, apparently, she's ready to show them off. I'm putting you on the list, Julia."

"Oh, well, I don't know. . ."

"If I have to go, you do, too," Mildred said. "Besides, I've heard that her house is palatial and the grounds out of this world. It'll be something to do, and a garden party will be different from the usual."

"You know what that'll mean, don't you? Even if we don't care for her, we'll have to invite her to something we're having."

"Oh, tell me about it," Mildred said in her world-weary way. "But that's the chance you take. Come on, help me with a list. Who else can we rope in?"

So I did, but carefully did not commit myself to attending a garden party given by a complete unknown. We decided on about a dozen women who were always invited to our social events, LuAnne Conover being one and Marlene Hargrove and Pastor Poppy Peterson being two others.

"What about Helen?" I asked.

"Helen Stroud? I think, yes, let's do. She's been out of circulation long enough. But, Julia, if she really does marry Thurlow Jones, what's that going to do to her standing?"

"Improve it, I'd think. Financially speaking, at least. And from what I've heard, she's well on her way to improving *him*."

"Okay, I'll put her down," Mildred said. "I've missed seeing her anyway. But too bad Emma Sue won't be here. She'd love it."

"She'll be back in a little over a week. When is the Whitman woman having this thing anyway?"

"Day after tomorrow."

"My word, Mildred. What's she doing waiting until the last minute to invite people? I don't want to go to something that's just been thrown together."

"Oh, I don't think it's that," Mildred said. "She apologized, but said she's having some more landscaping and building done soon and wanted us to come before the grounds are torn up. She's decided to build a guesthouse that will be a replica of the main house—smaller, of course, which may or may not turn out to be tacky. I told you about it when I told you that Adam Waites will build it. Anyway, it doesn't surprise me that she's suddenly decided to give a party and invite people she doesn't know. She's a little different—the normal rules don't apply. So it should be interesting if nothing else. You'll go, won't you?"

"I don't know, Mildred. I'm not fond of garden parties. When you walk on grass, your heels sink down in the dirt. The last garden party I went to was after several days of rain. My heel got stuck and I walked right out of my shoe. Yet you can't get all dressed up and then wear flats, either."

"I know what you mean, but I want you to go. Besides, you need something to keep you occupied while Sam's gone."

I'd been fairly well occupied already, but Mildred knew nothing of that and I didn't tell her. I distracted her by letting her know that Adam Waites and Tucker Caldwell were working on my house and thanked her again for her recommendations.

"Even more reason for you to go to the party," Mildred said. "I understand that Adam did most of the finishing work out there, so you'll see what he's capable of. And I wouldn't be surprised to learn that Tucker is her architect. He's well-known throughout the state and beyond. You can't miss this chance, Julia."

Then something Mildred had said earlier came back to me. "Wait a minute, Mildred. You said the Whitman woman is having this party in such a hurry because her yard will soon be torn up and Adam will be doing the work. Something's out of kilter here because he's working for me and will be for several more weeks. I have him committed to finishing the upstairs, and Tucker Caldwell has him lined up for the new downstairs library."

Mildred laughed. "Looks like he'll be whipsawed between the two of you then. But possession is nine-tenths of the law, and you've got him. Just keep him busy and don't give him any free days—she'll snatch him up and no telling when you'll get him back."

"Oh, my," I murmured. I'd already realized that all the remodeling I was planning would not be completed by the time Sam returned home. But the thought of everything coming to a complete standstill while Adam worked for Agnes Whitman was most disconcerting. Why, the house could be in a state of disarray the whole summer long. Maybe I should go to the garden party and at least meet the competitor for Adam's services. And maybe drop a hint or two that she should rearrange her work schedule to coincide with the completion of my projects.

"All right," I said, "I'll go. What time should we be there and how do I get to her house?"

"Four o'clock and I can pick you up."

"No. Thanks anyway. I may need to leave before you. So much is going on here, you know." I didn't go into exactly what was going on at my house, but for all I knew a certain sheriff would be in town by then. And if that were the case, I might not be available for any kind of party—garden or otherwise.

Mildred gave me directions to the gated community out in Fairfields, which was some ten miles or so from Abbotsville. "Just go past the gatehouse and stay on the main road until you see another set of gates on the right." Mildred tittered. "You might say the house is gated within the gates. But you can't miss it, Julia. They say it's enormous—the largest and most outstanding house in the county, bar none."

After hanging up, I stood there wishing I hadn't agreed to go. In the past few days, I'd about met my quota of people who were a little different and had little stomach for meeting any more of the same. And I couldn't help but wonder: if Agnes Whitman's house was so magnificent, why was she having an outdoor party?

Chapter 27

The day of the Whitman woman's party arrived with a cloudless sky, high temperatures and heavy humidity. By early afternoon the thermometer registered well into the nineties, and all I wanted to do was stay in my air-conditioned home and drink iced tea with lemon.

And that sense of impending doom I've spoken of? It was heavier than ever. There'd been no word from Sheriff McAfee, and even Coleman was at a loss as to what the sheriff's intentions were.

"I'm thinking," Coleman had said to Mr. Pickens, "that maybe I'll call him. At least let him know you're here and available if needed."

The three of us—Coleman, Hazel Marie and I—had gathered around Mr. Pickens's bed the day before to discuss the problem. Even though Mr. Pickens had a pale and peaked cast to his face, his looks were considerably improved by a shave that had been administered by James—a procedure undergone only by a man of courage. Mr. Pickens was propped up in bed with several pillows behind his back while he sat gingerly on one of Hazel Marie's best eiderdown pillows—a position that indicated to me that he was well along in the healing process. At least he could look us directly in the face now instead of out from under his arm while he lay on his stomach. And I'm happy to report that his mind had cleared considerably. After being told a half-dozen times how he'd gotten home, he'd begun to exhibit some well-deserved appreciation toward his liberators. He'd sent both Etta Mae and me huge bouquets of roses with thank-you notes scribbled in his own handwriting. Mine read: *Can't begin to thank you for the risks you took on my behalf. You can work in my kitchen anytime you want.* Which just goes to show that he was pretty much back to normal.

"Hold off awhile, if you can," Mr. Pickens said, responding to Coleman. "You've not had an official request for information, have you? No BOLOs or APBs?"

"Nope," Coleman said, shaking his head as I worked out Be On the Lookout and All Points Bulletin. "Nothing about you at all. In fact, the only contact I've had with the Mill Run sheriff was when I was trying to get information out of him about you."

Mr. Pickens squirmed a little to ease one of his four sore places. "I'd like to wait before stirring the pot until I get copies of my licenses, credit cards, and so forth. I sent some faxes to Raleigh this morning—with the help of my wife." He smiled at Hazel Marie as she leaned across the bed to take his hand. "Right now I'm still as stripped of identification as I was when they found me."

"We know who you are," I said, "but our word, apparently, means nothing to Sheriff McAfee. Etta Mae and I both told him your identity, but he kept saying he had to wait for official confirmation. But how would he get that when he wouldn't let anybody see you?"

"Fingerprints," Mr. Pickens said. "He probably ran them through the federal identification system, then contacted Raleigh. It wouldn't surprise me to find that he's sitting up there now with copies of everything I had in my pockets, including the two-for-one coupon from McDonald's."

Mr. Pickens turned to Coleman. "If he calls, go ahead and tell him whatever he wants to know. I've got nothing to hide. But I'd rather have my identification in hand before reaching out to him."

Coleman nodded. "Suits me."

"Well, none of it suits me," I chimed in. "I'd like to know just exactly what you were doing to get yourself in such trouble. And just who took your original identification and who shot you and, well, how you got in that situation in the first place. A situation, I remind you, that exposed several of us to a great deal of peril in order to get you extricated."

Those black eyes of his gave me a long look, then he said, "It's not a story I'm proud of, but it started out as a simple missing person's case." He grimaced, then shifted his position again.

"Oh, J.D.," Hazel Marie said, "if you need to rest, you can tell us about it another time."

Before I could enter a protest, Mr. Pickens said, "I'm all right, honey. It started with my client, a Mrs. Hanson, in Winston-Salem, who hired me to find her son who'd been missing a little over six months. The local cops had investigated and sent out bulletins, but she felt they'd given up on it. And they had because, come to find out, this wasn't the first time the boy had gone missing and not the first time he'd been in trouble with the law. He'd been arrested at least once on a marijuana charge and several times for vandalism and joyriding. Mrs. Hanson blamed it all on his getting mixed up with the wrong crowd." Mr. Pickens stopped and seemed to gather his thoughts. "I keep saying 'boy,' but he's twenty-two or -three, so with no evidence of foul play, the cops treated him like an adult who was free to come and go as he pleased. And also, come to find out, I was the third PI she'd hired. The others, she claimed, had just taken her money and done nothing. But I had something they hadn't had: a ransom note that the mother had just received. It demanded twenty-five thousand dollars for his safe return, and a picture of the kid dated a couple of days before it came was sent along with it.

"Well, the mother was beside herself, but she wouldn't call the cops in again. 'They won't do anything,' she said, and told me she'd pay me the twenty-five thousand if I'd bring him back to her. Well," Mr. Pickens said somewhat wryly, "that was a pretty good incentive, although I would've done it for my usual fee. See, the picture gave me an idea of how I could find him. Part of a sign on an old store was in the background, and the note itself gave me a starting point. That and the picture told me I wasn't dealing with the sharpest knife in the drawer."

"Why, J.D.?" Hazel Marie asked. "What was in the note?"

"Well, first off, it was written on the back of a gas receipt from a station in Beckley, West Virginia."

"Why, we went right through there!" I said.

"You sure did, and that's where I headed. I put out some feelers and began looking around from there."

Coleman grinned and shook his head. "Sounds like he'd been picked up by some real dummies."

"That's not the half of it. I figured from the first that this Harold Hanson hadn't been abducted. He was part of it. Who else would send a picture of a kidnap victim standing out in front of a store sign and eating a popsicle?"

"My word," I murmured.

"Well," Mr. Pickens went on, "it took me awhile, but I finally found where the picture had been taken. I'd spread out my search from Beckley, going through some of the surrounding towns. Anyway, I was tooling along a state highway outside of Mill Run and saw it. Drove right past it, then it hit me. I turned around and there it was."

Hazel Marie was holding one of his hands in both of hers, sitting on the side of the bed, entranced with the story of her husband's expertise. "Oh, J.D., you are so smart. How in the world did you recognize it?"

He smiled at her. "Well, in the picture, it looked to be a sign across the top of an open structure of some kind, but all the picture caught was CEPT SUNDAY in big letters."

"Oh, my goodness," I said. "It was EXCEPT SUNDAY, wasn't it? LUTHER'S FLEA MARKET OPEN DAILY EXCEPT SUNDAY. Etta Mae and I saw the same thing. Mr. Pickens, it's just remarkable that you would recognize the place from that little bit in the picture."

He shrugged to show it was all in a day's work. "It was right on the side of the road, so I could hardly miss it. Then, well, I won't go into how I narrowed it down, but I spent some time in bars and roadhouses, and picked up a few leads."

"We didn't see any bars or roadhouses," I said, "and we drove around the town a lot."

Mr. Pickens gave me a quick grin. "They're there, all right. You have to have a nose for 'em. Anyway, I got a line on a sorry group that was trying to buy, lease, borrow or steal a couple of delivery trucks to move some merchandise, which, from the way they were going about it, I figured was stolen." Mr. Pickens grimaced at the recollection, looking a little abashed. "I never found out exactly what they had or where they'd gotten it—probably broke into a warehouse somewhere. But they had whatever it was stashed in this old, run-down barn back in the mountains because the truck they'd carted it in on had given out. I followed a couple of them back from a bar one night and spent a miserable few hours in the bush watching them. I was just waiting till sunrise to find my way out and report to the sheriff, but they found me first. One of 'em came out to relieve himself and came right toward me. I couldn't move because he'd know I was there, so I stayed still and he stumbled over me. I ran and he shot. Shot wild because it was still dark, but he got me. Why they didn't track me down—because I *was* down—I don't know. Probably scared them as much as it did me. The next thing I knew, I was in the hospital without a thing to my name. Not even my name. I lost a couple of days somewhere in there before somebody found me."

"Oh, J.D.," Hazel Marie cried—literally, because tears were welling up in her eyes. "I don't know what I would've done if they hadn't found you. Why, you could still be lying out there on the cold ground to this day!"

"Yeah," Coleman said, "but you know, they must've tracked you down, because somebody searched you. Probably scared them even more when they saw your license, so they just took off."

"That's what I figure, too," Mr. Pickens said. "But I sure don't come out of it looking too good. The doc said I probably hit my head falling after I got shot. Some hunters found me in a gully, and I guess I was lucky not to get shot again."

"Don't you worry about it, Mr. Pickens," I said, trying to put his mind at ease. "I think you did Sheriff McAfee a favor, because right before we left Mill Run the other night, Etta Mae saw a bunch of ATF men at the sheriff's office getting ready to go on a raid. So, see, you did a good deed in spite of getting shot."

"ATF, huh?" Mr. Pickens got a thoughtful look on his face. "That could mean a lot of things. So, Coleman, maybe it'd be worth going ahead and making a call to the sheriff. I'd sure like to know if they picked up the Hanson kid."

I couldn't blame him if it was that twenty-five thousand dollars that troubled his mind. The man deserved some compensation for the pain and suffering he'd endured. And the embarrassment of not only getting shot, but of *where* he'd gotten shot. It wasn't as if he'd be able to show off his scars.

Chapter 28

As that previous day's conversation ran through my mind, I stood before my closet trying to decide what to wear to a garden party I didn't want to attend. I wished Hazel Marie were going with me, but she wasn't ready to leave either the babies with a babysitter or Mr. Pickens with James. I knew she wouldn't when Mildred put her on the list, but she'd been pleased to get an invitation—hand delivered by a chauffeur, mind you, because the Whitman woman had waited too late to post them.

I decided on a voile frock—a flower print—because of the heat and a pair of white Naturalizer pumps because of their wide heels, which I hoped would keep me aboveground. Some of the younger women would wear sundresses, I was sure, because it was so warm, but when you reach a certain age and your skin reaches a certain level of wrinkled sag, you put aside anything that lacks adequate coverage.

Then, on a whim, I took down several hatboxes that were high on a shelf. Why not? I asked myself. It had been so long since I'd worn a hat, but what better reason to wear one than an outdoor party on the hottest day of the year? I lifted the lids of several boxes and wondered why I hadn't gotten rid of all the hats that I no longer wore. There was a time, I mused, when I would never have darkened the door of a church without obeying Paul's admonition to cover my head. He'd not said anything about covering anything else, but I'd considered both hats and gloves essential to being appropriately dressed. I couldn't recall when those two essentials had faded from use, but they had and now it was the odd woman who wore either or both to church.

But why not gloves along with a hat for the garden party? I rummaged through a drawer until I found my short kid gloves wrapped in tissue paper. They were a little stiff from being unused for so long, but with some smoothing over my hands and fingers they looked quite nice, and I hoped the Whitman woman appreciated my efforts.

As for a hat, I of course decided on a wide-brimmed one, quite suitable for such a party, even as I hoped there'd be an awning or a tent or a pergola or some form of shade. A large tree would do, if nothing else.

I declare, though, the hammering and sawing that Adam Waites was doing upstairs was enough to give me a headache and make me more willing to leave the house in spite of not wanting to go. But the cabinets and bookshelves in the sunroom were coming along and the room was beginning to look like a working office. I hoped Sam would be pleased with it, even though if we had an overnight guest we'd have to set up a cot in a corner.

No, I realized as my spirits dropped, overnight guests could use Lloyd's room because he'd soon be gone. Thinking of what it would be like when he was no longer with us put a damper on the whole day, as if a cloud had suddenly covered the sun. I sat down to let the lonely feeling pass, reminding myself of my blessings even though the long list didn't quite compensate for the loss of one item on it.

The trick was to stay busy, I reminded myself, and the following day would be full of decorating decisions. Something to look forward to, if I could. I would be meeting with an interior designer—not the one who'd helped Hazel Marie with her pink room, but a more conservative one in Asheville. Paint color for the upstairs bedroom along with fabrics for curtains, bedcovers and chairs had to be selected and ordered. Oh, and carpet for that room and the sunroom. Then I needed to decide on furnishings for the new English library that would take the place of the downstairs bedroom, where I was now sitting.

A lot to do, especially with little heart to do it. Still, I owed it to Sam to make the house as suitable and comfortable for the two of us as I could. The two of us! That thought brought tears to my eyes as I realized that I was suffering from a favorite topic of the women's magazines Hazel Marie loved: empty-nest syndrome.

And with that, I sprang from the chair, determined not to be a victim of every popular psychological or medical problem that came along. And why did it need a special name in the first place? Couldn't you simply miss someone without having a medical label stuck on it? A plain, simple word like "heartache" would come closer to describing what I felt at the thought of losing that boy. Then I reminded myself that I had lived for forty-something years in an empty nest with Wesley Lloyd Springer and didn't know I was missing anything. Well, yes I did. I just didn't know *what* I was missing. Now I knew, and its name was Lloyd.

❧

The drive to Fairfields was an easy one, although it was my first trip there since it had been built up, it being somewhat off the beaten path. I'd heard about the fine estates in the area and when I turned into the gated area, I was not disappointed. Not disappointed, but somewhat rattled because of another reason that kept me from fully appreciating the large homes and spacious lawns. I'd forgotten how carefully a large-hat-wearing woman has to maneuver herself when moving about. For instance, when I'd attempted to get into the car, the hat's wide brim had struck the door frame, unsettling the whole thing and messing up my hair. It had taken almost ten minutes of sitting in a blistering hot car to readjust both hat and hair, and because I was using the small mirror on the back of the visor, I wasn't sure how well I'd done it. Then when I'd slipped on my sunglasses, the hat canted to one side and I had to do more adjusting. Added to that, I found that the hat was so wide that every time I moved my head to check for traffic, the brim grazed the headrest, knocking the hat off kilter again. So I drove the whole way hunched over the wheel to keep that blasted hat in place. I was in no mood for a party by the time I arrived.

But the Whitman estate was a sight to behold. Mildred had been right—I couldn't miss it. I turned off the main road of the community and drove through an open wrought-iron gate onto a straight, tree-lined avenue, with lawn on one side and a rail-fence-enclosed horse pasture on the other. The drive proceeded a quarter of a mile to the châteauesque mansion at the end of it, although the closer I got, the less Frenchified it looked. In fact, it was a mishmash of different colored stones and stucco with a lot of Gothic windows, one huge Palladian window over the double doors and a slender tower at the far end. A huge fountain spurting water like a geyser stood in the middle of the front court. I thought to myself that if Tucker Caldwell had designed this monstrosity, I would unemploy him forthwith.

I slowed and stopped beside a young man who waited at the paved courtyard. He wore black trousers and a long-sleeved white shirt buttoned all the way up to a black string tie. Almost blinded by the sun's glare, I lowered my window and asked where I should park.

"I'll park it for you, ma'am," he said, opening my door as I wondered how large a party this was to be if it required valet services.

As I stepped out of the car, bending way over so I wouldn't scrape off my hat, I got a closer look at the young man. My smile froze on my face as I smothered a gasp. That poor misguided boy was absolutely studded with rings and bolts and safety pins, and I don't mean just his ears. I mean all over his face from eyebrows to nose to bottom lip to his tongue. And creeping up from his shirt collar, tattooed swirls wound around his neck all the way up to his chin.

It's rude to stare no matter how bizarre someone looks, so I tore my eyes away from the sight that must have had his mother in tears, thanked him and proceeded to the walkway beside the house that he pointed out to me. It was a lovely walk under a wisteria-covered pergola that led to an extensive lawn at the back of the house.

From the corner of the house, I could see a gathering of women across an expanse of grass near what appeared to be a cabanalike structure beside a pool. I stood for a moment to take in the back of the house, which looked much better than the front. From this aspect, the house formed a shallow U, which allowed for an open terrace bounded by a stone balustrade. A few wide stone steps opened onto a broad walkway that bisected the lawn and led to the pool area. Miniature boxwood hedges lined the parterres on each side of the walkway, making a lovely vista. I stood for a minute, taking it all in.

Off in the distance, beyond the pool, two horses grazed in a white-fenced paddock next to a barn. To my right was a garage with four bays, all occupied by vehicles of one kind or another. Farther away, almost hidden in a copse of trees and laurels, I noticed the roof and a side of a large rustic building, the purpose of which I had no idea. Gazing at the lawn, the fields, and all the outbuildings, I was entranced with the beauty and extent of the Whitman compound.

"That way, ma'am," a young woman said, pointing toward the pool.

She had walked up behind me and it was just as well I hadn't seen her coming—I might've run for the car. If I'd kept my eyes on her fresh and comely face, I would've been all right. But who could miss the rest of her? At first, I thought she was wearing a long-sleeved tie-dyed undershirt beneath the short sleeves of her gray uniform, and I wondered how she could stand it in the heat.

When I realized that what I thought were long sleeves was instead a multitude of black, yellow and red tattooed designs completely covering her arms and neck, I audibly gasped. Shocked and embarrassed, I murmured my thanks and hurried on my way, wondering why in the world someone would do that to herself. Didn't she know she'd have those things for the rest of her life?

And wasn't she aware of what would happen when her skin began to sag, a condition I was more than familiar with? A rising sun on a young shoulder would be setting on an elderly elbow.

Maybe, I thought as I walked toward the party, the maid and valet were a couple. Maybe they'd gotten in with the wrong crowd when they were younger and hadn't known any better than to have themselves inked over. Maybe they were now settled into stable jobs and regretted their misspent youths.

Then again, maybe they'd been in the navy.

However it had happened, I was saddened for them, stuck as they were with indelible dermal designs.

Shuddering a little at the thought, I was glad to approach the gathering of ladies, many of whom smiled and waved at me. As I joined them, I felt relieved to be among familiar faces and unadorned arms and necks. Well, except for strings of pearls, lockets, a few diamond tennis bracelets and several charm bracelets, all of which were perfectly normal and appropriate, and could be removed at any time. I put the pitiful young couple out of my mind and set about to enjoy the party—until I met our hostess.

Chapter 29

Mildred watched with a peculiar smile on her face as she introduced me to Agnes Whitman, and I must say that it took an act of will to keep my composure and respond courteously to Miss Whitman's welcome. The woman was skinny as a rail, one of those thin edgy types whose eyes bore into you. On that hot day, she was dressed in a long-sleeved, high-neck silk blouse with a long flowing skirt that flipped around her ankles. And sandals—sandals that revealed long toes with rings on them. And after I had gone back and forth about the kind of shoes I should wear. Her hair was pulled back tightly from her face, then fell long and straight down her back all the way to her waist. It was dark with plenty of gray, which might make you think she cared little about her looks, but you'd be wrong. When she turned her head to speak to Mildred, who was still silently amused at my reaction, I saw scars behind her ear. *Face-lift*, I thought, having seen such scars a few times before, but to my mind this one hadn't been too successful—her eyes had a definite slant to them and her face was so tight that her lips looked like two thin lines.

I don't mean to be critical. If somebody wants a face-lift and can afford it, why, go ahead and have one. I, myself, was just waiting for an arm lift.

But Agnes Whitman's drastic face-lift wasn't the worst of it. It was her earrings that drew my eyes and kept them there, in spite of my trying to look everywhere but at them. They were so long that they dangled to her shoulders and so heavy that her earlobes were stretched. But the absolute worst was how those earrings were attached. I stared—I couldn't help it. Her earlobes were filled with . . . well, I don't know what to call them . . . *plugs*, I guess, or maybe round corks from which a number of jangling chains and disks hung. I declare, the woman looked like a Zulu chieftain in a *National Geographic* magazine.

"Thank you for having me," I managed to say, shaking Miss Whitman's extended hand. "Your home is lovely." A more descriptive word would have been *impressive*, which wouldn't have expressed a personal judgment on a matter of taste, but courtesy had been too long ingrained in me. So I lied, which in a social setting is entirely forgivable.

"I'm so glad you like it," Agnes said, her eyes, which I noted were slightly popped, whether from birth or from surgical intervention I couldn't tell, giving me the once-over. "I designed it myself."

"Remarkable," I murmured, inwardly relieved that I wouldn't have to find another architect for my project.

"Please," Agnes said, indicating a linen-covered table in the shade of the cabana, "have something to eat. And drink. There's wine and mint juleps, or if you'd like something straight, just tell the barman." Then turning to give me that pop-eyed stare again, she abruptly said, "So glad to meet you, but I see someone else coming. Excuse me."

I glanced back toward the house and saw Helen Stroud walking toward us. "Mildred," I said as our hostess moved away, "why didn't you warn me?"

"I *did*," she whispered. "I told you I hadn't seen her in years and didn't know what to expect. And I told you she was a little strange. But you have to admit she's interesting. I told you that, too."

"Well, yes, you did. But let's get out of the sun. I'm about to melt." As we wandered toward the table, I went on. "I hope the something straight is lemonade."

Just as we arrived at the table, which was covered with trays of fruit and vegetables as well as a variety of cheeses and nuts, without a ham biscuit in sight, LuAnne Conover came rushing over.

"Julia, Mildred," she whispered, her eyes bright and darting around, "did you see that valet? Have you ever seen anything like all that metal on his face? I nearly died. And the maid! Honey, she is *covered* with tattoos."

"Sh-h-h, LuAnne," Mildred said, laughing. "Not so loud."

"Well, I don't care," LuAnne returned right smartly. "If somebody wants to freak herself out like that, she has to expect to be talked about. But let me tell you what Marlene told me." She leaned in close as the three of us huddled to hear the latest. "She said she'd heard that Agnes *herself* is covered with tattoos and that's why she's wearing that blouse in this heat. She didn't want to shock us at first meeting."

My head, along with Mildred's, swiveled around to look at our hostess, who was chatting with Helen.

"Surely not," I said, although I had wondered at the long sleeves and high neck of Agnes's blouse—not exactly what one would expect at an outdoor party.

"Well, I'm just passing on what Marlene said," LuAnne went on. "She said Agnes has full-sleeve tattoos, like that maid. That's what it's called—full-sleeve because it runs from shoulder to wrist, and it's considered body art, of all things."

"Art, my foot!" Mildred said, drawing back in surprise. "Art is what you hang on the wall."

"I'm just telling you what I heard, but we'd better be careful before getting too close with her. You never know."

As soon as I got a look at the young man tending bar, I was inclined to agree with her. Having walked over to the table set up with drinks, intending to ask for something cold and unlaced, I turned on my heel, deciding I could do without. The bartender had a two-inch metal rod stuck straight through the septum of his nose, and all I could think of was how it must've hurt going through. I also wondered how in the world he kept it clean.

I walked out of the cabana into the shade of the awning and

met Pastor Poppy Peterson, who was heading for the table. Poppy was an assistant minister and one of my favorite people, even though she was a Methodist. She was her usual luscious-looking self, dressed today in a sundress that revealed her smooth, creamy shoulders and a discreet décolletage. Apparently having given no thought to the perils of walking on grass, she had on high heels that almost qualified as stilts—three inches at a minimum and open toed to display bright red toenails.

"Miss Julia!" she said, a smile lighting her face. "I'm so glad to see you. How are you?"

"Hot, ill at ease and disturbed. How are you?"

Her laughter, always close to the surface, bubbled up. "I don't need to ask you why. My only question is why I was invited."

"Because Mildred and I put you on the list," I told her and went on to explain how that had come about. "We had no idea what we were getting into and, frankly, I still have no idea. What is it with these people, Poppy?"

"Let's walk over here out of the way," Poppy said, taking my arm and moving toward a table with an umbrella. "I've already filled my plate once and don't need to again. It's all vegetarian anyway."

We sat at the table beside the pool, and Poppy scooted her chair close to mine so we could talk. "It's like this—I think," she said, her voice pitched low. "I got here fairly early, so I had the benefit of a long talk with Agnes, or rather of *listening* to a long talk by Agnes. In fact, I think she was just waiting for me. She started by asking me how I'd decided to become a Christian minister—that's the way she put it, with the emphasis on *Christian*. But instead of letting me answer, she announced that she's a minister, too, but a minister of a much older religion than the Christian church. Then she went into this long song and dance about the necessity of strengthening the bond of mind, body and soul, which I gather are inclined to fly apart if you don't. According to her, if you want to become a complete human being and experience the divine, you have to enhance your life by celebrating certain ancient rituals that she would be happy to explore with me."

"What in the world was she talking about?"

"Beats me," Poppy said, shrugging her shoulders. "I just told her I was already celebrating an ancient ritual every day in my devotions and once a month with Communion. Then I invited her to the Methodist church, which didn't go over too well. I think," Poppy went on with a conspiratorial grin, "I've lost my place on her invitation list."

"I'm taking my name off as well," I said, although I wasn't as sanguine about it as Poppy. I was still distressed by what I'd seen and by what might be seen under Agnes's blouse if she took it off. "Well," I went on, "she may be off on a tangent as far as religion is concerned, but we do have to give her credit. Not many people would employ those poor misled refugees from a motorcycle gang. I know I'd hesitate to have them around every day."

Poppy crossed her arms on the table and hunched closer. "I don't think they're from a motorcycle gang. They may be members of that church Agnes was talking about. I mean, if you can call it a church, given that it's nontheistic, but it's probably part of some New Age movement that's essentially pagan, which means not new at all but as old as the hills. If it's what I think it is, they're into ritualistic manipulation of the body with piercings and tattoos and even cutting the skin to make decorative scars. The idea is to test the limits of what the body can take."

I was horrified. *"Why?"*

"Well, obviously, I don't understand it. But we studied cults a little in seminary, and there is one that encourages a kind of alteration of the body. You know, by decorating it and changing the way it looks."

"You mean like having a face-lift?"

Poppy laughed. "I doubt cosmetic surgery qualifies as a religious ritual, but I guess it could. I'd certainly do a lot of praying before having any."

I nodded, thinking of something Hazel Marie had said. "What about having surgery on a woman's stretch marks?"

"You mean a tummy tuck?" Poppy smiled and patted my arm as if she knew what I was thinking. "I wouldn't worry about something like that. That's putting things back the way they were, not adding things like whole sleeve tattoos or covering your back with designs or piercing yourself everywhere. And even those don't always have a spiritual dimension—probably most don't." Poppy thought for a minute, then sat up straight, a frown on her face. "I wish I could remember what we studied—well, not studied—it was just mentioned in class along with a number of other cultic practices. But if Agnes really is a minister, then these people out here could be part of her congregation."

An intense look passed across Poppy's face. "I'm going to look up my notes and do some research as soon as I get home. I sure don't want our young people getting involved in it. We have a hard enough time with the Baptists' enticing them with basketball courts and game rooms and so on."

"Let me know what you find out," I said, thinking of the Presbyterian young people and, of course, of one in particular. And thinking also that I should warn Pastor Ledbetter about this hotbed of freakish behavior in our midst. If, that is, he could ever get world travels off his mind.

Chapter 30

As soon as the tattooed valet brought my car around, I hopped in as spryly as I could manage, took off the hat that kept grazing everything in sight and threw it on the passenger seat. I drove away disturbed and saddened by the strange ways that people sought meaning in life, or perhaps sought attention by being different. I could've told them a better way to have both meaning and attention, but I wasn't asked and doubted I ever would be.

The strangest thing, though, was that Agnes Whitman, after greeting me warmly enough, seemed to avoid me the rest of the afternoon.

But maybe I was being too sensitive. There had been a lot of guests—maybe thirty or so—not only from the list that Mildred had given her but also many of her Fairfields neighbors as well, and as the hostess, she'd had to mingle. But every time I had approached a group she was with, she'd moved away to another one. I couldn't think why she didn't want my company—she had invited me, after all—but perhaps I was reading too much into her actions. Perhaps the way she always kept one step beyond me was unintentional.

One other possibility occurred to me. Maybe she'd seen Poppy and me huddled together and assumed we'd discussed her, which, I must admit, would've been a correct assumption. But she would not have had to worry about defending her beliefs to me, in spite of her efforts to proselytize Poppy. I am a firm believer in avoiding discussions of politics and religion in a social setting and simply would not have put up with it.

Besides, what I'd wanted to talk to her about wasn't religion, but Adam Waites and the fact that he was committed to me for some weeks to come. I'd wanted to make sure she understood that he wasn't available until I was through with him. And, actually, when it came right down to it, I *needed* Adam working at my house. I needed things to progress, to see changes, to have something new and different to think about—like how well a new room or two were shaping up. The fact of the matter was that Lloyd had had his last final exam that very day, and more than likely, he had started packing up his stuff while I was out partying.

Trying not to dwell on the emptiness I was feeling, I drove home with all that Poppy had said running through my mind, wondering how anybody would willingly undergo the pain of an electric needle on sensitive flesh, much less the agony of piercing metal stakes through nose, eyebrows, lips, ears and who knows what else. If such procedures came under the heading of worship, I was doubly glad I was a Presbyterian, which only required sitting through boring sermons and mumbling through hymns I couldn't sing.

Well, of course there was more to it than that, but I'm talking about just the outward observance in a Presbyterian service. When you got down to the real requirements like treating others as you want to be treated, feeding the hungry, clothing the naked, visiting the sick and loving the unlovable, they might, in the long run, prove harder and more rigorous than having a metal rod jammed through your nose, although I wouldn't want to do a comparison test.

🐝

I went into the house through the front door, castigating myself for not telling Lillian to go home early. I would be the only one for supper, and after attending such an unappetizing social gathering, all I wanted to do was have a snack and sit around feeling sorry for myself, alone and lonely for Sam and Lloyd.

Well, that would have to wait. Seeing that Lillian was still there, I could tell her about the party and what I'd learned about people who believed that nuts and bolts and safety pins stuck into and through tender places would get them to heaven.

So I sailed into the kitchen, saying, "Lillian, you won't believe this, but . . ." And stopped as I saw who was sitting at the table with her. "Why, Lloyd, I thought you'd be at your mother's."

He grinned and ducked his head. "I got lonesome for Miss Lillian's cookin'. James can't hold a candle to her, and, well, you know how Mama is in the kitchen." He turned his empty cup around in the saucer, glancing up at Lillian.

Lillian laughed, got up from the table and brought a cup and saucer for me, along with the coffee pot. I sat down with them, pleased to have them both with me.

"Supper'll be ready in a little bit," Lillian said as she poured coffee. "Latisha gone on a day trip—a long day trip—with her class, so I'll fix her a plate an' heat it up later. Lloyd," she went on, "tell Miss Julia how Mr. Pickens doin'."

"Oh, he is something else," Lloyd said, delight beaming on his face, "I can't help but laugh, 'cause he's a mess. I mean, in a good way. He can't stand to stay in bed, but it hurts too bad to walk around and he can't sit in a chair too long, even with that pillow he carries everywhere. James has to go to the kitchen so he can laugh, and Mama wants J.D. to stay in bed, so she gives him back rubs all day to keep him still. She says he'll never heal if he keeps moving around like he's doing."

"She gonna spoil that man," Lillian said. "But 'bout the onliest time you can keep a man like that still is when he sick or gun shot. So I guess she makin' the most of it while she can."

I laughed at the thought. "At least he won't be running off looking for missing persons anytime soon. She'll have him home for a good while now." Then, sobering at a memory, I went on. "Lloyd, do you know if he's heard from that sheriff yet?"

"No'm." He shook his head. "I don't think so. He told Mama that it was like waiting for the other shoe to drop. I know Coleman was going to call the sheriff, but so far he's not been able to get him."

"Sheriff McAfee is a hard man to pin down. It took hours for Etta Mae and me to even get in to see him, then he avoided us by sending us to the wrong church, and now it's like he doesn't know or care that he's lost his prime suspect or witness or whatever label he's hung on Mr. Pickens. I don't know what to think, but I wish he'd do something so we could put this behind us."

"Jus' watch," Lillian said. "He be showin' up here sooner or later, or sendin' somebody 'cause I bet he want Mr. Pickens back up there."

"Well, if he does," I said, "I hope he has a better way to transport him than we had. I don't think Mr. Pickens could stand another trip like that, even if he is on the mend. Anyway," I went on, "let me tell you about the garden party."

I briefly described Agnes Whitman's house and grounds, then went into detail describing her valet, maid and barman. And her, as well. "I tell you, I've never seen anything like it. They've just ruined their bodies and, as far as I'm concerned, their lives as well. And the strangest thing was that, according to Poppy, all that metal and ink could be connected to some kind of religion. Have either of you heard of anything like that?"

Lloyd's frown had gotten deeper the longer I spoke. "No'm," he said, "but our tennis coach has a tattoo up high on his arm. I guess it could be something religious, but I don't think so 'cause he goes to the Episcopal church. It kinda looks like an anchor, but I'm not sure. He always wears shirts with sleeves."

"Well, see," I said, sure that my point had been proved, "he keeps it covered up. I expect he wishes he hadn't gotten it, but he probably did it when he was in the service and didn't know any better. And now he has to live with it, and those poor souls at the Whitman place will, too."

"No," Lloyd said, slowly shaking his head. "They might not have to. I think now those things can be removed with laser surgery or something. I think it takes a long time, though, and it's pretty expensive. Probably painful, too."

"Well, from what Poppy said, enduring pain is part of it—you know, while they're getting stuck or cut or pierced, so I guess they wouldn't mind a little more. But I'll tell you the truth, I've never felt the least bit religious when a doctor comes at me with a flu shot."

"Law," Lillian said, getting up from the table, "all this talk about needles an' safety pins give me the shivers. It all I can do to wear clip-on earbobs of a Sunday. Y'all 'bout ready for supper?"

I stood, too. "I'll set the table. You're eating with us, aren't you, Lloyd?"

"Yes'm, and staying the night, too, if that's all right."

I beamed at him, my heart lightened. "It's always all right, and you don't ever have to ask."

"Well, good, because I thought I'd wait to move my stuff until J.D. can help me. He offered to, just as soon as he's well enough."

"That was thoughtful of him," I said, at once serene and comforted. I began laying out the place mats. "We don't want to rush his recovery, though, do we?"

Lillian suddenly turned from the stove. "Oh, Miss Julia, I forget to tell you. That carpenter been up yonder hammerin' all day, an' he say 'fore he left to tell you he can't work tomorrow. He promised a lady to do something for her, but he be back soon as he can."

"What!" I spun around, immediately upset at being left in the lurch by someone I was depending on. "He can't do that—just walk off the job without a fare-thee-well. He's supposed to be reliable and professional, at least that's what I was told. Now what am I going to do?" I stood there with a handful of silverware, just so put out with this turn of events. "I'm calling Mildred."

Chapter 31

A lot of good that did, for Mildred had no solution for me.

"He didn't say who he'd be working for?" she asked.

"No, but you know who it has to be, don't you? Agnes avoided me all afternoon, so I think she already knew he'd be at her house tomorrow. I am just done in about this, Mildred. I expect people to do what they say they'll do when they say they'll do it."

"I don't know what to tell you, Julia," Mildred responded. "It's not like Adam to walk off a job. So if it is Agnes, he must feel obligated to her in some way. Maybe he made her a promise, and she called him on it sooner than he expected." Mildred paused as we both thought about it. "What are you going to do?"

"I've a good mind to fire him. Except I don't know who to get in his place. Not many people want to come in and complete a job somebody else has started. But, Mildred, Sam'll be home in less than a week and I just hate for him to come back to the mess this house is in. He might talk the pastor into jumping on another plane and going to Africa."

Mildred laughed. "Oh, I doubt that. Did Adam tell Lillian when he'd be back?"

"No, just said as soon as he could, which could be weeks, for all I know."

"That is strange. It's just not like him at all. You know he's so religious, and I'm not talking about *talking* about it. He tries to live it, too. He once told me that he dedicates every job he does to the Lord. I think something's going on that we don't know about."

"You may be right," I said, calming down a little as I thought about Adam Waites and what might be happening in his life. "I tell you, Mildred, it's like he hasn't had his mind on what he's doing from day one. I gave him specific instructions, all written out and everything, and still he was going off on tangents, planning to stain instead of paint and make a built-in desk when a built-in desk is not on the plan. I asked if he was having trouble at home, but he said no and shrugged it off. But the whole thing put me on alert. I figured I'd have to watch him closely, but now I can't even do that."

"Well, speaking of trouble at home, that daddy of his keeps all those boys on a tight rein. They're all super religious—I mean that's how they were raised—very fundamentalist with no television or movies or parties or anything like that. But the interesting thing about those boys—the ones I've met, that is—is that none of them are rebellious. They're just as happy as they can be." Mildred stopped again, then said as if it were hard to believe, "joyful, even."

After a little more back and forth that produced no answers for my problem, we hung up, leaving me still fuming. I immediately dialed Adam's home number, determined to demand that he return to work and finish what he'd been hired to do. His mother, however, answered the phone and told me that he was working late, which almost sent me into orbit because he wasn't working late at my house. She was so pleasant, though, that I had to be satisfied with leaving a message.

"Please tell him that I am expecting him to be here in the morning," I said as calmly as I could under the circumstances, considering that I was speaking with his mother.

"Lillian," I said as she prepared to leave after cleaning the kitchen, "would you believe that Adam is working late? But it's a settled fact that he's not doing it where he's supposed to be doing it."

"He put in a good long day here," she said. "Wonder where else he's workin'."

"I can guess," I said bitterly. "He's at that Whitman woman's house, I just know it, working night and day for *her*."

"Yes'm, maybe so, but 'member he been workin' Saturdays for you an' not many folks do that."

"You're right," I conceded, trying to be fair about it. "Maybe he's working tonight so he can finish her job and be back here in the morning."

With that hope, I joined Lloyd on the front porch, where we waved to Lillian as she left. It was still hot, but a nice breeze had come up and as dusk settled in, I settled myself in a wicker rocker. Lloyd, wearing a polo shirt and khaki long shorts, was sitting on the front steps so he could take note of the few cars passing along the street. My view was partly blocked by the wisteria vine that grew around the porch.

We'd often spent the last hours of the day on the porch, enjoying the company of each other and discussing whatever came to mind or whoever happened to pass by.

"Remind me, Lloyd," I said, "to have those crepe myrtles trimmed back this winter. They're about to take over."

"Okay. They sure filled out this year, didn't they?"

"Yes, and the boxwoods ought to be pruned, too." That was the kind of thing we talked about as I gently rocked on the porch and he stretched out his skinny legs. Unless, of course, there was some worrisome matter that was weighing on our minds.

"Mr. Sam'll be back in about a week?" he asked, glancing over his shoulder at me.

"Yes, and I'm counting the days. I can't wait to hear all about the trip and, well, just have him back again. I miss him."

Lloyd nodded. "I do, too. But I was wonderin', I mean I kinda thought I'd stay on here while he's gone. You know, not move to Mama's yet."

"Why, Lloyd, that would be fine," I said, thinking, *More than fine.*

"Well, Mama doesn't like to stay by herself at night, so I thought you might not, either."

"Well, I don't. I'll certainly sleep better with you here, if it's all right with your mother."

"Oh, it is. When I told her I was gonna stay on till he gets back, she said she should've thought of it herself."

I rested my head against the rocker, a smile on my face as I thought that maybe Lloyd was having a problem with his move, just as I was. I certainly wanted what was best for him, but what was best for me kept getting in the way. It wasn't that I was glad the boy might have a troubled mind about where he should live, I was just grateful to have him a few more days.

We both looked up as a little red car slowed at the stop sign on the corner, hesitated for a minute, then reversed itself to park at our curb.

"That's Etta Mae," Lloyd said, standing up and waving as she got out of the car.

Still in one of her colorful scrub suits, she came bouncing up the walk. "Hey, Lloyd," she called, then as she approached the steps and saw me, "And Miss Julia. I was just passing by and saw y'all sittin' out here and thought I'd stop and see how you're doing."

"Come on up and have a seat," I said. "We're glad to see you."

"I'll just sit here with Lloyd." She sat down on the top step, then swung around to lean against one of the pillars on the porch. "I had to be over this way today, so I stopped by to see how J.D.'s getting along. I could tell he's a whole lot better, because he wouldn't let me check his bandage." She threw back her curly head and laughed. "He is so modest."

Lloyd began telling her how Mr. Pickens couldn't walk, sit or lie on his back and how Hazel Marie kept trying to rub his back to keep him still. "I'm just gonna stay with Miss Julia till things calm down over there."

"I don't blame you," Etta Mae said, and they laughed together. "So school's out for the summer? You going to be doing anything special?"

"Just a lot of tennis, I expect," he said. "I think they want me to help with some clinics again this year. You know, with the little guys."

They went on talking in this manner for some while, and even though it was pleasant to sit in the lengthening dusk and listen to them, I had noticed something that was unsettling me.

Etta Mae, as long as I'd known her, had had pierced ears, always adorned with earrings of various sizes and designs. She usually wore fairly simple ones—small hoops or studs—when she was working, but I realized that she'd begun to branch out a little with things that dangled or sparkled. I'd often looked askance, though I would never have said anything, at the little bells or stars or reindeer that she wore on her ears around Christmas. More recently, though, she seemed to have earrings that celebrated every holiday that rolled around—dangling hearts on Valentine's Day, shamrocks on St. Patrick's Day, and once, when we were in Florida, she'd come out with little green frogs on lily pads. Her patients, she'd told me, those shut-ins that she took care of, enjoyed seeing what she'd have stuck in her ears each time she visited.

"They'll say," Etta Mae had said, " 'Turn this way, Etta Mae, and let me see what you have on today.' It's something they look forward to, so I try to come up with the cutest earrings I can find."

Hazel Marie loved earrings, too, and she had a number of nice gold ones and some pearl ones as well as a pair of diamond studs. Hazel Marie wasn't given to wearing anything outrageous, except when it came to the length of her skirts.

But here we were resting at the end of a busy day, conversing and enjoying one another's company, while I grasped the arms of my rocker tighter and tighter, and tried to calm the dreadful fear that Etta Mae somehow had gotten mixed up with that bunch of body alterers I'd met that afternoon. For not only was she wearing a little silver crescent moon in each lobe, but she also had tiny stars stuck in three separate holes running up the curve of her right ear.

Chapter 32

Now, I am not against piercing one's ears for decorative purposes. Obviously, because my own were pierced, but only once to a side. I think that when you go beyond one hole in each ear, you're teetering on the edge. On the edge of what, you may ask, and I say on the edge of too much, which is my opinion and my right to hold it.

Still, I probably wouldn't have had such a reaction to Etta Mae's superfluity of holes if I had not seen those prolifically perforated employees of Agnes Whitman, and Agnes Whitman herself.

The fact of the matter was I was worried about Etta Mae. I didn't want to see her mixed up with some outlandish cult and end up with a safety pin in her eyebrow or with her beautiful skin covered with hearts and flowers and Harley-Davidson insignia. But even as I told myself that the posssibility of that happening was just too far-fetched, especially to someone as levelheaded as Etta Mae Wiggins, the thought of staid, reliable Adam Waites being lured away from his job sprang to mind. I came to the realization that Agnes Whitman was a force that would have to be reckoned with.

Which immediately reminded me of another force—Sheriff Ardis McAfee—who sooner or later would also have to be reckoned with.

"Well," Etta Mae said, standing and reaching over to ruffle Lloyd's hair, "this is nice, but I better be going. Been a long day."

"Oh, Etta Mae," I said, walking over to her, "I haven't even offered you anything. Have you had supper?"

"Yes'm, I had something at McDonald's between patients. I usually get through in time to fix a decent meal, but today's been busy."

"Yes, and you went out of your way to see about Mr. Pickens,
which was thoughtful of you. But you need to take care of yourself
and eat right so you can fight off viruses and flu bugs and bad
influences."

She glanced at me with a quizzical expression, but then
laughed and said, "I probably need a keeper. See y'all later." And
she walked out to her car.

As we watched her drive away, Lloyd asked, "What kind of bad
influences?"

"Oh, you never know what you'll come up against. There're
people who'll talk you into anything if you're not strong enough to
resist." I was going to leave it at that, but decided to ask his opinion. "Did you see those extra earrings Etta Mae was wearing?"

"Yeah, they looked pretty cute, didn't they?"

My word, I thought as I sank back onto the rocking chair, bad
influences just kept rippling on and no telling how far they'd go.

I rocked for a while without answering, then said, "When Etta
Mae and I found ourselves in a snake-handling service, I noticed
that those snakes were left alone until just one person got the
nerve to pick one up. Then everybody else began to crowd around
to get one, too. What I'm saying, Lloyd, is that most people don't
think for themselves. They simply follow a leader or a fad or what
have you. And along those lines, have you seen the girl who runs
the cash register at the drugstore? I was in there last week, and I
couldn't understand a word she said."

"Oh, you mean the one with a stud in her tongue?" Lloyd said,
and then laughed. "I've seen her, and she does lisp pretty bad."

"I don't know what comes over people to make them do a thing
like that, and I hope Etta Mae stops with what she has. Enough
is enough, I always say. But at least she hasn't marked herself up
for life with tattoos."

"I kinda hate to tell you this, Miss Julia, but Etta Mae already has a tattoo. Just a little one, though. At least that's all I've seen."

I stopped rocking. "Where does she have a tattoo? I've never seen it."

"Well, it's on her back, kinda."

"You must be mistaken, Lloyd. I've seen her in sundresses and there's nothing on her back."

He squinched up his face, then mumbled, "It's lower than that. Hardly anybody would ever see it."

"So when did you?"

"Remember when we went to Florida that time? I went swimming with Etta Mae in the hotel pool and I saw it then. It's just a little tiny butterfly nobody'd ever see unless she had on a bikini. Which she did."

"Well," I said, dismayed at learning what was under Etta Mae's clothes. But if she'd had it when we were in Florida, it couldn't be the handiwork of Agnes Whitman. Which gave me some comfort. "Well, maybe she was young and didn't know it wouldn't come off. Maybe she regrets it now, and maybe she ought to wear a one-piece bathing suit from now on."

As the streetlights began to glow, I gathered myself to go inside, then decided that I couldn't leave the subject without adding a moral.

If I should ever be so full of myself as to declare a teachable moment, this would have been the perfect time for it. But I don't see myself as a puffed-up teacher strewing pearls of wisdom before the less astute. Lloyd, however, was still young and needed guidance, so I preferred to call these times *learnable* moments, especially since nine times out of ten I learned something as well. Someone, long ago, said that he didn't know what he thought until he wrote it. That's the way I am, except I'm never sure what I think until I say it.

Now, I certainly don't mind saying what I *think* I think, even though I might change my mind as I'm saying it. I could never, however, set myself above anyone in order to pronounce from on high something they needed to be taught.

Well, actually, I guess I have done a little of that in the past, but not knowingly and not without being sure I knew what I was talking about.

Nonetheless, I couldn't let this teachable or learnable opportunity pass without subtly making my views known, so I did.

"I hope, Lloyd, that you will steer clear of snakes wherever they are, and I hope you will never come home with holes punched in your ears or nose or tongue. And I hope and pray that you'll never go to one of those parlors where they jab ink under your skin that will be with you for the rest of your life."

Lloyd stood and stretched himself, yawning as he did so. "No'm, I'm not about to get mixed up with snakes. And you don't have to worry about me sticking pins and such in my face, either." Then with a glint in his eyes and a sideways glance at me, he said, "But what about a girl with a belly button ring? Can I come home with one of them?"

"Oh, you," I said, standing and opening the screen door. "Let's go in and see what those tacky *Housewives* are up to."

"Okay, but I think a soccer match is on. Maybe in Portugal or somewhere."

Chapter 33

After a restful night, morning came but Adam didn't. When breakfast was over and Lloyd had left to run errands for his mother, I walked upstairs to the sunroom and surveyed the chaos, determined to hold myself in check. There was no use whining and stomping around because work wasn't progressing on my timetable. The situation was what it was, and I had to put up with it.

I took one look around the sawdust-covered room and walked out. It was a mess, not even half done and so full of building material that I could barely get in the door. So instead of wasting my time fretting over Adam's disloyalty, I put my mind on the full day ahead of me, meeting with my new decorator and making selections to transform Hazel Marie's dream room into an appropriate setting for Sam and me.

As I surveyed her room, I was somewhat mollified. It wasn't so bad—the pink wallpaper had been stripped off, the walls had been primed and the carpet was gone. It was ready for a new decorative scheme, except, I suddenly realized, for her bathroom.

What had I been thinking? There could be no new decorative scheme with a pink soaking tub, pink basin with gold trim and a pink commode that Hazel Marie had had to special order because pink had gone out of style a few decades ago. Thank goodness her decorator had drawn the line and talked her into using ivory-colored travertine tiles on the floor. The tiles on the shower and tub surrounds were another matter—less than pink but not quite ivory.

"Lillian," I said as I went back to the kitchen, "I don't know where my mind has been. I completely overlooked Hazel Marie's bathroom—it's as feminine as her bedroom was, and something will have to be done. There's no way that Sam will be satisfied much longer with a pink tub and commode."

She leaned down and slid a skillet into a cabinet. Straightening up, she said, "I 'spect Mr. Sam be satisfied with whatever he get."

"Well, yes, I guess he would. But I can't very well decorate the bedroom in blue or green or whatever and leave all that pink in the bathroom." I sat down at the table. "Maybe I should've left everything the way it was, even without any masculine touches. It's all getting to be too much, especially since I've lost my carpenter."

"No use cryin' over spilt milk, so why don't you go on an' do what you got to do an' first thing you know, he be up there sawin' an' hammerin' again." She wiped off the counter with a sponge, then went on. "You s'posed to go see that decoratin' lady today?"

"Yes, and I better get ready. She's over in Asheville."

"Then why don't you jus' go on an' see the plumbin' people while you at it, an' see can they order you whatever Miss Hazel Marie got upstairs, only in a different color."

"White, and that's a good idea. They can look up their records and order the same model numbers. Then the fixtures will fit perfectly without tearing up the walls or the floor." I sat back in the chair, relieved. "Shoo, Lillian, you ought to go into the construction business. That's the most practical and easiest suggestion I've heard yet."

Then, as I visualized a sparkling white bathroom, my relief spurted away. "Oh, my word, I wasn't thinking of the tile on the shower wall and around the tub. To take that off and replace it will be a major undertaking. There'll be tile dust all over the house and the way Adam is going—or *not* going—it'll be Christmas before it's done."

"Miss Julia," Lillian said, somewhat sternly as she came over to the table and put her hands on her hips. "You jus' thinkin' up things to worry about, an' they's no need for it. You jus' pick out something to go with them tiles an' let 'em stay on the wall."

"Well, I guess I could. I mean, maybe the decorator could work with them. They have just the barest tinge of pink to them, what I'd call blush, maybe. Maybe we could find a fabric for the bedroom with that color in them." I sat up in my chair with a renewed interest in decorating. "Brown! Shades of brown from very light to maybe a deep chocolate. That would be masculine enough for anybody, and it's as far from pink as you can get. Lillian, you ought to be in the decorating business, too. I declare, you come to my rescue every time."

"No'm, not ev'ry time, but I figure when you can't climb over something, you have to go 'round it. And while you gettin' ready, I think they's some leftover tiles out in the garage. I'll find you one to take so you can match it up to whatever yard goods you find."

🌸

So that's what I did, and it all worked out beautifully. I drove home from Asheville some four hours later, having spent most of the time with a lovely young decorator who not only listened to me, but also mainly agreed with me. It was a most refreshing experience after dealing with an architect and a carpenter with minds of their own.

Ms. Allie Parker had immediately understood my concern about blush-colored bathroom tiles in a master bedroom suite for both a master and a mistress, but she wasn't as enthusiastic as I'd been about brown.

"It's a very *in* color right now," she'd said, pushing back her long strawberry-blond hair, "but I don't think it's going to last long—too dark and depressing. I wouldn't want to get up in the mornings."

"Exactly what I was thinking," I said. "But I do so want a room that my husband will like. He's put up with pink for so long, and a brown room would be the exact opposite."

"Well, of course we can work with brown, but I don't think you want to go *too* masculine. You'll be living in it, too." She opened a wallpaper book and began to flip through it. "Let me suggest something else. If we use blush as a neutral, there's a wide range of colors that will complement it. Green, for instance, although you have to be careful with shades of green and pink—they can get Palm Beachy real quick."

As she talked, she got up and started sliding hanger after hanger of fabric swatches that hung from racks along the walls of her place of business.

"Here's a possibility," she said, laying a swatch before me on the long table where I was sitting. "And here's another."

Before long there were so many choices—all with blush somewhere in the plaid, striped or floral designs—that I was about to be overwhelmed. Who knew blush was such a popular color? I'd certainly never considered it and here I was basing the entire decor of a bedroom and bathroom that Sam and I would use every day of our lives on that one color—condemned, one might say, by Hazel Marie's choice.

But at least it wasn't pink, so I drove home with my spirits high. Ms. Parker—Allie, as she insisted—helped me decide on a lovely faded floral design on a background of the lightest shade of blush for the curtains and bedspread—a copy, Allie said, of a fabric in one of the great houses of England. And from what it cost per yard, the house might well have belonged to the queen herself.

We decided that the curtains would hang from fairly simple cornices instead of the swagged and fringed valances that Hazel Marie had chosen. Then we selected a striped fabric for the chairs that blended beautifully with the curtain material and balanced the floral with a hint of masculinity. When Allie found a gorgeous linenlike wallpaper with just enough blush in it to keep it from being ivory, I quickly discarded the thought of paint and decided on it.

After going to a showroom and ordering new bathroom fixtures, I was highly pleased with the morning's decisions, although I'd had to call Allie and ask her opinion about a new shade of white they were offering. Who knew that what they were calling biscuit would be the *in* thing in fixtures? And when I saw that the color was nowhere near that of the beautiful brown tops of Lillian's biscuits, which was what had come to mind, I knew it would be perfect. And to top it off, Allie assured me that biscuit fixtures would blend with the tiles much better than pure white and would also pick up the ivory tint of the wallpaper.

Much relieved to have all that behind me, I came to the conclusion that decorating was a mind-boggling process that involved second-guessing one's choices until it was simply too late to change anything.

Now to get Adam Waites back on the job, I said to myself as I took the Abbotsville exit and headed home.

Chapter 34

"Look at this, Lillian," I said as I excitedly spread out swatches and samples on the kitchen table. "Just look how everything goes together. I am so pleased. It'll be a beautiful room."

"Yes'm," she said as she surveyed the display and fingered the fabric swatches. "It'll be pretty all right. But I thought you was fixin' up a brown room for Mr. Sam."

"Well, not completely, because I live in it, too. But see, it has some masculine touches. All the background color is neutral and look at these flowers—the stems are brown. That's masculine enough. And the bathroom fixtures, Lillian—look at this little sample—would you believe they call that biscuit?"

Lillian laughed. "If my biscuits come out that color, I put 'em back in the oven."

The telephone rang then and when I answered it, Pastor Poppy Peterson said, "It's called the Church of Body Modification, Miss Julia. I looked it up on the Internet and, apparently, it qualifies as a real church, although who or what they worship I can't figure out. But they do have ministers and you can apply to be one online. All you have to do is answer about four pages of questions about yourself and send them in." Poppy paused, then said, "Sure beats three years of seminary if you just want to call yourself a minister."

"My word, Poppy. It is a legitimate church then?"

"Depends on your definition of a church, I guess. But listen to this: it involves body manipulation, ritual body suspension, hook pulling, play piercing, fasting, binding, corsetry, firewalking, and so forth, which test and push the limits of flesh and spirit. I'm quoting."

I didn't have an immediate response, visualizing what would've added up to torture if inflicted by one person on another. But if one did it to oneself, what would that add up to?

"Well," I cautiously admitted, "I used to wear a corset and it certainly tested my limits. I never thought of it as part of my religion, although I expect every church-going woman back in those days wore one, too."

"Oh, Miss Julia," Poppy laughed, "you are too much. Anyway, just wanted to tell you what I found. I'll talk to you later."

❦

Late that afternoon, after a call from Hazel Marie asking me to drop by, I strolled over to see her and the walking wounded. I took the long way because I needed the exercise and wanted time to clear my head. I had waited all day for Adam to show up or to call or in some way let me know when he'd be back, but I'd heard nothing from him. The whole thing was getting to me to such an extent that I'd contemplated calling his mother again. Then I'd had a better idea, but finally restrained myself because it would've been too much like tattling to run tell his daddy.

But if he wasn't soon back on the job, heads were going to roll and that Whitman woman's would be the first to go. Except she'd probably enjoy it.

The day hadn't been a total waste as far as work moving along, however, because about midafternoon a crew of chimney builders had shown up along with that prissy architect. Tucker Caldwell had carefully outlined with yellow spray paint a large rectangle on the grass where they were to dig the foundation for my big fat chimney, then he set them to work.

I almost missed him, for by the time I got outside, he was already heading for his car and I had to call to him to wait.

"Good morning," I said, panting a little from my dash as I reached him. "Are you just leaving them to it?"

"They know what they're doing," he said, somewhat shortly. "They don't need me around."

"Well, I need somebody around. Adam Waites has abandoned me, Tucker, and he's left a mess. Do you know where he is?"

He gazed off as if he were suddenly interested in crepe myrtle blooms. "He may be at the Whitman estate, staking off the dimensions of a new building."

"That's exactly what I thought. Is he in the habit of leaving jobs before finishing them?" I stared at him, or rather at the extra stud in his left ear. That made two there—one more than he'd had the last time I'd seen him. I wondered when he'd have enough.

Squinching up my eyes to block out the sight, I asked, "And are you working out there, too?"

He gave a short nod. "I'm designing the guesthouse." Then meeting my eyes in a challenging manner, he said, "You know, Mrs. Murdoch, I have several clients. I can't offer my services exclusively to just one."

"I don't expect you to," I replied, "but I do expect my work to be done in a timely manner, and so far you've done just that. But Adam is another matter, and if you and Mrs. Whitman have colluded to take him away from an *incomplete* job, then we're going to have a problem."

He drew himself up, which wasn't very far, and said with some indignation, "Adam is an independent contractor, so I have no authority over him. Where and when he works is between him and his clients."

"That's good to know, Mr. Caldwell. I will take this matter up with him, now that I know that you aren't pressuring him to choose one client over another."

"No," he said thoughtfully, as if he'd just realized how it might seem, "I wouldn't do that. But Adam is a compliant soul, and, well, Ms. Whitman has a strong personality." He reached up and fingered the extra ear stud. "He likes to please people."

Murmuring "Don't we all," I ended the conversation and returned to the house, thinking that Tucker Caldwell had told me all I needed to know. Adam was enthralled in some way or another by Agnes Whitman and could be needing help to get *un*enthralled.

I might just have to call his daddy after all.

❧

When I got to Hazel Marie's house, I found both her and Mr. Pickens sitting—he quite gingerly—in the room that Sam had used as an office, but which now was their family room. They'd been watching the late afternoon cooking shows, or at least that's what was on the television. I don't know how much actual watching they'd been doing.

"How're you feeling, Mr. Pickens?" I asked as Hazel Marie led me into the room.

"I'm fine," he said, somewhat testily, and squirmed a little on the eiderdown pillow underneath him. "But if you want to know the truth, I'm tired of this."

"Oh, J.D.," Hazel Marie said as her eyes watered. "I hope you're not tired of us."

"No, honey, I mean I'm tired of not being able to do anything. Have a seat, Miss Julia, you'll need it." He squirmed a little more, trying to ease whatever was bothering him. "Thought you'd like to know that I got a call from Coleman. Sheriff McAfee's on his way."

"Oh, my goodness, when will he be here? Do you know what he wants? Is he going to arrest anybody?" My immediate thought was to let Etta Mae know so she could take some vacation time and get out of town.

Mr. Pickens gave a short laugh. "You've had some experience with that office, so you should know. They didn't tell Coleman anything except that the sheriff has some other business to take care of along the way. He's expecting me to be available when he gets here, whenever that is."

"I hope you've alerted Binkie," I said. "You shouldn't say one word to him without your lawyer present—all the shows tell you that."

He ran his hand through that thick mass of black hair and said, "I can handle it. I'm the victim here, which is something new for me."

"That sheriff thinks you're more than that—a witness at the very least. So you ought to be prepared: be in bed when he comes, have Dr. Hargrove tell him you can't be moved, whatever you have to do. I tell you, Mr. Pickens, they do things differently in Mill Run, West Virginia, and I don't think you want to go back there."

"Oh, J.D.," Hazel Marie said again as she wrung her hands in her lap. "What if he's coming to arrest you?"

"Look, honey, if he wanted to do that, he'd tell our sheriff to hold me. And Coleman said it sounded more like a courtesy call. He'll just take my statement and that'll be the end of it." Mr. Pickens turned to me. "I expect he'll want to talk to you and Etta Mae, too, about getting me out of the hospital. You two better have your stories straight."

I looked around the room, so different now from the way Sam had had it, wondering as I did so why the sheriff would make that long trip just to take a statement. Couldn't our sheriff do it for him? Or couldn't Mr. Pickens mail him a notarized statement? There were too many questions and too few answers, and one possibility after another ran through my mind. "Did they say when he'd be here?"

"Just that he's on his way with a stop off or two before he gets here. Which could mean anything. He could be here today, tomorrow or later in the week."

"Well, I might be going out of town for a while. I thought I'd ask Etta Mae to go with me."

Mr. Pickens gave me one of his knowing grins. "You better put that on hold for the time being." Then he grimaced and squirmed again.

Hazel Marie jumped up and ran to him. "Let me straighten your pillow. You can't keep twisting around like that, J.D. You'll hurt yourself."

"I can't help it," he complained, frowning. "The blamed things itch."

❦

Well, I thought as I walked home, the other shoe has finally dropped—Sheriff McAfee was on his way. I went over and over in my mind all that Etta Mae and I had done when we were in Mill Run and, I declare, I couldn't come up with one thing I would've done differently or that anyone else wouldn't have done in our place. We had contacted the sheriff and gotten no help. We'd contacted the hospital and gotten no help. I had specifically asked if Mr. Pickens was under arrest and had been assured that he was not, so we couldn't be accused of abetting a jailbreak.

The only thing I could see that we might be held responsible for was ignoring a NO VISITORS sign on his hospital door. But then again, it wasn't as if we'd gone in and sat around chatting with him for an hour or so. I wouldn't call what we did *visiting*.

One thing was for sure, though. I would have to call Etta Mae and warn her, and I hated to do it. She would worry herself sick until the sheriff got here and we learned exactly what he would do.

And one more thing was for sure—I would have to have Binkie primed to take care of us. She was the best lawyer I knew for snapping "Don't answer that" in the nick of time.

Chapter 35

After moaning to Lillian for a while about our impending inter-
rogation, then having supper and worrying about the sunburn
Lloyd had gotten on the tennis court, I called Etta Mae to put her
on notice about Sheriff McAfee's imminent visit.

"But J.D.'s not worried?" she asked.

"He didn't seem to be, but of course with Hazel Marie there
he'd play it down to keep from upsetting her. He just said the two
of us should have our stories straight." I thought about that for a
minute and so did she. Then I said, "I don't know what he meant
by that because I've always found that telling the truth is the best
policy. Besides, what did we do wrong?"

"Well-l-l," she said, drawing out the word as she considered the
question. "We did take him out of the hospital against a doctor's
orders, but I don't think that's an arrestable offense."

"I don't, either, because it was the sheriff's orders, not a doctor's. Wouldn't that make a difference?"

"Gosh, I don't know, Miss Julia."

I suddenly had an inspired thought. "I think it would! So if he
gets us on that, we can get him for practicing medicine without a
license. What do you think of that?"

She sighed. "I think we're up a tree without a paddle. Maybe a
creek. Anyway, I guess all we can do is just wait and see."

"I know, but if you have an urge to leave town, don't go without
me." I almost brought the conversation to a close, but then thought

of something to cheer her up. "Listen, Etta Mae, the sheriff may not get here for days and if he holds off long enough, Sam'll be home. Binkie's already said she'll be there for us, but with Sam *and* her, we would slide right through this whole mess."

After hanging up, I sat for a while, longing for Sam, while at the same time hoping we could satisfy Sheriff McAfee and see the last of him before Sam got home. I never like disturbing my husband's peace of mind.

❧

I was slow getting up the following morning, having been troubled by dreams of courtrooms and jail cells half the night. As I went through my routine ablutions, I took special care in my clothing choices because I might have to face Sheriff McAfee sometime during the day. I wanted him to be aware that he was not dealing with a run-of-the-mill Saturday night barfly—the kind I assumed a sheriff usually dealt with—but rather with a dignified woman of a certain standing who was not without friends in high places.

So I took care in my selection, even though I was unsure that he would notice. Or if he did, that it would even matter to him. I declare, I still hadn't figured out Sheriff McAfee. He gave the appearance of being a laconic backwoodsman with little on his mind but getting through the day. At the same time, he wasn't above skirting the law, at least to my mind, by isolating Mr. Pickens in a hospital room and preventing access to him by his loved ones. And all the time he was cutting his eyes at Etta Mae, he was also making sure that we knew he was a church-going man.

Which brought up another matter: Was he a snake handler or not? Had he deliberately sent us to that church with following signs, knowing full well what we'd run into? Had that been his idea of a joke? Or had it really been his church and he'd been prevented from attending by another call at the last minute?

As I said, I couldn't figure him out, yet today might be the very day he showed up in Abbotsville and we would all have to answer to him. If, that is, he had jurisdiction in this county. Or even in this state. *That* was something to look into, so I'd be on firm legal ground if I needed to take the Fifth Amendment.

As I opened the bedroom door to go to the kitchen, I realized that I'd been hearing the murmur of people talking as well as doors opening and closing. Lloyd and Lillian, I thought, and hurried out to remind Lloyd to put on suntan lotion every time he stepped out on a tennis court. The poor little thing had Wesley Lloyd Springer's fair complexion and would burn to a crisp if he wasn't careful.

"Good morning, Lillian," I said as I walked into the kitchen and looked around. "Where's Lloyd? I thought I heard him."

"No'm, he already gone. They playin' early 'fore the sun get too high. Coffee's ready." She pointed at the pot and I headed for it. "Who you heard was Mr. Adam, which I know you glad to hear is upstairs workin'."

"Oh, thank the Lord," I said with heartfelt gratitude. "Did he say what he's been doing?"

"No'm, when I say, 'Good mornin',' he say, 'Praise the Lord, it is a good mornin'.' He don't ever have much to say for hisself."

"Well, that's certainly true. I'm not sure I'll get any more out of him, but I'd like to know his plans. I'd like to know if I'm going to have to put up with him going back and forth between that woman's job and mine. Sam will be back before we know it and I expect to have that sunroom finished by the time he gets here. I mean it's not as if Adam has to build those cabinets himself. We're using ready-made ones and all he has to do is nail up the framework and install them. How hard can that be?"

"You better eat some breakfast 'fore you go up there all grouchy an' light in on him." She put a plate of eggs and bacon on the table and pointed to my chair. I sat.

All through breakfast, I could hear the sound of hammering from upstairs and, I tell you, it was music to my ears. The longer Adam hammered, the calmer I became. I was even able to linger with Lillian as we prepared a grocery list for the weekend.

"We may have a guest, Lillian," I said, "and if we do, we'll need to have the Pickens family and maybe Etta Mae, unless it'll put her in jeopardy. But I'm not about to entertain that sheriff by myself." I sighed, then looked on the bright side. "But with the house so torn up, I won't have to offer him a room. He can stay in a motel, for all I care."

"I 'spect he plannin' to do that anyway."

"Well, he should! The idea of coming down here ready to interrogate and perhaps arrest somebody and expect us to provide him with room and board. It's beyond thinking of."

"Yes'm, an' you don't need to. An' if he act up like you think he might, I wouldn't even ast him to supper."

"You're right," I said, tearing the list off the pad I'd been writing on. "But get a large roast, just in case. No, wait," I said, striking through several items, "let's have chicken, fried chicken, and if he wonders what it really is, he can just wonder."

We rose from the table and began taking plates and dishes to the counter by the sink. I looked out the window at the beautiful day, noting how green everything was—the boxwoods in the back were covered with bright new growth and the ornamental fruit trees were in full bloom.

"Listen," I said, turning to Lillian. "Do you hear that?"

"No'm, I don't hear nothin'."

"That's just it! It's too quiet." I raised my eyes to the ceiling. "What's Adam doing—or not doing—up there?"

"Maybe he doin' something that don't need hammerin'. Or maybe he takin' a rest."

"He better not be taking a rest," I said, slinging down a dish towel. "He hasn't worked long enough to need one."

✿

I hurried upstairs, taking no care to approach the sunroom quietly. I wanted him to know I was on the way, hoping he would bestir himself and get back to work. It was not my desire to catch him loafing on the job. I didn't want to have to upbraid him, so with that in mind I walked firmly up the stairs and down the hall, weaving my way through the boxes stacked along the way. I even tapped on the sunroom door before opening it, giving him every opportunity to be up and doing and busily working.

But did he take that opportunity? No, he did not. When I walked into the lumber- and sawdust-covered room, I found him sitting on a boxed cabinet reading a book.

He looked up at me, making no effort to hide what he was doing or to appear busy. "Good morning, Mrs. Murdoch, and the Lord's blessings on you."

"And on you," I replied, slightly stunned that he seemed not the least embarrassed at being caught flat-footed without a hammer in his hand. "Adam," I went on, "Mr. Murdoch will be home in a few days and he'll be most unhappy if this room isn't finished. It was bad enough that you didn't come to work yesterday, and even worse that you're here now but not getting anything done. Remember that I'm paying you by the hour to work, not to read."

"Yes, ma'am," he said with a sigh. And carefully closing the book which I now saw was a Bible, he laid it aside. "My brother's coming to help me catch up, but I just felt the need to turn to God's word for a few minutes. I won't charge you for the time it took."

Stricken by the troubled tone in his voice, I began to feel bad about my strident behavior. "I'm not worried about what you charge, Adam. I'm worried about you. Is anything wrong?"

"No, ma'am, everything's fine." He got up from the box he was sitting on and adjusted his tool belt. "I just find that my work goes better if I study the Word off and on throughout the day."

"Well," I said, at a loss for a response. "Well, good. I'll leave you to it." And I left, feeling chastened even as a rather sharp observation flitted through my mind: *better to have been studying my plans, considering the state of that room.* Then felt worse for having thought it.

Chapter 36

Adam was true to his word about bringing in help. Before the hour was past, another pickup drove in and a younger brother, Josh, as he introduced himself, hopped out to help finish the sunroom. He was about twice the size of Adam, a blond giant of a man, with an open and pleasant expression on his face. Up and down the stairs the two of them went, carrying out the table saw and odds and ends of leftover lumber, then bringing in the rest of the cabinets. With both of them working, we had a double dose of hammering, which I bore stoically because it meant that things were moving along. They gave me a full day's work with no stopping except for lunch, which had been brought from home, even though Lillian invited them to our table.

"Mr. Adam say thank you all the same," Lillian said as she came back downstairs, "but his mama fix meat loaf san'wiches an' they jus' stick with that."

"Well, we tried," I said, sitting down to a fruit salad. Just as I finished, the telephone rang.

I answered it and heard Hazel Marie say without taking a breath, "The sheriff's coming, Miss Julia! The sheriff's coming!"

"I know, Hazel Marie, you told me yesterday."

"No, I mean we know when he's coming and it's Friday, day after tomorrow, at nine o'clock, and I won't even be dressed!" She had to stop to catch her breath, then with a little more control, she said, "Coleman just called and told us. And J.D. said that means it'll be an official interview, because Sheriff McAfee has gone through our sheriff to set it up. It won't be just a drop-in-and-visit kind of thing. Oh, Miss Julia, I am so worried I don't know what to do."

I had to think a minute, half ashamed of myself for feeling relief that no one had officially notified me or Etta Mae. Maybe that meant we weren't wanted and wouldn't have our pictures tacked up on post office walls.

"Well, Hazel Marie," I said, "maybe it's better to know than to have it hanging over our heads. What does Mr. Pickens say?"

"Oh, you know him. He's not a bit worried or at least that's what he's telling me. But I am. He's not at all well, though he puts up a good front. They just *can't* make him go back up there. It could ruin him for life!"

"Surely it won't come to that. He seems better every time I see him."

"But you haven't seen his *scars*. I was finally able to look and he's got *four* of them on his . . . you-know."

"But just think, Hazel Marie, how fortunate he is to have them there. You're the only one who'll ever see them."

"Oh, I *hope*."

After giving her a few more encouraging words, I hung up without asking what I wanted to know. And that was, had Etta Mae and I been included in the official interview that Sheriff McAfee had set up. I assured myself that she would have told me if we had been or if she had known. Or else Coleman would've called me.

Maybe he still would. Maybe he hadn't gotten around to it. And maybe I should've been more concerned about Mr. Pickens's predicament than about my own.

The day after tomorrow, I thought, and was finally able to draw some ease of mind from that. Only a few days afterward, Sam would be home and Sheriff McAfee would've been and gone by then.

Surely he was not coming to arrest Mr. Pickens—that was

unthinkable. For one thing, if that'd been his intent, he would've had our sheriff do the honors. Wouldn't he? Hazel Marie had said *interview*, not intervene or interrogate or intercept. He only wants to talk, I assured myself.

And, I went on, thinking up one possibility after another, we were told he had other business to take care of on this trip—which could mean that he wasn't after Mr. Pickens specifically. Maybe he wanted to visit that niece of his and just tacked Mr. Pickens on to make the trip official and have his expenses reimbursed. I wouldn't put it past him.

But whatever his intentions were, I intended to warn Etta Mae as soon as she got home from work. Just to be on the safe side.

❧

"Etta Mae?" I said, my call catching her, she told me, just as she walked in the door of her single-wide after a long day of caring for the sick and ailing. "I hate to tell you this, but Hazel Marie called to say that Sheriff McAfee will be in town the day after tomorrow. He's set up an interview with Mr. Pickens, but I don't know if that's all he's planning. He may have a few other interviews in mind."

"Yes, ma'am," she said in a slightly subdued tone, "I know."

"You know? Did Hazel Marie call you, too?"

"No'm. He did."

"He, who? Coleman? Mr. Pickens?"

"No, that sheriff."

"Sheriff McAfee? Why, Etta Mae, why would he do that? He hasn't called me, and if anybody's at fault with what we did in his jurisdiction, I am. Besides, how did he find you?"

"I don't know. Maybe Coleman told him. He called on my cell right in the middle of me clipping Mr. Avery's toenails. Made me so nervous, I almost nipped his little toe. Anyway, I don't think he wants to interview me. At least, not the way he'll interview J.D."

"Well, I don't understand why he'd want to talk to you and not to me. I was the instigator and I take full responsibility for everything we did. You're completely in the clear, Etta Mae, I want you to rest easy about that. So unless he wants to turn you against me, I can't see why he'd come after you."

"I don't think that's what he has in mind," she said. Then, as if unburdening herself, she went on in a rush. "Actually, I think he's just interested in dinner and dancin'."

That stopped me. "A *date*? He asked you for a date?"

"That's pretty much what I figured. I hope you don't mind that I said yes."

"Oh, well, of course not. It's entirely up to you who you see, but, Etta Mae, be careful. That man is sneaky. Remember how he sent us to that church, so he may have something more up his sleeve than dinner and dancing. And if it's a snake—I mean if he's a snake handler—you don't want to be involved with him."

"Ugh, don't worry," Etta Mae said. "That's the first thing I'm going to ask him, and if he is, I'm not going anywhere with him. I would've asked him on the phone but I was so surprised to hear from him, I didn't think of it."

"I think I'm surprised to hear he's a dancing man. Maybe that speaks well of him, because, I grant you, those snake handlers did a lot of prancing and dancing around, but they did it by themselves, not with each other. Where will you go? There's no place to dance around here unless you belong to the Cotillion."

"Well, I don't belong to that," she said with a laugh. "Whatever it is. No, there's a steak house out on Highway 64 with a dance hall next to it. Ardis said he likes steak and he likes to line dance, so that'll be the best place to go."

Ardis? One phone call had certainly gotten them off on a fast track. And steak and line dancing? She'd found out a lot about him even in the midst of cutting toenails, but she hadn't found out the most important thing: namely, his church affiliation. That would've been my first question, but then, I hadn't been asked to dance.

"That sounds nice," I said, which is about like saying an ugly baby looks interesting. "Well, Etta Mae, I know he'll be in town

Friday because that's when he'll interview Mr. Pickens. But do you have any idea when he'll actually get here? You know, so I'll know not to answer the phone."

"Yes, ma'am, he's already here."

"He *is*? You mean he's *there*?" I could just picture that tall denim-and-boot-clad vibrating man in Etta Mae's tiny single-wide. They wouldn't be able to move without touching each other.

Etta Mae laughed. "Our date is tomorrow night, but he got in today. He's visiting that niece of his. So, no, he's not here yet."

Thank goodness for that, I thought, then thought of something else. For several days I'd been wondering how to bring up the subject, and the only way I could come up with was just to jump in and do it.

"Well, I hope you have a good time, but, Etta Mae, even though I know it's none of my business, I have to ask you about something else." I paused, hesitating to pry into her affairs or to criticize her in any way. But I cared about her, and knowing how easily led she was—just witness the numerous times I'd talked her into one escapade after another—I simply had to warn her. And as reluctant as I always am to interfere in the lives of others, a mental picture of those little stars running up the rim of her right ear gave me the impetus to press on. "Have you ever met a woman named Agnes Whitman?"

"I don't think so. Why?"

"No reason," I said, attempting to back off. But Etta Mae was naive in many ways—again, witness her willingness to go out with a man who'd already proved to be tricky and underhanded. So, deciding to issue a warning whether or not it was heeded, I went on. "Well, yes, there is, and your mention of Sheriff McAfee's niece reminded me. Remember he told us she lives in Fairfields? Well, so does this woman and she is somebody to stay away from in case you're ever invited to her church. Don't go, Etta Mae, because if you think handling snakes is bad, you won't believe what those people do."

"Worse than *snakes*?"

"Well, when you get right down to it, I don't know if it's worse, but it's certainly just as bad. Etta Mae, they cut, pierce and tattoo themselves from one end to the other. And it's all in the name of getting the body in touch with the soul. Or something of the sort."

"Phoo, Miss Julia, I wouldn't get mixed up in something like that. I'm Baptist to the bone."

"Good," I said, relieved. "But I don't want you to think I'm singling you out, Etta Mae. I'm warning everybody I know to stay away from those people. They seem nice enough, but they might run a metal rod through your nose before you turned around good." I didn't mention puncturing a line of holes up the side of an ear because I didn't want to get personal. He who has ears to hear, as they say, let him hear.

I was reassured, though, that she'd had no contact with the Church of Body Modification, which meant that all those little stars were purely for decorative, not religious, purposes, which is a matter of taste, not faith.

As soon as I'd hung up, Adam and his brother made their last trip downstairs, both of them smiling and looking pleased with themselves. The odor of fresh paint followed them down.

"All through, Mrs. Murdoch," Adam said. "Me and Josh got it finished."

"Wonderful," I said, heading for my checkbook. "It just goes to show what can be done when you keep your mind on what you're doing. I can't thank you enough."

Adam handed me a stapled stack of receipts, along with his bill. "You didn't tell me what you wanted done about the floor, so we just swept and mopped it."

"That's fine. The carpet people are supposed to be here tomorrow, which was another reason for wanting the room finished. Now, Adam," I said as I handed him a check, "that bedroom upstairs needs the woodwork painted. I hope to have the paperhangers in here soon, so we need to get that done right away. Here's the name and number of the paint you'll need."

His face fell as he hesitantly accepted the paint sample. "Well, I sorta promised another lady I'd give her a couple of days."

"That's fine," I said again. "Give her a couple of days when you finish here. You knew I had two rooms to be done, and it won't take long to paint the crown molding and baseboards. You can send Josh to her while you do that."

"Oh, no, ma'am," he said, his eyes widening in alarm. "Josh can't go out there. He, well, he's just learning. I can't send him by hisself. But don't worry, I'll put her off and get that room done tomorrow. Josh'll work here with me."

I glanced at Josh, who grinned and blushed, apparently un-aware of his brother's concern. But I knew of it, or thought I did. Adam had just made it apparent that he wouldn't send his brother to Agnes Whitman's house alone—and I was sure that she was the lady he'd promised to help. Was he afraid that Josh would be influenced by those strange body manipulators? And it suddenly followed, it seemed to me, that Adam's troubled mind was be-cause he himself had come under their influence.

Something ought to be done about that, but I didn't know what. I did, however, intend to give it some thought.

🕸

I was on edge the rest of the evening, disturbed by my sudden realization of the source of the spiritual crisis Adam seemed to be undergoing, wondering what could be done to help him and won-dering also if Sheriff McAfee had checked into a local motel or was staying with his niece, if he'd called Mr. Pickens to confirm their meeting, if he'd called Etta Mae again and, most especially, if he intended to apprehend and arrest anybody.

I knew that was unlikely, given the fact that as far as I knew, Mr. Pickens wasn't worried about being shanghaied back to West Virginia. Actually, I figured Mr. Pickens was fairly safe, at least until Sheriff McAfee had squired Etta Mae around a bit. But when you're anxious about something, your mind flies off in all directions and almost anything seems possible.

Twice I went to the phone to call Hazel Marie to reassure myself, but thought better of it both times. No need to add to her anxiety just to relieve mine. Once, I picked up the phone to call Etta Mae, then put it down again. What was there to say? I wished for Sam, then was glad he wasn't involved. I dreaded having to tell him what I'd done in rescuing Mr. Pickens and, by doing so, putting the man in jeopardy with Sheriff McAfee.

Then I had another disquieting thought. If it came right down to it, Mr. Pickens had a reasonable defense if he needed one. He could disclaim any responsibility for his precipitous exit from the Mill Run hospital. He had not been mentally competent at the time and had therefore been incapable of formulating such a plan, much less carrying it out. Nobody knew that better than Etta Mae and me after what we'd gone through to get him out of there.

But Mr. Pickens wouldn't shift responsibility. Would he? No, certainly not. He thought too much of himself to admit to any loss of his faculties. And he was too much of a gentleman to lay the blame at the feet of two women.

At least that's what I told myself, for I also knew that you could never tell what Mr. Pickens was capable of doing.

Finally, as I took myself to bed, I was comforted by the thought that if we could get Sheriff McAfee in and out of town within the next few days without arresting anybody, Sam would be home and he'd know what to do about Adam and the strange hold that Agnes Whitman seemed to have on him.

Chapter 37

Early the next morning, I had another reason to want to leave town: too much was happening at one time. Tucker Caldwell showed up at seven o'clock, along with two crews of workmen—one for the exterior and one for the interior. Right behind them came a huge flatbed truck with some sort of crane on it that unloaded pallet after pallet of bricks that would eventually be my Williamsburg chimney.

And when the pallets had been unloaded and stacked in my yard, I realized my next call would be to a landscaper to resod and replant.

Tucker led his interior crew inside and straight back to the future library, which I, barely dressed, had barely vacated before they tromped in.

"Mrs. Murdoch," Tucker said, "we have to get this furniture out of here. Where do you want it?"

"Oh, my word," I said, pushing back my hair in agitation. "I haven't thought that far ahead. Let me see, maybe out here in the hall? The mattress can go in the dining room against the table, and everything else, well, anywhere you can find space."

When he pursed his mouth at my lack of preparation, I added, "I assumed you'd let me know ahead of time when you were coming."

He ignored that, walked into the bedroom, and said, "The closets have to be emptied. They're coming out first."

Lillian, who'd just walked in, said, "We can do that, Miss Julia. Where you want all them clothes?"

"I don't know," I responded, feeling frazzled and it hardly seven-thirty in the morning. "Upstairs, I guess. In Hazel Marie's closet."

Then to add to the commotion, Adam Waites pushed through the front door with a ladder, along with Josh, laden with paint cans and brushes, right behind him. Adam nodded to me, but one glance at Tucker sent him scurrying up the stairs.

Which reminded me, so I followed Tucker down the hall. "Mr. Caldwell? Tucker? What about Adam? I thought you were going to have him do the library."

"Just the finishing work," he replied. "He's booked solid for a while, and I figured you wouldn't want to put this off until he's free."

"You figured right, because I don't. But we did have an agreement with him, and I'm inclined to hold him to it. Besides, I don't want to hurt his feelings by using someone else."

"I've already spoken to him," Tucker said, somewhat shortly. "And he's fine with it. Besides, the men I brought are true craftsmen. You'll just have to trust me on that because I know what I'm doing. Now the best thing you can do is get those closets emptied so we can get on with it." Then, dashing over to two men who were lifting a chest to move it out, he yelled, "Wait a minute, wait a minute! Be careful with that. It's eighteenth century."

Well, I wasn't sure it was, but it had come from Wesley Lloyd's grandmother so it might've been. I was gratified, nonetheless, that Tucker was looking after my belongings.

Lillian was already going in and out with armfuls of clothes, both mine and Sam's, taking them upstairs, and I began to do the same. By the time we were finished carrying out hanging clothes as well as plastic bags full of shoes and shoe boxes, weaving around and between the workmen who were moving out furniture, all I wanted to do was sit down and rest.

The kitchen, in fact, was the only undisturbed and restful

room in the house. Well, Lloyd's room stayed the same—I'd put it off-limits. But the rest of the house began to look as if a wrecking crew had been at it. Adam and Josh were painting in Hazel Marie's room; her walk-in closet was filled with extra clothes; the sunroom was finished but not furnished; Sam's boxes that had been moved from his house crowded the upstairs hall; and bedside tables, bed frame, lamps, chests of drawers, easy chairs, mattress and boxspring were taking up space in the living room, the dining room and the downstairs hall. Twice I'd tripped and almost fallen on the Oriental, rolled up and left in the hall.

"Why did I ever think of remodeling?" I asked Lillian as we collapsed at the kitchen table. We were just having our first cups of coffee that morning, which was another reason I was feeling tired and washed out.

"Don't ast me," she said, pushing the cream toward me. "But here's something you better think about: where you gonna sleep tonight?"

"That is a question, isn't it? And the answer is I'll sleep in your room." There was a small guest room behind Lloyd's bedroom that I kept for her and Latisha on those nights when the weather was too bad for her to drive home. It had also come in handy after Hazel Marie's twins had been born and we needed all the help in the house we could get—day and night.

"You gonna have a time gettin' in there," Lillian said. " 'cause Mr. Sam's desk an' swivel chair an' his big leather chair an' some lamps already in it."

"Oh, my goodness." And almost put my head on the table in despair. "Well," I went on, straightening up, "I'll just climb over stuff till I reach the bed."

"Maybe you an' Lloyd better stay with Miss Hazel Marie. Least, till you can walk around in here. Look to me like if we ever go out the door, we won't never get back in."

"Yes, and I thought I could have it all done by the time Sam got back. That shows how little foresight I had, doesn't it?" I stirred cream in my coffee, then tried a sip. "I'll just make do here, at least until Sheriff McAfee leaves town. It seems the better part of discretion is for me to stay out of his sight, so I won't be going to Hazel Marie's."

We looked at each other as an awful wrenching sound split the air. Then what sounded like sledge hammer blows followed it.

"Sound like they tearin' down the house," Lillian said.

"No, just demolishing the closets. At least I hope that's all they're doing." I went over to the coffeepot to refill my cup. "You want a refill?"

"Yes'm, I guess another cup won't hurt. But I don't feel like cookin' or eatin' with what all's goin' on. They's some muffins in the freezer I can put in the oven. You think that do you?"

"I'm not that hungry, either, so muffins will be fine. Lillian," I went on as she opened the freezer, "did you get a good look at Tucker Caldwell?"

She glanced at me. "You mean that prissy little man tellin' everybody what to do? I seen him but I didn't look too hard."

"I didn't, either, but I kept trying to because I'm wondering how close he is to that Whitman woman. I know he's in contact with her, because he's designing some new building she wants. But something's going on with him. When I first met him, he was as professional looking as a man of stunted growth can look—in fact, almost too much so. Overcompensating, probably. But the next time I saw him, he had an earring stuck in his ear and, believe me, that woman is big on earrings."

"Lots of men do that these days. It don't have to mean anything I know of." She put four muffins in the oven, then came back to the table with butter and jelly.

"I know, but it seems unlike him. Or unlike the little I know about him. Anyway, if he shows up with a tattoo or another earring or two, I'll know that woman has her claws in him."

"Nothin' you can do about it, if she do. A grown man ought to know what he doin'."

"But, Lillian, that's just the thing. I'm not worried about him—he's cocky enough to take care of himself. It's Adam I'm concerned about. And, yes, I know he's a grown man, too, but he's an inno-cent and he doesn't have a smidgen of worldly knowledge. It's a fact that something's bothering him, and I think Agnes Whitman is trying to wheedle him into that church of hers. Lillian," I said, leaning over the table to put my hand on her arm, "I think his faith is being tested."

"That happen to all of us, one time or another," she said, nodding judiciously. "They's not much anybody can do about it, neither."

"I know, but I feel protective of him. If Agnes can sway a con-ceited little man like Tucker Caldwell, she could eat somebody like Adam alive." I stopped and looked around as a crash of lum-ber resounded from the future library. "I hope they know what they're doing. Are those muffins ready yet?"

They were, and while we ate, I continued to mull over the problem with Adam. I'd noticed how he'd hurried up the stairs as soon as he saw Tucker, neither speaking to him nor acknowledg-ing him in any way. And of course they knew each other, having worked together in the past and, apparently, still doing so at the Whitman estate, so it was all the more strange that Adam had made the effort to avoid him.

And later in the morning when I'd walked upstairs to see how Adam and Josh were doing and to offer some refreshments, the door to Hazel Marie's bedroom had been closed. That probably hadn't meant anything—just an attempt to keep the noise level down so they could hear the Gospel music on their radio.

But it had meant something when after greeting me from the top of his ladder, Adam had asked, "Everybody about cleared out downstairs?"

"Oh, no, not everybody. The brickmasons are working outside and the inside crew is, well, I don't know what they're doing—I'm afraid to look. Getting ready to open the wall for the fireplace, I guess." Then, realizing that Adam's question might have had a more specific meaning, I said, "Tucker Caldwell's back at his of-fice, working on specifications. He said he'd be back at quitting time to see how far the crews had gotten."

Adam nodded as if he'd received the answer he wanted. "We'll be through with the first coat about midafternoon. We'll let it dry overnight, then be back in the morning to put on the final coat."

"Thank you, Adam. And you, too, Josh." Josh looked up from where he was sprawled on the floor painting the baseboards and smiled bashfully at me. "I know you were supposed to be working somewhere else, so I doubly appreciate your getting this done for me."

Adam dipped his brush into the paint can, then glanced down at me. "Just as soon put off that other work, but when a man gives his word, he has to hold to it."

I agreed and left, thinking that he'd just told me that he was not all that eager to be working for Agnes Whitman again.

Chapter 38

"Miss Julia," Lillian said as I entered the kitchen the next morning and closed the door behind me, "I know you thinkin' 'bout asting that sheriff to dinner, but you might not ought to now. They's a king-size mattress in the dining room, so nobody gonna be able to get to the table."

"What a lovely thought, Lillian! It's the perfect excuse for not extending hospitality, which I hadn't wanted to do in the first place." I rubbed my hands together, pleased to discover this unexpected benefit of remodeling. "In fact, I'd been wondering why on earth Tucker would start a job on a Thursday, only to leave the house in a mess over the weekend, but now I see it as a blessing in disguise. If I work it right, I might not have to see Sheriff McAfee at all."

"Uh-huh, 'less he want to see you."

"True, but I'm hoping for the best. Oh, did I tell you that he called Etta Mae for a date? He's taking her out to eat and to a dance tonight, then interviewing Mr. Pickens sometime tomorrow." I pulled out a chair and sat down. "Which means he could be leaving town tomorrow afternoon. I plan to make myself unavailable from now until then and hope I can avoid him altogether."

Lillian laughed. "If he got Miss Etta Mae on his mind, I wouldn't count on him leavin' real soon. But I tell you one thing," she went on, sitting down beside me, "if you don't have a dinner party, we gonna be eatin' chicken till doomsday. I went to the store on my way here an' now we got enough to feed a army."

"Just divide it up and put it in the freezer. We'll eat on it as long as it lasts."

🐝

When the phone rang, Mildred Allen was on the line. "I see you have workmen there, Julia. Why don't you walk over and visit for a while?"

"Why, I'd love to, Mildred," I said, as another crash resounded throughout the house. One good thing about Adam and Josh putting on the second coat in the upstairs bedroom—painting was a quiet occupation that wasn't adding to the din. "I won't stay long, though, because the carpet people could show up anytime. I'm afraid they'll lay it in the wrong room if I don't watch them."

Feeling slightly guilty for leaving Lillian with the noise, I asked her to call me if the carpet men came. "Take it easy today, Lillian, put your feet up and read the paper. Nothing can get done anywhere in the house."

Leaving the sounds of hammering, men's voices, the tromp of feet going in and out the front door and their blaring radios relieved me considerably. I could even hear birds singing as I walked over to Mildred's serene household, where she met me at the door.

Thanking her for the respite, I followed her out to the side porch, where a tray with a full pitcher of tea, tall glasses and a dish of fresh mint leaves waited for us.

"I declare, Mildred," I said, accepting a glass from her, "I didn't know what I was getting into when I had the bright idea of remodeling. So I better get it right, because I doubt I'll ever do it again."

"Sure you will," she said. "The trick is to go somewhere, take a few weeks at the beach or go to New York and shop. When you come home, it's all done."

"You have more trust in your fellow man than I do. I'd probably come home to find the kitchen upstairs or out in the garage. I hate to complain, Mildred, but let me just tell you that I've had to watch both Tucker and Adam like a hawk. I don't think either of them has his mind on his work. And furthermore, I think Agnes Whitman is the reason for it."

"Well," Mildred said, taking a sip of tea, then setting down her glass, "that's what I wanted to talk to you about."

"What? Agnes?"

"Yes, she called me to complain about you."

"Me? What have I done? I hardly know the woman. And why did she call you?"

"She knows we're friends and, of course, she's upset about how long you're keeping Adam."

"Why, Mildred, you're the one who told me to keep him busy so she couldn't get him. Besides, he has left me and gone to her at least one day and he's worked for her after hours, as well." I fumed for a minute or so, then said, "And if she's upset with me, she should've called me. I think it's tacky that she called you to complain about me."

"I know," Mildred said somewhat complacently, "and I don't blame you. I told her she should talk to you directly. I didn't want to be in the middle of it, but she insisted that I at least speak to you about it. So that's what I'm doing and that's the end of it as far as I'm concerned." She patted her lips with a linen napkin, then said, "I told her, just as I told you, that possession is nine-tenths of the law, and there wasn't much she could do about it."

I could hardly speak, I was so disturbed. Don't you just hate it when somebody has a complaint against you and sends the message secondhand? The more I thought about the whole thing, the more incensed I became.

"So what am I supposed to do?" I demanded. "Stand at attention and salute? I don't think Adam wants to work for her, so her problem is with him, not me." I paused. "Or you. I have enough on my plate these days without adding Agnes Whitman's inability to keep help."

"I know, Julia. I'm just passing it along."

"Well, I wish you hadn't."

"I wouldn't have," Mildred said, looking directly at me, "except for the last thing she said."

"What'd she say?"

"She said she was not accustomed to having her plans disrupted by either a menial worker or a small-town upstart."

"*Upstart!* She called *me* an upstart? Why, I'll have her know . . ." I couldn't get enough breath to continue.

"Julia, it's all right." Mildred reached over and patted my clenched hand. "Don't distress yourself. You have to consider the source. I wouldn't have told you, but the more I thought about it, the more it sounded like a threat, so I thought you should know. But what can she do to you, other than keep Adam so busy you never get him back?"

"Well, that's another thing—calling him a menial worker. There's nothing wrong with working with your hands. In fact, there's honor in it, and her saying that just shows how little respect she has for him or anybody else who works for her." I took a deep breath. "I resent it for him, as well as for myself. I'm insulted and highly offended, especially since it comes from a tattooed woman who ought to be in a circus sideshow. Who is she to criticize or judge anybody?"

Mildred started laughing. "Well, she claims to be a minister, so I guess she's doing what they all do."

"Oh, Mildred, that's not fair. They're not all that way. Think of Poppy. But listen," I said, leaning toward her, "there's not a thing she can do to me—she ought to be worried about what I can do to her. Just wait till she wants to join the garden club or the book club or anything else in this town, then she'll find out. But I am worried about what she can do to Adam. He's already indicated that he doesn't want to work for her anymore, but honorable man that he is, he feels obligated. Mildred, I tell you, something strange is going on out at her place and I think Adam is being drawn into it. Against his will, I might add."

"Oh, I don't know, Julia," Mildred said. "Agnes has led a strange life, I grant you, but I don't think she's actually *wicked*. Why don't you just tell Adam he doesn't have to work for anybody he doesn't want to work for? He may *feel* obligated, but he's not legally obligated. We've all had people walk off a job or refuse a job, haven't we?"

Well, no, I hadn't, but Mildred was a lot more picky than I was, so I expect she'd had experience with people who wouldn't work for her. I decided not to point that out.

"I think," I said after giving it some thought, "that I should speak to Adam about this. I'm not sure how much good it'll do, but he needs to at least know she's upset with him because of me. Then," I went on with a bright idea, "I'll give him enough to do so that he can work at my house for as long as he wants to. He can even read his Bible on my time, I don't care. And Agnes can keep on blaming me, but maybe she'll leave him alone."

Mildred opened her mouth to say something, but Ida Lee appeared in the door. "Excuse me," she said, "but Miss Lillian just called to say that the carpet men have arrived."

"Oh, my goodness," I said, getting to my feet. "Thank you, Ida Lee. I have to run, Mildred. Thank you for the tea and the warning. I'll let you know how it turns out."

Chapter 39

After checking the roll of carpet to be sure they'd brought the right one, I led the two men up to Sam's new office in the sunroom. I had selected a tightly woven, almost commercial grade of carpet so Sam's executive chair would roll smoothly over it without needing plastic mats and runners strewn everywhere.

Leaving the men to it, I tapped on the bedroom door, then walked in. Josh was painting in the bathroom while Adam was putting meticulous strokes on the window trim. He turned and gave me a tentative smile as I entered.

"Almost through,' he said.

"It looks lovely," I said, surveying the soft ivory paint on the woodwork. "So much more soothing than pink. Adam," I went on as I walked over to him and lowered my voice, "I don't mean to interfere in your business or your work schedule, but if you'd like to make a full week here, I could use some help putting furniture and boxes of books into the sunroom. And the carpet will be laid in here tomorrow, so furniture can be moved back in then." Before he could respond, I hurried on. "Before you decide, I have to tell you that Ms. Whitman is most upset with me and you—you for not dropping everything and going to her, and me for preventing you from going. Frankly, I think she has some nerve for making such demands, and I want you to know that I can find work for you and Josh for as long as you want it. If you stay here long enough, she might get tired of waiting and leave you alone."

A worried frown creased Adam's forehead as his eyes darted around the room, looking everywhere but at me. Fearful that I had overstepped, I immediately regretted speaking so openly about one of his clients. My first thought was that I had misinterpreted what I had perceived to be a reluctance to work for her.

Yet he was reluctant about something or somebody, and what else could it be? Certainly not working for me.

Looking distressed, Adam said, "She already called me. I told her I had to make the week here."

"Why, that's perfect. It's all settled then, and you don't need to give it another thought."

"No'm," he said, shaking his head miserably, " 'cause I lied about it."

"Lied? That's hard to believe. How did you lie?"

I thought if his shoulders slumped any farther, they'd soon be on the floor.

"I told her you wanted me to stay on here."

"Well, I do! How could that be lying?"

"Because," he said, giving me a quick glance, "I told her that before you asked me to stay. So I guess I better go on out there and, maybe, make up for it."

Scripture verses began flitting through my mind as I searched for some redeeming reference about lying in a good cause. I wasn't having much success in finding one.

"Uh, well, Adam," I began, thinking furiously, "you know that the Bible gives us some stern warnings against drunkeness. We're warned over and over about it. On the other hand," I went on as his frown deepened, "we are also told to take a little wine for the stomach's sake. So it seems to me that that's a good analogy for lying under duress. We shouldn't do too much of it, but a little now and then can be helpful under certain circumstances, even if we don't have stomach problems."

"Ma'am?"

"All I'm saying is that you weren't lying, you were making a presumptive statement because you knew I'd need you. You were thinking ahead on my behalf and should be commended, not condemned, for it. So you'll be here tomorrow and maybe on into next week?"

"Tomorrow," he said, nodding with some hesitancy. "Don't know about next week."

"We'll see about that later, then. But if Agnes Whitman gives you a hard time, you have my permission to blame it all on me. I'm not afraid of a skinny tattooed woman who thinks she's the boss of the world."

That brought the flash of a smile, but it didn't last long. "I'll probably pay for it, though," he murmured.

And, I thought, I probably would, too. I'd taken scripture out of context to prove that a little lie wasn't as bad as a out-and-out lie. The fact that we all tell little white lies every day didn't exactly absolve me. But what do you do when a friend needs reassurance about what she's wearing? I was in good company, though, because I was reminded of some of Pastor Ledbetter's less efficacious pronouncements after a convoluted effort to find a scriptural basis for some of his opinions.

I didn't let it worry me. There were too many other things rushing through my mind. As far as I was concerned, Adam was safe for a while and I could focus my worries on Etta Mae, who'd be in the clutches of that possibly snake-handling sheriff in a few hours, and on Mr. Pickens, who would be facing an official grilling by that selfsame treacherous law officer.

So I showed Adam where Sam's office furniture was stored and explained where I wanted each piece in the sunroom. Then I took the newspaper into Lloyd's room, where I could occupy myself in a semblance of peace and quiet to await supper. Gradually, I began to hear the sounds of workmen gathering their tools and leaving. When all was quiet downstairs, outside and in, I went to the kitchen, where Lloyd had just come in.

We had supper at the kitchen table by ourselves, for I had told Lillian to go on home, that we'd clear the table and do the dishes. It was something to help me while away the long evening, which didn't get any shorter when Lloyd went out to ride his bicycle after we finished.

I wandered around the house, looking at what had been accomplished—not much—by the work crews during the day. The new library was larger by a good two feet where the closets had been removed, and a tarp had been stapled over the hole in the wall where the fireplace would be.

I walked outside to examine the brickmasons' work and was pleased to see that the fat part of the chimney was coming along nicely. Of course the lawn was a mess with pallets of bricks, wheelbarrows and discarded cement bags ruining the grass and one of my hybrid rhododendrons.

I saved the best for last and went up to Sam's new office. There was his large mohagony desk and chair, right where I wanted them; his easy chair; his lamps, which needed better placement; and the boxes of books and papers, which he would have to shelve himself. But the room was ready for him, so at least one part of my project had come in on time.

For the rest of the evening and on into the night after Lloyd and I went to bed, my mind was filled with concern about Etta Mae and Mr. Pickens. And all because of one lanky and laconic sheriff of an out-of-state backwoods county who had the power to wheedle his way into Etta Mae's heart, arrest and remove Mr. Pickens from the arms of his family and totally disrupt my sleep.

Chapter 40

My anxiety hadn't lessened during the night. In fact, by morning, it was worse. My overriding concern at the moment was for Etta Mae: had she gotten home all right, had the sheriff been a gentleman, what was his attitude toward snakes, had she put him in a good mood, although not *too* good, before he interviewed Mr. Pickens this morning?

As nine o'clock approached, Mr. Pickens took first place on my hit parade of worries. I was tempted to go over there and sit in on the interview if they'd let me. And if they wouldn't, I'd be there to comfort Hazel Marie if Mr. Pickens was led away.

"Lillian," I said, as I paced the kitchen floor, "I can't stand this. I thought Etta Mae would call and let me know how the evening went, but she's at work now so I hesitate to call her. And I'm so distraught over Mr. Pickens, I don't know what to do."

"You done had four cups of coffee. It's no wonder you so antsy. Jus' set yourself down an' wait till somebody lets you know something."

"Easier said than done." But I did as she told me and sat down, only to begin drumming my fingers on the table. The noises of the work crews didn't help my nerves, other than to reassure me that work was progressing. Adam and Josh had come in earlier and were putting the finishing touches on the room upstairs, and before I could find any peace the carpet men were knocking on the door, ready to install carpet in the new bedroom.

Adam came down, tapped on the kitchen door, and asked if I had anything for them to do while the carpet was being laid.

"We'll move furniture in when they finish," he told me, but I reminded him that the paperhanger had to have room to work, so we couldn't move all of it.

I walked through the house with him, pointing out which pieces could go upstairs, some stacked in the middle of Hazel Marie's former bedroom, but most of them in the hall that had been cleared of Sam's office furniture. Eventually, all the furniture from what had been our bedroom downstairs would go into the new bedroom upstairs, which meant we'd finally have the living and dining rooms back to normal.

Adam nodded agreement to everything I said, but he didn't have much to say for himself. He seemed, in fact, morose and heavy laden, which I put down to an overactive conscience about avoiding work for Agnes Whitman—lying to her, he would call it, while I would term it finishing the job he started for me.

"At least," I said, "we'll have room to walk when part of this is upstairs." I was trying to carry on with Adam as if I'd noticed nothing wrong, then I nearly tripped again over that old Oriental that was still rolled up in the hall. "This thing is going to break my neck. It needs to go to the cleaners so I can give it away." Maybe Hazel Marie could use it at her house as a memento, so to speak, of the night her babies were born.

❧

Sam called just as I got back to the kitchen to remind me that he'd be home Tuesday, as if I hadn't been counting the days. The thought of his being home lifted my spirits, although I had to hold my tongue in order not to tell him that Mr. Pickens was being officially interviewed even as we spoke, and who knew what would happen after that?

"I be glad when he come home," Lillian said as she went into the pantry to get a broom. "Maybe he calm you down."

"I'll calm down when this mess is over. Of course, having him home will help, but I'm hoping it'll be over by the time he gets here."

She just shook her head and started out with the broom. "Gotta sweep off that front porch," she said. "An' run the vacuum in the front room. Them men tracking dirt all over the house."

So nine-thirty came and went with no word from Hazel Marie, then ten, then ten-fifteen, and it was all I could do not to pick up the phone or else dash over there to find out for myself.

At ten-twenty the phone rang and I nearly killed myself getting to it.

"Miss Julia!" Hazel Marie wailed as I thought my heart would stop. Images of Mr. Pickens being led away in handcuffs flashed through my mind.

"Oh, Hazel Marie, what happened?"

"You won't *believe* what J.D. just did."

"What? What did he do? Has he been arrested?"

"No! He's fine, but he invited Sheriff McAfee to supper *to-night*, and James is gone and I can't cook and the babies are crying and I'm at my wit's end! I can't believe he'd do such a thing!"

"Wait, wait, Hazel Marie. Slow down and tell me what happened."

She took a deep breath and tried to pull herself together. "Well, you know the sheriff came to interview J.D. at nine this morning—."

"Yes, I know, I know. But how did it go? Did he believe Mr. Pickens?"

"I guess, 'cause they're in there talking about fishing and hunting and I don't know what all. I just left after J.D. asked him to supper, because I nearly fainted when he did it."

"Well, but you were in the room when the interview was going on? How did it go? Was the sheriff upset?"

"Oh, it went fine," she said, passing it off as if the interview hadn't been a source of anxiety to us all for days on end. "I told J.D. he ought to stay in bed. I had him propped up with pillows, and I put all his medications on the bedside table so the sheriff could see how sick he is, and I told him not to shave or comb his hair. You know, so he'd look like he was too sick to be moved. If the sheriff wanted to move him, I mean."

"Good thinking, Hazel Marie," I said, pleased that she'd had that much forethought. And even more pleased that Mr. Pickens had followed through, which meant that he'd been more concerned about a possible arrest than he'd let on. Mr. Pickens wouldn't do anything he didn't want to do or that he didn't see the need to do.

"All right," I went on, "so the interview is over and they're just chatting? That's reassuring but, Hazel Marie, you must have a long talk with your husband when this is over. He should never issue an invitation before talking it over with you. But where is James? Why can't he fix supper?"

"J.D. did that, too!" Hazel Marie's voice was showing the strain as it went up an octave. "He gave James a long weekend off to go to a homecoming at his family's church. In South Carolina! So he's gone and I'll be all by myself in that kitchen!"

"You really need to have a talk with your husband," I repeated, but what was done was done and no amount of talking would help the current situation. "Maybe we could ask Lillian."

"Oh, *would* you? She would save my life, Miss Julia, because it's either that or hot dogs, which is the only thing I can cook without ruining. Or maybe peanut butter and jelly sandwiches." She stopped, seemed to consider the matter, then went on. "Any other time, I'd get J.D. to grill something outside because I can bake potatoes and make a salad, but I don't think it'd look too good for him to get out of his sick bed and cook. Do you?"

"No, that wouldn't do," I agreed. "He needs to limp around as long as the sheriff is there, maybe even have his dinner on a tray in bed. But listen, Hazel Marie, I'll see what Lillian says. But you need to speak to her, too. If she can do it, you should plan the meal, let her know what you want."

"Anything, anything," Hazel Marie cried. "Whatever she wants to cook will be fine. Tell her I'll pay her double, triple, anything she wants, because who knows but that sheriff could have a change of heart and take J.D. with him."

Well, I didn't think that was likely, because if Sheriff McAfee had arresting on his mind, he wouldn't hang around to see what kind of supper he'd get. Still, I could understand Hazel Marie's concern. No woman wants to make a poor showing at her dinner table.

"Here's Lillian now," I said as Lillian came into the kitchen to put up the broom. "I'll see what she says."

I covered the phone and explained Hazel Marie's problem to Lillian. "So she wants to know if you'd be available to fix supper at her house tonight. If you can't do it, Lillian, just say so. She can order out. Get pizza or something."

"Law, no!" Lillian was horrified. "That ole sheriff might take Mr. Pickens off an' we never see him again. Tell her I be glad to do it, 'specially since Latisha spendin' the night with a little friend. Oh, an' tell her what we got a whole lot of in the freezer."

"Chicken!" I said. "That's perfect. Hazel Marie," I went on, turning back to the phone. "You think the sheriff would like fried chicken?"

"He better, 'cause *I* would."

"Good, and don't worry about side dishes. Lillian will know what to fix, maybe some corn and a few other things. You go ahead and set the table—that's all you need to do. Well, except see to the babies."

"Oh, I can't tell you what a load is off my mind. But, Miss Julia, would you come, too? I think it'd be a whole lot easier if there were other people around the table. You know, to make conversation."

"Why, yes, I could do that." And, I thought, find out at the same time what went on during that interview and hope to goodness that Etta Mae had deflected the sheriff's interest away from anything I might've done in his jurisdiction. "And here's another thought, Hazel Marie, why don't you ask Etta Mae, too? If she says no, then we'll know their date last night didn't go too well.

But if it went okay, then he'll be too taken up with her to give Mr. Pickens much thought." Or anybody else.

"That's a wonderful idea," Hazel Marie said. "I'll do that right now. And tell Lillian I love her to death for doing this. Tell her I'll dance at her wedding."

After hanging up, I told Lillian what she'd said.

"Huh," Lillian said, smiling in spite of herself, as she wiped off a counter, "that be a long time comin', 'cause I don't have no more marryin' on my mind."

I sat down and started making out a grocery list while Lillian took the frozen chicken out of the freezer, then began mumbling as she rummaged through the kitchen cabinets.

"Wonder she got flour," Lillian said, talking mostly to herself. "She got to have salt an' pepper. Miss Julia, what all she got in her kitchen? Do you know?"

"I wouldn't count on her having everything you'll need. Although surely James has the kitchen fairly well stocked with the basics."

"Huh," she mumbled, putting a jar of paprika on the counter. "Maybe. An' maybe not." She began bagging the odds and ends that she would take to Hazel Marie's house. "If you got that list ready, I'll go on to the store."

"It's ready except we need to think of something for dessert. What would be quick and easy to fix? You don't have enough time to make anything fancy."

Lillian studied it for a minute, then said, "I got a pound cake in the freezer. What about if I toast some slices, put ice cream on 'em an' some chocolate syrup on top of that?"

"Perfect. This is all so last-minute that nobody could expect an elaborate meal. Besides, that sheriff should count himself lucky to get anything." I jotted down ice cream and chocolate syrup, then handed the list to her. "Now, Lillian, I want you to make time to put your feet up and rest—you can't work from sunup to sundown without a rest. And if you get over there and find you need something, call me. I'll run to the store for you or bring it from here, whichever."

After we loaded her car and she got off, I returned to the kitchen and heated up my fifth cup of coffee. I didn't know what I'd do for the rest of the day, relegated as I was to the only room in the house where I wouldn't be underfoot of the workmen. And without Lillian to talk to.

But at least my worries about Mr. Pickens's fate had been eased. Sheriff Ardis McAfee surely would not have the gall to sit at his table, then arrest him. I decided that all my fretting over the sheriff's intentions had been for naught and that I could enjoy my first worry-free day in some time. And I continued to feel that way until Hazel Marie called again.

Chapter 41

"*Miss Julia!*" Hazel Marie wailed. "You won't believe what he's done now!"

"What! Who! Mr. Pickens?"

"No, that sheriff!"

"Oh, my Lord, has he changed his mind?" That would teach me not to let my guard down—you can never tell what will happen when you stop worrying and begin thinking that all is well.

"No, that's not it," Hazel Marie said, as if she had to think it over. "I don't think he changed his mind exactly. It was more like he just thought of it."

"What, for goodness sake?"

"Well, see, he just called and, I give him credit, because he called me and not J.D. He asked if it'd be all right to bring his niece to supper tonight."

"Oh," I said, relief flooding through me. Although asking to bring an extra to a dinner party indicated a certain lapse of etiquette, it wasn't as bad as I'd feared. "Of course, upsetting a hostess's table placement is something you and I would never do, Hazel Marie, but I guess we can understand. I got the feeling when he mentioned her to Etta Mae and me that she'd been out of touch with her family, so maybe he's trying to remedy that. And, of course, he won't be in town long—at least I hope he won't—so I expect he wants to see as much of her as he can."

"I guess so," Hazel Marie agreed, "but I just got the table set and now I'll have to rearrange everything. Thank goodness, Lloyd's here and not playing tennis. He's sweeping the front porch and the walk for me. But the babies are so fussy today, I had to give them to J.D. just to get anything done at all."

"Were you able to reach Etta Mae? Is she coming?" I crossed my fingers, hoping she'd be there to keep Sheriff McAfee's mind off enforcing the law.

"Oh, yes, and I'm so glad she is. She sounded thrilled to be asked. I tell you what, Miss Julia, I think she really likes him."

That was one thing, then, that I didn't have to worry about, but on the other hand, it opened up a whole new can of worms. Or snakes, as the case might be.

"And," Hazel Marie went on, "Lillian is here, and I am just so grateful to her. And to you, too. Oh, my goodness, I've got to go. J.D.'s calling me. He has *got* to learn to change diapers."

Well, I thought, smiling as I hung up the phone, lots of luck with that.

I spent the rest of the afternoon thinking up things for Adam and Josh to do, learning at the same time that the two of them were the handiest of men. Adam fretted that I was making work for them, feeling that he was taking ill-gotten gains just so he could honestly tell Agnes Whitman that he hadn't finished at my house.

But it was the truth, because there were any number of things to be repaired, touched up with paint or cleaned out. My gutters, for instance. And a crack in the plaster in the hall. The longer I looked around the house, the more I found for them to do. In fact, I told Adam that if he wanted to fill his Saturday—in case Agnes called him again—the outside of the house could use a pressure washing.

As the morning neared eleven o'clock, there was a noticeable diminishment of noise around the house. I had quickly learned that workmen start their days so early that lunchtime for them is an hour before a normal person would eat. Some of them left to go to a local diner, but others—mainly the bricklayers—brought their own lunches. I glanced out the kitchen window and saw three of them sitting in the shade of the arbor, opening brown paper bags. Then I saw Adam and Josh walk over to a garden bench on the other side of the lawn and begin unwrapping sandwiches from their lunch boxes.

Interesting that they did not join the bricklayers, but I supposed that there was a hierarchy among working men.

So I thought I might as well eat, too, and looked in the refrigerator for sandwich makings. I'd just smoothed a layer of mayonnaise on two slices of bread when the front doorbell rang.

"Now what?" I wondered, and put away the mayonnaise before going to answer the door.

"Mrs. Murdoch," Tucker Caldwell pronounced, as if I didn't know who I was. "I've come to see how the work is progressing."

I was so taken aback at what he'd added to his appearance that it took me a minute to respond. I stood there, holding the door open and staring at the dapperly dressed little man, bow tie and all, while focusing on the gold stud stuck below his lower lip, making a matched set with the two in his ear.

"All right," I said, cleared my throat and stepped back. "Yes, come in. The men are taking a break for lunch, but several . . ." I had started to say, "are in the backyard," but amended it to, "have gone out to eat."

He nodded smartly, then marched past me and headed for the new library. I followed, noticing again his firm way of walking and his rigid posture—a man in control. Or trying to be.

Tucker stood in the middle of the library, looked around, touched a few seams in the paneling, then pursed his mouth. "I'll speak to the foreman about a few things. Nothing for you to worry about. I'll handle it. Now, Mrs. Murdoch," he turned on me so swiftly that I stepped back. "We have to come to an understanding about Adam Waites. He was supposed to be through here two days ago, and I know that you have him doing odd jobs just to keep him on. He is holding up everything at Mrs. Whitman's, and I tell you frankly that she is not a patient woman."

By this time, I'd regained my composure and added a little outrage. "And just what does Mrs. Whitman's lack of self-control have to do with me?"

He heaved a deep breath, as if exasperated beyond belief. "You are keeping him from an excellent job, one that will pay him well. He's too timid to tell you he needs to get out of here and move on. You'll have to do it. Tell him that she is expecting him today. This afternoon, in fact."

My posture suddenly got as good as his. "I certainly will not. Adam is fully employed here for as long as he wants to be. And I'll tell you another thing." I took one of those deep breaths. "I resent Agnes Whitman's domineering attitude. Who is she, or *you*, to tell me what to do? I resent your interference in this matter, Mr. Caldwell. It's none of your business. And here's something else that neither you nor Agnes seems to have considered: maybe he doesn't *want* to work for her. So while you're transmitting orders from her to me, here's one you can carry back to her: hire somebody else."

"*Well!*" he said, drawing himself up as far as he could, which wasn't far. "Well, I'm not sure you and I can work together under these circumstances."

"You better be sure, and you better see that this work is done as it should be, or I will not hesitate to see my attorney. Now, Mr. Caldwell, you have had your mind more on Mrs. Whitman's project than on mine from the start. If you are determined to put her work ahead of mine, just say so and I'll sue your little pants off."

"Oh, well," he said, losing a good deal of the steam he'd started with. "We don't want to go that far. Of course I'll finish this job, and to your complete satisfaction. There's no need to be thinking of lawsuits. I was, ah, just passing along Mrs. Whitman's concern."

"Well, stop passing it. Every time I turn around somebody is passing along something from Agnes Whitman and I'm tired of it. Tell her to get down off her high horse and stand in line like everybody else."

He patted the air in a futile effort to calm me down. "I didn't mean to upset you. Sometimes I let my passion run ahead of me. Agnes, I mean, Mrs. Whitman, is deeply concerned about Adam. As am I. She is helping him work through some spiritual matters. She's a minister, you know, and she's leading him into new ways of connecting with the spiritual world. Old ways, actually, but they're new to him. It would be detrimental to his journey toward unification for you to interfere with his progress." He leaned toward me, as if to pass along something in confidence. "He is a seeker, you know."

"I *figured!*" I all but yelled. "Listen, you haven't *seen* interference, now that I know what you're really doing. And I'll tell you this, Adam is not seeking anything. He's already found it. And another thing," I went on as I waved my hands in the air, "sticking studs all over your face is about the silliest thing I've ever seen in a professional man. *Un*stud them when you come back to my house. If you come back. And if I let you in."

He could barely leave quickly enough, red faced and muttering apologies or arguments—I couldn't tell which—as he hightailed it out the door.

So, I thought, as I shut the door behind him, I may have lost an architect along with my temper, but I wasn't about to stand still for a lecture from a bossy little man who needed a little correction himself. Although my hands were still shaking from my outburst, I didn't regret a word I'd said and went back to finish making a sandwich before the bread dried out.

Chapter 42

Poor Adam, I thought as I sliced roast beef for my sandwich, coming close to slicing my hand as well. No wonder he'd been moping around, what with that woman and Tucker Caldwell, too, undermining his childlike faith, which is exactly the kind we're supposed to have.

I stopped with a lettuce leaf dripping in my hand as it came to me that there'd been a noticeable lack of singing around the house in the past few days. Those two must have really gotten to him. I sat down with my sandwich and a glass of tea, the words of an old hymn running through my mind: "Rescue the perishing . . . Lift up the fallen," or something like that, and began wondering what I could say or do to counteract the pressure they were putting on him. At least, I reminded myself, Adam might be naive and unworldly, but so far he'd withstood having his chin pierced, unlike another I could name.

As the afternoon wore on toward the time to dress for Hazel Marie's dinner party, I was still dithering over what to wear, mainly because I couldn't get to anything without running into somebody in overalls. By that time, the sky had begun to darken, so much so that I went around turning on lamps. Then the wind picked up, scattering petals across the lawn as thunder rumbled in the distance. The brickmasons started covering the half-finished chimney with a tarp, then they gathered their things and piled—three and four at a time—into the cabs of their pickups. And off they went.

Adam and Josh had been tying up the wisteria vine on the arbor, and they hurried in, ready to leave, as well.

"Comin' up a cloud," Adam said, just as a streak of lightning seemed to hit nearby. We all flinched, then tried to pretend we hadn't. Rain began pelting down as the wind blew it in sheets across Polk Street.

Adam handed me their hours and I sat at the desk to write the checks. "Wait till it slacks off," I said. "You don't want to go out in this."

"I sure don't," Josh said, which may have been the only words I'd ever heard him say.

The lights in the house flickered on and off, and as I glanced out the window, I saw hail bouncing on the lawn and power lines swaying in the wind. Lightning continued to flash and crackle overhead. Josh and Adam sat gingerly on my Duncan Phyfe sofa, but only after I insisted they do so. I didn't want them to be driving in such a storm, and, well, I didn't want to be alone in the house.

We sat without speaking waiting out the storm, and gradually the hail stopped and the wind died down to the occasional gust. Rain continued to come down so heavily that I could hardly see the church across the street.

Just as the worst of the storm seemed to have moved past, the telephone rang. I looked at the set on the desk, not wanting to touch it for fear that lightning would strike a pole somewhere and run down the line to knock me off my chair. But it continued to ring, so I did, especially since Josh seemed to be wondering if I was deaf.

"*Miss Julia!*" Lillian yelled. "A tree jus' fell on the house! It come right down on Mr. Sam's house!"

I thought my heart had stopped. "Who's hurt? Anybody hurt? The babies? Is Lloyd all right? Tell me, Lillian. How bad is it?"

"It's bad," she said, her breath coming in gasps. "That big ole tree in the backyard jus' split in two, an' half of it come crashin' 'cross the corner of the house! Right there in the back. It sound like Judgment Day a-comin'!"

My Lord, that was the corner where Hazel Marie's bedroom was, right where Mr. Pickens was laid up in bed.

"Call an ambulance, Lillian! Get some help. I'm coming over."

"No'm, you don't have to. Everybody all right, 'cept the back bedroom upstairs. Tree branches stickin' through the roof an' rain pourin' in like sixty up there, an' both babies cryin' their eyes out, an' Miss Hazel Marie runnin' 'round lookin' for pots an' buckets, an' Mr. Pickens, he crippin' 'round givin' orders, an' . . ." She stopped to catch her breath.

"And Lloyd?" I asked, gripping the phone. "Where's Lloyd?"

"He tryin' to mop up water 'fore it come through the ceiling, but it doin' it anyway."

"And you, are you all right? Nobody's hurt?"

"No'm, 'cept I almost burnt the last batch of chicken, an' we got comp'ny comin' pretty soon."

"I'll be there in a few minutes. I'm bringing help." Turning from the phone, I said, "Adam, Josh, we have a problem."

❧

We left in an international convoy—me in a German sedan, Adam in a Japanese pickup with a camper shell on the back, and Josh bringing up the rear in an American, partly made-in-Mexico pickup. Rain or water dripping from trees or maybe both was still falling, steam rose up from the wet streets, and the neighborhood looked ghostly in the murky light. I parked at the curb in front of Sam's house, jumped out struggling with an umbrella, and waved to Adam to turn into the driveway. Josh followed him in, and both trucks pulled in toward the back.

I hurried around the house, looking up toward the back where it seemed a tree was growing out of the roof. Just as I reached Adam and Josh, who were out of their trucks surveying the damage, we heard the growling throb of a heavy motor.

I peeked around the edge of the house and saw another pickup—a big one—pull to the curb. Sheriff Ardis McAfee, dressed in his Sunday clothes—jeans, boots, white shirt with a string tie, and that black sports jacket—climbed out. He adjusted his hat, then walked around and opened the passenger door. A young woman in a green raincoat—the niece, I surmised— hopped out, and another young woman—Etta Mae in a low-cut dress—was lifted out by the sheriff. I saw the flash of her teeth as she smiled up at him. They headed for the front porch, and I turned back to Adam. I didn't have time for greetings.

"What do you think, Adam?" I asked, wondering if we should call some kind of emergency workers, although I didn't know who they would be.

"That's a big 'un, all right," he said. "Look, it split right in two." He pointed at half the huge hemlock that was still standing. "It'll have to come down, too, but you can do that later. Josh, get the ladders and all the rope you got. You got your chain saw?"

"Yep," Josh said, and the two of them hopped up into their camper shells and began pulling out the tools they'd need.

Then everybody—Lillian holding one twin baby, Hazel Marie with the other one, Lloyd, Mr. Pickens leaning on a cane, Etta Mae, Sheriff McAfee, but not the niece—came pouring out of the back door and stood on the porch, watching.

The sheriff kept on coming, walking straight up to me with his hand out. "Ardis McAfee, Mrs. Murdoch," he said. "Looks like we got a problem here."

"It sure does." I shook his hand, introduced him to Adam and Josh, then, lying through my teeth, said, "It's nice to see you again, Sheriff."

"Ardis."

I nodded, then stepped back, hoping to avoid any further conversation lest he bring up some archaic penalty for impersonating a hospital employee.

The sheriff cocked his head this way and that, studying the lay of the land, or rather the lay of the tree. "Boys," he said to the two brothers, "if you don't mind a little help, we gonna need more rope than that. Hold on, I got some in my toolbox." And off he took in a loping run to his truck, coming back with a thick coil of rope.

I declare, I've never seen the like of what those three did. They threw a couple of ropes up over limbs still attached to the hemlock, making, it seemed, some sort of pulley that Josh was to handle from the ground. Then Ardis, after removing his tie and jacket, and Adam climbed the ladder to the roof. Each had a power saw tied by a short rope to his belt, so that the saw swung free but was close to hand.

Lloyd came out in the yard to watch. With a worried frown, he said, "I hope those saws don't have automatic starters. Somebody could lose something."

Etta Mae, joining us, looked up at the men with dangling power saws, and said, "Don't even think that."

We were craning our necks to watch, and were soon reassured by seeing Ardis wrap the end of a pulley rope around a branch, pull a cord to start his saw, zip through the branch and let it fall free as Josh, at the other end of the rope, eased it gently to the ground. Adam followed suit, and within thirty minutes all the branches were piled on the ground, leaving only the large chunk of the tree trunk leaning against the house.

Adam called to Josh to bring a tarp and a couple of staple guns, and before long the gaping hole in the roof was covered. The two men came down the ladder and, with Josh's help, pushed the remaining part of the trunk off the house. It fell with a heavy thump to the ground, where it would stay until we could get someone to clear the yard.

"Boy, that was something to see!" Lloyd said, admiration lighting up his face as the men, covered with wet leaves and sawdust, joined us.

"It really was," Etta Mae agreed, but her admiration was for only one of the men.

Ardis McAfee smiled and winked at her as he passed on his way to the porch to speak to Mr. Pickens. "That'll hold 'er for a while," he said, indicating their Band-Aid approach to roof repair, "but you gonna need some carpenters and a roofer out here pretty quick."

"Soon as I can find somebody," Mr. Pickens said, while I jabbed the air, pointing toward Adam, who was loading up his truck. "Can't thank you enough, Ardis. I count myself lucky for getting shot in your jurisdiction."

"I been around some," Ardis said, modestly. Then cocking his head in the direction of Adam and Josh, went on. "Them two boys know what they're doin'."

So Mr. Pickens, with Hazel Marie cautioning him about doing too much, limped out to talk with Adam.

Lillian stuck her head out the back door and called, "Supper's ready. Y'all better come on."

Adam began shaking his head, as I issued a specific invitation to the table. "You most certainly are going to stay for supper," I said. "Now go on in and clean up as much as you can. Giving you supper is the least we can do, although of course we'll pay you, so you can't say no." Then when he looked up and saw Josh stepping up on the porch and going through the door, there wasn't much he could do but follow.

We all trooped inside, the babies crowing at the entertainment and Mr. Pickens still looking somewhat chagrined at not being able to climb a ladder to mend his own house. Men yearn to cut things, especially if a howling chain saw is involved.

I took the baby from Lillian so she could begin dipping up food, and Hazel Marie gave hers to Etta Mae.

Hazel Marie had not regained her color from the fright they'd had. She was still shaky and as white as a sheet, but still able to twitter around, thanking the good Samaritans who'd appeared almost out of the blue. She pointed the men to the downstairs bathroom, then said, "Almost every towel in the house is upstairs sopping up water. Etta Mae, would you mind taking some dish towels to them to dry off with?" Then she turned to me. "This'll be the third time today I've set the table, but, oh, I am so thankful you had somebody to help us. I've never been so scared in my life."

After we had unset the table, put another leaf in, then reset the table, people were crowding around, ready to eat fried chicken, creamed corn and all the other good things, including her world-famous biscuits, which Lillian was placing on the sideboard.

Hazel Marie put the babies in their little carriers and placed them in a corner out of the way, then told everybody to sit wherever they wanted. We began lining up with our plates at the buffet when Hazel Marie's country raising came to the fore. She arranged for the men to go first.

As I stood next to her at the end of the line, I glanced through the arch into the living room and saw the sheriff's niece put down a magazine and rise from the sofa to join us. And what I saw of her made my teeth hurt and my skin crawl.

Chapter 43

Her skin—what I could see of it, except her face—was absolutely covered in bold, graphic designs that swirled and blended into one another. If she'd been a wall, deputies would've been out looking for a spray painter.

"Y'all," Sheriff McAfee said as the young woman walked into the dining room, "this is Nellie McAfee, also known as Cheyenne. At least, locally. Come on, honey, and get you a plate."

I stared, then quickly turned away, wondering if I'd be able to eat with my stomach knotting up like it was doing. She had, of course, removed her raincoat, although she'd have been better off to have left it on. The white sleeveless, low-cut dress she was wearing served only to make the red and blue tattoos on her arms, across her shoulders and down on her chest stand out more starkly. The designs were so thick it took me a minute to focus on the swirling patterns that were filled in with different colors. There were flowers—roses, I thought—blooming on each shoulder, and leaves on a vine that climbed each arm, and like an optical illusion, little animal faces gradually appeared to peek out from behind a scroll. When she turned toward the sideboard, I was able to make out the head of a unicorn on her back.

As my eyes traveled over her ornately covered torso, they finally landed on her clear and pretty face. With a jolt of recognition, I realized that the sheriff's niece was the maid who'd directed me across the lawn at Agnes Whitman's garden party.

Right then, it all came together. That arrogant Whitman woman had had a hand in the desecration of this lovely girl, and would do the same, or worse, to Adam if she got her hands on him. And all in the name of religion. I felt sick to my stomach.

The only good thing I could say about Nellie—I refused to think of her as Cheyenne—was that her face was not ruined by piercings. She wore earrings, like most women, and though they were large hoops, they were no larger than I'd seen on more conservative types. I, for instance, was wearing my good pearl earrings—the plain ones, not the ones with diamonds—and so was Hazel Marie, although hers dangled a little. Etta Mae, I noticed, wore tiny gold hoops with small gold studs in the three holes where stars had once been.

But wouldn't you know it? By the time I'd filled my plate, the last empty chair was right across the table from Nellie. It was all I could do to keep my eyes aimed in any direction other than straight ahead.

Fairly soon, I realized that everybody else was having the same problem. Other eyes kept straying toward her, then quickly shifting away. None of it seemed to bother her. She had nothing to say for herself, attending only to her food and ignoring everybody else. Except Adam, who sat next to her. I saw her cut her eyes at him and give him a few shy smiles. He, on the other hand, seemed ill at ease, perhaps because he was eating with strangers, which can be hard on a shy person under the best of circumstances.

"Well, I come down here," Sheriff Ardis McAfee announced, "thinkin' I was gonna get me a first-class witness against that crew of thieves we arrested. An' all J.D. can tell me is that one of 'em had to relieve himself in the bushes. Beats all I ever heard."

It shocked me that the sheriff would bring up such an unsavory subject at the dinner table or, for that matter, anywhere in mixed company.

"Well," Mr. Pickens said, grinning, "I could've told you more if he hadn't shot me. I was getting close, too close as it turned out, but I never saw what they were trying to move out of that barn."

"You pretty much led us to 'em anyway," the sheriff said, giving Mr. Pickens some credit. "When those hunters told me where they'd found you, I knew there was an old barn back in there somewhere, and figured they had them a meth lab. But we scoped it out while you laid up in the hospital, and didn't see or smell any evidence. Figured then they were trying to move something they had stored there. We called in the ATF, and that was all she wrote."

"What was in the barn?" Lloyd asked, the very question I wanted answered, as well. "TVs and stuff they stole?"

"Cigarettes!" Ardis said. "Cartons and cartons of cigarettes, stacked to the roof." He started laughing. "Only problem was. . . well, except for a truck that wouldn't run, that barn leaked like a sieve. And we'd had us some downpours. Those cartons got soaked through, and if you've ever seen a wet cigarette, you know what a soggy mess they had on their hands. They couldn't of sold 'em even in New York City."

"And that young man Mr. Pickens was looking for," I asked, "was he part of it?" Although I was hesitant to draw the sheriff's attention my way, I spoke up for Mr. Pickens's sake, hoping he'd get paid for his efforts, pitiful though they'd been.

"Arrested him along with the rest of 'em," Ardis said, "but he's out now. He had a mama who went his bail."

Everyone at the table was fascinated with the tale of a police action against thieves, especially one involving Mr. Pickens. He, however, laughed off his part in finding and identifying the crooks, as well he should've, because he'd had to get shot to pinpoint their location.

Then, in spite of my effort to keep my eyes averted, I saw Nellie McAfee's ink-covered arm slide toward Adam, and, I declare, I do believe she laid a hand on him under the table. Her expression didn't change—she looked as innocent as one of Hazel Marie's babies. But Adam's eyes popped wide open. He almost choked as he shifted away from her.

I was astounded at her audacity—she was moving in on him,

254 Ann B. Ross

and right in public, too. Forwardness in a young woman is so un-
attractive. But it did make me reconsider the conclusions I'd previ-
ously jumped to. Maybe I'd been wrong all along about the source
of Adam's concerns. Maybe it wasn't Agnes Whitman who was
after him for religious purposes, but Cheynne McAfee for roman-
tic purposes.

Or who knew? Maybe it was both of them—each coming from
a different direction to snare him into whatever strange rituals
and ceremonies that were going on out at that Fairfields estate.
And I couldn't leave out the influence of that little pierced architect who'd taken it on himself to lecture me about Adam's spiritual welfare.

And I'll tell you the truth, I'd had enough lectures from Wesley
Lloyd Springer, the deceased husband I'd lived with for forty-
some-odd years, to last me a lifetime. Every time I thought of
Tucker Caldwell's nerve in berating me for standing in the way of
Adam's so-called spiritual growth, my blood pressure shot up a
mile.

But Sheriff McAfee continued to hold forth, telling in detail
about the confiscation of pounds and pounds of moldering tobacco.

And I'd thought he was the tall, silent type—he certainly
hadn't had much to say in Mill Run, West Virginia. But maybe it
was Etta Mae's admiring face turned up toward him that kept him
going on. Or the eager questions from Lloyd and Josh. Or Mr.
Pickens's leading comments that kept our guest talking.

Not wanting to draw the sheriff's attention to a certain escape
from hospital custody, I'd mostly kept quiet, hoping that Etta Mae
had put that little escapade in perspective for him. Still, there was
a matter for which I felt he needed to be held accountable.

So in a lull of the conversation, I ventured to ask, "You like
fried chicken, Sheriff?"

"Do I ever!" he said. "And this is about the best I ever had. You
folks know how to make real southern fried chicken."

"Etta Mae and I had some in Mill Run that was quite good, at
least while we were eating it. It didn't sit so well later on."

"Bet you had it at Bud's. Sometimes he uses his grease too long."

I put down my fork at the thought. "No, actually we had it at your church. Dinner on the grounds, you know."

"Well, I don't . . ."

Etta Mae jumped in. "Oh, I think we got the directions wrong, Miss Julia. We were at the wrong place, I'm pretty sure of it."

Uh-huh, I thought, pretty sure but not completely so. But I didn't pursue the matter because talk of religion, along with politics, were not suitable topics for a dinner table discussion. Such controversial subjects can upset one's digestion, you know, and mine was already upset enough by seeing what was going on across the table.

Little Miss McAfee quickly lifted her hand as Lillian, with Lloyd helping her, circled the table, removing our plates and beginning to serve dessert. Adam kept his eyes down, refusing to even glance to the side. Josh, however, was as avid a listener to the sheriff as Lloyd and as hearty an eater as Mr. Pickens.

"Well, I tell you," Ardis said, pushing his dessert plate away when he'd finished the pound cake and ice cream, "that was as good a meal as I ever had." He went on to thank Hazel Marie, who glowed under his compliments, and to praise Lillian to the skies. Then he tilted his chair back and proceeded to entertain us— feeling, perhaps, that as a guest, he was beholden for the meal he'd been served.

Lloyd got him started again by asking, "Have you always been a sheriff, Sheriff?"

"No, son, I was with the Charleston Po-lice for a few years, then decided I'd had enough of city life. So I moved to Mill Run, where the fishin's good, and got on with the Sheriff's Department as an investigator. Then when the old sheriff retired, I ran for the office, got voted in and been there ever since. But I tell you, boy, it was a wonder anybody ever voted for me, 'cause I got known as a joker. Couldn't help myself, 'cause if you can't laugh, you don't last long in law enforcement.

"I'll give you a for instance. Not long after I was hired on as a deputy, I got a call to an area on the outskirts of town about a big ole horse that was galloping loose up and down the road. This was in the middle of the night. Well, by the time I got there, a man in a pickup had stopped and caught it—and it was a big 'un, lemme tell you, some seventeen or so hands high, like one of them Budweiser horses you see at Christmas. And lying underneath it was this woman—looked like a witch with her hair stringing out everywhere—and she was too inebriated to crawl out from under. Come to find out, it was her horse. She'd been trying to get it home, but it had stepped on her foot, so she was laying there cryin' and carryin' on, with that horse still high steppin' around her. Well, I got the EMS guys out there and they dragged her out and got her to the hospital. Then a neighbor offered to keep the horse in his lot till somebody could come for it. And that was the end of it, until I got back in the squad car to let the sergeant know I was leaving the scene. When he asked how I'd handled it, I couldn't help myself. I told him, I said, 'Well, I got the woman taken care of, but I had to do something with the horse 'cause, you know, Sergeant, I couldn't just leave it runnin' loose. I had to do something. And with all that activity, it had gotten kinda skittish and was about to step on the reins that were trailin' on the ground. It took me the longest to grab the bridle, but I finally got it and led the horse over to my squad car, meanin' to bring it in to you. So I tied it to the rear bumper, and everything went real fine till I got up to about sixty. . .'"

We all burst out laughing, and even Adam, as miserable as he was looking, managed to laugh.

Chapter 44

"That reminds me," Mr. Pickens said, "of the time I was on the Charlotte-Meckleinburg force, working the third watch. It'd been a fairly quiet night, but cold, man, it was cold. So there I was coming out of a residential area, about to go up a ramp to I-77, when I saw a scraggly little kitten right on the curb. I stopped and picked it up, thinking I'd give it to one of the family guys when the watch was over. I swung back around and stopped at a McDonald's and got it some milk and a hamburger."

"I didn't know kittens ate hamburgers!" Lloyd said, laughing.

"This one did—it was about half starved. I told 'em to hold the ketchup and pickle, and I didn't give it much, afraid it'd get sick in the car. Anyway, after it ate, I let it wander around in the car and pretty soon it found a warm place under the passenger seat and, I guess, just went to sleep. Then I got busy and, to tell the truth, I pretty much forgot about it until I picked up a drunk who was walking along the interstate, weaving on and off the traffic lane. He was smelly and filthy, and, man, he was out of it. He kept mumbling about "ale-yuns," which I finally figured out meant *aliens,* who were pinching and scratching him and hovering around with blue lights flashing all over the place." Mr. Pickens stopped and laughed. "That was the light rack on my car, I guess. Anyway, I put him in the cage and headed for the city jail with him talkin' and mumblin', not knowing who or where he was. I wasn't paying much attention to him—he'd given me no trouble—and I was just cruisin' along, when all of a sudden he let out this blood-curdling yell that nearly gave me a heart attack. 'Git 'em off me!' he yelled. 'Help, po-lice, the ale-yuns is on me!' Well, I swung off the road, hopped out of the car and flung open the back door, thinking he was going crazy on me. And all it was was that little kitten had come flyin' up out of nowhere and landed in his lap. It had clawed its way up his chest and was licking his face and beard, looking for more food."

While we laughed, Mr. Pickens began his awkward rise from the table, carefully standing upright as he suggested we move to the living room. Hazel Marie and Etta Mae took the sleeping babies to their cribs, and Lloyd and I cleared the table, taking dishes into the kitchen. Lillian then shooed us out, saying that she could clean up better by herself.

When I got to the living room, I saw Josh talking with Ardis and Mr. Pickens, asking them about going to the police academy. Adam was fidgeting in a chair by the door, more than ready, it seemed to me, to leave. Little Miss McAfee had moved a chair next to his and was whispering to him. She was sitting demurely with her ankles crossed, and my eyes almost crossed when I saw that she had more tattoos on her feet and ankles. If the ones on her arms were called full sleeves, then I supposed she also had full socks.

I'd about had enough of tattoos and piercings and enticements designed to lure an unsuspecting young man into who knew what kind of freakish behavior—all in the name of a spiritual quest of some sort. Don't you just hate it when you've already said no, and people won't leave you alone?

Adam suddenly jumped to his feet. "We got to go, Josh. It's late, and we thank you for supper, but we got to go."

Mr. Pickens managed to rise again, shook Adam's hand and thanked him for his help. "If you and Josh can repair the roof, I'd sure like to see you out here bright and early tomorrow."

"Yessir, be glad to. Let's go, Josh."

As Josh disengaged himself from his intense conversation with Ardis, Lillian walked into the room. "Somebody's telephone ringin' its head off in a raincoat back there."

Nellie McAfee hopped up. "Must be mine. Don't leave yet, Adam, I'll be right back."

Mr. Pickens walked Adam and Josh out into the hall, discussing what would be needed to repair the roof. Adam seemed intent on getting out the door before Nellie returned, but he didn't quite make it. She came running back, calling to him.

"That was Agnes," she said, almost gasping. Addressing Adam and ignoring everybody else, she went on, "There's a power line down at her place and she's been calling everywhere, looking for you. She wants you tonight, right away, because she's been without power for hours and the generator won't start. You have to go, Adam, she really needs you." Then turning to the sheriff as she slipped into her raincoat, she said, "No need for you to drive all the way out there, Uncle Ardis. I'll ride with Adam."

There was nothing Adam could do but agree to go to the Whitman place and take Nellie with him. It wasn't in him to refuse help to someone in need, although I wondered how dire the need actually was and also wondered why Agnes didn't have enough help already. There had been at least two decorated, yet able-bodied, young men at the garden party. Was this sudden after-hours need of help designed to entangle Adam even further?

While good-byes were being said, Adam walked out onto the porch and I followed. It was hardly late, for a dusky light lingered across the wet grass of the lawn and steam from the street blended with the evening mist.

"Adam," I said, lowering my voice, "you don't have to go if you don't want to. Just because somebody calls doesn't mean you have to answer."

He gave me a bleak look, then shook his head. "It'll be all right, I guess."

"I'm not so sure about that, but what you have to do is put on the whole armor of God and call me if you need me."

I didn't know what I could do if he did call, but I could certainly try something. He was wrestling, it seemed to me, with spiritual wickedness in high places and he was no match for it.

Why he couldn't just turn her down, I didn't know or understand, unless he had such a strong work ethic that he couldn't refuse to get an ox out of a ditch, regardless of who the ox belonged to. I just didn't think Agnes Whitman needed help, or if she did, why she couldn't find it closer to hand.

I stood on the porch and watched the three of them walk out to the driveway. Adam spoke to Josh, while Nellie waited impatiently beside Adam's pickup. Then Josh got in his truck and left, apparently having been sent on home. Adam and Nellie got in his truck and turned in the opposite direction toward Fairfields.

I hoped she'd keep her hands to herself while he was driving.

"What was that?" Mr. Pickens was standing next to me, watching his guests leave.

I realized that I had murmured my concern aloud. "Oh, nothing. Just wondering if Miss McAfee is quite the demure little thing that she appears to be."

"Nope," he said with a wry grin. "Tattoos make a statement, and anybody with that many is making a loud one."

"I don't understand why anyone would want them," I said, noticing that we were the only ones still on the porch.

He shrugged as if he didn't know, either. "Lot of people have them—one or two, maybe. I've got one on my arm."

"You do?"

"Yeah, got it when I was runnin' wild and didn't know any better. But these days, even a lot of women wear ink, kinda as beauty marks, I guess, like flowers or hearts or something. Nothing like Miss McAfee's, though."

"Well, in my opinion, hers aren't beauty marks," I said. "I understand that she's involved with some kind of religious group that encourages subduing the flesh in order to strengthen the spirit."

"Huh," he said. Then turning to go back inside, he said, "From the way that girl looks, her spirit must be pretty strong by now."

"That's what I'm afraid of." I followed him toward the door, then touched his arm. "Mr. Pickens, if Adam doesn't show up in the morning to fix your roof, give me a call."

He gave me a quick grin as he opened the screen door, motioning me inside. "Think she'll keep him overnight?"

"I wouldn't put it past her," I said as I walked in past him. "Or Agnes Whitman, either."

Soon afterward, I made my excuses and left early so I could get home before full dark. Mr. Pickens and the sheriff had settled in to swapping cop stories, as they called them, so Lloyd decided to stay on to hear them, which meant he'd stay the night.

✦

Lying in bed later, unable to sleep for wondering what was happening at the Whitman place, it suddenly occurred to me to also wonder why I was so exercised about Adam Waites's welfare. He was a nice young man, hardworking and dependable, but he was only a temporary employee. I'd had many of those over the years with never a thought of their personal lives or problems. They had come and gone and stayed out of my mind until I needed their particular expertise again.

What was it about Adam that so troubled my sleep? His apparent innocence about the ways of the world? Maybe, except he was a grown man and should be able to take care of himself. And if he could, why was I lying there with visions of circus women chasing him with needles and pins and plugs?

Nellie Cheyenne McAfee was one reason I was feeling so protective of him. She was the kind of woman that a man needed to build up to, not to have to tackle as his first experience. She'd be a handful for any man, even one who had a tolerance for bold women.

But here was a thought: maybe Adam wasn't very bright, although if true, being backward certainly hadn't prevented him from learning his trade.

"Oh, Sam," I whispered, "I wish you were here."

✦

When the phone rang, it jerked me out of a deep sleep and for a second I was so disoriented I nearly knocked the lamp off the table.

"Yes? Hello?" My heart was thumping away for fear that something was wrong somewhere—was it Sam? Lloyd? The babies? Another tree across the house? When the phone rings at one-thirty in the morning, you can be fairly sure it is not a social call.

"Um, uh, Miz Murdoch?" It was a man's voice, but not one I recognized.

"Who is this?" I demanded, still afraid of hearing bad news. "Who's calling this time of night?"

"Uh, it's me. You said, uh, I could call, so . . ." The words were slurred and mumbled, trailing off into moaning incoherence.

"*Adam?*" My hand tightened on the receiver. "Is that you, Adam?" It didn't sound like him. It sounded like somebody in pain.

"Yesh, ma'am. M'truck's gone." More mumbling and a few gasping breaths ending with ". . . need to go home."

"Speak up. I can't understand you."

"Hate to ask," he said, fairly clearly, then fell to mumbling again, ". . . get home."

"Where are you?" I said it loudly and forcefully, as if that would shake some information out of him.

"Agnesh's." There was a beep on the line, then a click, then nothing.

"Adam! Are you there? Speak to me."

I heard a hum on the line, then his voice came through with one word: "dyin'."

Good Lord! I sprang out of bed, still clutching the phone and calling to him. The line was dead or he was, one. Jerking open the drawer of the bedside table, I rummaged around for the phone book. I'd call Agnes Whitman and tell her. . . well, I didn't know what I'd tell her. But she could start looking for Adam and get him some help. But there was no phone book, and no wonder, with the house as torn up as it was.

I dialed information and was told that the Whitman number was unlisted.

"*Unlisted!* But this is an emergency!" It did no good, for you can't argue or plead with a robotic voice.

I began dressing, my mind running over possibilities, the first of which was who I could call for help. Adam's father? No, or Adam would've called him instead of me. Mr. Pickens was out. He could barely get around his own house, much less run around the countryside looking for a dying man. I thought of calling Coleman or 911, but what could I tell them? That I'd gotten a strange phone call from a man who was either half dead or already there?

If his truck was gone, he could be stranded on the side of the road somewhere between Fairfields and his home. But no, Adam had said he was at Agnes's, or that's what it sounded like.

Then I thought of Sheriff McAfee. He'd know something of Agnes Whitman from his niece, and if I'd read him right, he'd not been all that enthusiastic about Nellie's association with her. Which was ironic, considering his association with snakes. Talk about a pot calling a kettle black.

But if nothing else, Sheriff McAfee could start with Nellie—wake her if necessary—and track down Adam from the last time she'd seen him. I pulled on some low-heeled shoes, thinking I might have to walk all over creation to find him.

But where was the sheriff staying? A motel maybe, or perhaps an inn, of which there were any number in and around Abbotsville. Too many to call if Adam was in dire straits.

Etta Mae! I should have thought of her first. She'd know where the sheriff was, or if she didn't, she'd go with me. Because I was going, there being no way in the world I could ignore a cry for help.

Chapter 45

She didn't answer. I let it ring long enough to wake the dead if she'd been at home. *Cell phone!* I thought and hurried down the stairs to the kitchen, where the number was written on a pad, the rolled-up rug in the hall nearly tripping me on the way.

Picturing Adam lying in a ditch somewhere, breathing his last, I shouted, "Etta Mae!" when she answered her cell. "Where's the sheriff?"

"What? Our sheriff or the other one?"

"The other one, McAfee. Ardis, where is he? How can I get in touch with him?"

"Well, uh, he's right here. We're in his truck on our way home. What's going on?"

"Adam Waites just called and he's either sick or hurt or something. He sounded near death, Etta Mae, and I need some help finding him."

"Who's Adam Waites?"

"You know! One of the men who climbed on the roof and ate supper with us and went off with that pitiful-looking girl to the Whitman place. And he's still out there somewhere and she's the sheriff's niece so I figure he can get her to help us find him." I took a deep breath and tried to state my case calmly. "I wouldn't disturb him, Etta Mae, if I didn't feel that he's the most likely one to approach Nellie or Cheyenne or whoever she is and get some answers." I took another breath as panic swept over me again. "She may be the last person to see Adam alive. Will he do it, Etta Mae? Adam needs help!"

"Uh, well, wait just a minute." The phone went silent, then I heard some muffled sounds of movement and whispering.

"Miss Julia? Ardis says we'll swing by the Whitman place and he'll talk to Nellie. Will that be all right?"

"Yes, yes, that'll be perfect. But I'm going, too. I'll either drive or go with you, whichever is easier."

"We're just leaving Asheville, so it's easier for us to go directly to Fairfields. But you stay home, Miss Julia. Let Ardis handle it, he knows what to do."

Well, so did I, which was to find Adam and get him home. So I didn't agree or disagree, just urged her to hurry, hung up the phone, grabbed my pocketbook, and went stumbling out the back door in the dark. Then turned around and went back inside, thinking *cell phone* again. Lloyd had mine charging on the kitchen counter, bless his heart, so I stuffed it in my pocketbook and hurried outside to the car, congratulating myself for thinking of it.

Heat lightning flickered around as I got in the car, and thunder rumbled off in the distance. Typical summer weather, I reassured myself, and merely the back end of the line of thunderstorms that had come through earlier. Nonetheless, I turned on my heel and ran back to the house, snatching up the yellow slicker and hat that Lillian kept on a hook by the door.

Surely by this time, I had everything needed to conduct a search if that was what I had to do. I couldn't understand why Adam hadn't turned to the people at the Whitman place or why they had not come to his aid. Something had gone on, or was still going on, out there that made Adam seek aid from an outside source—namely, me. And that thought made my heart race and my hands tremble.

There were a few cars out and around on the streets as I drove through town, but as I gained the state highway that led to Fairfields they were few and far between. In fact, on long stretches, my car was the only one on the road. And as sprinkles of rain dotted the windshield, a lonely feeling swept over me, but at least I was dry while Adam might be lying out with no shelter at all.

My eyes swept the sides of the road, looking for stranded pick-ups in case it had been taken, then abandoned. Adam had said he was at Agnes's but, apparently, his truck wasn't. Who could've taken it? Or had he left it somewhere that he couldn't get to? Whatever had happened, it stood to reason that Agnes Whitman's estate had to be the starting point in any kind of search.

Maybe I should've called his daddy instead of Ardis or instead of taking it on myself. It had crossed my mind earlier to do just that, but Adam could've called home just as easily as he'd called me. Yet he hadn't. I'd surmised that the elder Mr. Waites was a hard man who might not understand the lure of a tattooed girl. So maybe Adam wanted somebody with a little more compassion for the weaknesses of the flesh. Like me, for instance, who'd once experienced a temptation on a green velvet love seat and lived to regret it.

Besides, far be it from me to interfere in family relationships. I'd find Adam, reassure him that whatever had gone on between him and Nellie would not mean eternal ruination, and send him home hardly worse for the wear.

My mind was running away with me as one speculation after another flitted in and out my brain.

Slowing as I reached the Fairfields community, I turned in and drove through the stone pillars that marked the entrance. Wondering how close Etta Mae and Ardis were, I drove carefully toward the Whitman place. There were no other cars on the street, no streetlights, and only a few security lights dotted here and there. One of the advertised features of this planned estate community was its rural atmosphere, and I could believe it. I could've been driving through abandoned countryside for all the human activity I could see.

But soon I began to see a glow above the trees as I approached the Whitman place—security lights on tall poles were scattered on the outskirts of the property. Either the power had come back on, or Adam had fixed the generator, who knew which? But the house itself was shrouded in darkness. I turned into the drive and came to a stop. Closed and undoubtedly locked gates blocked my way.

I sat in the idling car, determining what my next step should be. In the glare of the headlights, I saw an intercom box set into one of the pillars that supported the gate. I could buzz myself in, I supposed. Or I could sit and wait for Ardis, who had a semi-legitimate reason—his niece—for disturbing the sleep of Agnes and her strange staff.

I strained to see up the driveway between the trees, hoping for signs of activity that would perhaps mean that Adam was getting help. But the drive toward the house faded into darkness, the security lights having been set too far away.

I sat there for a few more minutes, hoping to see Ardis and Etta Mae pull in behind me. Then deciding that if there was a dying man on the property, I could never forgive myself for having dithered over the propriety of ringing a doorbell in the middle of the night.

I couldn't stand it any longer. I got out of the car and buzzed the buzzer. And kept on buzzing it until finally a sleep-filled male voice answered.

"Who is it?" he growled.

"It's Mrs. Julia Springer Murdoch. There's an emergency somewhere on your property and I need to get in to see about it."

"Who?"

I repeated myself, ending with "Let me in this minute! Somebody may be dying while you're trying to wake up."

He mumbled something about waiting a minute, so I began walking back and forth between my car and the gate, getting more anxious by the minute. I'd left the car running and the door open, so I had plenty of light, but still the night seemed to close in on me. I kept looking over my shoulder, thinking something might spring out of the blackness. The rumble of thunder and flickering lightning weren't helping my feelings, either.

With relief, I saw headlights coming down the drive toward me. An old, mud-spattered Jeep stopped on the other side of the gate, and a young man with mussed-up hair crawled out. As he approached the gate, I recognized him as the valet who'd parked my car at the garden party. But he didn't have on his nice car-parking outfit. All he was wearing was a pair of drawstring pajama bottoms and a lot of ink on his chest, including a hollow-eyed death's head. In the glare of the car lights, I caught a glimpse of metal here and there on his face.

That answered one question: no, he didn't remove all his bolts, nails and screws when he went to bed.

He walked to the gate and clasped a bar with each hand. There was no welcoming smile this time. "What do you want?"

"I want Adam Waites. He called me from here, saying he needed help to get home. Where is he?"

"He left. Hours ago."

"Well, could you just let me in to look around a little? He sounded ill or hurt. Dying, in fact. You may think he left, but he could be lying somewhere in desperate need of help."

He studied me through the bars, and I thought for a minute that he wouldn't answer. Then he said, "Mrs. Whitman's orders say that once this gate is locked for the night, we're not to open it—not for you, not for anybody."

"Well, wake her up and get some new orders! Tell her Adam's in trouble. I'm sure she'll reconsider if she knows that."

"He's not here—how many times do I have to tell you?" And that rude and unfriendly man turned his back on me and headed for his Jeep.

"Young man, look here!" I scrounged around in my pocketbook and pulled out my cell phone. "In less than fifteen minutes, there's going to be a swarm of deputies, a search-and-rescue squad, a K-9 team, an EMS vehicle and a firetruck sitting out here with red and blue lights waking up not only Mrs. Whitman but all her neighbors. Now you can either let me in or you'll certainly be letting them in."

He stopped, turned around and put his hands on his hips, glaring at me.

"Oh, quit posturing," I said. "Those pajamas are about to fall down as it is. Now open this gate and get out of my way."

And he did. He went to one of the pillars, opened a niche and, using a key, unlocked the gate. The two sides began to slide apart as he got in the Jeep, calling, "Follow me."

As if, I thought, but didn't say, getting in my car and putting it in gear. He'd been giving me the runaround, so I was through being courteous. Besides, taking orders didn't sit well with me.

As soon as the gates parted and while he was turning around, I drove on through, heading for the house.

Chapter 46

I whirled the car around the courtyard, making a circle to look for Adam's truck in the beam of the headlights. The courtyard was dark and empty, so I pulled to the side, got out and put on the raincoat and hat against the misting rain.

I looked around, seeing little but shadows thrown by the distant pole lights. The house loomed over me in the dark and so did the four-door garage—no lights were on inside or out. Where was everybody?

Two sets of headlights swept across the front of the garage, one after the other, as the gatekeeper sped into the courtyard with, I hoped, Sheriff Ardis McAfee right behind him in a seriously large pickup with a growling engine. The Jeep stopped with a squeal of brakes on the wet pavers, rain flickering in its headlights. The metal-pierced driver hopped out, hopping mad. "You were supposed to follow me."

"I don't have time to dillydally around, young man. What's your name anyway?"

"Uh, Carl."

"Well, Carl, I'd like you to meet Sheriff Ardis McAfee." I flung out my arm toward Ardis as he descended from his truck, settled a hat on his head and ambled over to us, Etta Mae, holding a pocketbook over her hair, hurrying after him.

"Evenin', folks, or maybe mornin'," the sheriff said, the light rain beginning to speckle his hat. "What kinda problem we got here?"

Before I could get out a word, Carl said, "No problem. None at all. This woman insisted on coming on private property to search for somebody who's long gone."

"That's not so!" I broke in. "Adam called from here, so he's here somewhere. It's a matter of finding him because he sounded desperate. And," I went on, rounding on Carl, "you ought to be eager to help, in case he's lying injured somewhere on this private property. Lawsuits abound, you know.

"And where is Agnes?" I demanded, having worked up a full head of steam. "Why isn't she out here looking for him? She was the one who called him—nothing would do but he had to get out here to fix her generator, and I guess now that it's fixed, she can just go to bed and forget about him."

"Okay, okay," Ardis said, patting the air, "let's see where we are before we call in the lawyers. Now, young man, where is Ms. Whitman? If she'll give her permission to do a little ground search, we can get on with it and leave the fussin' for later."

Carl glanced up at the dark house. "She doesn't like to be disturbed."

"Well, now that's too bad," Ardis said, "because I 'spect we're gonna have to disturb her. Why don't you go wake her up, tell her why we're here, and ask her for permission to look over the grounds. Then she can go back to bed. Oh, and turn on all the outside lights while you're at it."

Carl stared at the sheriff for a second, then he nodded and walked off toward the house. Before he got fully into the shadows around the house, I saw him put a cell phone to his ear. She wasn't asleep! He was reporting to her, while she stayed out of sight. Didn't want to be disturbed, my foot!

The sheriff and Etta Mae drew close, as the sheriff's sharp eyes peered at me from under his hat. "I'm a little ways off my stompin' grounds here. How 'bout bringin' me up to date."

"Well, see," I said, straining to make my case, "Adam called me a little while ago, and I didn't know who it was at first, he sounded so distressed." And I went on to recount the phone call, ending with his last words. "He said he was at Agnes's, which I assume meant at her house or on her grounds somewhere. Then the very last thing he said was a string of mumbles that ended with the word *dying*. Which scared me to death."

Ardis responded with a low grunt, the meaning of which I couldn't interpret. "And you think Nellie might know where he is?"

"It was all I could think of. I mean, coupled with the fact that he left with her to come here and that he told me this was where he was. So I thought of you, her being your niece and all. I didn't want to come barging in here on my own." Which, of course, was exactly what I'd done, but not without knowing that backup was on the way.

"Uh-huh," the sheriff said.

Etta Mae leaned in, lowering her voice. "Looks like," she said, "if he's still here, they would've helped him if he's sick or something. At least help him find his truck."

"It's all very strange," I said. "And all I know for sure is that for the last week or so he was more and more reluctant to come out here and work for that woman. But she kept on and on at him, thinking up things for him to do." I stopped and thought about that. "Of course, I tried to help by thinking up things for him to do at my house. You know, so he'd be too busy to leave."

"Well," the sheriff said, casting an eye around, "I see what you mean, but that boy ought to get some backbone and stand up for himself. But I give you this: the Whitman woman has a way about her. I met her when I came to see Nellie the other day, and I saw the way she rules the roost around here. Look what all she talked Nellie into. Her mama's gonna bawl her eyes out when she sees her. If Nellie ever gets home. From what she says, they got some weird worship services goin' on out here."

I gave him a sideways look, thinking that it took one to know one. Of all the weird worship services I'd ever seen, it had been the snake-handling one he'd sent us to.

"That's what I understand," I agreed. "And I think they're pressuring Adam to join in, but you know, Sheriff," I went on, "there're all kinds of strange and unusual worship services going on if you just look around."

Ardis let that little jab go right over his head and looked instead past my shoulder toward the house. "Wonder where that boy got to. He must be having trouble waking Miss Agnes up. I kinda get the feelin' they don't much like night visitors. Might have to do a little threatenin'."

"With what?" Etta Mae asked, shivering a little. Etta Mae never liked confrontations on the edge of the law. "You don't have any authority here, do you?"

"Nope, but I got professional courtesy," the sheriff said with the assurance of a man with a badge. "I b'lieve I could get us some help if we need it. And if Carl don't get movin', I may have to call on it."

Just then lights came on all around us—floodlights on the corners of the house, garden lights, lights over the garage doors, and lights along the drive. Water started spurting out of the fountain and all four garage doors went up.

"Look!" I said, pointing past Etta Mae's head. "There's Adam's truck." The truck with its camper shell sat lonely and abandoned in the last bay of the garage.

"You ladies stay here," Ardis said as he went over to the pickup. Etta Mae and I followed, but not closely, and watched as he opened the cab door, looked around and shook his head. Then he walked to the back, opened the shell and searched the truck bed. "Not here," he said, jumping down.

By that time Carl, having finished reporting in, walked over to us. "I told you," he said, all in a huff. "Waites is not here. He left hours ago."

"Not without his truck, he didn't," I said, stepping up in his face. "That truck holds everything he owns and he wouldn't leave without it."

"Well, I'm telling you he did," the nail-studded man said right back at me. "It wouldn't start, so he walked away. He left the windows down, so I rolled it into the garage when the rain started."

"And you didn't offer him a ride? What kind of people are you?"

"The kind," a strident voice out of the dark said, "who don't like strangers invading private property."

We all turned to see Agnes Whitman, fast-walking and furious, appearing in a pool of light. She was wearing a long, filmy peignoir that revealed she was also wearing ink up one arm and down the other.

"Where's Adam?" I demanded. "His truck's here, so he must be, too. Where is he?"

Agnes propped her hands on her hips and said, "I don't know and at this time of night I don't care. You are on dangerous ground to come in here and start throwing accusations around."

I opened my mouth, but Ardis put a hand on my shoulder. He had a smile on his face, but it wasn't particularly pleasant. "We have reason to believe that Waites has been injured," he said. "He made an emergency call asking for help, and said he was here, at your place. Now, we can handle it ourselves by looking for him or we can turn it over to the local sheriff, whichever way you want."

Well, that was reasonable, I thought, and would probably be more effective than pulling the Tattooed Woman's stringy hair out. So I subsided and let Ardis handle her.

"Go to it then," she said, flinging out her arm. "Look for him all you want." Then with a sly smile, she said, "To save you a little time, though, I'd suggest you look in Cheyenne's bed first."

Oh, Lord, I thought, *the boy has been compromised.* But would he be dying, too? It didn't make sense. I'd heard of old men kicking the bucket on their wedding nights, but Adam was awfully young to be having a heart attack, regardless of whose bed he was in.

"Good idea," Ardis said, without turning a hair. "We figured to start with her anyway. Where is she?"

Chapter 47

"Show him, Carl," Agnes snapped, as if she'd had her fill of us. She turned—that see-through robe billowing out around her—and headed back to the house. "They can look around, then get them out of here."

"Well, I never," I mumbled, stunned by her rudeness. If people had shown up at my house on a mission of mercy, I would have at least invited them in for coffee. But to add insult to injury, she turned off all the outside lights, even the security lights on the far reaches of the property. Only the headlights of my car were still on, which made me worry about running down the battery.

Even Carl seemed startled to have been left in the dark. But he'd been given his orders, so he hooked a thumb at Ardis and said, "Easier to take the Jeep. Cheyenne's in the women's quarters over beyond the church."

The church? That was a surprise. I hadn't known that New Agers believed in churches, church services being relatively recent compared to the centuries of pagan worship. I would've thought they'd have oak trees or corn circles or temples or maybe piles of stones to dance around.

I started to follow Ardis to the Jeep, but he said, "Etta Mae, you and Miss Julia better stay here. If the boy's with Nellie, I'll bring him back. If he's not, I'll deal with her. Y'all get in the car and wait for me."

I started to protest, but he raised a finger and shook his head. "No tellin' what we'll find. Stay here."

Ardis, I decided, had a highly developed sense of what was appropriate for delicate women to know. I understood what he expected to find, but Adam had not sounded like an exhausted lover on the telephone. And I didn't believe for a minute that he'd given in to the wiles of a girl with hyperactive hormones.

Etta Mae and I stood there in the mist, watching as Carl drove the Jeep off the courtyard onto a track that went behind the garage and led to the expanse of the estate beyond the house. Ardis was off on either a rescue mission or a fool's errand, and I was fairly sure I knew which it was.

"Let's sit in the car, Miss Julia," Etta Mae said. "We're getting soaked."

So we got in, but I didn't like it. How could I sit in a dry car, doing nothing, while Adam might be dragging himself through a muddy ditch, trying to find a helping hand? We were wasting time waiting for Ardis to discover that Nellie was sleeping alone.

"Etta Mae?"

"Ma'am?"

"Can you drive Ardis's pickup?"

She gave me a sharp glance. "I don't know, but I wouldn't touch that truck. It's his personal vehicle and he loves it to death."

"What's so special about it? As far as I can tell, if you've seen one pickup, you've seen them all."

"Not hardly," she said. "It's a heavy-duty Ram truck, Miss Julia, fully loaded with HEMI power, a four-door mega cab, off-road action, quad headlights, a Ram toolbox, a trailer hitch, center console, Sirius radio and a navigation aid. You'd need a training course to be able to drive it."

I tapped my fingers on the steering wheel. "Off-road action sounds interesting, but I guess what I'm asking is, can you drive a truck in general?"

She squinted at me. "I've driven one or two. Why?"

"Look there." I pointed toward the open garage, lit up by my headlights. "See that thing in the second bay? Looks like a buggy of some kind? I bet it'd be easy to drive."

Etta Mae sat up and strained to see through the rain-streaked windshield. "That's a golf cart. You're not thinking. . . ?"

"I certainly am. Adam's not with Nellie, and I doubt he even has been. He's out in the weather somewhere, unable to get inside. The grounds are what need to be searched, not somebody's bedroom. And that little go-cart thing is just what we need to look for him. Come on." I opened the car door and stepped out.

Etta Mae just sat there, a deep frown on her face. "I don't know, Miss Julia. Ardis told us to wait."

"Leave him a note. Come on, if you can drive a pickup, you can drive a golf cart. It even has a canvas top to keep us dry. We'll just drive around the front yard and along the back where the pool is and in and out of the trees along the edges—you won't believe how big this place is."

I walked into the garage with Etta Mae reluctantly following. We stood for a minute gazing at the open-sided two-seated cart with its little fat tires and no windshield.

"Try it, Etta Mae. See if it'll start."

She crawled in, but she did it gingerly, then she studied the unadorned dashboard. "There's a key in the ignition."

"Well, see. It was meant to be." I got in on the passenger side and held on to a roll bar. There were no doors or seatbelts. "Crank it and let's see if it'll run."

"You think we'll get in trouble?"

"Agnes said we could look around, so that's what we're doing. Crank it up."

"Well, okay." Etta Mae turned the key and the little motor started up and began purring away. "Oh, that's neat. But where's the gearshift? I can't find it."

I helped her feel around the dashboard and the steering column, then felt around the floor and the seat. "Wonder what this is," I said, moving a lever, thinking to adjust the seat.

The little cart spurted backward out of the garage, with Etta Mae yelling, "Whoa!" She hit the brakes just before we hit my car.

"Oh, my goodness," she said, resting her head on the steering wheel. "It got away from me." She sat up and blew out her breath. "We better figure this out a little better."

After a few minutes of trying this and that, consisting mostly of searching around for driving instructions, she said, "It's got two gears—forward and reverse—and I was looking for first." She giggled nervously. "And guess what? No lights."

"*No lights?*" I said, feeling defeated before we'd even started. "How're we going to search woods and fields without lights?"

"Yeah, and how're we going to stay out of holes and ditches with no lights? It won't work, Miss Julia. We'll just have to wait for Ardis."

I could've cried until something else came to mind. "Etta Mae, you know that big, heavy flashlight that Coleman has? You know, like all the deputies carry? Wouldn't you think Ardis has one, too?"

"You mean a heavy-duty Maglite? I expect he does."

"Run get it. If that Ram truck of his has everything you say, it'll have a flashlight, too."

She sat for a few minutes, considering the matter—probably wondering how free she should be with her date's property. Of course she was prepared to drive off in who knows whose go-cart, so I didn't think borrowing a flashlight should hold her back.

"Well, shoot," Etta Mae said, and turned off the ignition. "If we're gonna do it, we might as well do it. Be right back."

She ran to the Ram truck and climbed up into the cab, and I do mean climb—I would've had to use a ladder. I could see her head moving around, ducking down then up as her hands searched high and low for the flashlight.

"Got it!" she said, running back and practically falling into the driver's seat of the golf cart. "He had it in a special bracket, close to hand. Now to figure out how to turn it on." She studied it from end to end, which was a good bit of ground to cover because the flashlight was at least a foot long. "Here it is. See, Miss Julia, you turn this dial then punch the button on the end."

She did it and nearly blinded me. Never had I seen such a beam as that flashlight put out—must've been about a million candlepower. "Okay," I said, trying to blink away the afterimage. "You drive and I'll light the way. Good gracious, this thing must weigh five pounds."

"A couple, anyway." Etta Mae fiddled with the gearshift. "I hope it's in drive this time," she said, with her foot on the brake. She turned the wheels, then cranked the engine.

And off we went across the courtyard toward the front of the house, Etta Mae hunched over the wheel, and me hanging half-way out of the cart, holding on to the roll bar with one hand and aiming the flashlight beam in front of us with the other.

"Throw it out a little farther, Miss Julia," Etta Mae yelled. "We've only got one speed, and I'm outrunning the light."

I half stood, trying to aim the beam far enough in front of the hood for her to see where we were going. "Watch out!" I screamed as the fountain loomed before us. The imminent collision had me swinging the beam all over the place.

Etta Mae swerved, almost throwing me out. "Aim it, Miss Julia! I can't see!"

I steadied the light as much as I could while holding on for dear life. Etta Mae swerved the cart away from the fountain and bounced us off the pavers onto the lawn, mowing down a bed of annuals as she went.

"Twist the knob, Miss Julia," Etta Mae said, straining to see what else she was about to run into. "See if there's a broader beam."

I did, casting the beam all around while I did it, and sure enough we soon had a beam that lit up a wide swath in front and to the sides of the golf cart.

After that, we began to get the hang of it and settled down to carefully search along the line of trees bordering the drive. Settled down, I say, except for when Etta Mae hit uneven ground, which had us springing up and down and in and out of the seats, and almost entirely out of the cart. When we reached the front gate, Etta Mae turned to follow the rail fence to the corner, where she turned again to run alongside it at the far edge of the property.

I occasionally swung the light to the side to look across the lawn for any lump that might be a dying man. Each time I did it, Etta Mae screamed that she couldn't see.

When we passed the house far to our right, a stand of evergreens blocked our way. Etta Mae slowed and stopped. "I don't think we ought to go in there. We might get stuck."

"It's not that muddy, is it?"

"No, I mean stuck between trees. Let's go along the edge and concentrate on the lawn. Because why would he go in the woods if he knew you were coming to pick him up?"

"You're right. But I tell you, Etta Mae, I've got to swap places with you. I don't know if I can drive this thing, but my arm's about to break off. This light is heavy."

"Okay, you can drive it. There's nothing to it really."

We exchanged places, and instead of sitting and holding the flashlight out to the side, she stood sideways so that most of herself was hanging out of the golf cart. She wrapped one arm around a roll bar and balanced the flashlight on the roof with the other.

"Don't hit any bumps," she said. "I'm hanging on by a thread."

After a few unintended spurts of speed, accompanied by shrieks from Etta Mae, I managed to gain some control and drove us along the back edge of the manicured lawn. We passed from some little distance the cabana and pool where the garden party had been held. Then a white rail fence began again, which at least gave me something to steer by. I could hear horses snorting behind it, and figured that was the last place Adam would be.

Actually, I had counted on finding him along the drive, assuming that he would've been trying to walk out. Not having found him there, the next most likely place, it seemed to me, would be a utility building of some kind where a generator would be housed. And that brought to mind the possibility that Adam had been burned or shocked when he was repairing it. Generators scare me anyway. Obviously, though, he'd fixed the thing, for Agnes had lights, even if she wouldn't turn them on.

I tried not to think of what could've happened, turning instead to trying to see and steer at the same time. Maybe, I hoped, Ardis had shaken some information out of Nellie, and we'd have a better idea of where to focus our search.

I declare, it was worrying me to death that we'd come up empty so far. Adam had said he was at Agnes's, and so were we. He'd said his truck was gone, yet we'd found it. He'd said he was dying, but where was he doing it?

I didn't know what else to do except keep on looking, but if we didn't soon find him and if Ardis had struck out with Nellie, I'd made up my mind to call in the professionals.

Chapter 48

"Watch out!" Etta Mae screamed. "Turn, Miss Julia, turn!"

I zipped left, just missing another rail fence behind a huge structure that I assumed to be a barn—a fairly good assumption considering the odor and the nicker of horses. Could Adam be in the barn, curled up in a dry stall? Maybe, but I wasn't eager to deal with large animals. Better to let Ardis handle that while we continued to search the grounds.

It was a fortunate turn I'd made in avoiding the fence, for we found ourselves on a wide gravel-covered path. It led away from the house and toward a cluster of shrubs and small trees with just the dark outline of what looked to be a shed of some kind. I slowed as we came abreast of it to let Etta Mae sweep the open structure with the light beam. Empty, except for a couple of bicycles and a wheelbarrow.

Etta Mae leaned under the canvas top of the cart to get my attention. "Slow down. I see some lights way over yonder."

I took my foot off the accelerator and came to a stop, wondering who had lights that worked in spite of Agnes Whitman. Etta Mae pointed the flashlight to the right, lighting up a thick growth of laurel under a stand of trees some several yards from us. "See 'em?" she asked, and straining to see over the bushes, I got a quick glimpse of yellow light glimmering through the trees and the roof of a long, low structure that looked like a roadside motel.

"I can't see doodly," I said, craning to look where she was aiming the beam.

"Looks like candles or something in a window," Etta Mae said. "I think I see the Jeep, too—the top of it anyway. So Ardis must still be talking to Nellie."

"Well, I'll tell you what's a fact, Etta Mae, the time for talking and tooling around in the dark is about over. We'll never find Adam this way, and the boy is dying. We've got to come up with something else."

She turned off the flashlight, surrounding us with a night as black as sin, and slid into the seat beside me. "You think we ought to call the sheriff, I mean our sheriff, and get a search party going?"

"Yes, I do. Where's your cell phone?"

"In Ardis's truck. You have yours, don't you?"

I leaned my head on the little steering wheel, just done in. "It's in my pocketbook, left in the car." I *knew* I should've brought my pocketbook. I never went anywhere without it, yet here I was, unarmed and unprepared.

"Let's just go on," Etta Mae said. "Ardis will have his, and we're closer to him than the car." She stood up again, holding on to the bar, and lit the way. "This path ought to swing around and come out where he is."

Almost in despair, I cranked up the cart and followed the light. The path swung around, all right, but not toward Ardis and the Jeep. It meandered away from the way we wanted to go, up and down small hills, curving and getting bumpier. "We're getting farther away, Etta Mae. I don't know where we're going."

She dropped back into the seat and swung the beam along each side of us. Trees lined the path with no break that I could see. Total darkness surrounded the light beam.

"We're in the woods," Etta Mae said, in some wonder. "How did we do that?"

"I don't know, but I'd turn around if I had room." The path had gotten noticeably narrower, and the trees were so close there was no space for such a maneuver.

"Maybe you can back out."

284 of Ann B. Ross

"In *reverse?*" I was appalled. "Etta Mae, it's all I can do to back out of my driveway. There's no way I can do it here."

"Well, me, either," she admitted. "Let's just go on. It has to come out somewhere. I mean we're still on the Whitman place."

Yes, we were, but we weren't on gravel any longer. The path had become a dirt track with mud holes and slick spots.

"Hey, look!" Etta Mae cried, as she steadied the beam off the track during one of her sweeps, leaving me as blind as a bat. I took my foot off the accelerator, bringing the cart to a stop. "There's a little path. See it? And look, there's something back there in the trees."

She aimed the light at a muddy but well-worn footpath leading off the track we were on. Heavy undergrowth bordered the path, but as she played the beam farther along it, I could make out a small weathered building almost hidden in the undergrowth.

"What would be stuck out here in the woods?" I said, not expecting an answer. "We better check it out, Etta Mae. With the rain we've had, Adam would've looked for some kind of shelter. Come on, we'll have to walk up. It's too narrow to drive on."

We got out of the cart, and Etta Mae handed me the flashlight. "You go first," she said. "I'll catch you if you slip."

I used the flashlight to pick my way around mud holes on the footpath, walking carefully. Etta Mae suddenly grabbed my shoulder, startling me so bad that I swung the beam around among the tree tops. "Look!" she hissed. "There's a light on. Somebody's up there."

It was a dim light from a window, barely visible in the dark, and not at all when the high-powered beam was on it. "Come on," I said, my heart lifting. "Maybe it's him."

The hut, for that's what it was, wasn't far, only a few yards from the main path, but a fairly steep few yards. I was breathing heavily by the time we reached what looked to be a one-room outbuilding. The footpath ended at a door made of wide boards.

I tried the doorknob, but the door was locked, firmly. It didn't even rattle when I rapped sharply on it. "Adam? Are you in there? It's me, Julia Murdoch."

With my ear against the door, all I could hear was the sound of rain dripping from the trees. I yelled his name a couple of times, but there was no response.

"Somebody has to be in there," I said. "There's a light on."

"Not much of one, though," Etta Mae said. "Hey, there's a little window over there. Maybe we can see in."

She pushed through a wet shrub to a small high window, barely large enough for both of us to look through at the same time. I followed, getting soaked in the process.

Standing on tiptoes, our heads next to each other, we looked through the dusty window and saw a single candle set on a saucer in the middle of a dirt floor.

"Throw the light on it," Etta Mae said, and I did. Lot of good it did, though, because the opaque glare against the dust on the inside reflected back at us.

"I can't see anything," I said, as I fiddled with the flashlight to dim the beam and cut down the glare. I played the light through the window, casting it around the floor. I kept expecting to find Adam curled in a corner awaiting help.

Then Etta Mae screamed. "Swing it back! Swing it back! Over the candle, oh, my Lord, look at that!"

Aiming at the candle, I could see dangling above it two long bare feet. I thought my heart would stop. Etta Mae's fingers were digging into my shoulder, but I hardly felt it. Fear of what had happened to Adam almost took me out of myself. Trembling, I tried to aim the light on the body, but I couldn't keep it steady. Perspiration popped out on my face, or it might have been rainwater. I couldn't tell.

"He hung himself!" Etta Mae cried, her voice trembling. "He's just . . . just hanging there!" She grabbed the flashlight from me and steadied the beam on the body.

My first full look as Etta Mae ran the light up and down the body made me sag against her in relief. It wasn't Adam. I knew without being able to see the man's face, for his head was bowed to his ink-covered chest. His long arms hung limply by his side, and he was as near naked as I'd ever seen outside a bedroom, with only a tiny Lycra brief covering what ought to stay covered.

"Good grief," Etta Mae whispered, tremors vibrating through her body. "Is that a Speedo?" Then she gasped and stumbled back, the light bouncing around the walls. "Oh, my goodness, he's not hanging, he's *suspended*!"

I grabbed the flashlight and saw it all—two leather thongs running from a block on the ground up over a rafter and down to two metal hooks sticking through the skin, one on each side of the man's chest. Blood dripped from the slits where the hooks were inserted.

One look was enough. Scrambling to get away, my own skin crawling with horror, I jumped back and bumped into Etta Mae. She grabbed me and held on.

"No, wait," she yelled. "Wait, Miss Julia, we have to do something. He could be alive." Etta Mae's limited medical experience was coming to the fore, and I was the better for it. She gave me a little shake to bring me to my senses.

"Okay, okay," I managed to say. Of course we'd have to cut him down. We couldn't just leave him there, suspending to death, while we went for help.

We knocked on the window, then banged on the door, but there was no answer and no movement from the man. Etta Mae pushed through the bushes around the hut to look for another way in—even a window big enough to crawl through—leaving me in the dark and none too happy about it.

Thoroughly soaked, she came back around. "Nothing. No way in at all. He's locked himself in or . . ." She stopped, took a rasping breath and went on. "Or somebody else hung him and left him locked up." I could hear her breathing—little whimpers coming with each breath she took. "That's what happened, Miss Julia, somebody strung him up!"

"Oh, my Lord," I whispered, looking over my shoulder toward the dark woods. "We better get out of here, Etta Mae."

"I know it, but he could still be alive. Hold on, let's try something." She pushed her way to the small window again, stood on tiptoe, and aimed the beam at the Hanging Man. "Bang on the door as loud as you can," she told me. "I'll watch to see if he moves."

I did, and she did, but he didn't. "It's too late," she said. Then grasping my arm, she said, "Let's get out of here. Whoever did it might come back."

Appalled and terrified, I scurried along behind Etta Mae and the light back down the path to the cart. But the farther we went on the slippery path, the more anxious I became to put some distance between us and the unspeakable sight we'd left. By the time we reached the cart, we were both half sliding, half running, and completely out of breath.

Chapter 49

"You drive!" I cried, falling into the passenger seat. "Hurry, Etta Mae, crank it, crank it!"

She did and we trundled off, still following the muddy track we were on and hoping it would lead back to civilization. I was trembling so bad that it took both hands to hold the light beam steady enough to light our way. It didn't help that the track was unpaved and ungraveled and the trees so close that it was like being in a tunnel.

We hit a bump on a little rise, then swooped down the other side and wallowed through a creek bed. Etta Mae was crouched over the wheel, urging us onward, still whimpering with each breath. Finally, after bucking over more bumps and slewing through the muddy patches, the trees on each side began to thin out and I could see a white rail fence running alongside of us.

"We're almost there," I said, and almost lost the flashlight when Etta Mae ran over a rock that tilted the cart to one side.

We both screamed, thinking we were rolling over, but the little cart righted itself and Etta Mae gave it the gas again.

Gradually, darker shadows began to loom out of the general blackness, so I dared to sweep the light around to see where we'd come out.

"Slow down, Etta Mae. I think that's the pool house over there. If you swing out around it, the garage should be diagonally across the lawn."

"Yeah, okay," she said, her voice quavering. "Okay, I just want to get somewhere safe."

"Look!" I cried. "Look over there." Some ways off, a moving glow lit up the garage, throwing into relief the huge bulk of the house and dimly illuminating the pool house, which we were passing. "It's the Jeep coming back. Hurry, Etta Mae, we've got to tell somebody about that dead man."

"Yeah, gotta hurry," she panted, then sideswiped a bush, overcorrected and almost ran into the rail fence. The golf cart stalled out, leaving us sideways of the fence, while Etta Mae whimpered some more and cranked the thing again.

Just as the motor started, she let out a blood-curdling shriek, levitated from her seat and stomped on the gas. The cart scraped along the fence with Etta Mae yelling, "Something's after us! Oh, Lord, it touched me!"

The cart bounced on and off the fence until Etta Mae gave it a hard turn to the right, almost throwing me out. Scared out of my wits, I screamed along with her and grabbed her with both hands, letting go of the flashlight. I saw it tumble to the ground, flinging the beam out into the pasture—not the way we were going. Horses thundered away from the fence, but I was too busy holding on and screaming to think of anything but getting to the garage, where there were lights and people and safety from whatever had followed us.

The cart careened across the lawn, bounded up onto a paved surface, struck a patio chair, and came to an abrupt halt. It teetered for a second, rocking back and forth, until the nose slowly tipped over and we hit the water.

The little cart began to sink as water flooded the floorboard and climbed into our laps. "Get out, Etta Mae!" I yelled, scrambling to get myself out. The raincoat billowed out around me as I leaned into the water, thankful for the doorless cart, and started dogpaddling to the edge of the pool.

"Help!" Etta Mae screamed. "I can't swim!" She thrashed around on the other side of the cart, flinging water everywhere and getting nowhere fast.

"I'm coming, I'm coming!" I was paddling as fast as I could, but sinking just as fast. Grabbing the cart to pull my way around to Etta Mae before she drowned, my foot touched the bottom of the pool.

"We're in the shallow end!" I cried, relief flooding my soul. "Stand up, Etta Mae, we can walk out."

I finally pulled my way around the cart to reach her, and together we made our way to the underwater steps and climbed out, drenched to the skin.

"Oh, my Lord," she said, leaning over and gasping for breath, "I thought I'd killed us both."

"No, I think we're saved. Somebody's coming." I pointed to two flashlight beams bobbing toward us.

"Waites! Is that you?" Ardis's voice carried easily across the back lawn.

"No," I called back. "It's us."

Ardis and Carl came running up, and Etta Mae, sopping wet, flung herself onto Ardis, sobbing, "I broke it or drowned it or something. We'll never get it out, and I'll never be able to pay for it."

"We'll fix it, little girl, whatever it is," Ardis said. "Don't you worry. What're you doing out here anyway?"

"Searching," Etta Mae said. She pushed back her wet hair and pointed at the swimming pool. "We've been all over the place in that golf cart and something chased us and licked me on my neck and I got so scared, I drove it into the pool, and I guess I ruined it."

"And," I added, "we borrowed your big flashlight because the go-cart didn't have lights. I dropped it when Etta Mae lost control, so she couldn't help driving into the pool—we couldn't see a thing."

"My *Maglite*?"

"Well, yes, and I thank you for the use of it." I think his eyes rolled back in his head, but it was too dark to tell.

Carl swung the beam of his flashlight around and centered it on the canvas roof of the golf cart—the only part visible. It looked like one of those floats that women lie on to sunbathe.

"Oh, shoot!" Carl said, except he used a different word that revealed his poor breeding. "Agnes is not gonna like this."

That just tore me up. Here we'd been driving half blind, found a hanged man, been chased by some dark creepy thing and come near to drowning, and all he could think of was what Agnes would or wouldn't like.

"Well, here's something else she won't like," I said, wringing out my skirttail. "There's a half-naked, tattooed dead man hanging from the rafters in a shack back in the woods. We couldn't get in to cut him down, but somebody better get down there."

"Oh," Carl said, shrugging his shoulders. "That's just Darren. He's doing a suspended meditation. I hope you didn't disturb him."

"*Disturb* him! We couldn't get a twitch out of him. I think he's meditated himself right out of his body. For all we know, it was his spirit that was after Etta Mae."

"Oh, don't say that," Etta Mae said, snuggling closer to Ardis.

"But," I went on to Carl, "if you're not concerned about him and if he's doing it to himself, then good luck to him. But he's in bad shape and somebody ought to see to him. And I'll tell you this," I said, pointing my finger at him, "if Agnes didn't want go-carts in her pool, she should've turned on the yard lights and kept them on. And you can tell her I said so."

Turning to Ardis, I asked, "What did you find out about Adam? Did Nellie know what happened to him?"

Ardis held Etta Mae with one arm and with the other hand, a flashlight—a normal-sized one, not the great long one he used in the line of duty because it was still lighting up the horse pasture—and it cast a dim glow around us. He shook his head. "She said she watched him fix the generator, then she offered him a snack. From the sound of it, they maybe had a little party and she tried to get him to spend the night. She's a bold one, all right—shameless, even—but he turned her down. She got mad and went to bed. And that's all she knows."

"You mean he's still out here somewhere! And nobody knows

anything? What're we going to do?" I'd finished wringing out my dress and started on my hands, just torn up over our failure to rescue Adam.

"Well, first I'm gonna get my Maglite, then get you ladies back to the truck, call in the sheriff and wait for help," Ardis said. "That's my advice."

I didn't particularly like his advice, but I didn't know what else to do. So we trudged back across the lawn, stepping over and occasionally into flower beds that lined the walkway. I was miserable in my wet clothes, which were clinging to me in embarrassing ways—a raincoat isn't much help when you drive into a swimming pool. And miserable, also, because we had not found Adam. We'd looked all over creation, except . . .

"Sheriff McAfee?" I said, using a formal address in case he was less than happy with me for appropriating his precious Maglite. He nodded to indicate he was listening, as we swerved to avoid a birdbath. "We haven't looked in the barn. Adam could be in there, in a stall or something. And," I went on, "nobody's searched the house, either."

"He's not in the house," Carl snapped. "Nobody goes in the house without Agnes knowing it."

That was interesting. Because if she knew that's where he was, it was no wonder she'd been so rude and dismissive of our search.

I opened my mouth to snap back at Carl, but Ardis intervened. "Let's get you ladies settled, and I'll search the barn. We'll leave the house for the sheriff." Then, in that easy way of his, he said, "I expect Miss Agnes will know it when a bunch of deputies tromp in."

I figured that had settled Carl's hash, so I focused on picking my way toward the garage without breaking my neck. Carl and Ardis were not very steady with the flashlight beams, and I was getting even more anxious about Adam, as I peered this way and that, looking for him instead of watching where I stepped.

We finally reached the paved courtyard in front of the garage, and Etta Mae and I, wet to the skin, headed for my car. Thank goodness for leather seats. I slid beneath the wheel and immediately turned on the ignition and the heater, hoping to dry us off.

The headlights came on when the motor did, and Etta Mae, who was walking around the car to get to the passenger side, suddenly stopped. "Look!" she screamed, pointing to Adam's truck. "There's feet sticking out!"

Chapter 50

And there certainly were. The driver's door stood open and whoever's feet were sticking out was sprawled across the bench seat.
But it wasn't just feet we saw, but feet clad in mud-caked, heavy-
duty work boots with a familiar green patch on the tongue.

"It's Adam!" I cried, scrambling out of the car, thrilled at finding him. "I'd know those boots anywhere."

Ardis strode toward the garage, holding up his hand as if he
was directing traffic. "Stay back, ladies. Stay back."

I declare, Sheriff McAfee was more concerned about the tender sensibilities of the weaker sex than he had any right to be. But
after searching all over Agnes Whitman's grounds, woods and
swimming pool half the night, I wasn't about to stay back.

Nor was Etta Mae. Both of us ran after Ardis, bunching up
around the truck door, trying to see inside.

"Where'd he come from?" Etta Mae said, peering around Ardis's shoulder. "He wasn't in here when we looked before. I mean,
we couldn't of missed seeing him. Could you, Ardis?"

"Nope. This truck was empty when I looked. Pretty obvious
that he crawled in while we were all out rambling around somewhere else."

I thought that might be a little jab at Etta Mae and me for not
obeying his orders to stay in the car, but I let it slide. *You're not the
boss of me*, I thought, especially because I felt I pretty much knew
the kind of judgment a snake handler would have.

"Is he alive?" I asked, trembling, as I tried to peer around Ardis's shoulders.

"So far," Ardis said as he leaned in and turned Adam over. Then he sat him upright and slid him to the edge of the seat with his legs dangling out. He was covered in mud and blades of grass, but it was his head that made my stomach knot up and my skin begin to crawl. Dried flakes of blood stained one side of his face and throat, with a little fresh blood dribbling down on top.

"Oh, my Lord!" Etta Mae cried, flapping her hands as she called again on the deity. "What happened to him?"

Even Carl looked worried as Ardis put an arm around Adam and stood him up, a cell phone sliding to the garage floor at the same time. "Is he all right?" Carl asked.

As Adam swayed and began to list to one side, Ardis steadied him, saying, "Whoa. Hold on there, son."

I was reluctant to touch him, but I did, holding on to one side so he wouldn't fall. "We have to get him to the hospital," I said, shivering with anxiety. "He looks near death, like he said he was."

Ardis reached down and picked up Adam's cell phone. He looked at it and punched a few buttons. "This is the only thing near death around here. There's nothing wrong with this boy that a good hosing won't fix," Ardis said. "He's as drunk as a skunk."

And just about then, I got a good whiff of powerful fumes emanating from Adam in waves, probably because I was right in line with his breath.

"But he doesn't drink!" I cried, hardly able to believe what was right under my nose. "He's been led astray by the wrong crowd." I gave Ardis a hard look, because it had to have been a member of *his* family who'd done the leading.

"Where's the blood coming from?" Etta Mae asked, peering closely at Adam's face. "Maybe he fell and cut himself on a rock or something. Let's clean him off and see if he needs stitches."

I hadn't noticed that Carl had walked away until he came back from the side of the garage, dragging a hose behind him. "Here's a rag I use to clean the cars," he said, handing Etta Mae a none-too-clean cloth. It occurred to me that my dress was both wet enough and clean enough to tend a wound, but I didn't have a mind to offer it.

"Sit him back down," Etta Mae said, as Adam's knees began to give way. His eyes were closed and his head lolled on his shoulders, as he mumbled something about his precious truck.

Etta Mae wet the rag under the trickle from the hose, wrung it out, then carefully began to clean the blood from Adam's face. "Hold still," she said. "I won't hurt you." Fairly soon, she had his face reasonably clean and began working around his hairline. "I don't see a cut or a scrape or anything," she said. "Maybe it's in his hair. Scalp wounds bleed a lot."

She leaned over Adam, frowning as she gently parted his hair and mopped at the dried blood. "Got to be coming from somewhere," she murmured, then suddenly sprang back, dropped the rag, almost stumbling over Ardis's foot. "Good gosh almighty! Look at that! I'm gonna be sick!"

As she whirled away from Adam, I stepped closer to see what was awful enough to turn a seasoned nurse's helper's stomach. Expecting to see a gash that had laid open his scalp, I steeled myself to look and cracked heads with Ardis who was doing the same thing.

I saw stars for a second, but not enough of them to block the sight of a large metal plug in Adam's left earlobe. I turned away, sick at heart that he'd taken the first step to becoming another Carl—an example of stomach-turning metalwork.

Ardis snatched up the rag, wet it again, and mopped around Adam's ear. "Well, I'll say this," he said, straightening up and gazing at what he'd uncovered, "I've seen a lot of strange things, but this is the first time I've seen a Phillips cross slot screw punched through an ear and backed with a wing nut."

"They've modified him," I moaned. "It's the work of that body-manipulating church out here, and just look what they've done to him."

Ardis threw down the wet rag and said, "Little Miss Nellie

about needs a whippin' for this. And I've a good mind to give her one, along with everybody else with a hand in it."

About that time, Carl eased back into the shadows, turned and ran. And a good thing, too, because as threatening as Ardis sounded, he didn't hold a candle to what I was feeling toward every pierced, tattooed and strung-up curiosity I'd seen, and especially toward Agnes Whitman, the instigator and perpetrator of it all.

"And I'll tell you this," Ardis said, as he stomped back and forth, "it's no wonder this boy's too drunk to stand up. I'd have to be in a flat-out coma before anybody could put a screw in my ear."

Well, so would I, but not before I slapped the daylights out of Agnes if she came at me with a hole puncher.

❧

We left the Whitman estate in a three-vehicle convoy—with me alone in my car; Ardis driving Adam's truck, with Adam strapped in tight to keep him from sliding into the footwell; and Etta Mae in the Ram truck. She could hardly believe it when Ardis had handed her the keys, saying, "We got to get this boy to the emergency room, and I don't want to have to come out here again. I'm shaking the dust off my feet. Mud, I mean."

None of us had had the stomach to unscrew Adam's new earring, especially after Etta Mae warned about the large hole it would leave. Then I chimed in, worrying aloud about a loss of brain cells because Adam had never built up a tolerance for any amount of alcohol, and he'd had a bait of it at one sitting. So Ardis had taken command as usual, deciding that he and Etta Mae would escort Adam to the hospital and I would go home and call the elder Mr. Waites. I think I got the short end of the stick.

When we reached Abbotsville, I peeled off and went home, going straight to the telephone when I got there, disregarding the time of night. I wanted that dreaded job over with as soon as possible. Nobody likes to hear the phone ring in the middle of the night, but I figured the Waites family would welcome news of

Adam's whereabouts. Until they heard he was in the emergency room, that is.

I didn't go into detail when I spoke with Adam's father, just said that his son had had a minor accident, and that I and some friends happened to be available to take him to the hospital because he'd seemed a little woozy.

That done, I went to bed, thinking I'd had my fill of going to the aid of grown men who'd gotten themselves into messes they couldn't get out of—first, Mr. Pickens, and now, Adam. And both had brought me into contact with people who had strange ideas about how and whom to worship. All I could think was that you'd better have a firm foundation when you go out into the world. There's no telling what you'll run into.

❦

Sunday morning I was with Lloyd in our usual pew at the First Presbyterian Church and thankful to be there. You can have your snakes and your tambourines, your hooks and screws and electric needles. Speedos, too. Give me the King James Version, a hymnal and Communion every quarter. Even with Pastor Ledbetter's sermons, I wouldn't trade a good traditional worship service for all the tea in China.

❦

That afternoon, after Lloyd left to play tennis, I walked over to Hazel Marie's. Mr. Pickens was in an expansive mood, looking healthier than he had since he'd left Mill Run, West Virginia. Hazel Marie was bubbling over with news that she couldn't wait to tell me about.

"Ardis and Etta Mae came over this morning," she said as I silently noted that the visit meant that none of them had gone to church. "And everything's all right with J.D. No further action needed, Ardis said, because, really, he didn't witness anything. But, Miss Julia, guess what! We're going to visit him in Mill Run in a couple of weeks. J.D. wants to go fishing, and I've never been to West Virginia, and we're just so thrilled!"

I looked from one to the other, wondering where their minds were. Mr. Pickens sat there on his eiderdown pillow, looking smug and satisfied, enjoying his wife's excitement.

"What will you do about the babies?" I asked.

"Oh," Hazel Marie said, "that's the best part. J.D.'s going to rent an RV and we'll take them with us. That way, we can take their stroller and their high chairs and everything they need. Ardis said there's a campground nearby with a bathhouse and grills and hookups and everything. Won't that be fun!"

For her sake, I hoped it would be, but if Sam ever came up with a vacation plan like that, I'd take to my bed.

Then nothing would do but that I had to hold each of the babies in turn. They were certainly growing, getting plump and wide-eyed and chewing on anything close to their mouths. I dandled and cooed to whichever one Hazel Marie put in my lap until one of them—Lily Mae, I think—spit up all over me and Hazel Marie relieved me of the honor.

While she took them back to their cribs, I took the opportunity to issue a discreet warning to Mr. Pickens.

"I'm glad to hear that things have worked out," I said to him. "It must be a relief to know there's not a warrant out for your arrest. But, Mr. Pickens, I wouldn't get too involved with that sheriff if I were you. He's not exactly what he seems."

"McAfee?" Mr. Pickens's eyebrows went up. "From what I hear, he was a good man to have around last night."

"He told you about that, then? So, yes, he was certainly a help and I was glad he was there. But," I said, leaning toward him and lowering my voice, "has he told you his church affliation?"

"Well, no. The subject hasn't come up."

"Well, you just watch out, and whatever you do, don't take Hazel Marie and the babies to any church he recommends. Mr. Pickens," I went on urgently, "he goes to *snake*-handling services or, if he doesn't, he *sends* people to them."

Mr. Pickens started laughing, but stopped short when he saw my face. "Sorry, Miss Julia. I did hear something about that. The story I got was that you and Etta Mae went to the wrong church. He feels bad about it, but he didn't do it on purpose. He's planning to leave for home this afternoon—if he can tear himself away from Etta Mae—and when he gets there, he's gonna make you an honorary resident of Mill Run to make up for the mistake."

My back got as stiff as a board at the thought. That was another honor I could do without.

"But what I want to know," Mr. Pickens went on, as he motioned to me to come close, "when you went to that church, were you moved to pick up a rattlesnake or a cottonmouth?"

I jumped back like I'd been bitten. "*Neither one!* How could you ask such a thing?" Of course, I soon realized he was teasing me, but I planned to check under the bed before crawling into it every night until Sam got back. Then he could do the checking.

❧

"Julia," Mildred said when I answered the phone, "you know what a time I have getting a member to lead the discussions at the book club? Well, I just had someone volunteer, and she volunteered not only to lead the discussion, but to select the book, too."

"That must be a relief for you," I said. Mildred was president of our book club for the year, and it'd been like pulling teeth to get a discussion leader for each month. Everybody loved the club, but nobody wanted to lead it. "Who's the brave soul?"

"Well," Mildred said after a slight hesitation. "It's not a member, but she wants to be. How would you feel about Agnes Whitman joining us? She's offered to take the next couple of months because she wants to do that bestselling book everybody talked about, but none of us wanted to read. You know, the one about a dragon tattoo? Agnes says she has a unique perspective that she'd like to share with us."

I'll just bet she would, I thought but remained speechless for so long that Mildred asked, "Julia? You still there?"

"Just considering the ramifications, Mildred," I finally managed to say. "And I've just finished considering them. All I can say is that I've never said a word against anyone who wanted to join us, and I'm not going to now. But if you let that woman in, I'm resigning. And if you want to know why, I'll tell you whenever you have time to listen."

"Come on over," she said, with a low chuckle. "I can't wait to hear."

❦

Monday morning, and the hordes descended before Lillian and I had finished breakfast. The brickmasons arrived first, immediately putting up scaffolding to continue, brick by brick, building my big fat Williamsburg chimney. Next came the paperhanger, who had to maneuver his cutting table up the stairs to Hazel Marie's old bedroom. I followed him up to make sure he had the slightly blush linen paper I'd selected, and not some garish stripe or floral that belonged on someone else's wall.

"You'll have this finished today, won't you?" I asked, after reassuring myself that the rolls of paper were the correct ones.

He adjusted a strap on his white overalls and shook his head. "Maybe tomorrow."

"No, Mr. Bailey. That won't do at all. My husband returns tomorrow from a trip abroad and this room has to be finished. Now look," I went on as he began shaking his head again, "there's no design on this paper, so you don't have to match anything. Just cut it to the right length and put it up. Surely you can do that in a day."

"Have to work overtime."

"Yes, I'm familiar with time and a half. It'll start at five o'clock if you'll stay until it's finished."

"Four's my usual quittin' time."

"Four, then."

For the first time he nodded. I nodded back and left him to it.

By that time, the carpenters had arrived and were beginning to put the finishing touches on the beautiful paneling in the new library downstairs. As I walked down the hall to speak to them, I could hear country music from the radio that seemed to be one of the essential tools of their trade.

Before I got there, Tucker Caldwell came flouncing through the front door in all his summer glory: a blue seersucker suit, yellow bow tie and a third gold stud, but this one was on the side of his nose. It was all I could do to keep from rolling my eyes, but I pretended not to notice. Why else do people do such things but to draw attention to themselves? So if he expected me to express shock, he was going to be disappointed. I'd seen worse over the weekend.

I followed him and stood by the door of the new library, observing as Tucker went over some of the finer points of installing the Adam mantel that had come with the paneling. I hoped they'd do it right, for the paneling had come from a very old house that had to give way for a Walmart Supercenter in an Alabama town, and it had cost me an arm and a leg.

Tucker had done no more than nod in my direction when he first came in, but soon he walked over and edged me toward the living room, both of us stumbling over the rolled-up rug in the hall.

"Uh, Mrs. Murdoch," he began, his eyes flitting around, "I have bad news for you." Then he rushed on before I could respond. "You'll have to do without Adam Waites from now on. He, ah, well, apparently, he's been through some sort of crisis as a result of working for Agnes—she can be quite demanding, you know. Anyway, I didn't get all the particulars, but his father called me last night to say that Adam would not be working for some time to come." Tucker took out a handkerchief and rubbed his nose, then winced as if he'd forgotten the new stud.

"I'm sorry to hear that," I said, although I wasn't surprised that Adam was in no shape to work. "Of course, he'd about completed my project, but I expect he's left Agnes high and dry." I smiled as sympathetically as I could manage.

"Actually, she's not taking it well, especially because she thought Adam was making great strides toward a new spiritual breakthrough. She hates to lose a true seeker."

I held my tongue, although I wanted to point out that Agnes had apparently gained *him,* if the gold studs dotting his face were any indication. But as we all know, some people are never satisfied with what they have.

"And even worse," Tucker went on with a flick of his eyes at me, "Mr. Waites said that Adam is moving away. He'll be attending an evangelical Bible institute somewhere in east Texas." Tucker twisted his mouth. "Studying for the ministry, if you can believe it."

"Oh, I can believe it. It sounds to me as if he's found what he was seeking, no thanks to Agnes or, I must say, to you, either. You might take note, Mr. Caldwell, that when you start messing with spiritual matters, you might be doing the Lord's work without realizing it."

✦

It was late when I finally got to bed that night, crawling thankfully between the sheets on the bed that was now upstairs in the new bedroom. Mr. Bailey, the paperhanger, had indeed finished in one day—one long day, that is. And because I was in the mood to pay time and a half, I offered the same terms to the carpentry crew to move the bedroom furniture up to Hazel Marie's old room.

That cleared out the living room and got the king-sized mattress off the dining room table, making the redone bedroom fit for occupancy. Of course, the coverlet and curtains were not finished, so I'd had to tack up sheets over the windows.

But that didn't matter. I lay in bed, almost too excited to sleep. Sam would be there with me the very next night. I'd meet him at the airport and bring him home to see his new office, still stacked with boxes, our new library with the Williamsburg chimney, still only half done, and our new bedroom, not quite finished, but sleepable and usable. I could hardly wait.

And would I tell him all that had happened while he'd been away? Yes, this time I would, but gradually—a little bit at a time—over the next few days so as not to distress him. As images of the strange people and practices I'd run into over the past several days ran through my mind, I recalled a conversation I'd had with Lloyd the evening before. He'd just told me of the living arrangements he'd decided on, which I must say were a balm to my soul. With his family's approval, he would live with them on weekends and holidays and with Sam and me during the school weeks because, he said, "Your house is four blocks closer to school." Any reason at all was good enough for me.

So anyway, we had been sitting on the front porch, watching lightning bugs flit around the yard, when I suddenly had an enlightened moment. "Lloyd, do you remember that snake-handling church I told you about—the one we went to in West Virginia?"

"Yes'm," he'd said with a shiver. "Don't remind me."

"Well, it seems to me that that's one end of a string of beliefs, while those body decorators or desecrators, depending on your point of view, are at the other end. But both extremes have something in common—they're looking for something beyond themselves, and they're doing it through pain of one kind or another. Snakebite and possible death for one, and mutilation and possible infection for the other. But when you get right down to it, there's not a nickel's worth of difference between them."

Lloyd said, "I never thought of it like that." He'd stretched out his skinny legs and watched a flock of night birds as they flew over the roof. " 'Course I've never given much thought to either one."

"Neither have I, and except for having both extremes thrown in my face during the last several days, I guess I never would've. But it's remarkable how far some people will go to avoid a church service done decently and in order."

❧

Sam would appreciate such an insight. He enjoyed finding parallels and analogies and such like in ordinary things. Besides, my having drawn such a meaningful conclusion would impress him and likely distract him from certain questionable actions on my part.

And when it was all said and done, we would settle down to

enjoy our remodeled home together, and the long summer days would be filled with the pleasure we found in each other as well as with friends and easy talk and warm companionship and lemonade on the porch and Lloyd going in and out most every day. I could picture us reading together on winter evenings in the new library, then glancing at each other in perfect accord before banking the fire below our lovely Adam mantel and walking up to the new bedroom, now so perfectly appropriate for Sam and me.

❧

Oh, and before I forget, I'm still a member of the book club.